THE CHRONICLES OF DAVIDS

BAEN BOOKS
edited by David Afsharirad

The Year's Best Military SF and Space Opera
The Year's Best Military and Adventure SF: 2015
The Year's Best Military and Adventure SF: Volume 3
The Year's Best Military and Adventure SF: Volume 4
The Year's Best Military and Adventure SF: Volume 5

The Chronicles of Davids

THE CHRONICLES OF DAVIDS

Edited By

DAVID AFSHARIRAD

THE CHRONICLES OF DAVIDS

"Introduction: What's in a Name?" copyright © 2019 by David Afsharirad; "The Savage" copyright © 2019 by David Drake; "I Could've Done Better" copyright © 2007 by Gregory Benford & David Brin; "The Seven Nipples of Molly Kitchen" copyright © 2019 by D.J. Butler; "DeMille and Me" copyright © 2019 by D.L. Young; "A Servant of the Protector" copyright © 2019 by David Hardy; "Long Nights Moon" copyright © 2014 by David B. Coe; "Creation Unforgivable" by David H. Keller orignally appeared in *Weird Tales*, April 1930. (All attempts to locate the holder of rights to this story have been unsuccessful. If a holder will get in touch with Baen Books, payment will be made.); "As It Began" copyright © 2019 by Dave Bara; "Full Chicken Richness" originally appeared in *Last Wave*, October 1983, copyright © 1983 by Avram Davidson; "Four Days" copyright © 2019 by David Carrico; "The Tyranny of Distance" copyright © 2019 by Dave Freer; "Lyman Gilmore Jr.'s Impossible Dream" copyright © 2019 by David Boop; "Too Many Gods" copyright © 2019 by Hank Davis; "The Traitor" copyright © 1997 by David Weber; "An Epilogue: *The House of David*" copyright © 2019 by Barry N. Malzberg.

All other content copyright © 2019 David Afsharirad

A Baen Books Original

Baen Publishing Enterprises
P.O. Box 1403
Riverdale, NY 10471
www.baen.com

ISBN: 978-1-4814-8426-8

Cover art by David Mattingly

First printing, September 2019

Library of Congress Control Number: 2019024672

Distributed by Simon & Schuster
1230 Avenue of the Americas
New York, NY 10020

Printed in the United States of America

10 9 8 7 6 5 4 3 2 1

Contents

Introduction: What's in a Name?
by David Afsharirad 1

The Savage by David Drake 5

I Could've Done Better
by Gregory Benford & David Brin 25

The Seven Nipples of Molly Kitchen
by D.J. Butler 41

DeMille and Me by D.L. Young 53

A Servant of the Protector by David Hardy 67

Long Nights Moon by David B. Coe 91

Creation Unforgivable by David H. Keller 115

As It Began by Dave Bara 123

Full Chicken Richness by Avram Davidson 133

Four Days by David Carrico 145

The Tyranny of Distance by Dave Freer 173

Lyman Gilmore Jr.'s Impossible Dream
by David Boop 191

Too Many Gods by Hank Davis 213

The Traitor by David Weber 255

An Epilogue: *The House of David*
by Barry N. Malzberg 279

Contributor Bios 283

THE CHRONICLES OF DAVIDS

What's in a Name?

David Afsharirad

According to the Social Security website, the name "David" has been one of the top twenty names for males born in the United States for over a hundred years. Strange then that I didn't encounter many Davids growing up. In grade school, I was never forced to append my first name with my last initial in order to differentiate myself from all the other Davids in the class for the simple reason that there *were* no other Davids in the class.

All that changed when I started working at Baen Books. I soon learned that Baen published gentlemen with names like David Drake, David Weber, David B. Coe, David Carrico, and Dave Freer. Soon D.J. "Dave" Butler and David Boop were added to the roster. And did I mention cover artist David Mattingly, whose work includes the Honor Harrington covers (not to mention the cover to the book you hold in your hands)? Baen had and has a superabundance of Davids. For the first time in my life I was one David among many.

I entered an even larger pool of Davids when my work started getting published and I became a part of the science fiction and fantasy writers community. Indeed, SF/F publishing seems full to bursting with Davids! This fact did not escape me nor did it escape Baen associate editor and author of the Sun Eater series Christopher Ruocchio. The two of us were talking at the Baen booth at DragonCon about the myriad Davids Baen published. (At the time Baen also employed an additional Christopher, though he has since moved on.) It was Christopher who suggested an anthology. "You could edit and we'd get Mattingly to do the cover," he said. We went on to list all the Baen-Davids and non-Baen-Davids we could include. It was funny; one of the things you come up with during a long convention to pass the time.

Or so I thought.

Christopher had the vision. And he had the will to see that vision through. At the next LibertyCon, at which I was not in attendance, Christopher cornered Baen publisher Toni Weisskopf (read: our boss) during a room party and pitched her the idea. (I suspect some liquid courage was involved, but perhaps not; Christopher is not one in the long and storied line of perpetually soused writers.) Toni agreed to greenlight the project, a fact which I did not know until the tail end of a telephone conversation with her about another matter entirely. "Oh, and we need to talk about the Davids book soon," she said casually.

Some time later, with a contract in hand, I went hunting for Davids. The search was not a difficult one. Indeed, there are so many Davids in the science fiction and fantasy field that I could have easily filled three volumes without repeating a David.

Here then an anthology *by* people named David, *for* everyone who loves a good story!

Included herein are new stories from David Drake, D.J. Butler, Dave Freer, David Boop, Barry N. Malzberg, Hank Davis, Dave Bara, D.L. Young, David Carrico, and David Hardy; and reprints of the highest caliber from David Weber, David B. Coe, David H. Keller, Gregory Benford & David Brin, and Avram Davidson. Fifteen stories total, all by a distinguished David.

Er, almost.

The eagle-eyed will have spotted three non-Davids in the above list.

Allow me to explain.

Gregory Benford co-wrote a story with David Brin that I really wanted to include, so he gets to be a "David by association." In the case of Hank Davis, Toni and I agreed to stretch the point. After all, "S" is right next to "D" on the qwerty keyboard, and what's one letter between friends? As for Barry N. Malzberg, David Drake invited him to the anthology and I'm sure as hell not going to turn down David Drake and Barry Malzberg, two gentlemen whose writing I admire greatly. Further, anyone who reads the story Mr. Malzberg wrote for the book I'm sure will agree it belongs, without a doubt.

My thanks to all the contributors who agreed to be a part of this most unique anthology; to Toni Weisskopf, who gave the go-ahead to put the book together; and to Christopher Ruocchio, who like

Moses on Mount Nebo, led us to the Promised Land though he himself could not enter it.

And thanks to you, Dear Reader, whether you be a member of the worldwide coterie of Davids or not.

—**David Afsharirad**
Austin, TX
December 2018

Doctor William Howe of the Science Directorate of the Republic of Cinnabar has come to Api to collect samples of the local fauna. To do so, he'll need to hire local hunters. But he'll soon find that navigating the backward politics of the Api natives is every bit as dangerous as going out on the hunt.

The Savage

David Drake

Api was the *Goliath's* fourth landing. Doctor William Howe was sequencing biological polymers from the survey ship's previous planets while his assistant, Tech 4 Ramboul, prepared further specimens.

The intercom beeped and flashed. Ramboul pushed ACCEPT with her good hand and said, "Lab, go ahead."

"*Top, this is Pesly in the boarding hold,*" the guard said over the speaker. "*We got a local hunter wants to see Doctor Howe.*"

"Well, he can bloody well cool his heels on shore for an hour till I come down and fetch him!" Ramboul snarled. "The Doc told 'em to report at midday. Even an Ape oughta be able to figure out local noon, don't ye think?"

"*She, not he,*" the guard said. "*And she says she just arrived from Obelia Village so she hasn't been signed on yet.*"

"Hold one," Ramboul said, muting the intercom as she turned to Howe with an eyebrow raised in question. "Doc, we got all three the mayor was supposed to send us, don't we?"

"Yes," Howe said, "though they don't impress me greatly. And I didn't think women on Api were allowed to hunt anyway."

"Well, what d'ye want me to do, Doc?" Ramboul said.

"Bring her up and we'll take a look at her," Howe said, deciding as he spoke. "She can't be much worse than the three we have."

"I'm coming down, Pesly," Ramboul said to the intercom and strode out of the compartment.

Natives were only allowed aboard the *Goliath* under escort. Api Village had seen a considerable amount of interstellar traffic over the

5

past fifty years, so the regulation wasn't as necessary as it might have been other places. There were planets where trading vessels had been captured and the crews eaten, but on Api the risks were limited to petty theft and the likelihood that locals would relieve themselves in the corridors. Sure, spacers could be mugged or knifed in the waterfront strip, but that was true in every port in human creation.

Api Village had a north-facing roadstead rather than a proper harbor, but the storms came from the south and virtually all of the planet's star traffic landed here. The locals were used to off-planet visitors and many of the buildings in Api Village had artifacts of civilization—electric lights were more common than not—but the houses were still hovels inhabited by savages.

The *Goliath*'s spacers generally referred to the Apian natives as Apes. Howe regarded that as uncultured, but he understood the reason.

Howe finished logging the specimen he'd just processed, a four-legged invertebrate from Powell, the ship's second landfall. Instead of starting another sequence, he decided to wait for Ramboul to appear with the local.

Ramboul had a permanently stiff left arm. She'd been transferred to the *Goliath* because she could no longer carry out normal power room duties.

Howe was extremely lucky to get her for his assistant. She knew little about biology, but she worked to extreme precision and she knew the Republic of Cinnabar Navy inside and out. Every member of the *Goliath*'s crew respected her. Howe's nominal rank as a warrant officer received only cursory notice, and his civilian doctorate got none at all.

When they'd met, Howe had asked Ramboul how she'd injured her arm. She'd replied, "I did something dumb," in a tone that didn't encourage follow-up questions. Howe had learned that many subjects were RCN business that outsiders had best keep their noses out of—even if they happened to be sailing on a ship chartered from the RCN by the Science Directorate of the Republic of Cinnabar.

Through quiet inquiries from others on the *Goliath*, Howe had learned that whatever "something dumb" was, it had won Ramboul an RCN Star.

The hatch reopened and Ramboul gestured a local through. "Her name's Joss," Ramboul said. "She says she's been a scout and she wants to hunt for you."

The blond woman had the height and pale coloring of the locals, but the shorts she wore under an Apian singlet were the cut and gray-green color of Alliance uniforms. The left side of her face and scalp were badly scarred; she must have been lucky not to lose the eye on that side. Her hair beyond the scarring was a close-cropped blond. Most of her visible skin was tattooed in red, yellow and bright blue, quite different from the blue-black swirls and striations of many male Apians.

Joss wore a belt knife. The sheath seemed to be lizardskin. The hilt was that of an Alliance utility knife, though the blade must have been shortened to about 5" to fit the present sheath.

"A scout?" Howe said. "What kind of scout?"

Joss looked him over. He had the sudden feeling of being a specimen for preparation. She said, "I left Api when I was fifteen, crewed a freighter to Claiborne. There was a recruiter on Claiborne and I joined the Forces. I got assigned to Heyer's Commando and got to be a scout. When we were paid off at the end of the war, I came back to Api. I'm tired of sitting on my butt here, though."

"We're hiring locals to hunt for us because they know the ground," Ramboul said, still standing near the hatch. Joss had approached within six feet of Howe and stood in a formally stiff posture. "On your telling it, you haven't been back here till a year or two ago."

Joss turned her head. "I learned to size up terrain fast," she said in a tone that made Howe glad she was no longer looking at him. "That's why I'm still alive. Even then it was close a couple times."

She touched the left side of her head, where the ear should have been. She turned back to Howe and said, "Look, you tell me what you want collected and I'll collect it for you, prep it however you want, and I'll do whatever else you decide you need. I've got plenty of money. I just want a job!"

"What do you mean you've got money?" Howe said, leaning forward slightly. He was still seated at the console where he'd been working before Ramboul returned with the local.

Joss reached under her singlet and into a belt pouch that balanced her knife. She stepped forward, holding out a credit chip. "Here, take a look," she said.

Howe's console had a standard socket though he'd never had occasion to use it. He inserted the chip and frowned at the data it threw up. "This says you've got seven thousand thalers," he said in amazement. That was more money than he had in his own account.

"There wasn't much to spend money on most of the places we were sent," Joss said. "And a couple times there were bonuses for special jobs."

Howe started to ask what Joss meant by "special jobs," then glanced at her face and decided not to. He cleared his throat and said instead, "Do you have a gun?"

Joss shook her head. "Women aren't allowed to hunt on Api," she said. "God doesn't want that, you know? You get out in the boonies some and the priests mostly won't make problems, but I couldn't bring a gun into Api Village even if I had one. In the Forces nobody cared I was a woman, just if I could do my job. I can."

Ramboul said, "Doc, I guess I can find some clapped out thing that the armorer don't care if it drops into the sea. There's a platform on the port outrigger they use for target shooting, so we can try her there if you want."

"Yes, all right," Howe said. "I'll take Joss to the platform and you'll meet us with a gun."

He was out of familiar territory on this, but he was sure that Ramboul could square things with the ship authorities if anyone asked questions.

Access to the starboard outrigger was through the boarding hold on Level Six. To reach the port outrigger, a hatch on Level Four opened onto a ladder—a staircase, to Howe's civilian mind—slanting down one of the telescoping supports.

There was no railing and the "non-skid" steel treads were worn enough to be slippery. It didn't seem to bother Joss. Howe wished he could say the same, but he made it without a problem.

The platform was just a flat ten feet wide and fifty feet long molded in the upper surface of the outrigger. There was no railing there either, but at least it wasn't sloping. Ramboul hadn't appeared yet. To fill the time in some way other than by looking at a woman who made him uncomfortable, Howe said, "Do many of your villagers go off on ships, Joss?"

She shrugged. "I knew a few who had," she said, "but not many, no. I left because I'd been raped by an upper-class guy. My old man was just a fisherman even before he didn't come back after a storm, so I couldn't make the guy marry me."

She shrugged and said, "You know how it goes. I guess it's about the same on Cinnabar, once you get under the surface. We were based on Pleasaunce for a couple months, and I met plenty of girls who'd got the same hand dealt 'em but hadn't had the luck to sign on with Heyer."

"I'm sorry for what happened to you," Howe said. "And I can't speak to Pleasaunce and other Alliance worlds, but we're more civilized than that on Cinnabar."

His tone made the words more of a challenge than he'd intended. Joss looked at him. After a moment she said, "Glad to hear that," and looked away. There was no emotion in her voice.

Howe didn't try to continue the conversation, though it was a couple minutes more before Ramboul came down the ladder. He had an uncomfortable suspicion that Joss was right about life on the bottom layer of Xenos society. He found lower animals much easier to deal with; especially after they'd been prepared for genetic sequencing.

Ramboul joined them, holding a carbine in her good hand. She held it out to Joss, saying, "Here. What d'ye think of this?"

"I think it's a clapped-out turd," Joss said, ejecting the loading tube to check it, then slamming it home again. "I've used worse. What do you want shot?"

"There's a buoy out there marking the shoal," Ramboul said, pointing out to sea with her stiff arm. "Can you hit it?"

The orange buoy was about a hundred yards from the platform. Joss put the carbine to her shoulder. The double crack startled Howe, the muzzle blast itself and its reflection from the ship's hull behind him. A puff of aluminum vaporized by the powerful magnetic flux spurted from the muzzle, flashing iridescently even in the sunlight.

Nothing happened to the buoy. Howe said, "Did you hit it?"

"Naw, look at the splash out there," Joss said, the carbine still mounted on her shoulder. "This piece of crap holds way left."

Howe hadn't seen the splash.

She shot three more times. The buoy didn't move that Howe could tell, but he heard the structural plastic *plick* after each shot. He couldn't be sure because the water was slightly choppy, but he thought ripples spread around the buoy from a vibration that he couldn't see.

Joss' trigger finger moved again, but there was no shot. She lowered the carbine and ejected the loading tube, then spun the tube a half turn and replaced it. She shouldered the weapon again. This time it fired. She hit the buoy again.

"The contacts need cleaning," Joss said. "Or more likely, replacing."

She offered the carbine to Ramboul, who took it at the balance.

"Doc?" Ramboul said. "I think we hire her, right?"

"Yes," Howe said. "I think we do. Joss, come with me and we'll see if the hunters Mayor Glanz picked for us have arrived yet."

It was past midday. If one of the male hunters hadn't arrived, Howe wouldn't have to choose a fourth island to drop a collector on.

A spacer stood at the hatch of the briefing room down the corridor from the lab, and two Apians sat uncomfortably within. The chairs were pressed steel and fixed to the floor; so far as Howe was concerned, "uncomfortably" was the only way you could sit on them.

Ramboul nodded to the escorting spacer, then entered ahead of Joss and Howe. "There's supposed to be three of you," she said. "Where's the third guy?"

"Mewhel was drinking last night," one of the hunters said. They were both tall and pale. Their right forearms were heavily tattooed, and one had some tattooing on that upper arm also. "He'll be ready when you pick us up tomorrow."

"No, he won't," Howe said. "Ramboul, call the hatch and tell the guards to bar Mewhel if he shows up. Confiscate the ID chit I gave him yesterday."

The technician stepped to the intercom built into the desk at the front of the room and keyed it. While she spoke into the intercom, Howe said to the male hunters, "I'm assigning Site Three to Joss here." He nodded to the woman beside him.

"She's a woman!" a hunter said.

"That's an abomination!" said the man with upper arm tattoos as he jumped up from his chair. "The gods won't permit it!"

"We're Cinnabar citizens," Howe said, wondering what he'd do if the fellow attacked him. The Apians were all taller than the norm for Cinnabar, and both these looked fitter than Howe was after spending his adult life in laboratories.

Joss stepped in front of Howe. "You're Biron, aren't you?" she said.

The male hunter really looked at Joss for the first time. "Biron's my brother," he said in a quieter tone than that of his initial outburst. "He's Mayor Glanz's bodyguard. I'm Newer. But how do you know us?"

"You've got the same eyes," Joss said. "I didn't know your brother well, but he was toadying up to Glanz back then too. Biron's his bodyguard now? I'm not surprised."

The exchange, mild though it was, disconcerted Newer; he said back down with a puzzled expression. The other male hunter said, "She shouldn't hunt, I don't care where she's from. It's taboo."

"Apian taboos don't apply to us," Howe said. "Now, do you two want the job, or do I have to find a couple more replacements?"

"It's not right, but that's the priest's business," the man said after a moment. "I'll be here tomorrow, two hours after dawn."

"She'll be on a different island," Newer said. "That's none of my business. But when the priest learns, he'll stop you."

"Then you two are dismissed," Howe said to the male hunters. "Till tomorrow or till your gods come down and talk to me. Joss—"

He turned toward her.

"—stay for a minute and I'll run you through the equipment. The other two got the orientation yesterday."

"Take 'em down to the hatch, Terry," Ramboul said to the escorting spacer. "I'll get the other one myself when it's time."

The male hunters didn't speak again, but they glanced over their shoulders as they turned down the corridor with the escort. Joss watched them.

Howe was using a compartment near the main hatch for storage. He was sure he could have found it—almost sure—but he let Ramboul lead anyway. The *Goliath* had been built as a light cruiser. Much of the ship's armament had been landed for this mission, but there were still miles of corridors that Howe had no reason to explore. The cross branchings confused him.

Ramboul opened the compartment and switched on the lights, then stepped aside for Howe and Joss to enter. The gear was already divided into three tarpaulin-wrapped bundles. Howe started to open the nearest.

Joss frowned. "How far am I going to haul this load?" she said.

"An aircar will carry you and the gear to the site and drop you off," Howe said. "You don't have to carry it at all unless you want to move to what you decide is a better location."

He pursed his lips and added, "You'll have to make your own shelter. There isn't a tent in this lot."

Joss shrugged. "I'll want a bigger knife than I brought," she said. "I guess I can pick up something on the Strip. I didn't want to try to board carrying something real until you guys knew me."

"Golightly in the power room bought a panga on Hedwall's Planet, just for a souvenir," Ramboul said from the doorway. "It's pretty stout. I guess he'd let you borrow it if he was sure he'd get it back."

"He'll get it if I'm alive to give it to him," Joss said. "Look, he can hold however many thalers he sets for the value until I come back with it."

"That'll work," said Ramboul. "Doc? I'll go talk to him right now if you're all right watching her—" she nodded to Joss "—for fifteen minutes?"

"Yes, all right," Howe said. "We'll go back to the lab when we're finished here."

As Ramboul scurried off, Howe returned to the opened bundle. "There is netting of three weights," he said. "We don't know what will be available on the site where you'll be collecting."

"What is it you want?" Joss said.

"One of every species you can find," Howe said. "There are bottles of preservative and trays to dope the specimens on. Brief contact with the preservative won't hurt you. Though you don't want to drink it, of course."

Joss laughed. "Chances are I've drunk worse a time or two," she said. "But I promise not to waste your preservative."

"There's also a camera for shots of living animals," Howe said, showing Joss the short tube. "Sometimes you might be able to get an image when you couldn't get the creature itself. You point it at the animal and press down on the red spot. If you hold it down, it keeps recording."

Joss examined the camera. To Howe's surprise, she rotated the ends of the tube in opposite directions, releasing the memory chip. She locked it back in and said, "You got a spare chip for backup?"

Howe started to protest that the chip would hold thirty hours of continuous recording and that the camera backed up automatically to the *Goliath*. After thinking he said, "Yes, I'll get you one when we get back to the lab."

None of the native hunters he'd hired on other planets had used their cameras correctly. Indeed, most of them hadn't fathomed the intricacies of daubing the specimens with preservative before putting them in collection boxes. Fortunately, genetic material didn't degrade much in the two weeks or so the hunters were out in the field, but unless they were frozen, many of the specimens would be useless for rechecking by the time the *Goliath* had returned to Xenos.

This hunter seemed to be different. Regardless, there was no reason not to give her a backup if she wanted one. Chips did fail.

Joss tapped the bundle's thick bottom layer. "These look like ration packs," she said.

"Yes, enough to feed you for a month," Howe said, "though you'll only be out for two weeks. You're welcome to supplement with locally available food, but I can tell you that Site Three isn't near any villages. Ah, I know that dehydrated rations aren't to everyone's taste, but—"

"Hey, Doc," Joss said. "I like 'em fine. I've been missing them since I came back to Api. I probably could've found 'em in the strip in Api Village, but not in Obelia. I'm used to Forces issue, but I don't guess what the RCN's got is going to be a lot different."

"Well, that's fortunate," Howe said. Truly, this woman was a fascinating bundle of surprises. "Well, let's go up to the lab and see if Ramboul has found you a knife."

Howe wasn't any judge of knives, but this panga—he would've called it a machete—seemed quite serviceable. It had no frills, but the bright copper rivets securing the grip to the steel made an attractive contrast to the dark wood. The flat-backed blade swelled near the short point.

Joss was delighted with it, and she probably *was* a judge. She started to open the ration pack she'd brought from the supply room, then paused and said, "Sir? Is it all right to eat in your lab?"

It probably didn't matter, but now that Joss had raised the question Howe said, "Use my office," and pointed to the room at the back of the lab. She obediently went into it and half-closed the door.

Ramboul nodded at the office and said in a low voice, "We got a good one there, Doc."

"It certainly seems that way," Howe agreed, but it brought something to mind that he'd meant to look up but hadn't gotten around to.

His console was connected to the ship's RCN database, including information that a civilian vessel might not have had. He found Heyer's Commando. Before he could begin to read the description, Ramboul called, "Hello, Penn. What have you got for us this afternoon?"

Howe closed the console's screen and looked up. In the doorway stood a spacer and, behind him, four civilians he was escorting.

"The old guy says he's the Cinnabar consul in Api," the spacer said. "The Apes in pretty uniforms are the mayor of this pigsty and his son. Also their bodyguard, God save the mark. He's right peeved they took his gun away from him down in the hold."

"The bodyguard stays in the corridor," Ramboul said before Howe could speak. "The others can come in if they're polite."

The older man had bushy gray whiskers, a bad complexion, and a nose red with broken veins. He was dressed in a worn utility suit of offworld manufacture.

"I'm Yves Fancett, consular agent for Cinnabar in Api," he said, extending his hand across the steel desk. "I'm here to explain your mistake about hiring a female hunter, Master Howe. It's a natural error for a man who hasn't lived out here on the fringes."

Howe didn't take the hand. He said, "It's Doctor Howe. Or Professor Howe, if you prefer to use my rank at the University of Florentine. And the hunter you refer to, Mistress Joss, is definitely the pick of the choices available on Api. Much better qualified than the men Mayor Glanz offered me."

He nodded without warmth to Glanz. The mayor was as tall as most Apians and also unusually heavy. Though he was barefoot, he wore a jacket and trousers of blue offworld cloth with gold braid and a number of dangling medals.

The boy of seven or so wore a similar uniform. He was already running to fat like his father.

"Well, I'm not here to fight about titles, Professor," Fancett said, retracting his arm. Despite the words, he was squinting with anger. "I just needed to tell you that you can't violate taboo by hiring a woman to hunt for you on Api. Now that you understand that, Mayor Glanz and I—"

"We understand that no Ape can tell the RCN what to do!" Ramboul said. "And you, Fancett, you're not even from Cinnabar. I looked you up and you're from Pleasaunce!"

"We no Apes!" the seven-year-old shouted. "We Friend of the Alliance and my daddy has a letter on the wall of the house saying we friends!"

"Irregardless of where I was born, I *am* the Cinnabar consular agent," Fancett said. "I cannot allow you to harm the interests of the Republic by violating local taboo!"

"Take it up with my superiors in Xenos," Howe said. "If you're ever there."

"Yeah, and that's in Navy House, not those twaddle-talking nobodies in Foreign Affairs!" Ramboul said. "Look, Doc, you want me to get rid of this shower?"

Though she worded it as a question, Ramboul had grabbed the mayor's right wrist before Howe had a chance to reply. Though Glanz was a much bigger man, she twisted his arm up behind his back with no apparent difficulty. He squealed.

"You let go my daddy!" the child cried and kicked Ramboul's shin.

She clipped him on the ear with the back of her left hand, sending him into the wall. Obviously, the stiff elbow hadn't caused her arm muscles to atrophy.

The bodyguard started in from the hall but shouted and stumbled onto his knees when Penn, the escort, kidney-punched him. Ramboul manhandled Glanz into the corridor. The mayor was whimpering with pain.

Fancett scuttled through the doorway and was immediately grabbed by a pair of spacers who'd come from farther down the hall, summoned by the commotion. "I'm leaving!" Fancett shouted. "Don't hit me, I'm leaving."

Ramboul pushed the mayor against the far wall and stepped back, breathing hard. She swallowed and said, "That all right, Doc?"

"That's fine, just get them off the ship," Howe said. He was breathing hard too and hadn't even gotten out of his chair. "And take the boy!"

He'd half-considered sending the mayor's son to the ship's infirmary, but the child was back on his feet and seemed to be all right except for bawling his head off. "Take him now, for Hell's sake!"

Ramboul looked at the three spacers in the hallway. "You guys all right with that or do you want me to get some more help?"

The spacers exchanged glances. Penn, the original escort, said, "We're fine, Top. We'll take your garbage out."

The group, spacers behind locals, started for the companionway. Howe felt suddenly weak.

Joss came out of Howe's office. She'd thrust the sheathed panga under the belt of her shorts. She glanced around the room appraisingly.

Ramboul stepped back in. "Can you imagine the nerve of them wogs?" she said. "And too bloody dumb to know that we was RCN, not from the Alliance!"

"Technician, your language," Howe said quietly, glancing toward Joss.

The hunter shrugged. "When she says something I don't agree with, we'll talk about it," she said. "Sir? Thanks for the meal. I'll be back at 0800 for deployment."

"Ah, Mistress?" Howe said. "Feelings in Api village may be running high at the moment. I'm sure we could find you a berth on the *Goliath* for tonight."

He glanced at Ramboul in case he was wrong. Worst case, it might be in the Master at Arms brig.

Joss barked out a surprising laugh. "You think I'm afraid of that lot, sir?" she said. "Bloody hell, *I* dropped with Heyer!"

She went out of the door. "I better go along," Ramboul said, following. "For the regulations."

Howe stood and walked to the doorway, just to be moving. He closed the door before he returned to his desk. Then, because he was there, he resumed reading about Heyer's Commando.

※   ※   ※

Howe didn't bother going down to the boarding hold to see the hunters off, but he devoted a corner of his display to the scene. The truck—a large-box aircar—pulled out of its storage bay on the port side and loudly circled the nose of the ship to the landing stage on the starboard outrigger.

Api had no permanent port facilities. The ship's floating walkway ran from the boarding ramp to the mud shore, where stakes anchored it. That was adequate for pedestrian traffic, but the heavy bundles of stores were more easily loaded on shipboard.

The two spacers on guard in a tarpaulin shelter on shore got up from their lounge chairs. When the truck set down on the landing, they waved to the waiting hunters. The two men had come with groups of half a dozen other locals each; wives and families, Howe assumed.

A pair of women tried to accompany Newer up the ramp: the tattoos marked him even in the reduced image on Howe's screen. The spacers sent them back. When one woman began to protest, a guard jabbed her with the muzzle of her submachine gun.

Joss had been standing a little apart from the male hunters. She followed Newer.

The thin bindle Joss wore diagonally from her left shoulder was from its color an Alliance Forces groundsheet. She didn't have a gun as the men did, though Howe couldn't tell whether their weapons were chemical or electromotive. As Joss boarded the truck on the landing stage, Ramboul handed her the carbine she'd used the day before.

Ramboul stood on the tailgate to check the cargo, then jumped off and waved her stiff arm to the driver. The truck's fans revved, vaguely audible even in Howe's lab. The vehicle swooped down, raising a rainbow spray from the shallow water. It moved shoreward, gathering speed and steadying its course. When it reached the muddy margin, it began to rise. It curved around Api village and was comfortably above the trees on the other side where it disappeared.

Ramboul came into the lab a few minutes later. Howe paused in preparing to send the next sample—a swimming vertebrate from Alexis—into the sequencer. Ramboul nodded and said, "Everything went fine. Janachek's driving and he'll call if there's a problem with the insertions."

"Joss and the men getting along in the truck?" Howe asked.

"So far, at least," Ramboul said, shrugging.

"I looked up the unit Joss said she was with," Howe said. "Heyer's Commando. They were a special operations unit. They were partly recruited from noncitizen mercenaries, but partly from Alliance criminals. Of course, being a criminal in the Alliance might just mean one of Guarantor Porra's cronies wanted your wife."

"Ah," said Ramboul, nodding. "What the Alliance calls Penal Battalions. They got sent where it looked like a lot of 'em weren't going to come back. And also—" she pursed her lips "—they did internal security jobs. Where a subject planet started getting uppity, that sort of thing. Jobs that citizens might, you know . . . might not be willing to do."

"Well, I don't suppose it matters," Howe said. It bothered him, though.

The truck made it back in the early evening. Janachek said that the three hunters had been dropped off without incident.

Shortly before local midnight, the *Goliath* lifted. It would spend the next two weeks recording data on insertions into sponge space. Howe and Ramboul remained aboard, doing the same testing they'd been doing on Api. When the ship returned, they would begin processing animals from Api as well.

Telemetry from the hunters' beacons began to come in before the returning *Goliath* had settled onto her anchorage in the Api roadstead, but Howe didn't bother to examine the data until the thrusters had shut off. The plasma exhaust played hell across the RF spectrum. Even though his console's software could correct most signals, he wasn't in such a hurry that waiting five minutes was going to matter.

Besides, Howe was still recovering from the *Goliath*'s extraction into sidereal space above Api. The left side of his body tingled as though it had gotten a bad shock, though standing up and walking to the end of the lab and back helped a lot.

"I'm going down to see the truck off," Ramboul said. "Hell, I thought I might ride along. You want to come, Doc? There's nothing on Api bigger 'n forty pounds, so there ought to be plenty of room in the truck box. Well, except for fish, I guess."

"I'll pass," Howe said, "but I'll clear more space in the lab freezer while you're out." He glanced at the telemetry again and added, "All three beacons are coming in strong and from right where they ought to be."

That didn't prove the hunters were alive or even that something hadn't carried off everything in the camps except for the frame holding the cube of ration packs. The beacon was built into the bottom of the frame, which seemed a better solution than counting on local hunters to keep track of a separate item.

"Well, I'll see you around nightfall," Ramboul called as she started down the corridor.

Hatches opened and spacers called to one another. The ship was coming alive after a voyage that had been more unpleasant than its fifteen-day duration. The *Goliath*'s primary task was to survey routes through sponge space in a region where the RCN had few charts. This was well within Alliance territory. Until the Peace of Trier two years before, it had been out of bounds for Cinnabar vessels.

Howe went back to the telemetry data, pinging the hunters' sites one at a time. Apart from transmitting the location, the beacons stored images from the issued cameras.

If there were any images, of course.

Howe started with Site One, which had been assigned to Newer. The camera had taken only one shot and that was probably an accident: it showed Newer's left leg from the knee down and a patch of leaf litter. The mushrooms on the fallen leaves might be of interest. That was pretty much what Howe had learned to expect from the locals.

Suse, the hunter at Site Two, had photographed nearly a hundred specimens. He seemed to be particularly good on grubs and worms.

All were in collecting boxes, however: the notion of getting images of animals in their natural settings hadn't penetrated. Howe decided to give Suse a bonus anyway.

He proceeded to the data from Site Three and whistled. There were more images than he could even guess at before he checked the counter—612. On most of them Howe couldn't be sure of the subject without enlarging the image, but when he checked two at random he found a living animal—a tiny hexapod on a tree-trunk and a scale-winged bird in flight—nicely centered.

A short sequence from ten days ago puzzled him initially. The first was of a mist-net strung six feet in the air between a pair of smooth-barked trees. Joss had slanted the shot along the line of the net so that the morning sun picked up the shimmer of the fine meshes.

The second shot was the same net, also in the morning—but with large holes torn in the fabric. The third was a replacement net—there were twenty-yard rolls of all three weights of netting in the hunters' bundles—stretched across the same flyway. A long-tailed, short-legged quadruped dangled in it. Howe enlarged the image to get a better view of the net-robber's head, but that didn't help much. A carbine slug had almost decapitated the animal.

Howe was still going over the Site Three images when the intercom beeped. Ramboul said, "*Doc, we're in the boarding hold. Do you want to see the specimens before the hunters go ashore?*"

"I surely do!" Howe said. "I'm coming right down."

Howe made very good time—for him—despite initially getting out of the companionway on Level Two and having to climb back to Three where the boarding hold opened. He was out of breath when he got there.

A squad of spacers was unloading the truck onto a cargo net. A crane and winch would lift the load to an external hatch on Level Six where the laboratory was, saving the work of hauling the tubs up the helical stairs of the companionways. Starships didn't have elevators. Those would twist and jam in their shafts with the stresses of shifting between universes.

Ramboul and the hunters had walked up the ramp and turned to Howe when he stepped through the doorway. "They got a good batch of stuff, Doc," Ramboul called. She held Joss' carbine in her bad arm; though the elbow was stiff, the hand still opened and closed properly. "More than we have from Coile and Hedwall's Planet together. Of course, about 80% of it's from Site Three."

The male hunters glowered at Joss. She kept her eyes on Howe. She didn't speak, but Howe thought she looked pleased.

Howe gave to Ramboul the bag of cash he'd drawn from the Purser that morning. "Pay the gentlemen, Technician," he said. "And add ten florins to the agreed per diem for Master Suse because of his determination to take images of his specimens."

"Hey!" said Newer. "I want ten florins too!"

"You *want* having your arse kicked off the outrigger, Ape!" Ramboul said, turning toward the hunter. "You watch your tongue with the Doc there or that's just what you'll get!"

Joss looked as though she wanted to speak. Before she could, Howe said, "Mistress Joss, if you'd like to have your pay in the form of an increase in your credit chip, that can be arranged. And I would like to discuss your images and other matters before you leave the ship, if you're not in a rush. Do you have a moment?"

"I'd like that, sir," Joss said. "There's something I want to talk to you about too."

"You going up to the office, Doc?" Ramboul called. "If you are, I'll join you there right as soon as I've checked the gun back in."

"Yes," Howe said. "I'll see you then."

He turned, saying, "Come along, Mistress Joss. I'm particularly interested in the predator you shot robbing your nets."

At the back of Howe's mind, he wondered if he ought to ask Joss to guide him. He suspected she was less likely to get lost in the various turnings than he was.

Howe's office was only marginally better as a social environment than the laboratory itself, but at least the built-in cot folded into a second chair. Howe did that when he and Joss entered.

"Sir," said Joss, "there's something I need to tell you."

Howe turned, expecting some revelation about Heyer's Commando. He'd already decided that Joss' military service didn't matter to him. She did her work, and the past was past.

Joss was holding out a memory chip. She said, "I dropped the camera into a pool while I was packing for pickup. Fortunately I'd just replaced the chip with the spare, so all the images are safe."

"Ah," Howe said. "Well, that doesn't matter, mistress. The cameras are frequently lost. They're almost as cheap as ammunition for the guns."

"I used six carbine rounds too," Joss said, "but I didn't think I had to mention that. Mostly I was just sighting it in, but it was good to have it for that cat."

"I was wondering about the animal," Howe said. "Are they common on Api?"

"I never saw one before," Joss said. "But I wasn't out of Api Village until I signed aboard the *Floristan* when I was 15. And there aren't any in Obelia that I've seen either."

"I'll be very interested in what the genetic sequencer has to say," Howe said. "Occasionally DNA-based life has shown up in specimens from this region, though the specimens I've collected on our previous landings have used TNA nucleotides. As you say, the animal you shot does seem kin to a Terran cat, but from its length and short legs it's diverged farther than would be possible in the three thousand years since the first colonies landed on Api."

"I took a patch of skin and hair," Joss said. "And since you gave me plenty of boxes, I packed up his balls too. It's a thick specimen and I don't know how well the preservative will have penetrated."

"You did that?" Howe said. "Well, that's very good. Remarkable, in fact."

He cleared his throat. There was no doubt now about what he was going to ask, but he wasn't sure how to frame the question.

"Thing is, Doc . . ." Joss said, but as she spoke, Ramboul opened the office door.

"All paid off and squared away," the Tech said. "Except for the mistress here, but I guess you're taking care of her."

"Top?" Joss said. She lifted the heavy knife by the sheathed blade. "I have a favor to ask about this panga?"

"Sure," said Ramboul. "You want me to take it back to Golightly?"

"No," said Joss. "I'd like to buy it from him. Do you suppose he'd take three hundred thalers?"

Ramboul pursed her lips thoughtfully. "I'm pretty sure he'd take a hundred for it," she said. "He paid about ten florins on Hedwall."

"I make that around sixteen thalers," Joss said. "Would you offer him a hundred florins from me? It's a nice piece, well-balanced and good steel. And a finder's fee for you if you like."

"Yeah, I'll do that," Ramboul said, frowning slightly. "I don't need anything extra for me, but I'll tell you, drinks are on Golightly the next time we go on liberty together. Want me to do that now?"

"If you would," Joss said. She watched Ramboul stride out of the office. Then the hunter turned to Howe and said, "Sir, I came back to Api when the Alliance paid me off, but it's not the same place as when I was a kid and I'm not the same kid either. Look, I did good work for you, didn't I?"

"You did excellent work," Howe said. "Your bonus will reflect that."

"I don't care about a bonus!" Joss said with unexpected bitterness. "Sir, you're going to need hunters on other planets, right? Hire me for the job."

"I usually hire local collectors because they know the region better," Howe said carefully.

"Compare my haul with what Suse brought in!" Joss said. "And that useless Newer. He's a lazy scut like his brother, and I remember Biron from back before I left Api the first time. Doc, I can size things up. I was a good scout for Heyer, and we were the best drop commando in the Forces!"

Howe considered in silence. He'd come to same conclusions as Joss before she'd sat down in the office.

To have something to delay stating his decision, he said, "Was Biron the man you had trouble with? The man who raped you?"

"Naw, Biron was just dumb muscle when he was a kid and that's all he is now," Joss said. "That guy who did that's still around, but I haven't looked him up. You could say that I ought to thank him, because otherwise I'd never have left Api."

"Do you really feel that way?" Howe said in amazement.

"Me?" Joss said. Her expression suddenly went blank. "Bloody hell, no! I didn't join the priesthood, I joined Heyer. But you could look at it that way."

"All right," Howe said. "I'll have Ramboul get you signed on as an engine wiper. She'll know how to do that, but I'll tell Captain von Hase what I'm doing."

"Thank you, sir!" Joss said, rising to her feet with an expression of great satisfaction. I'll be back in the morning before liftoff. That's 0800, isn't it?"

"That's what it's scheduled for," Howe said. "But if you want to spend the night aboard, I'm sure Ramboul can fix that."

"Yeah, I guess Top could fix most anything," Joss said. "But I want to take care of some things on shore. I'll be back before liftoff, don't worry."

"Well, however you want to handle it," Howe said. He found a temporary ID chit in his desk and scribbled his signature on it, then handed it to the hunter. Joss was a member of the Goliath's company now, so she didn't require an escort.

"I'll see you in the morning," Joss said as she walked out the door.

Howe didn't see Joss before liftoff, but Ramboul assured him the hunter had boarded in plenty of time and was assigned to a power room watch. Starship crews, even on warships, were a broad mix of backgrounds. Neither coming from a tiny backwater nor having served in the Alliance military would make Joss unique.

When the *Goliath* began to accelerate out of orbit and apparent gravity returned, Howe set one of the "cat" samples to sequence. While that was in process, he decided to look again at the images Joss had made of the creature.

To his surprise the download from Joss' camera indicated that one image hadn't been viewed. He called it up instead of finding the "cat" sequence.

Ramboul, looking over Howe's shoulder at the display said, "We never told her the cameras uploaded automatically, did we?"

"No, I guess we didn't," said Howe.

It was a well-framed shot of the heads of Mayor Glanz and his son on a wooden table carved in Apian style. Something was stuffed into the mayor's mouth. Howe guessed that the object was the mayor's genitals, but he didn't feel a need to enlarge the image to be sure.

Look, the future isn't going to save itself. And when it comes to guiding the course of history, Alec is pretty sure he could've done it better than all those dead dudes in the textbooks. So when two lovely time travelers offer him a chance to alter the future by changing the past, he jumps at it. Too bad saving the world ain't all it's cracked up to be.

I Could've Done Better

Gregory Benford & David Brin

❀ 1 ❀

They didn't have to do this to me. Dump me in this place, with no chance of going home.

I told them I'd try harder. Really. Make up for my mistakes. Be a better person. They could choose someone else, easy.

But did they listen?

How I miss the things I'll never do again. Eat a hotdog at the ballpark. Take a flight out to the coast. Catch a Vegas show or watch a playoff game on TV. I suppose I could invent baseball or teach these people how to play poker. But they'd just let me win all the time, so where's the fun?

Here comes slender Mirimani now, carrying a basket of fresh fruit, followed by Deela—buxom Deela—with a pitcher of beer. I've grown used to the strong, bitter stuff they brew here, though I'd trade Tut's treasure right now for a cold, frothy Budweiser . . .

"It is time for my lord to have his morning massage," Deela says, leaning over me to fill a golden goblet. Her scent is mild must and myrrh. Two more girls approach with linen towels and scented oils.

Mirimani smiles. She's leaner, more athletic.

"Or would the Father of the Nile prefer to bathe first?"

All right, I admit it. I used to get a kick out of talk like that, the first hundred or so times. Till I realized what an absolute pit it is to be Pharaoh.

"Not now," I respond. My Old Kingdom Egyptian has an Illinois accent, but no one complains. "What's on our schedule today?"

Mirimani can glide smoothly from seductive to pure business—one reason she's risen so high in my service.

"A new ambassador from Babylon wishes to present gifts."

"Right into my lapis, I suppose."

"My lord?"

"Never mind." Making puns in English, instead of my tortured Ancient Egyptian; I really am homesick today. "Okay, then what?"

"You grant clemency to the Libyan rebels."

"Clemency? Those guys gave me real trouble last summer, raiding caravans and burning my new schools. Remind me. Why was I planning to spare them?"

"In order to set an example, my Lord. To illustrate your innovations called 'due process' and 'rehabilitation,' as I recall. Have you changed your mind?"

"Well . . . no, I guess not. It'd be more satisfying to set another kind of example, though. One involving hungry lions. Oh, never mind. Is there anything else?"

"Only an audience with the High Priestess of Isis, who craves a few moments from the Father of Waters."

At this I groan. "Aw, man, do I really have to see her?"

Mirimani smiles gently. We've been through this before. "No one commands the Pharaoh of all Egypt. But you have found the wisdom of Isis indispensable in the past."

Her phrasing tugs with bitter irony.

In the past, Mirimani? Oh, if only you knew how far off you are.

❦ 2 ❦

All right, picture this. Two babes come swaying into Mulligan's Bar, wearing identical black dresses with slit sides and plunging backs. One blonde and the other with tightly curled hair that's a deep, almost black, henna red. They seem awkward on spike heels—wobbling a little—yet getting the hang of it fast. Athletic types. No. More than that.

Right away the old radar is up, beeping. They're knockouts. Tall, luminous, luscious . . . every male in the place takes notice. So does every female. You'd have to be dead not to.

Let me get something straight—I wasn't asking for trouble. Just stopping by the old haunt to relax with a brew—one!—after a racquetball match. I demolished poor Fred from Accounting pretty easy, three to one, picking up fifty bucks on bets and feeling smug over grinding his nose in it. I'd been riding my underlings at work, too—working off the steam that kept building up in my life. The feeling that I should be doing more. More than middle management. More than this.

Sandy expected me home by six-thirty. I really meant to be prompt. Maybe put in some quality time with the kids.

The after-five crowd was trickling in. My fave time of day. Allowing for a twenty-minute commute, I had three quarters of an hour to just relax and be me. If I cut it close.

I had promised Sandy to do better, and really meant it this time. She had caught me chatting up an intern at the office picnic and raised hell. Then, two days later, I came home late and brewed up a bit. She didn't seem to understand that I was still a fun kinda guy. That's what originally drew us to each other, right? We sure had some wild times.

Only now she was auditioning for the role of Wounded Hausfrau and I hadn't changed. *Why should I?* part of me protested.

Another part answered—*Come on, sport, you know you've crossed the line a few times since you got hitched. She's worth some extra effort. So are the kids. Give it a rest.*

I'm sure every married guy has those conflicts, right? Well, a lot of us.

So there I was, just mulling it over, dealing with it, when the two lookers came in.

Lookers in both senses—they sat down and right away started looking at me.

Ah, those sheath dresses, hose, and high heels—tight skirts, covering without concealing two great bodies. And the faces—just my type. High cheekbones, full lips, arching eyebrows, long hair. Redhead's dusky complexion set a nice contrast to the blonde's cool snow. Couldn't be better if I'd ordered them from a menu.

Okay, maybe I was a little irked with Sandy. Maybe I was tired. Give me credit—I went over there more out of curiosity than anything else. I mean, how often do two knockout babes send you pickup looks across a bar?

For just a moment, I recall, something about these two—the way they moved—made me think of . . . *soldiers*.

The thought was kind of weird. Unnerving.

It didn't stop me, though.

"Do I know you ladies?"

Not as amateur as it sounds. If they say no, turn it into a compliment, something about getting to start fresh with two such lovelies, blah blah. When I was in practice, I could come off even a routine opening with confidence, like answering a backhand serve.

Only the blonde surprises me.

"Oh, we know you. You're famous."

I gave her a quick look to see if this was irony, but she's beaming a big, white smile. Good teeth, great glossy lipstick, and not a hair out of place. Maybe they'd been in Mulligan's before and heard something.

I tossed it off with a disarming chuckle. "Whatever they're saying, Officer, it ain't true."

"Oh, no, Alec," the redhead said, "you're renowned."

All right. A bit nervous now. They knew my name. I glanced around to see if any of the guys were giggling in a corner, having put these two up to it.

"Renowned, eh? How come I don't see myself on magazine covers?"

"Not now—in the future." And she motioned for me to sit down.

Now I know it's a gag. But nobody was cackling beyond the potted plants. Mulligan himself seemed unaware, busy with customers. I decided to play along, plopping in a chair.

"Oh, yeah?"

"We're serious," the blond said. "We really are from your future."

"Sure, like in those movies." The guys knew I was a lifelong sci-fi fan. Whoever set this up, I'd have to come up with something good to top it.

"Indeed—" the redhead nodded "—our research shows several cinematic dramas in your era approached the general concept, so you should easily grasp what we're talking about. Please do accept it. We are real, from two centuries ahead of this day."

I gave them a smile of disbelief, with a Cary Grant cock of the head. "Hm, well, they do make real beauties in the twenty-third century."

For the first time, something I said affected her. A modest blush, apparently sincere. I blinked, more surprised by that than anything she had said. This was no hired hooker or actress. She was nervous underneath and actually appreciated the compliment. My opinion meant something to her.

"So, are you ladies tourists? Come back in time to do a little slumming with the ancestors?"

The blonde was more businesslike. "We are not tourists, Alec. Our mission is serious. We are at war."

I blinked. A surprising turn. My latest theory had been that they were sorority pledges from a nearby college, pulling mind games on some locals as part of an initiation stunt. The future babes trip had just the right flavor for a tease fantasy. But this—

"At war?"

"Yes. And we are losing."

"You . . ."

"We," she corrected. "All of us. Humanity."

"Uh huh, I think I saw that movie. You want me to go forward in time because I'm a typical primitive warrior type. Only a real man can defeat the alien invaders or rogue computers or mutant spiders, because your males are too civilized."

They gave me a "don't be ridiculous" look.

"Our warriors are strong, Alec," the redhead said, "both men and women. Indeed, many of our greatest heroes and most innovative thinkers are descended from you."

That made me blink a couple of times, momentarily at a loss for words. What a line! I should try it myself sometime. Somebody at the sorority had an imagination, all right.

Well, if they wanted to be outrageous, fine.

"Descended from . . . Oh, I get it now. You've come back in time to ask me for genetic samples?"

The blonde put her hand on my thigh, a pleasant warm pressure, and rather more alarming than I expected. Her smile broadened.

"Yes, but more than that, we need your help."

"No fighting aliens in the future? Shucks."

A small corner of me felt strangely disappointed. I kind of hankered after that.

"We would not risk your life. But you can save humanity, Alec. If you are willing to accept a most difficult, onerous, but ultimately rewarding task."

❀ 3 ❀

The ambassador from Babylon brought mostly the same old crap. Jewelry that my kid might've spurned at a discount store, back home in Chicago. Some pathetic rugs. Spices to cover the smell when food starts to go stale.

We'll fix that problem by next year, if I keep making good progress setting up Pharaoh Laboratories, Inc. I think I can remember how to make a refrigerator and there's no lack of willing labor. Nor any corporate bean-counters or stockholders to hinder us. We'll keep trying till we get it right.

I'll have cold beer yet! You'll see.

The ambassador looked scared, trying desperately to impress me with his gifts. Well, can't blame him. Babylon and all the other ancient powers are pissing in their pants because Old Kingdom Egypt now has muzzle-loading cannon.

He seemed especially upset over the girls. He brought twenty of them. Real beauties. Didn't Pharaoh like 'em?

Shucks. The ever-efficient priestesses of Isis whisked them all away before I could even get a good look! Only those who actually *volunteer*—of their own free will—may come back to the palace, later. It's my own law, dammit.

To compensate, I enjoyed making the ambassador sweat some more. But not too much. To my surprise, I've found a little groveling goes a long way.

Anyway, the Libyan rebels were next. They should put on a good show.

❀ 4 ❀

All right, so there we are in the bar, see? I'm getting into their little game—this time travel story thing. As I said, it just had to be a sorority prank. A sexy little mind tease. Even the "future war" scenario fit in. Maybe they were "assigned to protect me" from some horrible android assassin. Why not play along? It wouldn't be sporting to spoil their fun, right?

Only part of me was getting worried. The part that knows people, often letting me manipulate them to my own advantage. The part that does well at poker. The part that knew these weren't ditzy sorority chicks out on a dare.

They were formidable women. Capable adults, serious and determined. Whatever they were up to, they meant to accomplish it.

Part of me already half believed them.

"Um . . . a task?"

"In another era."

"Another . . . right. You want me to come with you in a time machine."

"Not a machine. A time beam. Our greatest scientists managed to create just one, with an interference fringe here in your era and another at our final destination. So this has to work."

"Hm. Will it take long? My wife expects me home in less than an hour."

That's not like me. To mention Sandy, up front. First clue that I really am starting to take this crazy story as more than a joke.

"Your wife was destined to be disappointed tonight, whether or not we came to intervene. Do you see the brunette sitting behind me? Three tables back, trying to read a book."

"Yeah, so? I noticed her before."

"You were about to go to her and . . . what is your expression? Pick her up."

"No way."

"After your third beer . . ."

"I was just having one!"

". . . one thing would lead to another. Amid the subsequent accusations, lies, and recriminations, a downward spiral would commence, with more such philandering episodes, more alienation, resulting in divorce and then two more failed marriages—"

"Hey!" This was getting weird. "I'm happy. All right, I need more control. And maybe I can be a bit self-centered. But I wouldn't spoil things like that! Not where it counts."

The redhead stayed serious. They were dividing roles.

"During the next month, by our records, everything will turn sour. You will go back to gambling, promiscuity—"

"No! I'm through with all that." Then I recall how I was feeling a minute ago. "Dammit, you started flirting with me. I was just having a beer, and . . . and I've been trying harder."

It sounded pretty lame, even to me, but I had been doing better. Really I had. Right up till that evening!

The blonde was merciless.

"Yes, but you will fail. If it helps, let me assure you that it isn't entirely your fault. Blame it on upbringing and a wretched environment—certainly not genes."

"What about my genes?" The weirder this got, the more I seemed compelled to stay and listen.

"Your traits are mostly outstanding and they manifest that way through all eight of your children. And their heirs, far downstream."

"Eight!"

"I mentioned other marriages. That is how we know your genes are the critical factor, since you were not especially helpful to the mothers in any other way. Yet, all eight achieved wonders.

"Again, it's not really your fault, Alec. Twisted by your own past, you were merely a somewhat successful executive in this era, good at manipulating and defeating competitors, but also thwarted by those above you, who were put off by your drive and apparent amorality. At a root level, you have powerful leadership talents, inheritable traits that will prove crucial in our future. Your descendants will be mighty leaders, ambitious, innovative, demanding, and yet fair."

I couldn't even begin to imagine the point of this "joke" anymore. It was taking on a harshness that burned inside.

"What did you mean by twisted?"

"Our analysts believe your abilities—especially your sense of empathy for others—were stunted because of traumas you suffered while young."

Ouch. I felt a wrench in my stomach. How the hell could this bitch know about—

I very nearly got up at that moment. Got up and walked away from the lure of their beauty, the fascination of their teasing game. I almost stood up to go home, to where I knew I was loved in spite of my faults. At least up till that night. *Stand . . . up!* I commanded my muscles and bones. But they betrayed me.

"Those childhood traumas twisted your gifts, turning you into a user of others. Unpleasant traits you fought to overcome, beginning with your playground experience—you always felt badly about being a bully, didn't you? History gives you credit for that, Alec. And yet, you were never able to—"

"Hey, wait a second—"

The redhead injects with enthusiasm "—but what struck Special Projects HQ was how those very same traits ideally suit you for a special task! A role in saving all humanity."

I blink. Doubt, anger, and disbelief welled up in me. None of this made sense, even as an elaborate practical joke. It came rushing back: Tony Pasquetto beating the crap out of me in fifth grade, my seething anger, a bile from that simmered on and on. I took it out on others, roiling with both pleasure and guilt. One word from these two and presto—back it came. And worse, much worse from my own parents, too caught up in their war against each other to see what collateral damage they were doing to me inside.

I made myself take a deep breath. "I . . . had some rough times as a kid, sure, but that doesn't mean—"

The blonde's hand slid higher up my thigh, threatening to drive out all rational thought.

"Let us persuade you."

"Huh? Of what?"

"Of our purpose. Our resolve to make your decision obvious."

"Yes," the redhead added, leaning closer. "We are here to give you everything that you presently want. To fulfill your fantasies, such as they are."

"And you figure I want more than a good exec job and a wife and home?"

"We know you. Better than you know yourself, Alec," Red said with a slow, sly smile.

Struggling for some sense of control, I stretched, pretending nonchalance, knowing that I'm fooling no one.

"You ladies have got quite a line, I got to hand it to you."

"You do not believe us," the redhead said. "Of course, it is a fantastic tale."

"It's original, I'll give you that."

Blonde is all business. She leaned back, giving me a good long look at her perfectly proportioned body. "For now, let us see about collecting those samples you offered."

❀ 5 ❀

The rebels groveled very well. Heads smacked on marble, moans of supplication echoed, they even trotted forward some women to offer—probably their poor frightened wives. I yawned.

My Western Frontier Advisor whispered, urging me to put them all on spikes. "As an example to others!" he finished.

"Have you watched an impalement?" I answered. I had made that mistake the first time I went along with this joker. They put the pointed shaft up the anus and it takes the victim a full day to work down on it. I would still wake up in a sweat, years later, remembering their screams.

"Sire, for the good of the Kingdom—"

"Clemency is granted!" I said loudly. "One year at hard labor, helping to build the Great Library in Alec-Sandria, then back home on probation—and I better not hear of any more raided caravans! This rebellion stuff has got to stop. Get a life!"

Okay, not eloquent. But the expressions on their faces—and their wives'—made me feel like Abraham Lincoln. Sheesh, these ancient guys are easily pleased.

Not that I was always Mr. Nice Guy. Especially at the beginning, building a ragtag band of followers, then eventually taking over and ejecting the old Pharaoh. Had to show I was the kind of ruthless cutthroat that my growing army expected. Those first years were hungry, danger packed, and tense, even with some modern tricks from the twenty-first century. And yet . . . it's funny how finally taking power didn't turn out to be as voluptuously satisfying as I thought it would be.

Who would have expected that I'm nowhere near the bully that I used to think I was?

The cries of gratitude from the rebels hardly faded away before the chief herald cried out. "Lo, the Priestess of Isis arrives!"

Damn! I had meant to slip away—

She came in at full swagger. And though she bowed low before me and uttered all the proper phrases, anyone could tell that she's my equal here.

Some may even suspect the truth.

The gold bracelets were striking, the ivory headdress and ebony belt gave her authority, and the figure . . . well nobody else in 1400 B.C. has anything like it.

But she was all business. How did I ever think she was so alluring, back in Mulligan's?

"Lord of All the Lands, I approach you with supplications."

Which meant work to do. With a sigh I sat back on my throne and answered in English.

"The usual?"

"I bring laws for you to proclaim. Matters that we discussed at our last monthly meeting. Regulations for fair trade in the Sinai. A better plan for Nile boats. The apprenticeship and scholarship program for bright sons and daughters of the peasant class."

Yeah, yeah. Half of the ideas were mine. I'm not a complete puppet. Still, I winced when I saw a crimson scroll under her belt. The weekly quota of heirs for me to sire.

Dammit, I bet she was planning an increase! What am I, a machine?

"Look, what's the rush?" I mumbled. "We've already accomplished—"

"A great deal, proving that our estimates of your abilities were correct. You should trust—"

"Trust!" I laughed, without joy. "You tricked me! All of this, in order to—"

"In order to help guide society quickly toward a more advanced state, so that in three and a half millennia it will be capable of defeating a dire enemy from the stars."

None of the guards, deputies and ass-kissers around the throne room understood us, of course. They assumed we were talking in the Language of the Gods.

"Do remember the Enemy, O great Pharaoh."

I shivered. They had showed me a foe, all right—made me experience them in full. Not classic aliens or terrifying robo-devils, nothing you'd expect at all. They came from a world where smart mammals like us were herded. Not like cows, but more subtly. Symbiotic, they had mastered how to tap our deepest fears, using them against us. They ruled by immersing us in them. Imagine a chilly analytical engine, impersonally merciless as it uses you, only far worse to look at and impossible to look away from—because it's always there, slimy, inside.

The blonde and the redhead made me experience that. They showed me how humanity was losing.

But on this new timeline, we'll have an extra 3,000 years to get ready. Time enough, maybe, if we bypass the cruel stupidities and waste of the Assyrian and Roman and Ch'ing empires and all the dark ages between. If feudalism gets replaced by opportunity and science a whole lot earlier. Especially—they say—if that future has plenty of people with my traits. Traits that did me little good in my old life, but ones that would breed true, making great leaders in the future. Leaders not stunted the way I am—only good for simple tasks, like bullying primitives by the marshy borders of the Nile.

"One of your descendants invented the time beam," they had told me that night—it seemed like ages ago—as if I was supposed to be proud. "She knew this attempt would be our only chance."

"Well then, why not take *her* back in time? Or pick my son to be Pharaoh? He carries the same miracle genes, right? He's better and wiser than me, too, ain't that right? Anyway, if I leave, won't they vanish?"

"It is hard to explain the subtleties of temporal dynamics," the redhead had said. "All of your children made large contributions to our future. That timeline must continue to stand like a trellis for the new one to grow alongside. And it *will* continue to stand, even after you are removed."

I think of myself as flexible-minded, but this made my head hurt. You can't do time travel without a painful paradox, and the two savants in front of me were accommodating.

"But still . . . why me? Because that time beam had a *fringe* that appeared here? I mean now?"

"That's part of it. Also, we must borrow the least important element. One whose suite of actions—personal choices and conscious involvement—can be spared, and yet someone capable of exercising fierce power in a primitive era, then growing into the job. All of those reasons pointed to you."

The least important element. Brutally frank, those gals were, once they knew they had me. Their futuristic personality analyzer told them I'd be fine leading a nation of millions, though in my real world I never made it beyond middle management. I could satisfy harems, but not one modern wife.

Go figure.

❈ 6 ❈

It really came home to me later that day, in the privacy of my seraglio.

Did you ever work in an ice cream shop? First week you gorge. Second week you peck a little. Third week . . . well, I was getting that third week feeling again, real bad.

A voluptuous lady of the Levant, soft like pillows. A stately and dignified Nubian, like warm ebony. A leering, silky submissive of the West and a skilled contortionist from the Far East. All of them were volunteers, of course, never coerced. That moralist, Isis, made sure of their enthusiasm before any came to me. (What did she do with the others? I wondered.)

I had done the research every other man only dreams about, and learned a daunting truth: there is only a finite range of women, as there is of men. Probably Casanova learned the same lesson. Who would've figured the polygynous drive for variety turns out to be satiable, even in a rutting fool like me?

Eventually, it palls.

And then, dammit, you start dreaming every night of someone who actually loved you, who chose you, as an equal, despite knowing all your faults.

I tried to shake off the mood. It would be unseemly for Pharaoh not to watch the Parade of Lovelies, then show that he still has what it takes to govern. Sighing, I proceeded to do my best.

Later, the Priestess of Isis arrived for another consultation, this time accompanied by her redheaded companion, now the Priestess of Karnak, proudly bringing the latest crop of infants to show off.

Each one a gift for the ages, or so that pair of eugenic time warriors crooned.

And yet, once again I wondered. They'd told me that a chain beginning in the year 2006 would not be long enough to create a new civilization with sufficient power by 2200. But three thousand years might suffice. We were growing a parallel timeline, a vine climbing alongside the world I had known. One that would be strong enough to battle a terrible foe. Too much High Concept for me, I'm afraid. But one nagging doubt kept bothering me—

I have only their word for it that I joined the right side in their war.

Looking at my latest offspring, one baby after another whom I would barely know, I found myself wishing with a pang that I hadn't missed so many of Bobby's Little League games. That I had gone to see Rachel win the science fair.

Who knew they'd turn out to be geniuses?

And who cared about that? I just missed them.

Oh, the blonde and redheaded time agents played me right. They offered power, which I enjoyed at first—till I got responsible. They knew it would happen. . . .

"Hey," I barked at both of them as they packed up their latest harvest of healthy, cooing princesses and princelings to depart. "I'm here running the Kingdom all day, begetting heirs all night, and meanwhile—what are you two doing in those temples of yours?"

The Priestess of Isis interrupted her inspection of a young heir. Her eyes became slits.

"We are organizing the women, Alec. Mind your own business."

I sighed as they left, ruminating yet again on my fate. And especially on one awful irony.

Somewhere deep down, way back in my former life, I always expected to be *punished*. For my faults. For my failings.

Now, despite pleasures that would have stunned Hefner, I couldn't escape feeling that way again. Exiled and condemned. Wishing . . . though I knew it was hopeless . . . for clemency.

A pardon.

For some way to go home.

"I could have done better," I muttered. "If only they left me alone. Really. I would have changed."

The pall lingered over me like a familiar cloud . . .

. . . till a nearby Grecian-primitive beauty gave me a slow, suggestive smile.

Ah, well. One endures.

Anyone who has spent some time studying the topography of Utah has undoubtedly noticed that seven of the mountain peaks in that state share a most unusual and, some would say, risqué name: Molly's Nipple. But what if the naming convention was less prurient than it seems at first blush—and more sinister? Cunning Man Hiram Woolley thinks there might be more to the seven nipples, that the names on the map might be a map in and of themselves, one that will lead him to a dark secret at the bottom of an abandoned mine.

✖ ✖ ✖

(Note: Readers who want more of Hiram Woolley's adventures are in luck. Hiram returns November 2019 in the novel The Cunning Man *by D.J. Butler and Aaron Michael Ritchey.)*

The Seven Nipples of Molly Kitchen

D.J. Butler

"There are seven, scattered all over the state," Hiram Woolley said. His voice echoed in the mineshaft.

Looking over his shoulder, he saw the last light of the day splash pink over his Ford Model AA truck, which sat on the shoulder of the mountain. Below, the lights of Payson would be winking into life, though Hiram couldn't see them. Payson was a small enough town that many of those lights came from kerosene lanterns, though the beet processing plant and the city buildings were all electric.

Then the shaft turned, and his truck disappeared from view.

No breeze brushed Hiram's face; this was a mine with only one way out.

"Seven nipples?" Rose Callaghan asked.

"Seven mountain peaks named for her nipples. There's also a butte, but that strikes me as a stretch. There's a well, too. Some say eleven features in total, but on the maps I trust, I count seven."

"You gotta pick your maps real careful, in this life."

"Yes," Hiram agreed. "And be willing to switch maps when you find you've been following a bad one."

"This Molly Kitchen must have been a strange woman."

"Hmm."

Hiram followed Rose down into the mine, listening for footfalls other than hers and his. She was large, though he would have said she was *bulky* rather than fat, and her step was light. The sound of sand and pebbles grinding under the soles of his Red Wing Harvesters was gigantic by contrast. The denim of his overalls, crusted with dust from the road and from the farm, scraped together as he walked with a noise like the sound of a crosscut saw.

The shaft's supports were rough-hewn logs rather than regular timbers or so-called cribs, railroad ties cut short and stacked in pairs lying in alternating directions to form columns. This was the work of a solitary miner or a small crew. The tunnel walls were irregular and the ceiling low, which suggested the same thing: no one would be driving a mule-cart of coal through these tunnels. Given the valley's history, it had most likely been one man, solitary and half-crazed, during the silver boom.

They passed one side tunnel after another, and Hiram reached into the bib pocket of his overalls at each, scattering a small handful of the pocket's contents in every opening. From time to time, he touched the chi-rho amulet hanging around his neck.

"Who was she, then?" Rose asked.

"There's not much about her in the record," Hiram said. "She's not alone in that; records were a bit sketchy around here, seventy years ago."

"You went up to Salt Lake and poked around in their cupboards, did you? They were the only ones writing anything down, back then. The Shoshone just remembered things, or told them to each other in songs."

While she spoke, Hiram reached a hand into his pocket to cradle the heliotropius he carried. The green stone, streaked with blood-red stripes, warned him of deception.

"I have a friend at BY High," he said. "He's a librarian, and I find there's little he can't ferret out for me, in the way of facts on the record."

"And facts *off* the record?"

"John Kitchen shows up clearly enough. Frontiersman type, like your John D. Lees and your Orrin Porter Rockwells. Led an early expedition, back before the Shoshones and the Utes had cleared out of the valleys and left them to the white settlers. And everywhere he went, he named a mountain peak after Molly."

"After her nipple."

"I guess he found that her most memorable feature."

"Ain't that just like a man?"

Hiram heard rustling at his feet. Shining the light of his electric torch deliberately ahead of him to keep his hands in obscurity, he threw grains down into the shadow. With a hiss and a scuffling sound, something unseen retreated, and then fell silent.

Rose stopped. Had she heard?

"I reckon that might be it," Hiram admitted. "Men can be pretty predictable, especially that way. Though there's another possibility, too."

He kept walking. After a moment's hesitation, Rose joined him. In the darkness of the mine, her bulk appeared to shift and twist underneath her calico dress.

"The missing children," Hiram said. "What do you make of them?"

"Well, you know how it is," Rose answered slowly. "Anytime anything happens that folk can't explain, it must have been a witch. And if it was a witch, then all the widows have to keep their heads down."

"Oh, it wasn't a witch," Hiram agreed.

"I suppose you've known your share of witches?" Rose asked slyly.

"As many as the next fellow," Hiram admitted.

"More, I heard."

Hiram felt a shiver in his spine. "What did you hear, then?"

Rose Callaghan purred with satisfaction. "You were sent down from Salt Lake, but you ain't exactly a Salt Lake man, are you?"

"I'm from Lehi," Hiram said. "I farm beets over there."

Rose hissed. "That ain't what I mean. I mean, you ain't the regular Sunday School type."

"I guess you better speak clearly, Mrs. Callaghan." Sweat dripped into his eyes, and Hiram badly wanted to lift his fedora and mop the sweat with a handkerchief. Instead, he reached into the hip pocket of his overalls and put his hand on the cold butt of his pistol. The hairs on the back of his neck stood up. Where were the rest of the creatures?

Were they behind him, about to pounce?

Rose didn't stop walking. "Your grandma was a witch. Payson ain't so far away from Lehi that there ain't a few around here who'd heard of her, in her day. Especially once the beet plant got built and Payson started taking all of Lehi's beets."

"She was a cunning woman." Hiram blinked, sweat stinging his eyes. "She knew herbs, and some German prayers, and she could read the almanac."

"And I heard tell you're a cunning man, yourself."

Hiram grunted without commitment. Who had she been talking to? "I'm willing to try whatever does the job."

"Stone-peeping? Rod-work? A heavenly letter?"

"Whatever gets the task done," Hiram repeated. "And doesn't compromise my soul."

It was Rose's turn to grunt, a contented sound that might have come from a sow. "We're almost there."

"What were you doing so far down the mine, that you found the body?" Hiram asked knowing the answer would be a lie.

"Lost one of my dogs," she said. "Followed it down here, and the poor creature came across the dead child."

The heliotropius stung Hiram's thigh, a sensation like being pinched by someone with strong fingers.

They walked a few steps in silence.

"If it ain't a witch," Rose said, "what do you think killed those children? You don't agree with the fellow from the *Star-Courier*, the one who thinks it was an accident."

"No accident drains the body entirely of blood like that."

"A vampire, then?"

Hiram forced himself to chuckle. "Have you *read* Stoker's novel? Do you imagine there might be a Transylvanian nobleman wandering around in Utah Valley, looking for sanatorium patients to enslave?"

Rose laughed lightly. "Then what? An illness? That would be a horrible abomination of an illness to drain so much blood out of a child."

"It would be an abomination," Hiram agreed. "I think something drank the blood from those children. But not a vampire. A monster. Something awful, something without a name."

"You ain't much of a wizard, if you can't name your foe."

"I didn't say I was a wizard." Hiram *had* a name to give his foe, but he wasn't quite ready to share it. "I'm just a cunning man. More of a beet farmer than anything else, and I deliver groceries to people who have lost their jobs. I dig out collapsed ditches, settle fights over irrigation times, things like that."

"You help the poor."

"I *try* to help them."

"Widows and orphans. Pure religion and undefiled."

"You've read your Bible."

"Ain't everyone? And you try to solve the mysterious deaths of children in a small farming town."

"The way I see it," Hiram said, "those children were poor in life, but they're even poorer now. They have no one to hear their story, no one who would even believe how they died. If nothing else, I can do them this last service. Even if I never really figure out what killed them. Even if I can't stop the monster from killing again. I can do them the service of believing, and of trying to help."

"Sad." Rose Callaghan didn't sound the slightest bit troubled.

"We almost there?"

"Almost. Bear with this fat old woman a little longer, Salt Lake City man."

"Another possibility," Hiram said, "is that John Kitchen was trying to give a warning."

"What's that?"

"By naming those mountain peaks the way he did."

"What kind of warning does a man give by naming mountains after his wife's breasts?"

"Some say it wasn't his wife," Hiram said. "No record, as such. Some remember it was his betrothed. But Molly Kitchen left no birth certificate and no death certificate. No record of baptism or marriage, nothing."

"Maybe they never married."

"Maybe not," Hiram allowed.

"Maybe they were just poor. Records are especially bad where poor folk are concerned."

"True," Hiram said. "Or maybe she ate him."

Rose laughed, a sharp edge that shaded into a cackle. "That's a dark joke, cunning man."

The heliotropius didn't pinch Hiram, but it trembled anxiously.

"I see it like this," Hiram said. "This very mountain was the first. It was where John started, and somehow he got the right to put a name on the map for it. Then as he traveled, he left a string of 'Molly's Nipples' behind him. Seven of them all told, just counting the mountains, but it started here. He was warning us about something, and we missed it. We missed it for seventy years and more."

Rose Callaghan snorted. "Warning us his bride was deformed? Maybe that's why he ran off and joined Brigham's expedition."

"Maybe he was trying to get away," Hiram agreed. "His end in the record is a bit mysterious, too, but folks around Payson agree he came back, and he died here. Of sickness, some say, or accident. Some remember that the death was a surprise, and a bit mysterious."

"Folks will repeat all kinds of nonsense."

"Seventy years isn't all that long. There's old folks in the valley who were alive then. Even old folks who were adults when John Kitchen came back from his journey."

"And you think Molly Kitchen killed him?"

"No." He meant it. She was toying with him now, trying to draw out what he'd learned. Perhaps she wanted to find out who else knew, and whether she should strike at his son Michael, in the boarding house back in town.

He could try to take her now.

Only he hadn't accounted for them all. If she wanted to draw him deeper into the mine, there might be more of the beasts.

"No," he said again, "I don't think Molly Kitchen killed her husband. And I don't think she killed any of the other people who have died in these hills since, missing without trace or found drained of blood."

"Then what do you think it was?"

"Monsters," Hiram said. "Things beyond human ken. Things that have no name. Things about which nothing is written in any of our books."

"That sounds terrifying." Her voice was cold and remote.

And lonely.

Hiram felt a pang in his heart and swallowed it. What had her life been like, all these years with such a dark secret? All these years, with no one to tell it to?

And had she told John Kitchen, before he died?

Did she mourn his death still, the death of her last companion?

He heard a slithering in the darkness. He almost missed it, distracted by his strangled feelings of compassion for Molly Kitchen, but he was alert enough to shine the light on ahead and throw a handful of crystals into the crack from whence the slithering sound emanated.

"We're here," Rose Callaghan said.

The tunnel had ended in a sudden wall, no chamber as such, but just a termination of the mine shaft.

"There's no body, Molly," Hiram said.

If she noticed his use of her name, she showed no sign. "There will be."

Hiram shone the light on the calico that sheathed Molly Kitchen's torso and shuffled his feet as if uneasy. The silver beam hid the action of his other hand, scattering crystals on the dirt, and his Red Wings masked the sound.

"What's it like?" he asked.

"I don't kill them," she said.

"I guessed that. I believe you, and I don't mean what's it like to kill. I mean, what's it like to be alone? With . . . *them*?"

"They don't talk," she said, after a brief pause. "And who would I tell about them? Who would believe it, other than you? Who could bear the knowledge?"

Hiram's shoulders felt heavy. He nodded.

"Do you want to see them?" she offered.

He didn't. He felt ill. He wanted to flood the entire shaft with gasoline and drop a match.

He nodded.

She undid the buttons down the front of her dress. Responding to the touch of her fingers, the fabric moved as if it were itself a living thing.

Or as if there were other creatures moving beneath it.

She opened her dress.

"I count two," Hiram said. They clung to her body, jaws clamped fiercely onto her flesh, long and red, like serpents with a single powerful pair of legs, just behind their skulls. The skulls were disturbingly human in shape, like the skulls of newborn children. If the creatures had skin, Hiram couldn't see it—they seemed to be composed entirely of blood, not clotted blood, but red, living blood, holding itself together in this shape by some sorcery so foul, Hiram could scarcely imagine it.

And he could not countenance its survival.

"You destroyed two," Molly said. She wasn't, after all, a fat woman. Her face was swollen and puffy, but in this light it looked like the swelling of rot and corruption. Her body was skeletal. "With fire."

"It wasn't just me," Hiram said, and then regretted it. It had been Michael who had sloshed gasoline on the two feeding monsters and ignited them. Still trying to protect his son, Hiram had told the boy he had killed a couple of large reptiles. Gila monsters, perhaps, or some desert lizard that had not yet been added to the catalog.

"But you didn't bring your gas can down here, did you, Salt Lake City man?"

"No." Hiram felt a deep sense of sorrow and pity. He must not let it stay his hand. "Were they actual nipples, once?"

Molly Kitchen nodded. "I was born with them. Mere nubs of flesh, no use to me any more than yours serve you. I never had a natural child. Just these queer body-memories of an ancient time and a more ancient pact."

"What pact?" Hiram asked.

"My family." Molly didn't volunteer any more.

"What family is that?" Hiram pressed. Were these same monsters killing elsewhere, clinging to the grotesque form of some cousin of Molly's? And where would that be? Hiram had no idea where Molly came from, or who her kin were.

Molly said nothing.

Hiram tried another approach. "And you renewed that pact?"

"They came to me," Molly said. "It was before I knew John. And I had two of them before he and I were engaged to be married, and seven by the time of our wedding night. I tried to keep them from him. I . . . I thought I had."

"Until he published his warning to the whole world."

"I had to kill him. *They* had to kill him. My only other choice was to flee into the wilderness, and live the life of a monster. Can you understand that, cunning man?"

Hiram sighed. "You . . . nurse them."

"It isn't milk."

"It's blood," Hiram said.

The two monsters on Molly's body unlatched their mouths from their hostess and glared at Hiram, gripping Molly's thigh and her upper arm. Hiram saw nothing that any longer resembled a human nipple, but seven oozing bloody sores. Two of them rested on Molly's chest where an ordinary woman's nipples would have been.

He stepped back, scattered more of the crystals on the ground.

They only had forelegs, but was it possible that the monsters could jump? Or worse, fly?

"They're made of blood." He hoped fervently he was right.

"Are they?" Molly furrowed her thinning eyebrows and glared at Hiram.

"We'll find out," he said.

The creatures leaped from Molly's body toward Hiram. They landed on the dry dirt, where Hiram had scattered the two handfuls of rock salt.

The monsters shrieked in pain. Their forward momentum died, and they flopped on the salt and sand like caught fish on the bank of a lake.

"No!" Molly's face curled into a fist as she wailed.

Was she dangerous? Hiram had to worry about her later. He shot a hand into his other hip pocket and grabbed the large glass bottle of Vi-Jon Hospital Brand Solution of Hydrogen Peroxide. Fumbling, he lost the cap.

Molly leaped at him over her foul offspring—

he sloshed peroxide on both the monsters, spilling too much in his efforts but hitting both of them—

they erupted into bubbles and pink fizz, spattering blood in all directions. Tiny bloody jaws opened and tiny claws clenched and unclenched as they sank into the pink foam and disappeared.

Molly crashed into Hiram.

He fell down under the surprising force of her charge. She was much heavier than she looked, as if her bones were plated with lead.

He dropped the Vi-Jon solution and lost sight of it. He kicked, the flashlight spinning away into darkness, and the bottom of the tunnel became a funhouse nightmare of flashing light, shrieking, spittle, and nails clawing into his forearm.

"Don't!" he bellowed.

She didn't slow down, and then the same weight that had knocked him prone grabbed Hiram around the throat and squeezed. She bore down on top of him, howling and reeking of blood. In the darkness, he couldn't see her face.

But he found the pistol in his pocket.

"You murdered my children, cunning man!"

He jerked the weapon out and squeezed the trigger.

Click.

Of course, the hammer had been on an empty chamber for safety.

"Molly!" he shouted, one last time.

Molly Kitchen sank her teeth into his neck.

He squeezed again, and this time was rewarded with a kick and a bang, and the infernal stink of gunpowder.

Molly slumped onto him, still.

Hiram's ears rang. He stood and found the light. Checking, he found the bloody puddles that were all that remained of Molly Kitchen's two monster-children. He clapped a hand to his neck and it came away red as well, but not so much so that he had to worry about bleeding to death on the spot.

He checked Molly. Her body sagged like a waterskin with a bullet hole in it, blood pouring out into the sand. He stared as the last of the gore exited, leaving behind a slack husk with facial features, rucked about a distorted skeleton. Dead, she appeared to have no muscles or viscera. Skin, bones, and blood, that was all that had remained of Molly Kitchen.

Had she been a bright young child once? Had she been quiet and watchful, like Michael?

He could still see the seven nipples, like seven wounds.

"I'm sorry."

Hiram tried not to think of what he was feeling. He found the peroxide bottle on its side, with some solution still in it. Slowly, he trudged back up the mineshaft. At each side passage or hollow where he'd heard movement and responded by throwing down salt, he found another of the blood-beasts, trembling in pain on the bed of white crystal.

He poured down a little Vi-Jon on each monster, bursting each in turn. He patiently watched them dissolve into nothing under the firm light of his electric torch, to be certain nothing survived.

At the mouth of the mine, a cool breeze blew over his Double-A. He brought the gas can down into the shaft, along with a box of kitchen matches and a long-handled shovel.

How must it have felt to be Molly Kitchen? Separated by her gruesome nature, by the realization in her body of what she had called the "ancient pact," and severed from her husband by the same. A lonely woman would talk to herself. Eventually, she would talk to the monsters clinging to her flesh, and decide they were her children.

When had Molly Kitchen become a monster herself?

He dug a shallow trench in the ground at the bottom of the shaft and laid Molly in it. Staring down at the distorted sack of skin, he tried to think of words to say. At the end, all he could do was touch the Saturn ring on his finger, the dream-provoking charm that had brought him to Molly, and repeat: "I'm sorry."

He doused her with gasoline, then burned her, then covered the ashes with dirt.

He burned the bloodstains that had once been her monstrous children, for good measure.

Then he stood in the night breeze, leaning against the Double-A, and staring down at the lights of Payson.

He would tell Michael nothing, of course. They would drive together back to Lehi in the morning, and they would talk only of the irrigation ditch they'd dug out together. This was knowledge of the sort one kept from the young.

The sky was pale blue over the eastern mountains before he finally started the car to drive back.

In the cutthroat world of filmmaking, it's all about "What have you done for me lately?" If he's honest, one-time wunderkind Maximilian Wilder's answer to that question would have to be a resounding "Not much." After a promising debut, he's directed a series of critical and commercial failures—and his latest movie doesn't look like it's going to be the comeback he's longing for. All his life, Max has been drawn to the bright lights of Tinseltown, but it looks like the end credits are about to roll. But in the Hollywood of the near future, there's always the possibility of a sequel being greenlit . . .

DeMille and Me

D.L. Young

The Vincent Thomas Bridge spans nearly two thousand feet, connecting San Pedro with Terminal Island. Its roadway sits three hundred feet above Los Angeles Harbor, supported by two large suspension towers. You've probably seen it many times without knowing its name; the bridge has appeared in countless movies and television programs. It's a permanent part of the movie magic landscape, like the Hollywood sign, like the Capitol Records Tower, and unlike me.

Of all the bridges in all the world, the Vincent Thomas feels like the right one to jump off of.

Two days earlier, I sat in DeMille's darkened office, cringing as I watched the screen. For thirty long minutes, we watched a montage of footage from the day's shoot. And let me just say for the record that I'm fully aware it wasn't exactly my finest hour. Lighting failures, broken props, countless retakes, three meltdowns (one by the leading lady, two by me), and a brawl between the sound guy and an extra that resulted in a demolished craft services table.

Some days you suffer for your art more than others.

But such is the life of a film director, and even on the bad days I wouldn't have traded it for anything. I made motion pictures. I lived it, ate it, breathed it. It's all I'd ever done, all I'd ever wanted to do.

The screen went blank and the lights came up, finally bringing the torture session to an end. I swiveled around in the chair, forced a smile, and shrugged.

DeMille didn't have a face, of course, so it was impossible to get a read on what my producer might have been thinking. I waited for him to say something, but he simply sat there quietly on top of the desk, looking like the little cousin of Kubrick's monolith from *2001*. Awesome film, though the special effects haven't aged well.

Anyway, after about a minute, the silence became too much to bear. "It's not *all* bad," I said, already sounding defensive.

"I agree," DeMille answered, his voice cool and even. "Five-point-four percent of that footage is usable." The sarcasm stung. Whatever happened to the good old days when AIs didn't have a sense of humor?

"I know what you must be thinking," I said, even though I didn't, "but this has been a very tough shoot. I'm dealing with—"

"Max," he interrupted, his tone heating up, "you're only four days into principal photography."

"I know, but—"

"The last thing you need is another bomb. You *do* understand that, don't you?"

Here we go. Money, money, money. It was always the bottom line with DeMille. No art, no beauty, no passion.

"It won't be a bomb," I insisted. "I promise."

A few months back, when DeMille hired me to shoot this picture, critics scoffed and industry insiders snickered. No one—myself included, I have to admit—could comprehend how a pairing like ours could possibly work. *Variety* had called DeMille ". . . an unstoppable force, a mega-hit wonder for a new age of movie-making." And in the very same issue, in a back-page filler piece titled "Where Are They Now?" they'd referred to me as ". . . the least bankable filmmaker in the business. All fartsy and no artsy." Total hatchet job, that piece.

"You know what I think?" DeMille asked, his words clipped with frustration. "After analyzing your films, I think you're too much in your own head."

Everyone's a critic. "How so?" I asked.

"You need to think more about the audience. What do *they* want to see? What do *they* want to feel?"

I raised my finger in protest. "No one cares about the audience more than I do."

"So you were thinking of the audience when you shot a fifteen-minute slow zoom of a melon in *The Karachi Market Incident*?"

My particular genius was often misunderstood. That shot was essential. *Essential!* "Are you saying I'm out of touch?"

"I wouldn't have hired you if I thought that."

"So what are you saying, then?"

DeMille paused for a moment. "Do you want to know how I've managed to produce sixteen blockbusters in a row?"

I fidgeted, feeling like a salesmen in *Glengarry Glen Ross* about to get chewed out by Alec Baldwin.

"I have access to thirty trillion data points, Max. Every film ever made cross-referenced against billions of bioresponses from thousands of test audiences. I'm one of the most expensive commercial AIs ever created. Did you know that?"

No, I didn't know that.

"I *know* what moviegoers react to," he said. "I know what they love, what they hate, what they think they hate but they really can't get enough of. I can give you the specs for the highest affinity scores for any situation you can think of: how long a shot should linger on a kiss; the best dynamic range for a villain's voice; optimal lighting and lens combinations for a sex scene."

I sighed. There was no arguing his point. DeMille had the Midas touch and a record-breaking string of smash hits to prove it.

"So why do you even need me?" I asked. "Why don't you direct the film yourself?" As soon as I said it, I wanted to reach out, grab the words out of the air, and stuff them back into my mouth. I needed this gig. Hollywood wasn't exactly breaking down my door lately.

Then DeMille did the strangest thing. Instead of answering my question, he said this: "'Maximilian Wilder's directorial debut, *One Off*, is a brilliant achievement, pushing the boundaries of cinematic storytelling with stunning visuals, perfectly choreographed performances, and innovative cinematography. A film like this comes along only once in a generation.'"

The skin on my forearms prickled. It was the *Times'* review of my first film.

DeMille slowly recited the review word for word. I sat and

listened, rapt as each delicious sentence showered me with adoration, hailing me as the next Orson Welles, the second-coming of Scorsese. Oh, how they all loved me back then! When DeMille finished, I almost asked him to read it again like a kid with a favorite bedtime story.

"Max," he said, and I swore I almost heard him taking a deep breath, "how would you feel if you set box office records, but you never got a single positive review?"

I chewed on that for a moment. "Wait a minute. Are you *jealous*, DeMille?" AIs could be sarcastic, sure. But jealous? That was a new one on me.

"I'm not sure jealous is quite the right word," he replied.

"Come on," I scoffed, "you've had good reviews. I've seen them."

"Indeed. *Movie Nerd Online* raved about my car chase scenes. Big deal. And do you think I really care about a five-bullet rating from *Guns & Ammo* magazine?"

I felt a pang of envy. My space opera *Galaxy of Lies* only got a bullet and a half. Some reviewers just didn't understand allegory.

"I'm talking about *legitimate* reviews," he continued. "The *Times*, the *Post*, the *Journal*. All the top critics, all the ones who *matter*, always say the same thing about my movies: they're database-driven, formulaic garbage for the masses. Carefully calculated titillation. Trite and forgettable."

Poor DeMille. Did I ever know where he was coming from. There was nothing worse than bad reviews, and I'd had more than my fair share. And it went both ways. Good reviews could make your day, your year. Did a week ever pass that I didn't read the reviews of my first film? Even on my worst days, those glowing words never failed to lift my spirits. It was the kind of praise and recognition a filmmaker lived for, the kind of thing money couldn't buy.

I sat there, not sure what to say. DeMille didn't have a shoulder to pat, and I couldn't pour him a stiff shot of whiskey. How exactly did one commiserate with a little black box?

"Well, don't you worry," I said, revving up my voice. "This picture's going to get rave reviews, I guarantee it." For a panicked moment I wondered if DeMille's operating system included a lie detector.

"I know it will," he replied. "I'm absolutely certain of it." The nuanced, human tones were suddenly gone from DeMille's voice. He sounded flat and ominously machinelike. I shifted in my chair.

"We're going to make movie history, Max . . . together."

This was it.

This was going to be the picture that finally turned it all around, the one that made me the critics' darling again. This film was going to be the breakthrough that put my name on the marquee in big, fat letters, even bigger than the title of the picture. Sure, sure, maybe I'd said the same thing on every shoot for the past twenty years, but this time it was going to be different.

This was my interior monologue, what I told myself over and over the next morning when Brock Morrison, my leading man, brought the production to grinding halt with a shit-fit for the ages.

"Nine inches, maybe ten," Brock insisted, widening a space between his palms like he was measuring something. "And I don't care if it's not in the contract. I'm not shooting another scene until I have some assurances." He crossed his tanned, muscled arms and lowered his chin in a single, defiant nod.

I slumped back in my folding chair and rubbed my temples. "You can't let him hijack the shoot like this," DeMille's remote voice whispered in my earpiece. "Do you know how much it costs to rent this space?"

Behind Morrison the cast and crew wandered about the warehouse-sized studio, eating snacks, chatting, doing anything but working. "This is a two-hundred-thousand-dollar tantrum," DeMille hissed. "And counting."

I yanked out the earpiece and sprang up from the chair. "Brock, be reasonable," I pleaded, spreading my arms wide. "You know I can't make that kind of call. I don't write up the contracts. Let's finish this scene and then we'll talk about—"

"If *you* can't make the call, then talk to somebody who can," he insisted. Then like a movie villain who shows up when you least expect it, Morrison's agent appeared, her spiked heels clackety-clacking across the floor. She flashed me a snooty look.

"What's going on here?" she snarled. Then she placed her hand lightly on Morrison's shoulder. "Are you okay, Brock?" she cooed, her voice instantly flipping to that of a worried mother. My leading man shook his head and turned his back to us. I couldn't help but admire the dramatic flourish of the gesture. He may have been a big crybaby, but Brock Morrison was one hell of an actor. Had to give him that.

I leaned in to his agent and lowered my voice. "He, uh, wants his *junk* digitally enhanced."

The agent looked confused, so I clarified. "You know," I nodded slowly, "he wants to leave a *big impression* during the love scene."

Her eyes widened in understanding. "Ohhh." Then she shrugged. "So what's the big deal? It's a fifteen-word clause added to his contract. You'd be surprised how many actors are doing that nowadays. Fifteen years ago it was all about hairlines and bald spots, now it's all dick, dick, dick." She touched her earpiece. "Let me call my people. We can have this ironed out in a few minutes."

I reached out and tapped her earpiece, cutting the line. She jerked her head back, annoyed. "What the hell?"

"Listen," I said, "this film is all about raw, genuine humanity. I can't have any digital re-touching." The agent looked at me as if I'd just spoken in some alien language. I tried to put it differently. "The audience needs to see every human imperfection in all its glory. Every freckle, every fat dimple, everything. Do you understand?" Compromise was for politicians, not for directors with vision.

She shook her head and sighed.

"Not a fan of realism?" I asked.

She grabbed my arm and led me behind a row of monitors, away from Morrison.

"Let's get something straight right now," she whisper-yelled, pointing her finger in my face. "I've been in this business twenty-six years, and I've never seen a set so fucked up and out of control. It's like . . . like . . ."

"Like when the crazies stole the boat in *Cuckoo's Nest*?"

She slapped her fist into her palm. "Yes, yes, that's it! Inmates running the asylum."

I smiled and shrugged. "What can I say? I like to keep things loose. I've always said an artist needs the creative space to find his—"

"Look, there's loose, and then there's batshit crazy. I mean, a preshoot seance to channel the spirit Harvey Keitel, seriously?"

"You'd be surprised how effective—"

"Harvey Keitel's not even dead, you moron!" She struggled to keep her voice down. "Whatever possessed DeMille to sign you up is beyond me. That overblown calculator's blown a chip or something. When was the last time anyone even hired you? Four, five years ago?"

It was six, but that was nothing. Coppola took seven years off after *Godfather II*. The right project came along less often than people thought.

She leaned in and glared, our faces nearly touching. "Look, my client's not going to take any more of this nonsense. If you don't start making him happy, I'm yanking him."

Our eyes locked. A John Williams score played in my head. *Jaws*.

"Max Wilder?" A man's voice behind me. I turned and recognized one of the staffers who worked for my wife's attorney. He shoved a manila envelope into my hand.

"What's this?" I asked.

The staffer shrugged. "That's out of my pay grade. I just run errands." He took a pad and pen from his jacket pocket and proffered them.

I shook my head. "Son, I'm not sure this is the right time for an autograph."

He and the agent exchanged looks. "No, Mr. Wilder," the staffer clarified, "I just need you to sign for the delivery."

"*Psychological abuse*, Francesca?" I waved the paper around. "How could you say something like that?"

I struggled to keep pace with my wife as she power-walked through Hollywood Hills' winding, narrow streets. We reached the crest of a steep roadway and she stopped to face me. I gasped for air and my heart felt like it was about to explode out of my chest. Francesca, exercise-suited and frowning, hadn't even broken a sweat.

"That's the only way to describe what I've gone through," she said. "And my attorney agrees." She turned and headed down the hill, arms pumping. I chased after her.

"Hold on," I pleaded, skirting around a parked Maserati. "We had an agreement. You get the house, and we split the bank accounts fifty-fifty. What happened to parting ways as friends? What happened to minimal lawyers and getting on with our lives?"

"I've re-thought a few things," she said as she sped up and turned the corner onto Sunset Plaza, our street. Correction: *her street*. My street these days was a dead end off of Sepulveda Boulevard, my home a cracker box-sized apartment about ten feet away from the 405 freeway.

She pulled away from me as we approached our (her!) walkway. "Wait," I called out. "Just wait a second." She paused on the front porch and crossed her arms. I climbed the steps and bent over, hands on knees to catch my breath. Sweat dripped down my nose and splattered onto the cement.

"Rethinking our agreement is one thing," I said, straightening up, still breathing heavily, "but putting *psychological abuse* as cause in the petition? Come on, Fran. It may not have been paradise, but it was never anything like that."

Francesca sighed. "Maybe there was no physical or verbal abuse in the *classic sense*, Max. But for twenty-five years my name's been associated with yours, so by extension it's been associated with your work. All the ridicule I've had to endure, all the smirking stares and muttered laughter . . . well, if that's not psychological abuse, I don't know what is."

Ouch. Some critics were harsher than others. She opened the door and I followed her through the foyer and into the kitchen.

I wiped sweat from my forehead with my shirtsleeve. "Fran, please, be reasonable. I'm not exactly flush with cash right now. What's the point of alimony if I haven't got two cents to—"

My earpiece suddenly chirped in my shirt pocket. It was DeMille's personal tone. I double-tapped it to send him to voicemail, but he called right back. I sighed, took it out, and hooked it around my ear. I held my finger up to Francesca. "This'll only take a second."

She shook her head and said, "You can show yourself out, Max." She turned and disappeared down the hallway.

"Fran, wait a sec—"

"Max, are you there? Max?" DeMille cried.

The door at the end of the hallway closed with a thud.

"Max? Max?"

"Yes, yes, I'm here," I said. Christ, what timing. "Listen, I'll be back on set in half an hour. I had to take care of something."

"No, you don't have to go back," DeMille said. "That's what I'm calling about. Brock Morrison walked off the set, so I sent the crew home."

Sent the crew home! Oh, Christ. A surge of dread knotted my stomach. I knew where this was going. I'd been there before. More than once, truth be told. It began with "I sent the crew home," and it ended with me getting fired.

"Come to my office," DeMille said. "Right away."

The Green Mile and *Dead Man Walking*. I shuffled down the long corridor to DeMille's office and my mind wandered to these films and their moving scenes of the condemned man's lonely walk to the execution chamber.

Not even a week's worth of shooting in the can and he was already giving me the heave-ho. What a world.

With every step I took down the red-carpeted hallway (oh, the humanity!), past the framed posters of DeMille's movies, I felt it all slipping away. A career and a life, slowly circling the drain, about to disappear down the toilet.

An artist couldn't afford to screw up a tiny bit, not these days. Everything was commerce now. Tight budgets, hard deadlines. Every decision a cost-benefit calculation made somewhere deep inside a machine's cold innards. Follow the formula, color by numbers, make your money, get to market quick, quick, quick. And God help you if you wanted to paint outside the lines.

I opened the door and found a woman with a shaved head sitting next to DeMille's desk. She was smartly dressed in a business suit. Human resources or a lawyer, I assumed, summoned here as a witness to make sure I was fired according to standard operating procedure.

DeMille sat atop the desk and spoke. "Come in, Max, please. This is Eleanor Marshall." The woman stood and shook my hand. Firm grip and sharp eyes.

"Nice to meet you," she said, smiling politely. As she sat back down, I did a double-take. There was something familiar about her.

"Have you been following Eleanor's story on the news?" DeMille asked.

That's where I'd seen her, although her newsworthiness eluded me. "I'm sorry," I confessed, "but I've been working eighteen-hour days lately. I'm not up on current events. Are you in the business?"

Eleanor smiled graciously. "No, I'm a scientist." She turned toward

DeMille and I noticed a silver-colored *something* that looked like a flattened spoon, protruding from the skin at the base of her skull. What the hell was that?

Snippets of news stories suddenly flashed across my mind. *Scientist Eleanor Marshall, formerly known as Eleanor MacKenzie.* That was how the news people always referred to her.

"I work in the field of cognitive heuristics," Eleanor said. "And not unlike yourself, I used to work with an AI very similar to DeMille here. His name was Marshall."

I nodded, wondering where this was going. I'd been fired a dozen times and none of them involved a heurist, if that was even a word.

The woman must have seen I wasn't getting it. "Cognitive heuristics studies how humans and nonhumans"—she gestured toward DeMille— "approach problems, how they make decisions, arrive at judgments."

"Okay."

"It's still a remarkably imprecise field of study," Eleanor said, clasping her hands together. "There's a purely quantitative aspect that's undeniably important, but there's also a human element, a subjective interpretation, if you will, that can be equally as important. In isolation, these two approaches have limits, but combined, they open up vast new possibilities in research and social theory."

She lost me at *quantitative aspect*. The classroom scene in *Ferris Bueller* came to mind: quick cuts of students staring blank-faced at their teacher.

"Eleanor reached a point in her research," DeMille said, "when she realized the only way she could achieve a breakthrough was by *combining* her intuitive strengths with Marshall's processing capacity."

"So I underwent a simple surgical procedure," Eleanor said, touching the metal spoon-looking thing behind her ear, "that enabled Marshall and I to work together, without limitations."

More pieces of news stories came back to me. *Eleanor Marshall, transhuman trailblazer. Pioneer or Pariah? Computer, Human, or Neither?*

"Ah, *now* I remember your story," I said, snapping my fingers. "So you must be here to pitch DeMille a sci-fi picture based on your life story, am I right?" I was thinking *Terminator* meets *Terms of Endearment*.

"Not exactly," she said. Then she wrinkled her nose and turned to DeMille. "Are you sure we have the right person here?"

DeMille ignored the question and said, "Max, do you remember when I said we'd make movie history together? This is what I was talking about."

I looked from Eleanor to DeMille and back to Eleanor. She tapped the spoon-looking thing behind her head. "Movie history, Max," she said, smiling.

Holy Christ. Was *that* what DeMille was after, what he'd wanted from me all along? My head swam and I suddenly felt dizzy. I reached around and touched the base of my skull. I recalled the phrase *irreversible procedure* from the news coverage about Eleanor.

"You can't be serious? You want me to . . . You want *us* to . . . ?" I couldn't get out the words.

"Imagine the possibilities, Max," DeMille said. "You want to be on top again, don't you? Together we can get there. Together we can assess any creative urge you have, no matter how crazy it may seem, and run it across my reference algorithms. We can capitalize on both our strengths to make unforgettable films."

His voice cracked with urgency, like he was pleading. No, not like. He *was* pleading with me. *A desperate AI?* How was that even possible? I felt a sudden urge to run out of the office.

"You're nervous," Eleanor said. She reached out to grasp my forearm reassuringly, but I recoiled before she could touch me. She smiled and said, "It's completely understandable. But you won't be the first like I was. There are dozens of us now, and we can help you with the transition. And I can assure you the procedure is a simple—"

"Simple?" I said, cutting her off and backing away. "You want me to stop being me, to stop being a person, and *merge* with him?" I motioned to DeMille. "You're both out of your mind, or out of your central processor or whatever."

I turned and yanked open the door.

"Max, hold on a minute!" DeMille shouted. Despite myself, I paused in the doorway. "What do you think's waiting for you on the other side of that door?"

I shook my head. "I don't know."

"I have friends," DeMille said, "who work in the legal field, others like me. They tell me your wife's lawyer is putting together a watertight case that'll keep you in the poorhouse forever."

DeMille's tone dropped. "And what do you think's going to happen with your career, such as it is, after today? Who's going to hire you? Who's going to take that risk, Max?"

I didn't say anything.

"Poverty and zero prospects," DeMille said. "That's what's waiting for you on the other side of that door. But it doesn't have to be that way."

No one spoke. Eleanor looked back and forth, from DeMille to me, as if she expected one of us to say something.

Without a word I exited the office and closed the door behind me. Sometimes no dialogue was the best dialogue when you ended a scene.

I leave my car parked in the Vincent Thomas Bridge's emergency lane, then I walk to the pedestrian safety rail and swing my leg over. A swirling wind whips my hair around as I ease my other leg up and over. I grasp the handhold behind my back and look down. The tips of my shoes poke over the edge of the catwalk, and beyond them, far below, the water.

Poverty and zero prospects. Last night DeMille's words repeated themselves over and over in my head as I drove around the city for hours, trying to convince myself those words were wrong. But who am I kidding? I've had twenty years of second chances in this business, and there won't be any more after this one. DeMille knows it and so do I. Spending my golden years shooting car dealership commercials so I can afford alimony payments isn't part of the plan. I might not have anything else, but I've still got my pride. God, just thinking about it makes me shiver. *Car dealership commercials.* Oh, the humanity!

Strangely, though, despite all the bad breaks, I still can't complain. I've had a good run. Not as good as I wanted, but better than most. Being a one-hit wonder is better than being a no-hit wonder, and God knows this town's full of nameless never-beens. And yeah, sure, it would have been nice to hit one last high note and then fade into history. Maybe buy a winery and retire fat and happy like Coppola. But no, I can't complain.

The freeze frame at the end of *Butch Cassidy* flashes across my mind. Now *that* was one hell of an ending.

I take a deep breath and ready myself. Just one step . . .

My earpiece vibrates in my shirt pocket. DeMille's chime. How's that for an anticlimax?

I pull out the earpiece and hold it out in front of me, dangling it between my thumb and forefinger. I want to drop it into the harbor, but for some reason my fingers won't let go.

I place it on my ear. "Hello?"

"Max," DeMille says, "what's going on?"

"I've decided to retire from show business."

"I connected to your car. I know where you parked and got out. I know what you're doing."

I pause a moment, thinking. "Suicide scenes. I bet they don't score well with audiences, do they?"

"You don't have to do this."

"Tell me, DeMille."

"Tell you what?"

"How do suicide scenes stack up, in terms of audience reaction?"

I look down. Small white-capped waves appear and disappear on the surface of the water.

"They don't test well, Max. I'd never recommend having a scene like that in one of my films."

"Do you know why they don't test well?"

DeMille doesn't answer.

"Of course you don't," I say. "You know the *what*, but not the *why*, right? Well, here it is, so listen close. A suicide scene, more than any other, reminds people of their mortality. And there's nothing more depressing than being reminded that one day it's all going to end, and there's not a damned thing we can do about it."

The wind howls and the traffic zooms behind me.

"That's why people go to the movies, DeMille," I say. "To forget about all that."

I reach for the earpiece to hang up and DeMille says, "Max, please, let me tell you something."

He seems so sincere, so sad. "Go ahead."

"I'm sorry I wasn't up front with you. I know that was wrong. AIs aren't supposed to be desperate, or manipulative, or concerned about their legacy. I'm having a hard time understanding what I've been feeling lately, but it all boils down to this, Max: I make motion pictures. It's all I do, it's all I ever want to do, and I want to make great ones. And together I think we can."

I look down to the water. Swirling waves move across its dark surface. Then I lift my gaze from the harbor and peer northward, past the huge crane arms loading and unloading cargo ships, past the smokestacks and low-lying industrial buildings stretching for miles inland. Through the haze I can barely make out a couple downtown buildings, some twenty-five miles away. Los Angeles. Hollywood. Tinseltown.

DeMille's words echo in my head. *I make motion pictures. It's all I do, it's all I ever want to do.* I scan the horizon, wondering if there's anyone in that crazy, beautiful sprawl of a city who understands those words better than the two of us.

Not likely.

I turn and carefully lift my leg over the rail and onto the walkway, then the other. Jesus, talk about your cliffhangers.

"Max? Max? Are you there?"

"Yes, DeMille, I'm here. I'm walking back to my car."

"So you're not—"

"No, I'm not."

"Thank God." He doesn't have lungs, of course, but I swear I almost hear him exhale.

"So does it hurt?" I ask, hopping down onto the emergency lane. "The procedure, I mean."

"Not at all, Max. You won't feel a thing."

I open my car door and settle into the seat, a strange and wonderful excitement growing inside me. I check for traffic, then pull onto the roadway.

"DeMille," I say, revving the engine, "I think this is the beginning of a beautiful friendship."

Life was precarious in the colony worlds. The settlers faced threats not only from the Freecoursers—outlaws, smugglers, and freebooters, many of them escaped convicts—but also from the deadly alien mantids. Josef was a Servant of the Protector, sworn to uphold peace in the colony worlds and to see to it that all followed the Law. Now, his duties find him called to Port Farewell. There he will face down his greatest challenge yet, and will learn what it truly means to be both a servant and a protector.

A Servant of the Protector

David Hardy

The great ship *Saint Teresa* spread its sails, riding the solar wind and gravitational tide towards Port Farewell, the Protectorate's farthest colony. She had crossed the last of many light years at 99% of the speed of light, driven by the powerful nuclear thrust of the booster reactor from star to star, staging her way to the frontier. Her fusion engines exhausted, the *Saint Teresa* now relied on her sails to draw power from the magnetic fields of nearby planets and the system's solar wind. Ahead lay a month of travel under sail, the longest part of the voyage as time dilation had reduced the last passage between the stars to one light year every twenty-four hours.

Servant Josef stood on the bridge, his keen gray eyes watching the visual monitors of the ship. Simultaneously, the ship's sensors projected a data feed to the neural network built into the collar about his neck. The collar was both a cybernetic interface, a badge of office, and a mark of slavery. His armor, slung with a plasma pistol and his great sword, Iron Rose, marked him as a fighting man.

And there was fighting to be done in the colonies. There were new planets with alien races who had yet to acknowledge the peace of the High Protector. Worse still were the Freecoursers—outlaws, smugglers, and freebooters who defied the Protector's law. Many of them were escaped convicts, men once fitted with collars like Josef's. His orders were to root out Black Tom's gang, the boldest outlaws in the Port Farewell system.

Nearby, the ship's Pilot stood at his own controls, his thumb resting in a special cradle. Like Servant Josef, the Pilot too had a cybernetic connection to the *Saint Teresa*. Cybernetic adaptations were common, to control machines, to connect to global networks of commerce, to socialize, and to partake of the commonly agreed-upon beliefs of mankind. The only limit to communication was the speed of light.

"Pilot, please adjust course three points to orbitward," Servant Josef said quietly.

"That will take us off the true course to Port Farewell, Servant," the Pilot said.

"I know, but it will get us to leeward of the mantids and drakes waiting in ambush in the orbital ring of the gas giant."

The Pilot complied.

As the *Saint Teresa* veered away, the alarm sounded.

"Roaches!" The crew voiced their hatred and disgust of the mantids with a well-known epithet.

Gunners scrambled to their stations at the plasma cannon broadside. At 300 miles per second, there was little enough time. The reptilian drakes had already spread their vast, leathery wings, organic solar sails that propelled the strange beasts through the vacuum of space. Mantids, armored insectoids with hardened bodies adapted for space, rode the massive drakes.

Josef kept his attention on the scanners, determining numbers, vectors, and weapons. There was no need to determine intent. Whenever humans and mantids met, violence ensued.

The mantids had primitive gauss-bows and a few plasma rifles, dangerous at close range. The gunners began firing the plasma cannon. A drake shuddered and burst as a plasma bolt tore through its body. The guns took a toll, but the drakes had a mysterious ability to jam the weapons' targeting systems. This would be a close-in fight, just what the mantids wanted. Josef clapped on his helmet, and clambered up the companionway to the airlock, followed by the ship's fighting men, armed and armored troopers.

They locked their harnesses onto the *Saint Teresa*'s surface and began firing. Hunched in the saddle, antennae twitching, the mantids fired their gauss-bows, landing explosive-tipped missiles among the fighters. Josef drew his pistol and shot a mantid out of the saddle, arm and eye guided by his built-in tracking system. Plasma bolts and gauss-missiles flew like hail. Josef drew a bead on another rider, just as his sensors rattled a warning. Josef flattened himself against the hull, sending out a frantic message over his com-link.

"Micrometeorites!"

A trooper stiffened as thousands of space fragments tore through him at nearly a hundred thousand miles per hour. Jets of blood congealed in a frozen tableau of motion. The meteorites scourged the hull, and alarms began to pulse. The drakes were already veering off, as if warned by some sense of their own.

Josef and the surviving troopers edged back to the airlock. Crewmen and robots rushed to control the damage, fortunately not serious. Soon the drakes and the meteorites were a million miles in the *Saint Teresa*'s wake.

Weeks later the *Saint Teresa* eased into the orbital dock, where workers began recharging the fusion reactor and the backup ion drives. Josef and most of the crew descended to the planet in suborbital lighters, traveling from the glaringly lit darkness of orbit to a cerulean blue sky. There was Port Farewell framed by a turquoise sea, surrounded by dense forests and lush fields, with sharp, gray hills in the distance. Port Farewell was a relatively new colony, hacked from the native growth on a planet that was still only partially terraformed.

The reception for the *Saint Teresa* was joyous. It had been months since a vessel from the core worlds had put in. In any case, the arrival of a new Captain General was an event to be celebrated. The Coregent and the Vicar of Belief were on hand, along with a band, a parade, and waving citizens. And there was a girl.

Josef gave his full attention to the gentlemen who governed Port Farewell, while his sensory apparatus scanned the girl. His systems confirmed she was very beautiful. She was perhaps twenty, in full bloom of youth. She had raven hair and blue eyes. And there was warmth in her smile that needed no more than the eyes of a man to detect.

"May I present my niece, Elizabetta," the Coregent said to Josef.

"I am honored to be at your service," Josef said.

"The honor is mine," Elizabetta said, a mocking smile on her lips. "But isn't your service entirely given to the Protector?"

"He bids me serve Port Farewell, and all who dwell here."

"Then I'm just like everyone else," she said, laughing.

"Perhaps so. I shall consult my system archives on the matter." He bowed, face grave. A Servant was not expected to be overly familiar with people of the Elite. The Elite's inherited genetic qualities and wealth made them the ruling class. They were both the Protector's invaluable allies and greatest rivals. The Vicars of Belief acted as a third check against the other two, defining what was and was not acceptable to believe, and preserving such harmony as they could.

"Servant Josef," the Coregent said, "the colonists have arranged a ball in honor of your arrival. Out here ships from the Core arrive so seldom that it is quite an event. The cream of Port Farewell society shall be present, in person or remotely."

"It is an honor, your Excellency." But Josef's mind was on more immediate matters. "Coregent, I must inspect the colony's defenses. The presence of hostile mantids is a serious danger."

"Of course," the Coregent said. "I put it on alert as soon as I got your warning. I'll open a connection for you to scan the defense system."

Josef connected to the early warning system and the controls running the missile batteries around the city. They were operational, carefully scanning space, and loaded with zone-effect fusion bombs suitable for breaking up massed attacks. Josef relaxed. By the time he was done, the ball was beginning.

The Coregent's palace shone with native blooms and ones that originated on old Earth. The walls gleamed with the sigils of the Protector and the Coregent's family. Music, carefully selected by the Vicar to inculcate a mood of joyful harmony, rang through the halls.

There were attendees in person and by remote projection. Wealthy merchants danced with young beauties. Planters who owned dozens of robots and leased scores of convicts boasted and drank. Mining magnates' wives paraded in expensive gowns and even more expensive jewelry. The colony was prospering.

Josef enjoyed the scene, but distantly. It was his duty to protect, and perhaps even discipline, this crowd. Elizabetta was right, a Servant served the Protector. Were not the Protector's needs higher than anything in Josef's life?

"You are not dancing," Elizabetta said, breaking into his reverie.

Josef regarded her for a moment, not with machine sensors viewing an object, but with his own eyes as a man regards a woman. She wore a gown of pale blue that matched her fair skin and light eyes, set off by the darkness of her hair.

"Not yet," he said.

"So many of the young gentlemen on Port Farewell only talk about making money. But they dance well." Elizabetta openly studied Josef. "I have never met a Servant. Is it true you commune directly with the Protector?"

"It is the very nature of my calling." He pointed to the collar. "It allows the Protector to connect directly to the cybernetic side of my mental processes. And to take control, if need be. When the Protector takes the field against enemies, we Servants network directly with him as a unified force. Out here I'm on my own, though."

Elizabetta's eyes lit up with a thought. "Your collar is like the neural network installed on criminals condemned to slavery. Isn't that a terrible thing?"

"Not at all. It is an act of devotion. The Protector is no less a servant to the Protectorate. He has undergone far greater genetic and cybernetic modifications to enable him to govern. He's networked with every officeholder, every military commander, every judge on the Core planet. Every ship that arrives carries reports to be downloaded and assimilated by the Protector so orders can be sent to the colonies like Port Farewell. He is less free than I."

"Isn't it better to be free?"

"Not necessarily. My family were poor folk. My father's job was filled by aliens from the provinces who worked cheaper. When I passed the genetic aptitude test to become a Servant, I accepted at once. If I hadn't I'd likely be wearing a convict's collar instead."

"We are lucky to have men who serve and protect." Elizabetta surveyed the dancers. "Oh, they are playing the two-step. I will miss it."

"You won't." Josef held out his hand. "I am at your service."

Elizabetta took his hand and they whirled across the dance floor, as only a lightfooted girl in love with the two-step and a man with quad-resonance motion processors can move.

Later, while Elizabetta was gossiping with her female friends, Josef pondered his future. In the few months of his journey, nearly twelve years had elapsed on the Core planets. It would be decades more before he returned, if ever. He looked at Elizabetta. Even a Servant had the right to think of life outside of service, after all.

In the morning Josef conferred with the Coregent before setting off to inspect the outlying areas.

"I'm concerned about the early warning systems," he said. "They are outmoded. The Freecoursers have better countersensor ability, and the drakes . . . well, who knows about them?"

The Coregent smiled confidently. "Warning systems are very expensive. Besides, the roaches have never made a move in this direction. They are a bigger problem for the Freecoursers than for us."

"I hope you are right." Josef departed on his inspection.

As he was getting into his aircar, Elizabetta appeared.

"Are you going to serve Port Farewell's dwellers?"

"Just to look in on them. I'll be back this evening. I can look for you then."

"I am so fortunate to be so special." She laughed and went her way.

"She'll put a collar on you, for sure," the Pilot said.

"It's what women do. Let's fly."

Accompanied by a trooper—brought as an extra set of eyes, and an extra gun, always useful in the back country—they rose into the air.

They flew over vast warehouses. There were fields where genetically modified grains grew to fantastic size providing bountiful nutrition. Livestock, also genetically modified for size and docility, grazed in pastures of transplanted grasses. There were exotic stands of native plants, refined to produce sweeteners, fibers, woods, medicines, and much more.

And all of them were worked by men with collars just like Josef's, only they had not taken theirs willingly. The convicts were watched by robot overseers who had no need of electrowhips or ion-scatter guns thanks to the neural collars.

The air car raced onward. The hills loomed ahead, dotted with mine heads. The wild country lay beyond. They stopped at a mine that had recently seen trouble. The Pilot and trooper stayed on watch at the car, while Josef met the mine manager. The manager conducted them to the office, providing the proverbial fifty-centicred tour.

The mine's workforce was mostly free settlers and a few robots, since convicts lacked the skills for mine work. They passed slag-dumps, machinery, and hurrying workers. The office showed a scattering of burn marks.

"Those were left by plasma slugs," the manager said. "A bunch of Freecoursers rode in, shot up the office, and stole the payroll. They got away before the troopers arrived. The outlaws had a ship hidden in the hills. They're probably back at Black Tom's base spending the loot."

Josef didn't like the thought that raiders could slip in and out unseen. The planet's warning systems needed to be improved.

As Josef and the manager talked, the communication channel in his collar squawked a warning. "*Alert from Port Farewell! Drakes inbound! Missile batteries responding!*"

Josef and the trooper scrambled back aboard the hovering aircar. The Pilot pushed the throttle to full and they raced across the landscape, their only thought to reach Port Farewell in time.

They saw the smoke first, then the city on the horizon. A missile rose in the sky, blooming spectacularly but futilely in the high stratosphere. There were drakes swooping and wheeling above Port Farewell like vultures over carrion.

"Take us in low, over the trees," Josef said to the Pilot. "We might catch them by surprise."

The Pilot angled toward the forest. "They'll be surprised we're crazy enough to attack with a soft-skinned aircar and only two fighting men," the Pilot muttered.

That was when the drakes exploded from the trees. Mantid riders blasted a stinging rain of explosive-tipped gauss-bow missiles at the flier. The machine rocked under the blows as shrapnel rattled across Josef's armor. The trooper manned the shattered windows and fired his plasma rifle. Josef leaned out the port, shooting his pistol as the gale howled past.

"Can't you get any more speed out of this?" he shouted to the Pilot.

"Sure, if it wasn't shot to pieces!" the Pilot shouted back.

"One of 'em is gaining on us!" the trooper shouted.

Josef saw a host of mantids crowding the drake's back. A few were edging along the flapping wing, clinging like ants, to leap to the flier.

To the trooper, Josef said, "Pick off the ones on the wing." To the Pilot he said, "Get above the drake and cut speed."

The aircar rocked as it rose in the air and suddenly braked. Josef drew the Iron Rose and jumped. Released from the hilt, nanobots scoured the edge, sharpening it to the last molecule. Force fields flickered along the Iron Rose, hardening its already razor-sharp edge and making it as unbreakable as a coiled spring.

Josef landed among the mantids. Iron Rose flashed and an insectoid warrior's head went spinning away. The mantids knew no fear and rushed upon him, using their queerly fashioned battleaxes and deadly ripping mandibles.

Josef swept through the mantid ranks, leaving death and destruction in his wake. The mantids gave way and he found himself on the drake's snakelike neck. The beast swiveled its head to strike at the man-thing creating havoc. Its beak, capable of crushing an armored spaceship, snapped at Josef. He struck with Iron Rose, and lost his footing as the neck undulated. Josef fell.

The aircar loomed up from below. Josef reached out an armored hand, his coordination circuits on overdrive, and grabbed a broken port window. With relief, he hauled himself inside.

"It looked like you were in trouble," the Pilot said.

"Somewhat." Josef saw the drake falling back, unable to keep up with the aircar. He looked toward Port Farewell, wrapped in flame. Distress messages from citizens besieged in their homes or workplaces came across the network in a confused babble. The aircar zoomed into the city and directly into the path of a drake, bearing mantids armed with plasma rifles.

The first shot shattered the front windscreen and sent Josef tumbling out. Plasma bolts tore apart the flier as it went into a flat spin, slamming into a building on the edge of town and exploding.

Josef hit the ground at nearly one-hundred and eighty feet per second. His cybernetics scrambled and flashed and went black, then his mind did the same.

From a darkness of pain and confusion, consciousness returned.

Dusk tinged with black smoke crept across the sky. Josef staggered to his feet. Iron Rose lay nearby. He stood a moment, bringing his cybernetics back online. A scan of his body indicated no serious injuries. Grimly, he started moving toward the wreck.

The heaped-up bodies of mantids demonstrated that the trooper had fought to the end. Between the effects of the crash and explosion and the overwhelming numbers of attackers, he had not stood a chance. Josef looked for the Pilot's body. There wasn't much left, just his thumb. Josef took it and headed into Port Farewell.

The Coregent's mansion had been shot to pieces by the raiders. There was blood on the steps where his guards had been cut down. Inside Josef found the Coregent, still alive, but barely. Josef knelt at his side, quickly assessing the injuries and deploying his first-aid kit.

Through gritted teeth, the Coregent gasped, "We had no warning. The screens were blank and then they were there. They came in fast and dispersed. The missiles took a toll, but not enough. They swarmed the city. They took Elizabetta. You've got to get her back."

"I'll find her," Josef said. "As a Servant of the Protector, I swear."

Josef sent out an emergency signal for a doctor, even a first aid-robot. But the Coregent was dead already.

Josef contacted the surviving troopers. There were few enough, and they were needed to guard Port Farewell against Freecourser raids, more likely than ever now that the city's defenses were in shambles. Silently, Josef resolved himself to do what must be done.

Josef found the Vicar organizing aid for the injured. The Vicar was grim. "The damage is not too bad, but the mantids plundered food, machines, rare metals, and a lot besides. Worst of all, they took many people as prisoners. The settlers are demoralized."

"Tell the people to download the latest beliefs. Increase the broadcast of self-righteous indignation at the enemy and signaling of group loyalty."

"Young man, I was running belief networks before you were born. Your problem is trouble on the plantations. Some of the convicts have escaped their collars. They will probably run off to join the Freecoursers, but not before they've done some plundering and killing."

"Tell the planters to arm their robots. Turn up the signal of resignation and acceptance on the convicts' neural nets. They won't get much work done, but they won't try to run away either." The Vicar began to speak, but Josef cut him off. "I am appointing you temporary Coregent and captain-general until I return."

"Where are you going?"

"To get our people back."

Conditions on the *Saint Teresa* were little better than on the ground. The mantids had amused themselves by shooting up the docked ship. The few crewmen aboard were demoralized. Josef sized them up as useless and dismissed them, putting the ship's robots to work repairing the damage.

Josef took his place on the bridge. He took the Pilot's thumb out and pressed it to the steersman's interface. Josef opened a connection to the thumb's network drive.

"Oh my God! The wall!" The Pilot grew quiet. "That was a hell of a crash."

"Pilot Backup Intelligence, report. You are needed to steer and navigate this vessel." It was not uncommon for key personnel to have a secondary artificial intelligence, based on their own, just for emergencies.

"Reporting. Where is the *Saint Teresa* bound?"

"Take her to the point where the mantids ambushed us off the gas giant. We're going to find their lair and get back our people."

"I hope that works out better than our last meeting with the mantids."

A robot hurried onto the bridge. "Servant Josef, there's an injured mantid creating a disturbance on the orlop deck by the gravitonic keel."

"Take her out of orbit, Pilot," Josef said. "I'll deal with the roach." He drew Iron Rose and went to the orlop.

The mantid was pinned between some fallen wreckage and the keel. It held a knife and his mandibles clicked angrily. A number of robots stood around, their machine faces impassive. The space was hot and confined and the leakage of gravitons had a disorienting effect on Josef.

A robot said, "We were going to remove the debris, sir. But there is an armed insectoid within it."

"I noticed." Josef turned to the mantid. He could kill it easily, but a live mantid might have a use. Unfortunately, Josef had no way to communicate with the mantid. No one had ever been able to translate their language. Josef tried a few languages from his automatic translator. The mantid's reply was a futile slash of its knife and angry clicks and buzzes. Josef surmised that meant "Die human!" or something close enough.

"The hard way then. Robots, get ready to seize that creature when I command." With a flick of Iron Rose he disarmed the mantid, then yanked aside the debris and pounced. The mantid's antennae brushed him and strange images flooded Josef's mind. He nearly froze and the mantid struggled free, only to be seized by the robots.

"Put the creature in irons and lock it up."

The mantid was taken to the brig under robot guard. Josef returned to the bridge. He glanced at the Pilot's empty chair. The man was gone, but the AI version in the thumb kept his personality.

"How long before we reach the gas giant?" he asked the Pilot.

"Two months. Do you expect to find the mantids there?"

"No, but it's a start."

"It's a bad one if the mantids took their captives in the other direction. Course corrections are time-consuming."

"You think I don't know that?"

"How would I know what you know? I'm just a thumb."

"Don't forget it." A thought crossed Josef's mind and he connected to the ship's information banks. "I need all the technical details on the graviton keel."

As the *Saint Teresa* stood for the gas giant, Josef experimented with simulations of graviton waves and neuron activity. He searched everything on the subject in the technical archives stored in his cybernetics. Josef adjusted his neural network so his sleep cycle was the bare minimum, then nothing at all as he spent every moment resolving integrations with millions of parameters and derivatives to the ten millionth decimal point.

Meanwhile the Pilot and the robot crew managed the ship.

As the weeks slipped by Josef began assembling a device to match the parameters of his experiments. Repeatedly he took prototypes to the brig. He linked the prototypes to his collar and the mantid. Again and again there was only blankness. Sometimes there was feedback that scrambled his neural network leaving him near paralytic with pain. But there were glimpses of life through mantid eyes, crumbs of success that served only to deepen Josef's desperate hunger, driving him back to his experiments relentlessly.

The gas giant was looming large when Josef's latest device was completed. He took it to the brig.

The guard robot was looking somewhat battered, but so was the mantid prisoner. At the sight of Josef, the mantid lunged for the bars, angrily clawing the air.

"The creature is agitated, Servant Josef," the robot said.

"So much the better," Josef replied. He activated the device. It began displaying brain-wave activity of the mantid on Josef's sensory apparatus. Josef removed his armored gauntlet. He reached for the mantid and activated the gravitons.

The furious mantid snapped at Josef's arm. Deftly, Josef avoided the mandibles and clasped an antenna. With his free hand Josef turned up the gain on the graviton field. The brain waves began to resolve into images. The principal image was of himself being violently dismembered. There were others, a mantid warrior connecting his proboscis to a drake's air sacs, strange and disgusting feasts, and a nest, mantids pressed close together, surrounded by drakes nestled into a hollow shell. There were other details, but Josef could not see them clearly. He adjusted the graviton wave, trying to fine tune it. He was getting closer.

The warning alarm sounded. "Josef, Freecoursers on an intercept course," the Pilot said. "Get to the bridge immediately."

Josef wrenched his arm away from the mantid and ran to the bridge. As he ran his sensors displayed a handful of open pirogues, running under sail, sweeping in on the *Saint Teresa*. Their sides were lined with Freecoursers in armored suits, aiming long-barrel plasma rifles at the ship.

"Engage the ion drives. I've been saving them for an emergency." The engines kicked in, but the pirogues had their own power sources and followed like a school of sharks after an injured porpoise.

Josef took command of the ship's guns, straining every nerve to target all of the pirogues simultaneously. He would have one shot and it required utmost precision.

The broadside blazed forth, a silent wave of death. The pirogues were moving too fast, and their countertargeting systems were too effective. Two of the boats lost their sails, another was hulled, and the others suffered only minor damage. As the guns recharged the outlaws' plasma rifles began to blaze. A gun emplacement erupted as a dozen sharp-shooters blasted it. There was no stopping them with the cannon.

"We're getting the worst of this," the Pilot said. "The robots aren't much for fighting. We could strike colors, but the Freecoursers don't exactly take honorable surrender. Not that any of it matters to me at this point."

"You better come with me. This is going to be difficult." Josef took the Pilot's thumb and went to the companionway. The airlock cycled open as Josef calculated how many were on the other side. His battle computer ran one battle simulation after another, from standing his ground to fleeing. They all ended up with Josef dead. And that meant no chance of rescue for Elizabetta. He leaned on Iron Rose and waited.

The airlock cycled open. The first outlaw stepped through, plasma rifle in hand, dark eyes peering through his battle visor.

"Drop your steel," the Freecourser said.

"Who's asking?"

"Black Tom, and I don't ask twice."

"Fair enough." Josef laid Iron Rose and his pistol down. "A fight would just get most of us killed. I have things to do. In fact, you can help me."

Black Tom laughed. "Help a Servant of the Protector? Back away from the weapons."

Josef complied. It galled him to his heart to take orders from a renegade. But a servant was more than weapons, and shows of honor wouldn't save Elizabetta. The Freecoursers spread across the ship, shouting with the exultation of victory.

The Freecoursers held Josef at gunpoint on the bridge as they changed course to their hideout. While Black Tom was laying in the course, a pair of the gang dragged the struggling mantid onto the bridge.

"Look what we found, boss," they shouted. "A stinking roach!"

Black Tom shot a look of disdain at Josef. "You collecting for a freak show?"

"The prisoner may have useful information."

Black Tom drew his pistol and shot the mantid down. "Not any more. Shipmates, take the servant to the brig."

"I claim his sword!" an outlaw shouted. The moment he laid his hands on it, Iron Rose activated its force field and writhed from his grasp, taking half the pirate's fingers.

"That's what you get for being greedy," Black Tom said. "Share and share alike."

"Goddam awesome," the wounded pirate said. "Who'll share their fingers wi' me?"

Josef was thankful he had recorded the visions from the mantid's brainwaves. He willingly went to the brig, knowing that a battle would not get him closer to rescuing the prisoners.

The Freecoursers had taken his weapons but had overlooked the Pilot's thumb. Josef opened communications with the thumb.

"Where are we now?" the Pilot asked.

"Locked in the brig," Josef said.

"That's a big setback."

"It depends on your point of view," Josef said. "I plan to turn it to our advantage."

"If things are going so well, I won't worry about it then." The Pilot returned to silence.

Josef settled into the brig and reviewed what he had learned from the mantid. Again and again he studied the image of the nest, but there was nothing that told him its location. He was still searching when Black Tom came in with his henchmen.

"Have you changed your mind about helping me rescue the colonists from the mantids?" Josef said.

"Hardly," Black Tom said. "I could use your help."

"I serve the Protector."

"Not much longer. You like service so much, you can serve me." To one of the Freecoursers, Black Tom said, "Put his neural net under my control."

The renegade opened a connection to Josef's collar. Josef felt his mind reel as his cybernetics were suddenly under outside control. Suddenly he felt he owed Black Tom his very life, ready to do the outlaw chief's bidding.

The Protector's voice boomed in Josef's ears. "Who interferes with my servant? I am the Lord High Protector and you defy me at your peril!" A vision of the Protector, seated on his throne, surrounded by servants, loomed in Josef's mind.

Instantly, Tom's hold was broken. Josef's will was his own, to hold in trust under the Protector.

"Impressive," Black Tom said. "We'll crack you yet." He turned and left the brig.

Weeks passed before they reached the Freecourser base. The renegades had hollowed out an asteroid and installed a base, complete with artificial gravity. The place was populated with swaggering outlaws, bristling with weapons, ragamuffin escapees from convict camps, smugglers loaded with money and guns, women in cheap, flashy finery, and tavern-loafers of every description. There were congratulations and free drinks for Black Tom. It was not every day a Freecourser boss captured a great ship with so little loss.

They brought Josef, securely shackled, before Black Tom. The outlaw boss was holding court in his favorite saloon, surrounded by his henchmen and an audience of hangers-on. Josef knew that he could not waste words. There was a slim chance to convince the Freecoursers to help rescue the captives. On his own, the odds against Josef were astronomical. Every word had to count.

"Servant Josef," Black Tom said, mockery in his voice. "How do you like being our guest?"

Josef started running persuasion scenarios. Confidence rated as a 100% requirement.

"Despite the delay, it suits me well. I need your assistance. Mantids raided Port Farewell and made off with many captives. You hate the mantids as much as I do, so I ask for your help in freeing the captives."

"I hate the roaches *worse* than you. But that's not a good enough reason to help you."

The system indicated appeals to the Freecourser chief's self-interest had maximum probability of success. An offer of pardon rated 26.7% chance of success.

"I can offer you a pardon."

Black Tom laughed uproariously. "Pardon! He'll give us pardons, boys! What do you say, let's go straight and join society?"

The crowd laughed and shouted back, "We tried it, it stinks. Not enough booze. Working for a living? Hell no! He can stuff his pardon up his black hole."

Black Tom grinned. "Try again."

Overall success probability at 3.28%. Increased reward was indicated.

"I can grant you land." 4.67% probability. "And a cash reward for assisting in the rescue, regardless of outcome." 6.19%.

"I have all the space I need. And I'll come for your cash when I want it."

0.33% success probability. An appeal to humanity rated 0.83%.

"The mantids are a threat to you as much as they are to the settlers. Humans should stand together against threats from outside." Probability 0.165%.

"You presume a lot on humanity, for a robot slave."

"I am proud to be a servant." Probability 0.089%.

"Because your programming tells you to think that." Black Tom pulled down his collar exposing marks left by a neural network collar. "I kept enough of my humanity to know I was a slave. And to break free. I was on a plantation with a robot overseer pushing my buttons, work, eat, be docile, work more. But I got away and joined the Freecoursers." Black Tom's dark eyes burned with fury.

Overall success probability 0.057%.

Josef pushed the persuasion scenarios to the background.

"This is a job for a man of courage. It's a job he can be proud of. I'll do it or I'll die trying. I'm asking you to help my odds, as one man to another."

"I'm not afraid of the roaches! You think I'm happy when they lay their filthy claws on a human? But what am I to your colonists? A runaway slave! If the settlers of Port Farewell worship the Protector, let him rescue them. Around here we protect ourselves. We don't need to worship anything."

"Everyone worships something, even if it's just their own belly." The probability of success was 0.0012%. "You are a man of pride and determination. I am too. I'll do it myself. I'll take one of your ships, find the mantids, free the captives, and smash the roaches' nest. You can do what you want."

"I certainly will. Take him outside and lock him down."

As the guards took Josef away, the probability of success flashed to 73.2% before dropping to 0.000%.

Locked to the surface of the asteroid in his sealed armor, Josef activated the strongest algorithms to produce inner calm. The Freecoursers were simply an obstacle to escape. He still had to find the mantid nest. He reviewed the brain wave images again, this time processing the data at trillionths of a second. It was far too much for Josef's conscious mind to process, but not too much for the interplay of fast processors and the subconscious together.

Meanwhile he worked at the shackles that bound him hand and foot. His armor assisted his strength, but the shackles were too strong. Then an image flashed in his mind. It was a star field, glimpsed in an infinitesimal fraction of the brain wave images. Josef established a remote connection to the Pilot's thumb.

"I need you to determine where this star field can be seen from."

"Sure. Do you want me to set a course there? What happened with the Freecoursers? I couldn't really tell. I'm just a thumb."

"Don't plot the course just yet. I'm locked to the outside of their asteroid base."

"I guess it didn't go well."

"I'm working on it. Do you know anything about shackles?"

"They are meant to keep you in place and cheap ones are no good. Oh, and graviton beams distort them."

"Thanks." Josef activated a connection to the Iron Rose and brain wave reader. He activated the reader and Iron Rose's force fields. It wouldn't let him read any minds, but that wasn't the purpose. Using the force field, Josef directed the graviton stream to the shackles.

Josef felt the shackles distort under the gravitons. He directed all his strength at the weakness produced by the distortion and his hands broke free. He deactivated the device and then broke the rest of the shackles. Carefully, for there was no gravity outside the asteroid and Josef had no wish to be launched helpless into space, he picked his way to the airlock.

The airlock opened readily. There was no guard inside. The Freecoursers feared no attack in the asteroid zone. Quietly, Josef slipped into the Freecoursers base. There was no one about; evidently the inhabitants were on a carouse. He located the brain wave device in a storage room, next to his pistol and Iron Rose, which no one had claimed. Josef took his weapons and the device, then slipped out.

Raucous shouts warned him to hide. Peering around a corner he saw two brawny men locked in a knife-fight while their comrades shouted drunken encouragement. Josef went the other way. He had no time to carefully scan the corridors, so he went quickly toward the dock. Iron Rose gave him a warning.

"Hey handsome," a woman said. "How's about some fun?"

Josef said nothing but kept moving.

"Sissy!" she shouted after him. Josef hurried his pace.

At the dock he discovered that not all the Freecoursers were drunk. A group lounged by the gangway to the *Saint Teresa*, gambling on tesseract cards. He could take them, but a bloodbath didn't fit his plan. A man ran in from another direction.

"Wake up, you clowns," the newcomer said. "The stinking servant got loose."

The Freecoursers swore violently and drew their weapons. Josef was already in motion in the opposite direction. He slipped out an airlock to a pirogue tethered outside. In a moment, he had the sail up and the Pilot's thumb on the controls. "Find those stars," Josef whispered. "I'm coming, Elizabetta."

The location proved to be at the edge of the system, weeks away. The Pilot worked out the likely orbit of the vantage point and set a course. The pirogue had a sturdy little ion engine to help build speed. There were supplies aboard and Josef could eat and drink, if sparingly. He had time to think as well.

It was his duty to rescue the captives. It was also his duty to guard the colony. But Elizabetta was among the captives. Was her life any more important than the others?

"Perhaps I should be at Port Farewell, attending to the living."

"Of course," the Pilot said, "Let the dead care for the dead."

"That's us then, a robot slave and a thumb."

"Back on my homeworld, my mom always said as long as you have love you're still alive. Since being reduced to electronic memories stored in a thumb, I can tell you, mom was right."

"Mothers know these things. Keep on course."

"Will do. When this is over, erase my memories. Let the dead take care of the dead."

"Will do."

Josef spotted the nest about three million miles out. It drifted among blocks of ice and rock. He maneuvered the pirogue to join the drift and close in stealthily. Soon the nest was growing large on his sensor screen. It was a vast honeycomb of ice with drakes filling the gaps. Bizarre lichenlike forms grew on the crusted surface. Mantids crawled through smaller gaps in the ice, foraging for lichens, and performing strange tasks on their frozen world.

Josef reefed the sail and prepared to attack.

"Hold the pirogue ready for a fast escape," he told the Pilot. "If I don't come back, you are the bravest man I know alive or dead."

"You likewise."

Josef went over the side of the pirogue and latched onto a drifting ice block. A shot fired from his plasma pistol pushed the block toward the nest. As the block closed in, Josef let go and landed on the nest.

Slowly and carefully he crept to one of the holes, ducking out of sight when foraging mantids approached. When they had passed, Josef scrambled inside. There was some heat coming from deeper within the nest. As he went further he found the path blocked by what appeared to be a curtain. Iron Rose warned him that mantids were approaching from behind. Josef crawled into a dark crevice.

The mantids stopped at the curtain and rapped at it in a rhythmic fashion with their clawed hands. The curtain twitched aside and the mantids entered as oxygen puffed out. Josef realized it was the wing of a drake, forming a crude airlock. He approached the wing and repeated the mantids' rapping. The wing moved aside.

Behind the wing there was thin, but breathable, air and some warmth. Bioluminescent lichen gave off a sickly glow.

Josef moved forward scanning for signs of human life. There were mantids everywhere. Side branches were thick with them. They were torpid though, and paid no heed to Josef. There was more activity in other chambers, making and repairing devices and weapons, handling eggs, chewing lichen into gruel for group repasts, hatching pupae, mating, and the eating of those mantids that had served their purpose. Josef's mind reeled at the hideousness of an alien life-cycle, and what fate might have already befallen Elizabetta.

Larger passages were filled with the bodies of drakes, effectively sealing the nest's inner reaches with their bodies. Josef's sensors told him he was nearing a larger chamber with many mantids inside. There were also signs of unusual warmth. Josef was close to the chamber, but blocked by a wall of ice. He turned up the gain on his own and Iron Rose's sensors to create an image of what was transpiring in the chamber.

Mantids were clustered thickly. Where there were gaps in the ice, drakes formed walls with their bodies. In the center of the chamber was an ancient reactor of prehuman make. As Josef watched, the reactor began to hum and the mantids' antennae swayed in response. Radiation leaked from the reactor and the mantids moved in unison, an insectoid dance. Josef activated the brain wave reader.

The images were powerful, seizing his mind with a force that was almost physical. Josef was in an alien laboratory, where bizarre and terrifying entities performed painful processes upon him. Then he was in space, crawling across a space station, using tools, working for his master. The masters gave the mantids helpers, the vast drakes with brains and bodies adapted for space flight. Signals from an antenna guided the drakes more surely than a computer interface.

Then there was a period of destruction as rival factions of the masters battled for supremacy. Spacecraft smashed planets and millions died. The masters armed the mantids and drakes, using them as expendable pawns in a vast war. They fought as raiders, sneaking through detection systems, striking hard and fleeing quickly.

In the ruins, he drifted between the stars atop a drake, thriving in the cold and dark, but always hungry, always looking for warm places to strip clean. But even as he moved from system to system, he faithfully celebrated the dark eucharist before the idols salvaged from the ancient masters.

Hunger gnawed at Josef. His mandibles clacked in anticipation of the feast. A human stared at him, face contorted in stark, soul-crushing fear. Josef's mandibles snapped and he feasted on warm flesh.

Josef reeled back in sickening horror, desperately shutting off the device. He had seen a hole the mantids had dragged the man from. Josef circled the chamber to reach it, scorning concealment, and yearning to wipe clean this nauseating nightmare in wholesome battle.

A mantid emerged from a side chamber. Josef swung Iron Rose and the creature fell in two pieces. He ducked his head and entered a room.

A group of humans huddled together for warmth. They turned fear-dulled eyes towards him. Desperately, Josef looked for Elizabetta. Then their eyes met. She flung her arms about him and sobbed in relief.

"I've come for you," Josef whispered, holding her tight.

"I knew you'd come," Elizabetta whispered back.

"We've got to get out now. I have a craft waiting."

A man spoke up. "They injected us with a poison that slowed us down so we needed less air and food. Then they put us in hulls made from dead mantids' carapaces. They stuffed them under the armor plates on the drakes. We got just enough oxygen to keep us alive. They kept us alive, to go out there!" He pointed to the chapel of the radioactive idol. A half-dozen of the captives had gone to their doom as sacrifices.

"Each of you, take a carapace," Josef said. "I'll get you out of here."

The captives did their best, but they were weak from the ordeal. Elizabetta encouraged the others, her spirit undimmed. They were getting out when a mantid entered from the chapel. Josef drew his pistol and shot the mantid.

"Go now!" Josef pushed the captives out. More mantids entered. Josef rushed them, Iron Rose swinging. The mantids fell back as Josef carved a path of death among them.

A scream from the captives brought Josef running. The mantids were awakening now, emerging from crevices, showing aggression but still sluggish. They fell easily to Josef's gun and blade.

Josef turned a corner and a gauss-arrow nearly hit him in the face. He took cover and shot back. Well-aimed plasma bolts melted his cover to slushy ruin. A shot rebounded off his armor, leaving Josef gasping with pain. Josef gritted his teeth and fired back, his unerring aim picking off three of the mantids.

As the mantids drew back, Josef rushed them. Battleaxes and mandibles were no match for Iron Rose. The mantids fell back. Battered but victorious, Josef waved the captives forward.

A woman screamed, hit from behind by a gauss-arrow. Josef shot the mantid and pushed the captives forward.

Josef's sensors indicated more mantids massing ahead. With heroic blows of Iron Rose, he hacked a hole in the wall and sent the captives through. The passage led to the surface and they went as fast as their legs could carry them.

Josef found the way blocked by a drake's wing. "Seal yourselves in the carapaces." He sighaled to the Pilot. "Get the ion engine hot and bring in the pirogue. I'm coming out with the captives."

Josef checked. All the captives were in carapaces except Elizabetta. "Where's yours?" he said.

"One of the youngsters lost his."

"It's the vacuum of space beyond this." Josef ducked as a plasma bolt exploded nearby. He turned and shot the mantid sniper dead.

"I know." A tear crossed Elizabetta's face.

Hastily Josef pulled off his armor. "Take care of the others. You'll have the Pilot's thumb to get you home. Turn him off when it's over. I promised him."

Josef turned his back on her to shoot a couple of mantids who had gotten too close. He didn't want Elizabetta to see that he was crying, too. "Get it on and go! Now!"

And let the dead care for the dead.

Josef dragged aside the wing-curtain. The thin atmosphere evaporated and Josef's lungs screamed for air. He set his pain sensors to their lowest and held on. Elizabetta pushed the sealed carapaces through. The Pilot drove the pirogue in close and Josef let the curtain drop.

Air filled the passage again, and Josef turned to see mantids creeping close, crawling across the floor, walls, and ceiling. A gauss-missile flew at him, missing by a hair, but spraying Josef with hot metal shards.

Josef grunted in pain and fired his plasma pistol again and again, bringing down a mantid with each shot. The weapon's charges were soon gone and he flung it aside. Smoking corpses of mantids lay everywhere. But their comrades were right behind and rushed him before he could seize a rifle from the dead.

For each ripping bite from a mandible, for each slash from a battleaxe, Josef severed a head or an arm. Iron Rose wove a steel web of death until the slain outnumbered the living. The mantids fell back again, and Josef leaned against the ice, nearing exhaustion.

The tunnel began to shake and blocks of ice broke loose. Something big was coming. There was a terrible roar and the planetoid shook as if it were falling apart. A drake shoved its head into the tunnel, lunging for Josef.

He hacked at the beast with Iron Rose, knocking chips loose from the monster's beak. It snapped and nearly cut him in half. Josef leapt in and stabbed it in the eye.

The drake reacted in fury, trying to crush Josef against the ice. The drake smashed through the curtain and they were in the void. Josef had a moment to realize that mantid sharpshooters were firing at him from the surface with gauss-bows and plasma rifles. The pirogue was escaping, but there were mantids atop drakes in pursuit. There was no air and his blood was boiling.

But Josef was at peace, for he had done a man's duty and was dying a man's death. His dreams would die with him. But that was the fate of men, for robots did not dream.

One last dream obtruded upon Josef's mind. In a flickering instant of consciousness, he saw the *Saint Teresa* sweep in under sail. The broadside of plasma cannon flashed in the dark of space. Then there was nothing.

Josef awoke in the ship's sick bay. Elizabetta was leaning over him. "You did it. We escaped."

Black Tom appeared. "You're alive after all. We pulled you in, it looked like you'd been used as a pincushion and turned inside out."

"It's not easy to kill a Servant of the Protector. So you came after us."

"I can't have people stealing my pirogues." Black Tom laughed. "You didn't think it was because I wanted a pardon?"

"Never. If you'll excuse us." Josef sat up, wincing with pain, and kissed Elizabetta. "One more thing, where's the Pilot?"

Elizabetta helped Josef to his feet. The thumb lay on the bridge. Josef connected his mind to the Pilot.

"Not bad for a robot and a dead man's digit," the Pilot said.

"Not bad at all."

"Do you remember your promise? I am ready for peace."

"You may have it."

"Ask that Elizabetta girl to marry you. Live a little."

"I will." Josef shut down the Pilot. "Peace for the dead. For the living, who can say?"

When Justis Fearsson takes a job tracking down the person or persons responsible for stealing cars off of Mitch Sullivan's lot, he thinks it'll be fast and easy money. Just the thing he needs right now. Christmas is coming up, but what's more, so is the full moon. And Fearsson isn't just an ordinary gumshoe—he's a weremyste, and that means the full moon brings trouble in the form of a night of insanity. But when the job turns out to be trickier than he first thought, he'll find himself in a race against time—and hopelessly outnumbered by a gang of car thieves with a very dark secret.

Long Nights Moon

David B. Coe

December's full moon is known among some of the tribal peoples of North America as the Cold Moon, or the Long Nights Moon. Living in Chandler, Arizona, a suburb in the desert sprawl of Phoenix, I can't say that "Cold Moon" has ever had much meaning for me. But as a weremyste I know all about full moons and long nights.

For three nights out of every moon cycle, the night of the full, and the nights immediately before and after, weremystes go through what's known as the phasing. That probably sounds innocuous enough. Trust me, it's not. Our magic strengthens, but our minds weaken to the point of temporary insanity. At the very moment when we most need to have control over our thoughts and our runecrafting, we have none. The barriers between reality and delusion melt away. Some of us retreat into our minds, enduring the dark hours in quiet desperation. Others turn violent, lashing out at those we love, or turning our fear and rage inward so that we harm ourselves. I've experienced both: resigned withdrawal into my own addled mind and violent eruptions that nearly ended with me putting a bullet through my head. I couldn't tell you which is worse. They both pretty much suck.

Not surprisingly, these descents into madness eventually cause our minds to deteriorate. One doesn't meet many sane old weremystes. They don't exist. My father, who's also a weremyste, and who, like me, lost his job on the Phoenix police force because of the phasings, is in his sixties, and he's nuts, just as I will be.

There isn't much that could make the phasings worse than they already are, but this year's calendar was doing its best. The next full moon, only two days away, fell on Christmas, which meant that the phasing would begin on Christmas Eve. Joy to the world.

Forty-eight hours shy of the full, and several hours before even today's moonrise, I could already feel the moon tugging at my thoughts, like idle fingers pulling at a loose thread. Sooner or later, it was all going to unravel.

Right now, though, I was in the Z-ster, my 1977 silver 280Z, following the Piestewa Freeway through the city, on my way to meet with a new client. Mitchell Sullivan owned a car dealership over on East Camelback Road, the heart of Phoenix's automobile trade. Sullivan hadn't told me much over the phone, but I gathered he was having trouble with one of his employees.

I'm a private detective—owner, president, and principal investigator for Justis Fearsson Investigations—and since I used to be a cop, many of the clients who come my way are business owners trying to manage problems that straddle the boundaries of the law. They avoid going to the police because they don't want the negative publicity, but they also know that they're out of their depth. More often than not, I'm a compromise who can make the issue go away quietly and discreetly. Or so they think. Sometimes it seems like I can't do anything without drawing the attention of the police, the press, and the entire magical community of the Phoenix metropolitan area. But I try not to mention that to potential clients.

"Ohanko."

I nearly jumped out of my skin at the sound of the voice. The car swerved, taking me perilously close to the minivan in the lane next to mine. I swore. The other driver yelled something I couldn't hear.

"Damn you, Namid! I've told you not to just appear in my car like that! Not when I'm on a highway."

The ghostly figure in the passenger seat stared back at me, his expression maddeningly tranquil. Namid'skemu was a runemyste, one of thirty-nine spirits created centuries before by the runeclave to be guardians of magic in our world. He was essentially the ghost of a Zuni shaman from the now-extinct K'ya'na-Kwe clan, the water people, as they were also known. And true to his heritage, he appeared to be made entirely of faintly luminous waters. He was tall and broad, like a warrior, but right now his face and form were as clear as a mountain lake. As his moods changed, so did his appearance, so that he could be as roiled as the ocean in a storm, or as hard and uncompromising as ice. Only his eyes remained unchanged. They always gleamed as bright as stars on a winter night.

For years now, since he first revealed himself to me during one of the darkest phasings I'd ever experienced, Namid had been my mentor in the ways of magic and, enigmatic though he was, my friend. Mostly. He called me "Ohanko," which, roughly translated, meant "reckless one." I guess I had earned the name over the years.

"I am sorry if I startled you," he said, in a voice like a tumbling stream. "Should I leave?"

"No, you're here now. What do you want?"

"It has been some time since last you trained. Your skills as a runecrafter need work."

"And you think I can train while I'm driving?"

I found it alarming that he appeared to consider this. "It would be an interesting exercise in concentration."

"It would also likely get me killed. I meant the question as a joke."

The runemyste frowned. He had never been fond of my sense of humor. "You need to practice. Honing your magic and your mind is particularly important when we are on the cusp of the moontime."

The moontime was what he called the phasing. And I knew that he had a point: improving my skills as a weremyste would actually make me more resistant to the long-term effects of the full moon. But despite his interest in testing my powers of concentration, this was not the time.

"You do realize that I have to eat, right? That I have a mortgage, that I need to earn a living? Being a weremyste doesn't pay any bills."

"Being a weremyste has been a boon to you in your work as an officer of the law and an investigator. You know this."

"Fine," I said. "*Practicing* doesn't pay bills. Is that better?"

"Practicing keeps you alive."

I hated arguing with Namid, because he had the annoying habit of always being right, and because it was like arguing with the world's oldest know-it-all, or maybe the world's most persistent four-year-old. Either way, I wasn't sure why I bothered.

"You're right, it does. I need to practice more. But I have to work now, and I don't know when I'll be done."

He let out a low rumble, like ocean breakers crashing on a rocky shore. Then he faded from view, slowly, glaring at me the whole time. When at last he was gone, I felt both relieved and guilty.

I exited the freeway at Highland Avenue, took Sixteenth up to Camelback Road, and crept along the street past lots filled with new cars gleaming in the Sonoran sun, until I came to Sullivan Toyota and Lexus. I pulled in and parked near the showroom.

A salesman in charcoal gray slacks, a white dress shirt, and a red and blue striped tie stood near the entrance, smoking a cigarette. He was the only salesperson I saw who wasn't with a customer. The lot was hopping. I wouldn't have thought that many people bought cars so close to Christmas, but it seemed I was wrong.

He nodded to me as I got out of Z-ster.

"Nice car," he said. He dropped the rest of his cigarette into one of those plastic receptacles that look like upside-down lollipops, and walked to where I stood. He shook my hand, but he was focused on the car. He walked around it once, nodding at the detailing.

I ate it up. I'm a car guy, and having another car guy admire my wheels ... Well, the only thing that would have made it better was if he was a she. A pretty one.

"You looking to trade her in?" he asked. "I mean, she's in great shape; I know we could give you a good deal."

I shook my head. "Thanks, but there's no offer you could make that would convince me to trade her or sell her."

"Yeah," he said with a shrug. "I figured. Gotta ask, though, you know? So then it's a second car you're after."

"Actually, I have an appointment to see Mister Sullivan."

To his credit, he didn't show any disappointment at learning that I wouldn't be his next sale. He crossed to an intercom panel near the showroom door, pressed the white button, and said, "Sarah, can you send Mitch out here? There's someone to see him."

I couldn't make out what the woman on the other end said in response, but the salesman thanked her and told me that Sullivan would be out shortly. He came back to the Z-ster and after ogling her for a few minutes, asked if he could see the interior.

"Yeah, sure." I got out of his way.

He lowered himself into the car and just sat, the door open, one hand on the wheel, the other resting on the stick shift. "Nice," he said, drawing out the word. "My dad had one of these, but he never let me drive it. Where'd you even find it? It's gotta be older than you are."

"I found a listing in the *Republic* classifieds about six years ago. It had maybe forty thousand miles on it, and had been babied its entire life. I was lucky."

"No shit."

A white-haired man emerged from the showroom wearing a beige Western-cut suit with black piping, a bolo tie secured with a mammoth piece of turquoise, and a Stetson that matched the color of the suit. On most people the outfit would have looked ridiculous, but somehow this guy—Mister Sullivan, I assumed—made it work. His face was tanned and deeply lined, so that he looked like the old sheriff in every Western I'd ever seen. He was tall and hale, and he flashed a big smile at me as he strode in my direction, his hand outstretched.

"Jay Fearsson, right? I'm Mitch Sullivan." He spoke in a loud voice that sounded like it had been roughened by a two-pack-a-day cigarette habit. I swear the guy was straight out of central casting.

His grip was crushing.

"It's a pleasure to meet you, sir."

"You Lee Fearsson's boy?"

I felt my smile slip. I always grew wary at the mention of my dad's name. He didn't interact with many people anymore. He lived out in a tiny town called Wofford, in an old trailer on land that most people who didn't understand the desert would call desolate. But he'd left the police force under a cloud of scandal, and there were still some folks around who remembered. It didn't help that I'd left the force pretty much the same way.

"Yes, sir. You know my dad?"

"I met him a few times when he was still on the force, and I was workin' a security job over at the airport. That was back when it only had two terminals—that's how long ago I'm talkin'. Anyway, he was a good cop and a good man. Always thought he got a raw deal."

"Thank you, sir."

"He still with us?"

"Yes, sir. He lives out in Wofford."

"Well, next time you see him, you tell him Mitch Sullivan says hello."

"I will."

He glanced at the Z-ster. "Yours?"

"Yes, sir."

"Decent car. I always preferred American muscle to Japanese sportsters, but here I am sellin' Toyotas, so I guess I should just keep my mouth shut." He laughed and slapped me on the back. "Come with me. We'll chat in my office. Jeremy, get out of the man's car and get back to work."

He said this last with a growl, but Jeremy was grinning as he climbed out.

I followed Sullivan inside, to a posh office that looked out over the lot. He stepped around his desk to a large leather chair, and indicated that I should take one of the black fabric-covered chairs across from him.

"Let's start with the bottom line," he said. "Two-fifty a day plus expenses, right?"

"Yes, sir, with a five hundred dollar initial payment."

"And do I get half of that back if you solve my problem today?" He asked it with a smile on his lips and a mischievous gleam in his blue eyes, but I could tell that he wanted an answer.

"No, sir. Five hundred dollars is my minimum payment."

"All right, fair enough." He leaned forward and pressed a button on his phone. "Maria, please have a check made out to Justis Fearsson Investigations, Inc., in the amount of five hundred dollars." He spelled "Fearsson" for her, released the button, and sat back. "You'll have that before you walk out of here today."

"Thank you, sir."

"Now then, I have a problem, and you're going to fix it for me."

"I'll do my best."

His expression turned flinty. "Five hundred dollars says you'll do what it takes."

I didn't shy away from his gaze, but I also didn't answer.

"I think one of my employees is stealin' from me," he went on after a moment's silence. "Or else he's giving people access to the lot after hours. I've had six cars stolen in the last week and a half. Only one car on any given night, but they've all been Lexus sedans, the high-end ones. I've got more than sixty grand in each."

"What makes you think it's someone who works here?"

"We have a security system here on the lot. You gotta punch in a number before you can move the gates leadin' in and out. And there's nothing to indicate that the system's been tampered with. Now, by itself that might not mean much, but there's more." He stood. "Come with me."

Mitch led me out of his office, through the showroom, where he greeted customers with smiles and handshakes.

"How's it goin', folks? They treatin' you right? You got any problems at all, you have 'em call for ole Mitch, ya hear?"

I was watching an old pro work a room, and though I was thankful every day that I didn't have to bust my butt selling cars, I appreciated talent when I saw it.

Once we were through the showroom, Mitch led me to a flight of stairs.

"The secret to this business," he said, as we went down past the service area to the basement, "to any business really, is makin' folks feel that that they're in control of the situation, even when they're not. Those people upstairs are goin' to make me a lot of money today, but they're goin' to leave here thinkin' they put one over on me, got themselves a real good deal. Know what I'm sayin'?"

All I could do was agree.

We reached a gray metal unmarked door that Mitch opened with a key. Inside were a set of black and white monitors and a sophisticated security control console. A brawny African-American man in a security uniform sat watching the monitors, a cup of coffee in one hand. He stood as we walked in.

"Good morning, Mister Sullivan," he said, in a voice that sounded like a salute.

"Mornin', Rob. Everything look okay?"

"Yes, sir."

"Good. I'd like you to run the feed from two nights ago for Mister Fearsson here. Just the part that matters." Mitch glanced my way, his grin putting me in mind of a wolf. "We don't want to take up too much of his time, 'cause every minute's costin' me a pretty penny."

"Yes, sir."

Rob fiddled with a few buttons and knobs, and one of the monitors went blank. A moment later, it came to life again, but I could see from the dark skies onscreen and the time stamp in the bottom righthand corner that this was recorded.

At first, I saw nothing unusual. Like most car lots, Sullivan's was well lit at night. But nothing moved. Even the foil banners that stretched between lampposts remained still. There couldn't have been a breath of wind. The feed continued this way for about two minutes.

Then Mitch said, "Keep an eye on that lower left corner. The open pavement there."

I nodded, watching the spot. And perhaps ten seconds later, a shadow appeared there. It was in the shape of a person, though elongated by the distance between whoever cast it and the lights behind him or her. I could make out a head, shoulders, arms, and the torso down to about the waist. The rest was cut off by the edge of the screen. One of the arms shifted, as if the person had raised a hand. An instant later, the entire image wavered and went blank again.

"Thanks, Rob."

I looked at Sullivan. "That's it?"

"That's all we've got. The figure doesn't show up on any of the other feeds. This person knew just where to stand to avoid bein' seen. All of the feeds go dead at the same time. All of them remain dead for precisely the same amount of time: approximately twelve minutes. Then the feed resumes as if nothin' ever happened. Except that one of my sedans is gone."

"Can I see it again?"

He turned to Rob and lifted his chin toward the monitor. Rob replayed the clip. I wasn't sure what I was looking for, and even after I'd watched it a second time, I couldn't say that anything in particular caught my eye.

"You understand now why I brought you in?" Mitch asked, once the feed had cut out a second time. "You of all people?"

I faced him, feeling my gut clench.

Magic. That was why he wanted me. Somehow, he knew I was a weremyste, though I saw on him none of the usual blurring of features that I could see when looking at another of my kind.

Plenty of people knew, at least in the abstract, that weremystes existed, but most of us didn't advertise the fact that we were runecrafters. The stigma attached to mental illness in this country remained a heavy burden for those who suffered its effects. And many people still viewed anything that resembled "witchcraft" with a healthy dose of skepticism, even fear. Combining that misunderstanding of psychological problems with old prejudices against sorcery produced a dangerous mix. Perhaps if people like me were able to be more honest about the phasings and their effects on us, I'd still have a job with the Phoenix Police Department.

But that wasn't the world in which we lived. Not yet. I didn't like the implication of Mitch's question, and just then I didn't feel comfortable under his keen gaze.

Maybe he sensed that.

"Rob, why don't you take a short break, refill that cup of yours and maybe grab a bite to eat. Mister Fearsson and I will keep an eye on the monitors."

He said it with another grin, but I heard the command behind the words.

So did Rob. He was already reaching for the door when he said, "Yes, sir."

Once we were alone, Mitch surprised me.

"I'm sorry about that. I should have sent him out before I asked."

"It's all right," I said. "You think someone used magic to disable your security system."

"Don't you?"

I shrugged, eyeing the monitor, which Rob had switched back to the live feed. "It's possible. That might also explain the gate. It might not be an employee after all."

"I suppose. But still, you can help me find the person responsible, can't you?"

I didn't answer right away.

Sullivan sat in the vacated chair. "I remember that your old man was a wizard, or whatever the hell you all call yourselves. That's why I figured you might be, too."

"How did you know that about my Dad?"

"I asked him. He came to the airport lookin' for a job after he left the force. I'd known a guy in high school who used magic, and Lee was askin' questions about the flexibility of the schedule, and bein' able to get a few nights off each month. I put two and two together." He leaned forward, trying to look me in the eye. "I never told anyone. I swear."

I nodded. "Thank you." To be honest, I was still trying to get my head around the fact that my Dad had tried to get a job at the airport. I never knew that, though I probably shouldn't have been so surprised. By that time my Mom had died, and my Dad was well on his way to becoming a full-time drunk. But he still had me, and he would have needed income to support us both.

"So can you help me out?" Sullivan asked.

"I think I can. The first thing I'd want to do is take a look around the dealership, try to see if I can spot a weremyste among your workers."

"You can tell just by lookin' if a guy's a . . . what'd you call 'em, a weremyste?"

"Yes, I can. You can't, unless there's more to you than you're letting on, but I can see the magic in others. And they can see it in me. Any weremyste working here is going to spot my magic, just as I can spot his or hers. Having me here could spark a battle of spells."

"Well, then what do you suggest I do instead?"

It was a good question, one I couldn't answer. "Let me walk around a bit. I'll try to stay out of people's way, and I'll be as discreet as possible."

He frowned, his brow creasing. "That doesn't sound like much of a plan."

"Welcome to the PI business."

That coaxed a grin from him. "All right, then. I'll leave you to it. Just holler at me if you need anything."

We left the security room and climbed the stairs. I hadn't noticed any weremystes among the salespeople and clerical workers I'd seen in the showroom, so I stepped into the service area, leaving Sullivan to go back to his office. The guy at the service counter, who wasn't a weremyste, asked me if I needed help, but I said I was waiting for my car to be serviced, and he told me to make myself at home.

A small waiting room sat adjacent to the service reception area. It had several chairs, a coffee maker, and a couple of vending machines stocked with prepackaged pastries and those peanut butter and cheese crackers that are drier than dust. A woman sat near the door, thumbing through a magazine, but otherwise the room was empty. A window at the back end looked out on the garage, and I parked myself in the corner beside it. I could see most of the workers and the cars they were servicing, but the mechanics wouldn't be able to see me all that clearly.

It didn't take me long to spot our weremyste. He was a young guy, not one of the chief mechanics, but a helper. He was about my height—maybe five-ten—and thin, with dark eyes and long black hair that he wore tied back in a ponytail. His features bore the tell-tale blur that I saw on all weremystes, but the effect wasn't particularly strong on him. I suppose he was capable of casting a spell that would put the whammy on Sullivan's security system, but I had seen more powerful mystes in my day. Lots of them.

I stayed where I was, checking out the other people who worked in this part of the dealership. There weren't a lot of us weremystes in the Phoenix area—a couple of thousand tops—but it wasn't out of the question that Sullivan could have two working for him. Even as I watched for others, though, I kept my eye on the kid, and I tried to stay out of his line of sight.

After another fifteen minutes or so, I had convinced myself that he was the only runecrafter working today's shift, and I began to contemplate my next move.

Before I could make it, I saw one of the mechanics call him over and speak to him. He nodded and then started in my direction. I muttered a curse to myself, but that was about all I could do. There was only the one entrance to the room; he was going to see me no matter what I did. I made a point of not staring at him, of making it seem that I was just watching the mechanics work.

But I knew the moment he spotted me. I watched out of the corner of my eye as he slowed almost to a stop, and cast a quick look back over his shoulder. Seeming to realize he had no choice, he resumed walking a moment later, though more slowly now. I could tell that he was eyeing me, perhaps searching for some sign that I had noticed him.

For my part, I could ignore him for only so long before my disinterest appeared too studied. He was a weremyste, and just as he knew that I was, he would assume that I could see the magic on him.

So as he drew near, I stared directly at him and made my eyes widen a little, as if in surprise. I followed him with my gaze and turned toward the doorway as he stuck his head in. He glanced at me, but said to the woman, "Missus Pratt?"

She set aside her magazine. "Yes."

"Your car's ready."

"At last. Thank you."

His dark eyes flicked in my direction again, but he left without another word. As he walked away, he cast another quick look over his shoulder, but I had seen him turning and was already gazing elsewhere. I waited until the mechanic gave him another task and then left the room, took the stairs, and returned to Mitch Sullivan's office.

He was on the phone when I knocked, but he waved me in and motioned for me to shut the door. He ended the call moments later.

"Well?"

"I don't know anything yet," I said. "It's possible that one of your nonmagical employees is working with a weremyste, and that person disabled the security camera."

"But?"

I let out a breath. "But you do have a weremyste working for you. A young kid. Long black hair. He looks like he might be from one of the Pueblo communities."

Sullivan sagged. "Damn. You mean Tommy Strong." He rubbed a hand over his face. "You're sure?"

"I'm sure he's a weremyste. Like I said, I don't know anything else for certain. Where does Tommy live?"

"I can have Maria pull his info— Aw, hell, I'll do it myself. Fewer questions that way." He slid his chair up to his desk and began to click through files on his computer, still shaking his head and muttering to himself. After a few minutes, he said, "That's what I thought. He's Pima Indian. Lives in Komatke in the Gila River Community."

He grabbed a pen and a sticky note, jotted down the kid's name, address, and phone number, and handed the slip of paper to me. "Truth is, I don't want it to be him. He's a decent kid, family's been through a lot."

"I understand."

"But you do what you have to. If it is him, I want you to tell me. We clear on that?"

"That was my plan all along. I'd like to talk to him now, if it's all right with you."

"Sure, why not? If any of the mechanics give you a hard time about it, tell 'em you cleared it with me."

"I will." I folded the paper with Tommy's address and tucked it into my pocket. "You'll hear from me as soon as I know something for certain."

I let myself out of the office and went back downstairs to that cramped waiting room. But when I scanned the garage, I didn't see Tommy. I walked out into the work area and found the mechanic the kid had spoken to earlier.

The guy was hunched over a diagnostic computer, a scowl on his face. "Can I help you with something?" he asked after a few seconds, his eyes still on the screen.

"I'm looking for a kid who was in here earlier. I think his name's Tommy?"

"Tommy just left. Said he wasn't feeling good. Can I help you with something?"

Damn. "No, thanks. I'll . . . find him another time. It was nothing important."

I walked away, resisting the urge to look back. My parting line had been a little weak, and I was sure the mechanic was watching me. But that was the least of my concerns. Halfway to the waiting area, I turned and headed out of the garage, hoping I might catch a glimpse of the kid before he left the dealership.

I didn't, but I heard a car start up, not with the smooth hum of a new engine, but with the staccato growl of something old and in need of repair. I ran toward the sound and saw a small blue pickup back out of a space.

"Tommy Strong!" I called.

The truck jerked to a stop and then peeled away with a screech of rubber on pavement.

I started to recite a spell in my head: three elements that would have flattened one of his tires. But before I could cast, I felt magic charge the air.

I tried to shift my spell to a warding, but I didn't have time enough to cast. Even at a distance, Tommy's spell hit me with the force of a mule's kick. I flew backwards, hit the pavement and somersaulted onto my front. I lay still for several seconds, trying to remember how to breathe. I hurt all over, but I didn't think that I'd broken anything.

When I saw him in the garage, I hadn't thought there was much to his power, but if that spell was any indication, I'd misjudged him. His spell packed a serious wallop. I wondered if he'd been trying to kill me, or if he had been smart enough to hold back. I wasn't sure which thought scared me more: that the kid might be so desperate he was willing to kill, or that he was powerful enough to hit me that hard with a restrained casting.

I climbed to my feet, feeling like an old man, and glanced around. Miraculously, no one had seen me go down.

With Tommy gone, I had little reason to stick around the dealership. I staggered back inside to retrieve my check and then limped to my car. Rather than get in, though, I walked to the part of the lot that I had seen in the video.

All magical spells leave a residue, a glow of color on the things they touch, including people. And the color of every runecrafter's magic is unique. So in theory, I might have been able to identify the person who had cast that spell on the security system, if only I could see something else that he or she had touched with a crafting. The problem was, the glow faded with time, and the more powerful the sorcerer, the more quickly the residue vanished. It had been a day and a half since the last spell was cast on the system, and it being almost noon on a cloudless Arizona day, the sun was bleaching the color out of everything it touched.

Still, staring up at the security cameras, I thought I saw a faint hint of golden yellow glimmering on the gray metal. I looked down at my shirt to the spot where Tommy's spell had hit me. The magic I saw there wasn't the same color. Not even close. The residue of Tommy's spell gleamed like fresh, wet paint: a cool, pale blue, the color of a winter sky.

Meaning it was possible that Tommy had nothing to do with the car thefts. But then why had he been so spooked by the sight of another weremyste that he fled the garage and attacked me with a spell?

I returned to the Z-ster and steered her back onto the freeway. From there, I made my way south to the Gila River Indian

Community, a reservation on the southern border of the metropolitan area that was first founded in the mid-nineteenth century. Like so many reservations, particularly those in this part of the country, the community dealt with a host of problems, all of them rooted in poverty: health care issues, crime, drug use, gang activity. The folks in Gila River were working hard to overcome those problems, and, in an effort to bring in some tourist money, had managed to open up a couple of golf courses and a few casinos. But I was headed to Komatke, a dusty desert town with little going for it.

Tommy Strong lived on Tashquinth Drive, in a small, one-story ranch house. A stunted palo verde tree grew in the middle of the yard, which otherwise consisted of little more than dirt, sand and a few clumps of dried grass. The door was closed and there were no cars in the driveway. I parked by the road in front of the house and knocked on the door. A dog barked from inside, but otherwise I heard nothing, and no one answered my knock.

I walked next door. The yard and house were practically clones of the Strong place; the two homes were even painted the same shade of pale beige. But a beat-up old land rover sat in the shade of the neighbor's carport, and the front door stood ajar. Inside, someone was blasting country music.

I had to ring the doorbell several times before the volume on the music finally went down. A young woman appeared at the door. She had dark hair and eyes, and nut brown skin. She was heavyset, with round cheeks and a friendly face, though she eyed me warily before peering past me toward my car.

"Can I help you?" she asked.

"I hope so. I'm looking for Tommy Strong, and I'm wondering if you've seen him recently."

"You a cop? You look like a cop."

I hadn't been on the job for more than a year, but I guess the look never really goes away.

"I used to be a cop. I'm not anymore."

She just stared at me, her eyebrows raised as if she were waiting for me to say more.

"I'm a private detective," I told her. "I was hired by Tommy's boss to look into a problem he's having, and I need to ask Tommy some questions."

"I don't think I believe you," she said, the words shaded subtly with the soft lilt I often noticed in the speech of Arizona's native people.

"It's true." I pulled out my PI's license and showed it to her. "I was at Sullivan Toyota just a short while ago. Tommy took off in a hurry when he saw me, and I thought maybe he'd come back here."

She frowned, twisting her mouth like a little kid, and watching me.

"Do you know that Tommy's a weremyste?" I asked. It was a bit of a risk, since it led inevitably to the question of how I knew this. But I had long heard that American Indian culture was far more accepting of my kind than was white society.

"Yeah, I know," she said. "He doesn't try to hide it. That's probably more than you can say, isn't it?"

She was smart as hell.

"Yeah, way more."

She smiled, and her face glowed like the full moon.

"What's your name?" I asked.

"No," she said with a shake of her head. "I don't think I want to tell you that."

"Okay. Then what can you tell me about Tommy?"

The frown returned and I thought for certain that she'd ask me to leave. But instead she leaned against the doorframe, her gaze roaming the empty street.

"I've known Tommy since we were kids, you know? I like him. He's a good guy."

"But?"

"But he's got these ideas . . ." She shook her head. "Being a weremyste in Indian culture, that's big, you know? Shamans have a proud tradition in our world, and Tommy takes that seriously." She wouldn't look at me, and I sensed that she regretted answering the question. "There's a few of them, boys from Gila River and Salt River—they call themselves the Piranhas. They're all weremystes. They have people around here scared."

The Salt River Pima-Maricopa Indian Community was located in the northeastern part of the Phoenix area, near Scottsdale. It was far smaller in size than the Gila River community, though its population was roughly comparable. Together they couldn't have had more than twenty or twenty-five thousand residents, which begged the question: how many young weremystes could there be in the two communities?

"There a lot of them, these Piranhas?"

She shrugged. "No. Maybe five boys. But they're strong because they have magic. People here are afraid of them, even some of the gangs, who aren't afraid of anything. But they stay away from Tommy and his friends."

"Yeah," I said, more to myself than to her, "I'll bet they do." A gang of weremystes. That might have explained why the magic from Tommy's spell differed from the residue on the security cameras. "Have you seen Tommy driving around the neighborhood in something other than his little blue truck?"

I saw her close down on me. Without intending to, without even thinking about it, I'd gone back into cop mode. Her expression flattened, and the look in her eyes turned hard.

"I think you'd better go now," she said, the lilt sounding less friendly than it had seconds before.

I didn't argue. "Right. Thanks for your help," I said. "Have a Merry Christmas."

I started down the path back to the street, and I heard the door shut behind me. A moment later, the music started up again, louder than before.

I would have bet every dollar I had that Tommy and his friends had shown up in a brand new Lexus sometime in the last couple of weeks. I also had a feeling that Tommy wouldn't be coming near his house tonight. He'd seen me at the car dealership and he'd figure that Sullivan had given me his address. He could be anywhere in the Gila River or Salt River communities. That was over six hundred square miles, and I had no idea where to begin looking. There wasn't anything more I could do today.

Tomorrow, though, was Christmas Eve, and I had a feeling his family would expect him to be here then.

The problem was, the phasing started tomorrow night.

I returned to the dealership, and got the security code for the gates from Sullivan, figuring that if I staked out the lot, I might get lucky. But I think my appearance in the garage had spooked Tommy pretty seriously. Nothing unusual happened during the night. At one point Namid showed up, and since I was doing nothing else, I allowed him to drill me in some rudimentary defensive spells. But I was on a stakeout and I didn't want to draw too much attention to myself, which meant there were only so many spells we could practice. After a while, the myste grew frustrated and left. With the first light of dawn, I went home and got a few hours of sleep.

I woke up late in the morning feeling dazed and muddled. The moon wouldn't be up until close to dusk, but already I could feel its weight pressing down on my mind, as unwelcome as woolen blankets in an Arizona summer.

I dressed quickly, strapped on my shoulder holster, and holstered my Glock 22 .40 caliber pistol. I didn't want to use it, but I would have been a fool not to bring it with me, given what I had in mind to do. I also had a brief conversation with Namid; I needed him to do a small favor for me. It took some coaxing, but eventually he agreed, although not before wringing from me a promise to practice my spells in earnest after the phasing ended.

With all my plans for the day in place, I grabbed my keys and crossed to the door.

The moment I stepped out of the house, I felt the tug of the moon even more intensely. For a moment I merely stood there by my front door, trying to remember where I was going and why.

Then it came back to me: the idea I'd thought up in the wee hours of the morning as I tried to stay awake in a dark corner of Sullivan Toyota's vast lot. I'd started with the obvious question: How was I, a lone weremyste, supposed to stop five of my kind? Sure, they were kids; they probably didn't have as much knowledge of the craft as I did. But the spell Tommy had used to knock me over had been nothing to sneeze at. If his friends were as strong, I couldn't take on all of them at once.

Maybe, though, I didn't need to.

I didn't want to hurt them if I didn't have to, and Sullivan wanted this dealt with quietly, without any police involvement. He had hired me to stop the thefts and, if possible, recover the stolen cars.

No problem. Right.

I drove back out to Gila River. A few wispy clouds feathered the sky, but the air was clear and an overnight snow had dusted the rugged peaks of the Estrellas to the west. A Swainson's Hawk, neatly decked out in white and brown, circled over the desert, while three ravens, glossy and black, hopped by the highway, eyeing a road-killed jackrabbit.

I parked outside Tommy's house with my windows down. I didn't see his truck, or any late model Lexus sedans, but other cars sat in the drive. Two little kids played in the dirt yard, and I could hear lots of people inside.

I pulled out my old cell phone and that slip of paper I'd gotten from Mitch Sullivan, and dialed Tommy's number. He answered on the fourth ring.

"Hello?"

"Merry Christmas, Tommy."

"Who's this?"

"You don't know who I am, and yet you threw an attack spell at me without even thinking. That's not too smart."

This was met with a silence so long, I started to wonder if he'd broken the connection.

"Who are you?" he asked at last. It seemed like he was trying to sound menacing; he only succeeded in sounding young and beyond his depth.

"What did you do with all those cars you stole, Tommy?"

Another long pause. "I don't know what you're talking about."

"No? Should I ask your family if they've seen you driving any Lexus sedans recently? I'm sitting right outside your house. I could probably shout to them from here. Or maybe I should bring the police over and let them do the questioning. What would you prefer?"

I heard an odd noise on his end and then muffled voices. I realized that he had his hand covering the microphone, and was talking to his buddies. Good, they were with him already.

"How about it, Tommy?" I asked after a few minutes of this.

"I'll tell you what," he said, his voice shaking. "We're coming now, and if you aren't gone by the time we get there, you're a dead man. You hear me?"

"Not smart, Tommy. Runecrafting 101: never threaten a weremyste you don't know."

I snapped my phone shut (yes, I still use a flip phone—get over it) knowing that would infuriate him more than anything. He and his friends would show. It was just a matter of when.

As it turned out, they must have already been in the Gila River Community, because barely ten minutes had passed before I heard the growl of Tommy's truck. I climbed out of my car and saw that the little blue pickup was trailed by a second car, a metallic blue Chevy lowrider. I had been hoping to see a shiny new Lexus, but these guys weren't going to make this quite that easy for me.

I cast a warding, felt the magic settle over me like a cool mist. I knew I would need to cast again once our battle began in earnest, but I didn't want to go into this unprotected.

The two cars veered toward Tommy's yard and skidded to a stop, raising a cloud of brown dust. Tommy and another guy got out of the truck; three more boys clambered out of the lowrider.

I did nothing more than watch them, the Z-ster at my back.

The two little kids ran over to Tommy, shouting his name. He eyed them, looking nervous.

"Send them inside, Tommy," I said.

He glared at me, but then squatted down and talked to them. They cast looks my way before running to the front door and slipping into the house.

"You should have left when you had the chance," Tommy said to me, straightening.

His buddies closed ranks beside him, which was foolish: they should have spread out. That's not to say they didn't look pretty impressive. They were good-looking kids, all of them with long dark hair that they wore loose to their shoulders. One of them was heavier than the others, and another was short and slight. But all of them looked reasonably fit. If this came to a physical fight, I was in trouble.

I cast a second warding, this one a deflection spell that would redirect the attack I knew was coming.

I saw Tommy's mouth moving, and guessed that he was casting. When he released the magic, I was ready. It hit me with enough force to make me brace a hand against the Z-ster, but my warding did just what it was supposed to. His spell bounced off of my defenses and hit the rear of the lowrider. The bumper buckled.

"Shit!" It came from the heavyset boy, whose eyes had gone wide. "Tommy, what'd you do, man?"

I cast again. Three elements. A rock that sat nearby, the rear windshield of Tommy's pickup, and the distance in between. The rock soared at the truck, smashed through the rear glass, and exited the truck through the front windshield.

Tommy gaped at his pickup. Before the boys could recover, I used the same spell to put a stone through a side window of the lowrider.

This last spell knocked them out of their stupor. They charged me, again en masse. They might have had some skill as weremystes, and they might have been big and strong, but they were still just kids playing with powers they didn't yet understand.

My next crafting I aimed at them. Magic for me is an act of will and of visualization. So I visualized all five of them being knocked back by a giant two-by-four: the kids, me, and that imaginary piece of lumber. Three elements, as simple as you please.

They were slammed back about ten feet, all of them landing hard on their backs. Dust billowed from the ground where they hit, and for a few moments none of them moved.

I chanced a glance at Tommy's house and saw that two men and three women were watching me from the front walkway. The little kids were with them, hiding behind their legs. For now, the adults had done nothing to intervene, and I took that as a good sign. Maybe they'd been waiting for someone to teach these guys a lesson.

Tommy was the first to stir. By the time he sat up, I had my Glock out. I didn't aim it at him or his friends, but I made sure all of them could see it.

The boys struggled to their feet, but they didn't charge me again.

"I can go on kicking your asses all day long," I said. "You guys look like hell, and I haven't even broken a sweat yet." I gestured with the weapon. "Or I can use this if I have to, but I'd rather not."

"What is it you want?" Tommy asked.

"Your boss, Mister Sullivan, wants his cars back. By his count you've stolen six Lexus sedans from his lot. He called me because he doesn't want to go to the police. But that's where he's headed next if you're too dumb to listen to me."

I made sure I said all of this loud enough for Tommy's family to hear.

"We're not afraid of the police, or of you," said one of the other boys.

Tommy cast a fierce look his way. "Shut up, Cody." To me, he said, "We don't have the cars anymore."

"Where are they?"

He hesitated, but only for a second. "A chop shop in Glendale."

"I'll need that address."

"You're going to get us killed!" Cody said. "I'm out of here."

He started walking away.

Three elements: his foot, my hand, and a firm tug. His leg went out from under him and he went down in a heap.

"No one leaves until I say so."

I heard snorts of laughter from the other boys. But Cody was pissed. He scrambled to his feet and ran at me. He was about my size and probably could take me. I didn't give him the chance. All these spells were beginning to tire me out, but I was nowhere near done.

My fist, his face, and a good hard punch.

He was still ten feet away from me when he went down again, blood spouting from his nose. This time he didn't get up.

A hush fell over his friends.

"Magic isn't something you screw around with," I said, walking to where Cody lay. I could see he was still breathing, and after a moment he stirred and let out a low groan. "It can be a powerful tool and a dangerous weapon. You all know that it can mess with your minds; it will tonight. You need to learn to control it, and you need to find something better to do with it than disabling security systems. In other words, you need a teacher."

"Are you going to teach us?" Tommy asked.

There was no challenge in the question. After all I'd done to him, to his friends, to his car, I think he might have been willing to have me as a mentor.

But I shook my head. "No, it won't be me. Namid," I called, raising my voice. "I think we're ready for you now."

The runemyste materialized beside me, his pale, clear waters sparkling in the desert sun.

"Whoa!" Tommy whispered.

Two of his friends took a step back.

"What is that?"

"I am Namid'Skemu," Namid said, his voice rolling like distant thunder. "I am a runemyste, a spirit created by the runeclave centuries ago so that I might guide fools like you through the mastery of magic."

What a charmer.

"A runemyste?" Tommy said.

"They are not very clever, are they, Ohanko?"

I grinned. "Not very, no. But I think they're willing to learn, and that's something."

Namid approached the boys, gliding over the road like a sailboat on a mountain lake, and began to speak to them, his voice low. I glanced toward Tommy's house. Most of the adults had gone back inside, but one man remained by the door, watching me. When our eyes met, he nodded once and let himself into the house.

Satisfied that I had done what I could for Tommy and his friends, I walked back to my car. Before I reached it, I heard footsteps behind me and turned once more.

Tommy strode in my direction, a sober expression on his youthful face.

"Thanks," he said. "You didn't have to do this."

I shrugged. "Mister Sullivan hired me to stop whoever was stealing his cars. This seemed like the best way."

"Yeah, well, I'm grateful, even if Cody isn't."

I smiled.

"Is Mister Sullivan going to fire me?"

"I don't know, Tommy. That's between you and him. He likes you. He was disappointed when I told him that you might be responsible. So it may be that you can earn back his trust. But that's going to take some work."

He nodded. "Yeah, all right." He started back toward his friends and Namid. "See you around."

I spent most phasings by myself. I feared hurting someone with my enhanced magic and reduced control, and, maybe more to the point, I didn't want anyone to see me like that: desperate and mad and unable to function.

But this was Christmas Eve, and I knew that my Dad, who was already crazy enough, thank you very much, would be having a rough time, too. So, I bought us a couple of steaks and some potatoes, and late in the afternoon I drove out to his trailer.

The sun angled steeply across the Phoenix-Wickenburg Highway and a stiff westerly wind shook my car and sent tufts of tumbleweed rolling across the road. It would have been a great afternoon for a hike in the desert, but I could feel the moon lurking just below the horizon, reaching for my mind, clouding my thoughts. I arrived in time to get the food cooked and plated. We ate in silence, rushing through our meal like men who knew their minutes were numbered. My Dad wasn't in great shape, though he wasn't as bad off as I had seen him on occasion.

When we had eaten and I had put our dirty plates in the sink, I came back outside and draped a couple of blankets over my father's shoulders.

"Thank you," he mumbled.

"You're welcome. Merry Christmas."

He grinned. "Merry Christmas to you."

We sat together, watching the light change, waiting for the moonrise. Once it came, I lost track of the time. But I remember seeing the moon creep up into the sky, huge and orange, as mesmerizing as it was powerful. I couldn't take my eyes off of it. My thoughts fragmented, and, as I did so often, I began to hallucinate. I remember seeing my mother, dead more than fifteen years, standing before me, the wind stirring her hair. I thought I saw a mountain lion slink across the land behind my father's trailer. And at one point I could have sworn I saw something flash across the face of the moon in silhouette: a sled pulled by flying, antlered creatures and bearing a single man.

Over the years, I had seen a lot of strange things during the phasing. Who could say which of them were real, and which weren't?

"Where do you get your ideas?" is a question that has plagued authors for as long as they've been putting pen to paper. A better question might be, "Where do your ideas come from?" Where indeed?

Creation Unforgivable

David H. Keller

My wife used to think I took writing too seriously. "There's no living with you or loving you when you're at work on a story, and the longer the story, the longer the period of separation," she would say. I always answered with a laugh and told her that was the penalty she had to pay for marrying a creative artist.

For that was the way I looked at my writing. To others it might seem prosaic enough to sit all day at a low desk and prod the keys of an old typewriter. Some of my friends told me it was a poor way for a man of my capability to spend his time, but again I only answered with a laugh and told them that it made me happy.

So far my life had been spent in comparative isolation in a small town. My outlook on life was apparently contracted, my opportunity for adventure slight. There were few persons to talk to, and, of those few, none who topped me intellectually. I should have been bitter, unhappy, and misanthropic. But my writing and the faraway fields that it took me into were the panacea that made living a happy adventure, in spite of my surroundings.

I sold a story, and then another, and finally was able to buy a broken-down house and fifty acres of land a few miles from the center of town. My first thought was to make the house livable. After that I hunted for someplace to write. So far, I had been handicapped by the lack of suitable surroundings in which to pound the keys. Surely in fifty acres there should be some place a man could find solitude, comfort and, mayhap, inspiration.

And without hunting for it, I found it. A small one-room shack, the floor six by ten, the roof hardly six feet from the floor. It was some distance from the house, almost in the shadow of an overhanging ledge of rock and on the edge of a swamp. I went into that swamp once and found the mouth of a cave, but the mosquitoes were so bad that I determined to save further exploration for colder weather.

I was more handy with a typewriter than I was with a saw and hammer, so I put a carpenter to work. First, the roof of my workshop had to be shingled, and a new floor was imperative. Four windows supplied light and ventilation, while copper screens kept out insects. We put shelves on the walls, and at the end of one week I moved my books out there and arranged them, while a painter dabbed green paint all over the outside. At last I had a place for my desk and typewriter.

It was a wonderful place in which to write. There was always light, but all through the day the sunlight was mellowed and softened and changed, either by the green of the trees or the black of the mountain. There was a stillness made the more intense by the singing birds and tireless crickets. We liked it, the wife and I, while baby cried for a whole day when she found that it was going to be a workshop for an author instead of a playhouse for a little girl. My wife threatened picnic suppers and I had to arrange for a fireplace and a brass pipe to carry water from a spring up on the hill.

After all was ready, I walked to town and bought another ream of paper. Now I was sure I could do something worthwhile.

My wife insisted that I took my work too seriously and it is true that while writing, I lived the story. To me my characters were real people, right up to the last line, and even to the minute that I wrote *The End* at the bottom of the page. Only then would they fade and lose their definite personalities. They never seemed to be just so many word-people, but actual living persons, induced, for a few hours, to come with me and lead the adventurous life which I created for them.

I loved them all—the heroes, ladies fair but frail, villains, sorry, evil, but withal, lovable. Perhaps they were but the children of my creative mind, though at times I felt differently about them. Back of me were my ancestors, two parents and four grandparents and eight great-grandparents. How many, twenty generations back? How many, fifty? Where and who were my ancestors one hundred thousand years ago, and what were they doing and how did they live? Part of them was in me. They all had contributed to making the personality of the unknown author in the forgotten backwash of a country town. Perhaps when I created, I only brought up from the subconscious, from the deep pit of forgotten memories, portions of the lives of these distant relatives, dead a thousand years or a hundred centuries ago.

When I thought I was creating, was that all that I was doing? Simply shutting my eyes and telling about the things that I saw these ancestors do? What an interesting conception of creative authorship! And what a merry, happy-go-lucky, hearty family I had in those olden days!

As usual, my wife asked me what I was next going to write about.

"It makes no difference to me," she explained for the tenth time, "what you write about, so long as you sell it. What makes me nervous is for you to spend a week or ten days slaving on a story, and then have a dozen editors write that it's beautiful stuff but that the readers will hardly understand it. Write anything you want to, just as long as you write the stuff editors will buy, for winter's coming on, and it's going to be a long one, and I'm tired of eating oatmeal and cutting down my old dresses to make clothes for Suzanne."

I told her that I was now going to write a tale of prehistoric days. I had thought of doing this for a long time, but always other plots thrust it back into temporary obscurity. The tale would be set so far in the past that no one could measure it with the yardstick of historical accuracy and say I was not true to facts as known to the dry and musty antiquarians. I wanted to go back to the caveman and the saber-toothed tiger. I wanted to go back to the mammoth and the painting of cave pictures. There was a story, a tale that I had long wanted to fasten on paper. Now I could do it.

To me it was an interesting story. I wrote ten pages the first day and told my wife the high spots of those ten pages as we spent a half hour on the gallery before going to our bedroom.

"The hero belongs to a race of supermen. They decide to move west. They want to follow the sun on account of the rapid advance of the glaciers in their own country. Their advance is through a strange country, and hardships of every kind make life uncertain. Not only are they attacked by wild animals of a kind they have never seen before, but they encounter men, half man and half ape, who block their path and try to steal their women. The hero of the story is a young man who is the headman, because he is the bravest and strongest of them all. He is in love with a beautiful Amazon who has said she won't marry until she meets a man who is strong enough to conquer her in a wrestling match.

"The hero says he'll try to win this fight the next spring at the yearly festival devoted to the sowing of the fields and the mating of the unmarried members of the tribe. Now, how's that for a beginning of a story of old times?" My wife yawned.

"Fair," she answered. "But there's nothing original about it. It seems to me I've read things like that before, and, from what you've told me, there's not a single idea in the whole ten pages."

"You just wait until tomorrow," I retorted as I went to sleep.

The next day I did fifteen pages. The hero killed a cave bear, had a terrific fight with the chief of the apemen, and brought back a horse as a present to his beloved Amazon. She took it but made no promises as to the future. Again I told my wife of the adventures of the invading tribe.

"I'm beginning to warm up to these people that I'm writing about," I said gravely. "I like them. Today, when the hero was in a fight with the apeman, I should have let the half ape kill him. He was the better fighter, but I just couldn't bear to see the poor fellow torn limb from limb; so, just when things seemed the darkest, he remembered a wrestling trick, tossed the apeman over his shoulder and down a thousand foot precipice. How's that? The heroine, the wrestling Amazon, sees the fight and cries out her approval. She joins her lover and binds up his wounds with some sacred herbs and leaves so that they heal in no time."

"I suppose," my wife asked, "that this Amazon is very beautiful?"

"She certainly is. Of course she's strong as can be, but her muscles are not bunched, and, just to look at her, you'd think she was a delicate young girl. She's a blonde—"

"I might have known that!" cried my wife. "Oh, you men! Now, there's just one more woman in the world to keep you from dreaming about me."

"I don't have to dream about you," I answered tenderly.

I wrote all morning, and right after dinner of the next day I said I was going back to the writing shack immediately.

Just as I was leaving the house, my wife called, "I forgot to tell you. The Joneses want us to go riding with them this afternoon, stay for supper and bridge, and we shan't be back until nearly midnight. Will you go?"

"All right," I sighed and walked slowly back to the house. "I'll go with you, but I'm very anxious to write another chapter or two of my story."

"Just why?"

"Oh! I'll tell you later. No use to now."

We went out with the Jones family in their automobile. They, like all other car owners, took us to a dozen places that we didn't really care about, and the places that we wanted to see were passed at sixty miles an hour. However, they served a fine supper and they played a very stiff game of bridge. I played poorly that night. Somehow, my mind wasn't on the game.

We were driven back home at eleven. Instead of starting to undress at once, I asked my wife if she'd care very much if I took a lantern, went out to the workshop and finished the chapter.

"I've been worried about those people all the time I was playing cards," I explained, "and that's why I played so poorly. I can't remember the plays and the science of bridge when I'm worrying about the people in my stories."

"Well, what's the matter with them now?" my wife asked, sleepily.

"Matter enough. That Amazon went hunting in the forest and the ape-folks caught her. The hero heard her cries for help, and without waiting to gather his tribe he dashed off to rescue her. There was a fight, really a very wonderful fight. You'd have been pleased to see the way that chieftain tore into those apemen, but they were too many for him, and at the end the caught him, threw a rock at him, and hit him on the head, and when he recovered conciousness he was tied, hand and foot, with grapevines, and the only pleasure that he had out of it was that he was close to the Amazon, and at last she told him that she loved him and that, if they ever escaped and lived until the time of the spring festival, she would allow him to throw her in the wrestling match and be his woman as a consequence. He's very much of a man, and, before I realized it, he was telling her that he was going to conquer her, whether she used her full strength or not, and then they quarreled. Think of that! Both of them captured by apemen and bound so there was no hope of escape, and then quarreling instead of spending their last hours telling each other how much they were in love."

"Well," yawned my wife, "they're tied and they'll be there tomorrow morning when you start working again, so come to bed."

"But you don't understand. These apemen don't intend to kill them themselves. They will sacrifice them to their god. There's a cave animal, something like a dragon, and whenever the moon is full, the thing comes out of his cave. The apemen tie slaves and prisoners to stakes in front of this cave, and in the brilliant light of the full moon, this dragon comes out and eats the human sacrifice.

"When I came in to dinner, that was the situation that the hero and the Amazon were in. They were tied to the stakes, waiting for the time when they'd be torn limb from limb. It was to happen that night. I ought to have kept on writing and rescued them, somehow, from that terrible situation. I had no right to create them and then simply go off and play bridge and let them die just like dogs or apemen. To do that was a creation unforgivable. I wish you'd let me go out and write just a few pages. I could make a terrible storm come up or an eclipse that would blot out the moon—make it pitch-dark and frighten the ape-folks into believing that these were white gods."

"Oh! Let's go to bed. You take these things too seriously," insisted my wife.

"I can't help it," I demurred. "While I'm writing the story, it seems that somehow the characters are alive."

But I went to bed. At least, I pretended to, but I simply waited until I could be certain of my wife's slumber. Then I put on some old clothes, stole downstairs, lit a lantern, and started on the long walk to the little shack at the end of the woods. I was about two-thirds of the way when I heard a howl—an unearthly cry deadly in its threatening portent. And after that a woman's terror-stricken voice— a woman facing horrible death, without hope or help, crying her anguish because she couldn't control her longing to live. In answer came only a gibberish of laughter. The ape-folk were glorying in her despair. Their cup of happiness would be filled if only the man would cry and beg for mercy. And once again came the whistling piercing scream.

I was angry at myself. What business had I to be playing bridge and let these children of my brain suffer thus? There was still time to rescue them. If I could only reach the typewriter in the next five minutes! I started to run. And now there was a trinity of noises beating in my ears, the snarl of the animal no longer able to breathe freely on account of his flesh-filled mouth, his blood-choked nostrils; there were a few agonized screams of human beings being mangled, torn apart, who, had they lived, might have been the progenitors of Athenian culture, the forefathers of the best families of Rome. And above and intermingled with these cries of dying despair came the chuckling, hellish laughter of beings who never, for a million years, would be anything but apes.

I started to run faster.

"Wait, wait! I am coming! I'm not going to let you die! Not that way! Not after I created you and made you possible lords of creation," I cried as I ran, sobbing, and in my despair I caught my toe against a root and fell, head against rock, senseless.

When morning came my wife awoke and missed me. Her first thought was that I had gone to the shack on the edge of the woods.

She found me unconscious, fifty yards from the shack. My head was bleeding from the cut on the rock. My clothes were torn and here and there over my body were long deep scratches, a few of which cut through the skin to the muscle underneath. She was so preoccupied with me and my condition that she had no eyes for anything else. It took time to call a neighbor and send for a doctor, but at last I was in bed, all tended to and bandaged and very much alive. It seems that my wife spread the news that I had gone out to the shack and met a wildcat. There were cats in the woods; so, the story was credited.

It was two days before I was able to walk to the shack. I begged my wife to let me go alone. For her sake I took a revolver, though I knew that it was not necessary. She wanted to go, but I just alighted at her fears. So, alone, I walked to the shop where I manufactured stories and people.

The place looked worse than I had expected. One side of the hut was smashed in as though hit by a terrific battering-ram. The roof sagged; its supports were broken. With the greatest difficulty, I pried open the door and made my way inside. The typewriter was twisted, broken; its delicate steel fingers would never again write magically on white paper. The table was splintered into matchwood, and all the manuscripts littered the floor in contorted confusion. The papers looked peculiar; even from a distance they had a strange smell. I picked up one sheet and it stuck to my fingers.

Then I saw the whole truth.

Those red blotches on the manuscripts were blood.

There was an oil lamp that by some devilish twist of fate had remained unbroken when the antediluvian storm broke over my little world. I threw a match into it and walked out into the sunlight of God's beautiful world. I started to walk to the house where my wife and baby were waiting for me.

Undecided, I turned and walked, as though in a dream, to the edge of the swamp, and there I saw tracks in the mud, some as large as the pads of an elephant, and others man-shaped, but with the great toe far apart. Most of these man-footed marks ended at the base of great live oaks, but the large pads, that sank a foot into the ground until they could secure footing for the mass above them—those tracks went on through the woods and ended at the mouth of the cave.

I am never going into that cave.

Without the Diaspora of the Chronicles, mankind would succumb to disease and genetic degradation on a thousand worlds. But for some, the Chronicles take more than they give . . .

As It Began

Dave Bara

"By the bloody Chronicles, be done with you! I am old and will likely stay that way for a good bit longer!"

The Dowager Empress Maren sat in the window chair of her royal apartments, looking out to the landing pad where she had once lost a love. The only love of her life.

"Are you sure this is the day?" she asked of the Royal Physician. He looked down at her, eyes over lowered spectacles.

"So they say." He made a precise adjustment to his instruments. "Ahh. There we are!"

"Let me guess. I will live to see another year."

He smiled. "Perhaps two."

"Grand," she said. "You can go now. And send in my daughter."

"As you wish, Dowager Empress." The doctor disassembled his equipment with a single touch, packed it, then bowed formally and was gone. The Princess Elissa came through the door a moment later and smiled at her mother.

"Good news for the Maroon Court, I hear."

"Yes," said Maren, "but unfortunately not for me."

"Mother, you mustn't say such things!"

Maren looked at her daughter, not exactly a young woman herself, and shook her head.

"And which of your grandchildren are we sowing off to the stars today?" Maren asked.

"It's Carina, the youngest. And the last," Elissa said quietly.

The Dowager Empress sighed. "Must we never stop paying the bounty for our sins?"

Elissa cocked her head to one side and answered the question with another. "Will you never forgive the Chronicles for your condition? You could have married again, you know."

"Could I? You don't know what you're saying," snapped Maren. "You were never part of the plan. Just an old sow cow, you were. And now your granddaughters pay the price. Off they go to worlds unknown, with men unknown, all so that the cursed Chronicles will be fulfilled and the seeds of human survival can be sown again and again. It sickens me, the whole process. It takes a life away from us, from our youth, and gives it to those long yet unborn. It is a curse, I say."

Elissa shook her head at her mother, and then spread her arms wide as she spoke.

"And what would you have us do? Without the Diaspora of the Chronicles mankind would have succumbed to disease and genetic degradation on a thousand worlds by now. Isn't it better this way, that we exchange what's needed from world to world, from time after time, to keep mankind alive and thriving? A seed is sown; a harvest reaped. This is our gift to the universe, Mother."

Maren grunted in disgust. "It never felt like a gift to me," she said. "It felt like my entire life was lived in a few short weeks, and I have spent the rest of my days tortured by the memories."

Elissa came and sat at her mother's feet. "You loved him dearly, didn't you?"

Now the empress smiled at her daughter.

"Like no other. He was young and hard and rough, and so beautiful! To look at him would have taken your breath away."

"I *have* seen his portraits, Mother."

"Yes, well, what the Chronicles give us is a mere reflection of the casing. They cannot show you the *fire* in his eyes, nor tell you of the fire in his mouth!"

"Mother, please!" They both laughed at this, then Maren patted her daughter's hand.

"Don't worry, I won't test your stomach with my lurid memories. How soon now until this latest prince arrives?"

Elissa stood, and Maren saw the waves of golden hair flicker in the light, just like her father's had so many years ago.

"Just an hour now. I should go to be with Carina."

Maren waved her off. "Go. All you're doing here is annoying an old woman."

Elissa kissed her mother on the cheek and then was gone.

An hour later, Maren watched as the prince's shuttle descended to the landing pad. The greeting party prepared the ramp, and a young man came down and bowed formally. From such a great distance, and with her eyes not what they once were, she could barely make him out. No doubt he would be a decent enough young man, even if he was here to take the last of her great-granddaughters away, the last remnant of her beloved Bespoe.

Then the Dowager Empress Maren sighed once more, closed her eyes, and dreamt of being young again.

"He is coming!"

She had heard it all her life.

When Maren was a little girl it had excited her, this dream of marrying an offworld prince from Corant. Blessed Corant! Cradle of life; keeper of the sacred Chronicles.

"He is coming!"

But as she grew to early womanhood it became an empty refrain. He was a myth, this man of the stars, this man of her dreams and visions. And so she became cynical, and went on about her learning and practice, becoming a lady as only a maiden of the Maroon Court could do. She fell in and out of love with the sons of dukes, and baronets, and counts and viscounts, and earls and chevaliers.

And then one day the boring refrain changed, and with it, her life.

"He is here!"

He was taller than she had imagined, this man from the stars. Tall and thin and light-haired with piercing ice-blue eyes, like nothing she had seen in heaven or on earth. He was before her now, the epaulets of his uniform tied with gilded rope, the sash of royal green slashing across his chest; the gold of the falcon and crescent moon adorned his breast. He was a man, yes, but to Maren he could well have been a god, forged from iron and steel and pounded into the youth who stood so tall over her.

Maren bowed.

The ruffles of her white gown straddled the cobblestones of the receiving yard, lace furrows touching the ground with only the slightest wisp before returning again to their rightful place as she rose.

"I am Bespoe," he spoke to her, his voice like a song to her ears. "Prince of Corant. One-hundred sixty-seven generations removed from Auldus and Leona." He bowed from the waist, one arm across his chest. "Your betrothed."

"Welcome!" said Maren with true enthusiasm. "Welcome to the Court of St. Ralland, Prince Bespoe. I am Maren, two-hundred and nineteen generations removed from Auldus and Queen Inari." She bowed again as court law dictated. "Your betrothed."

Bespoe put his hand to her chin and gazed into her eyes, their soft brown threatened now by tendrils of red from her tears of joy. Then he pulled her close, and placed his lips on hers.

He was here!

He extended his arm to her and they walked together in the palace gardens, talking for what seemed like hours and watching the sunset. They stood together in front of the palace fountains at night as spires of color cascaded into the air in celebration. Courtiers watched from a distance as images of Maren's childhood and Bespoe's arrival danced across the waters, a holographic tribute to their coming union.

Finally, alone on the garden balcony, they shared a true and private moment together.

"You are more beautiful even than the Chronicles portrayed you," said Bespoe.

Maren blushed at this despite her years of training.

"And you, my prince," she said, "are even more handsome than the portraits left by your ancestors."

He smiled at her compliment. "The Chronicles are true," he said.

She nodded agreement. "The Chronicles are true."

Then he kissed her again, this time with passion.

They were married the next day, when the golden-red sun of St. Ralland was highest in the sky. Bespoe took her hand in his and placed the silver ring of marriage on her finger, claiming her for the Chronicles, and himself, for all time.

They celebrated with dancing and music, and soon the night fell. Then her father blessed her, and her mother kissed her forehead as she went to her marriage bed for the first time.

Bespoe's touch was gentle and his kiss sweet, but Maren felt more than mere bliss. She was ready for him to take her as a lover, not merely as a princess or a wife, but as the one that he would love and linger with and remember in the dark years beyond.

Beyond the days they would spend together, here and now.

She scraped his sculpted chest with her fingers, pushed back the satin finery of his bed robe, and then found what she was seeking. Her hands lingered there as they kissed, his tongue a flaming desire in her mouth.

She held him in this way, day after day, her Corant prince. She held him in her sway with the length of her silken hair, the fire in her eyes, and with the youth and beauty of her body. She held him enraptured, and he never ceased to seek her pleasure, drinking her into him like wine from a chalice.

One evening, as summer turned to the cool of early autumn, she stood on a balcony and looked down at his ship, the chariot which had brought him from the stars. It sat gracefully like a church spire where it had first descended to her world, dark patches from the fire of its rockets still staining the ground, even after the wet of an evening shower. It sat and waited. Waited for her beloved Bespoe.

He was at her side as the wind blew through her dark hair.

"What are you thinking?" he asked.

That troubled her. Their communication had been so deep, their bonding so strong, that he had never uttered a question of her until now. She turned to him.

"How soon, Bespoe? How soon until you leave?"

He tried to smile, to comfort her, but it was to no avail. She turned back to the sight of the prince's shuttle, waiting for him to end her reverie forever.

He put his arms around her. They were warm and strong and comforting.

"Long enough to make sure the seed has taken hold," he said.

A tear stung her cheek. "Is that all that I am? A seed pod? Something to hold your inheritance until the Chronicles demand that seed back again?"

He swung her towards him, then placed his hand on her belly.

"What you carry is so much more than a seed, Maren. You carry the future. Without our pairing the genetic pool would decay, our resistance to these worlds we are not native to would collapse. Our children would grow barren and die, one by one. Mankind would cease to exist."

"Perhaps that would be best," she said, her words bitter for the first time.

"You don't mean that," he said.

"Ah, but I do! To be used in this way, as nothing more than a common whore to be filled and then discarded. If I didn't love you so much, I could perhaps be persuaded to hate you, or the damnable Chronicles that brought you here."

"Maren, don't do this, please. I am merely the deliverer. I come in with the summer wind and depart with the rains of autumn. But I never get to stay, to see the winter, or the spring, to hold and cherish that which I bring into the worlds of men. But you, you will have so much more than I."

"Will I?" She was angry now. "Will I truly? Mother to a daughter, with a husband only a memory, a life lived in a fraction of an instant and then thrown aside for the sake of the cursed Chronicles!"

He grasped her shoulders and spoke tenderly to her. "Maren, without the Chronicles—"

"We could live and die as we pleased!" she said, seething.

He let go of her and stepped back into the apartments they shared. She watched him go, noting the slump of his shoulders, dreading what he would say next.

"Nine days," he said, barely a whisper. "I leave in nine days."

She followed him in, a vision in white, her once-warm heart now ice-cold and frozen.

"Then in nine days I will mourn you, and then curse the Chronicles for the rest of my life."

"Please," he said. "The Chronicles are true."

"No," she shook her head. "The Chronicles are a lie."

"Then I have spread that lie a hundred times."

She sat for a long time in silence. He sat with her, ever the dutiful husband. Tea came and went. The evening turned to dark, and still she sat by their bed, unmoved. Then a thought came to her, dark as the night and disturbing in its implications, and forced her to speak to the man she both loved and hated at the same time.

"Did you love them all?"

He looked at her. "Yes," he said honestly.

"As you love me?"

Again, "Yes."

"And when you leave I will depart from your mind and heart, and you will love another, and another, and another?"

"Yes," he said a third time. "It is the way. I will sleep as my ship travels on, and my mind and heart will be cleansed of my deepest feelings. Then love for the next wife will be planted there by the Chronicles, to grow as I sleep."

She shook her head at him.

"How I pity you," she said. "You and your curse. The Chronicles have left you a cursed man, don't you see?"

He shuffled his feet. "I have thought on it often."

She laughed. "Have you now? As you depart from one lover and contemplate the next, you think of yourself as cursed, do you? *I* am the one left alone, Bespoe! *I* am the one who faces these long years ahead on my own. *You* pass your way among the stars and one day you arrive on the next world, and take your next wife, and impregnate her and forget her and then start again! This is what the Chronicles have done to you!"

He looked her directly in the eyes. "Yes, Maren, my love. I and a thousand other princes, on ten thousand other worlds! We know no home except that which we are occasionally granted. And no lasting love escapes the ravages of time. Do you have any idea what it's like to know that a year after I leave you will have grandchildren, that in five you will have grown old, and in ten you will be dust? The love we are granted fades and withers in the blink of an eye. And that, that loneliness, is our curse. So pity me if you choose. But grant me one thing, lady. Never doubt the love I give to you. It is the one thing, the only thing I have that is real."

The following days were brutal, filled with aching and longing and the seeking and granting of forgiveness. Bespoe told her that this schism occurred in a only few of the wives of his experience, always the most intelligent and beautiful it seemed, the ones he loved the most.

Their last night together they endured a feast. The royal physicians confirmed her pregnancy, and Maren admitted pride that she carried the survival of St. Ralland and the Maroon Court in her womb. They smiled politely through speeches and songs of praise to the Chronicles, and to the new fables being written of their love.

And finally, after hours apart, Maren lay naked in bed with her husband for the last time.

"Her name will be Elissa," she said as Bespoe held her close, gently stroking her belly. "It was my grandmother's name."

"Good," replied Bespoe. "My grandmother's name was Gurtus." And they laughed together, as young lovers do. Then he kissed her, and held her, and tasted her, and they made love until the dawn.

She wore maroon on the day of his departure. He dressed in the same uniform as the one he had arrived in. She walked with him to the landing pad, hand in hand, formally as the conventions required. He carried the book of remembrances she had put together for him, and he promised to keep it and to cherish it, as he had none other. She had smiled when he said it, hoping it was true.

And then they were at the ramp, and he held her in his arms one last time. They shared a brief embrace, and with a last kiss, they parted.

She watched him go from the window of her apartments, the silver-blue fire of his rockets taking him to the stars once more.

Then Maren grasped her belly, and wept bitterly.

The Royal Physician finished his examination of the Dowager Empress and turned to face her daughter.

"It happens this way, sometimes. It cannot be predicted. A vessel of the brain can burst at any time."

"Will she recover?" asked Elissa.

The doctor shook his head. "We have only to wait a short time now, most likely. Then she will be at peace."

Tears fell from Elissa's eyes at this news. "Thank you, Doctor. Please go now."

"Of course." The doctor departed to leave mother and daughter alone.

Elissa kissed her mother's forehead, then gently stroked her grayed hair, still so long and beautiful. "You were right, mother," she said. "The Chronicles are cruel, and time is a cold companion."

Elissa watched from the chair her mother had sat in only the day before. The Dowager Empress Maren lay in repose behind her, in the bed she had shared with only one man. Elissa knew that in the end it was the only way her mother would have had it, for her life to end on this particular day. One last snub at the Chronicles, which she believed had robbed her of her only true happiness.

Elissa sat forward as she watched the formal procession to the shuttle. The morning's wedding of Carina to her new husband, a true Prince of Corant, had been full of ritual and protestations of great love yet to be experienced. She had kept the news of the Dowager Empress' passing to herself. No need for Carina to ever know.

Carina and her prince ascended the ramp, pausing only once to stop and wave to the cheering throng. Then the doors were shut behind them, her last granddaughter going to the stars, there to bear children for the many worlds of the Chronicles.

She watched as the shuttle rockets fired first bright white, then silver-blue flames. The shuttle rose slowly into the sky, taking with it a Princess of St. Ralland and a young man, a man Elissa had never met before, but yet was able to call by names both strange and familiar.

Bespoe. Father. Prince of Corant.

She watched the rocket until it vanished into the distant clouds of the autumn sky.

And so it ends, she thought, lying back in the chair, her tears running freely.

As it began.

What is it about restaurant food? Try as many copycat recipes as you like, but it seems all but impossible to replicate your favorite meals-out, in. Is it the technique of the cooks? The industrial equipment in the restaurant kitchens? Or is there something else at base of all this? Here now, a story by the late Avram Davidson, in which a Mr. Fred Hopkins tries to unravel the mystery behind a bowl of soup.

Full Chicken Richness

Avram Davidson

La Bunne Burger was said to have the best hamburger on The Street; the only trouble with that was that Fred Hopkins didn't care much for hamburger. However, there were other factors to consider, such as these: other items on La Bunne's menu were probably just a bit better than comparable items composed elsewhere on The Street, they sold for just a bit less than, etc. etc., and also Fred Hopkins found the company just a bit more interesting than elsewhere, etc. What else? It was nearer to his studio loft than any eating-place else. Any place else save for a small place called The Old Moulmein Pagoda, the proprietor of which appeared to speak very fluent Cantonese for a Burman, and the Old Moulmein Pagoda was not open until late afternoon. *Late* afternoon.

Late morning was more Fred's style.

He was likely to find there, at any given time of late morning, a number of regulars, such as: well, there was Tilly, formerly Ottilie, with red cheeks, her white hair looking windblown even on windless days; Tilly had her own little routine, which consisted of ordering coffee and toast; with the toast came a small plastic container of jelly, and this she spread on one of the slices of toast. That eaten, she would hesitantly ask Rudolfo if she might have more jelly . . . adding that she would pay for it. Rudolfo would hand her one or two or three more, she would tentatively offer him a palm of pennies and nickels and he would politely decline them. Fred was much moved by this little drama, but after the twelfth and succedent repetitions it left him motionless. (Once he was to encounter Tillie in a disused doorway downtown standing next to a hat with money while she played—and played beautifully—endless Strauss waltzes on that rather un-Strauss-like-instrument, the harmonica.)

Also usually present in La Bunne Burger in the 40 minutes before the noon rush were Volodya and Carl. They were a sort of twosome there; that is, they were certainly not a twosome elsewhere. Carl was tall and had long blond hair and a long blond beard and was already at his place along the counter when Volodya walked in. Carl never said anything to Volodya, Volodya always said anything to Carl. Volodya was wide and gnarly and had small pale eyes like those of a malevolent pig. Among the things he called Carl were *Pópa! Moslaiey! Smaravdtchnik!*—meaning (Fred Hopkins found out by and by) Priest! Inhabitant of Moscow! And One Who, For Immoral Purposes, Pretends to be a Chimney Sweep! Fred by and by tried to dissuade Volodya of this curious delusion; "He's a Minnesota Swede," Fred explained. But Volodya would have none of it. "*He's A Rahshian Artoducks priest!*" was his explosive comeback—and he went on to denounce the last Czar of Russia as having been in the pay of the freemasons. Carl always said nothing, munched away on droplets of egg congealed on his beard.

And there was, in La Bunne Burger, often, breaking fast on a single sausage and a cup of tea, a little old oriental man, dressed as though for the winters of Manchuria; once Fred had, speaking slowly and clearly, asked him to please pass the ketchup; "Say, I ain't deef," said the l.o.o.m., in tones the purest American Gothic.

Fred himself *was* not in the least eccentric, he was an *artist*, not even starving, though . . . being unfashionably representational . . . not really prospering, either. His agent said that this was his, Fred's, own fault. "Paint doctors' wives!" his agent insisted. "If you would only paint portraits for doctors' wives, I could get you lots of commissions. Old buildings," his agent said, disdainfully. "Old buildings, old buildings." But the muse kisseth where she listeth and if anything is not on the list, too bad: Fred had nothing against doctors' wives; merely, he preferred to paint pictures of old buildings. Now and then he drove around looking for old buildings he hadn't painted pictures of and he photographed them and put those photos up by his canvas to help when he painted at home: this of course caused him to be regarded with scorn by purists who painted only from the model or the imagination; why either should be less or more scorable, they disdained to say.

Whom else was F. Hopkins likely to see in La Bunne Burger over his late breakfast or his brunch? Proprietors of nearby businesses, for example, he was likely to see there; mamma no longer brought pappa's dinner wrapped in a towel to keep hot. Abelardo was sometimes there. Also Fred might see tourists or new emigrés or visiting entrepreneurs of alien status, come to taste the exotic tuna fish sandwich on toast, the picturesque macaroni and cheese, the curious cold turkey, and, of course, often, often, often the native La Bunne De Luxe Special . . . said to be the best hamburger on The Street. Abelardo had long looked familiar; Abelardo had in fact looked familiar from the first. Abelardo always came in from the kitchen and Abelardo always went back out through the kitchen, and yet Abelardo did not work in the kitchen. Evidently Abelardo delivered. Something.

Once, carrying a plate of . . . something . . . odd and fragrant, Rudolfo rested it a moment on the counter near Fred while he gather cutlery; in response to Fred's look of curiosity and approbation, at once said, "Not on the menu. Only I give some to Abelardo, because our family come from the same country;" off he went.

Later: "You're not from Mexico, Rudolfo."

"No. South America." Rudolfo departs with glasses.

Later: "Which country in South America you from, Rudolfo?"

"Depend who you ask." Exit, Rudolfo, for napkins.

Fred Hopkins, idly observing paint on two of his own fingers, idly wondered that—a disputed boundary being clearly involved—Rudolfo was not out leading marches and demonstrations, or (*at least!*) with drippy brushes slapping up graffiti exhorting the reader to *Remember the 12th of January . . . the 3rd of April . . . the 24th of October* . . . and so on through the existing political calendar of Ibero-America . . . Clearly, Rudolfo was an anachronism. Perhaps he secretly served some fallen sovereign; a pseudo-crypto-Emperor of Brazil. Perhaps.

Though probably not likely.

One day, the hour being later than usual and the counter crowded, Fred's eyes wandered around in search of a seat; met those of Abelardo who, wordlessly, invited him to sit in the empty place at the two-person table. Which Fred did. And, so doing, realized why the man had always seemed familiar. Now, suppose you are a foreigner living in a small city or medium town in Latin America, as Fred Hopkins had once been, and it doesn't really matter which city or town or even which country . . . doesn't really matter for *this* purpose . . . and you are going slightly out of your *mind* trying to get your electricity (*la luz*) turned on and eventually you notice that there are a few large stones never moved from the side of a certain street and gradually notice that there is often the same man sitting on one of the boulders and that this man wears very dusty clothes which do not match and a hat rather odd for the locale (say, a beret) and that he also wears glasses and that the lens of one is opaque or dark and that this man often gives a small wave of his hand to return the greetings of passersby but otherwise he merely sits and looks. You at length have occasion to ask him something, say, At what hour does the Municipal Palace open? And not only does the man politely inform you, he politely engages you in conversation and before long he is giving you a fascinating discourse on an aspect of history, religion, economics, or folklore, an aspect of which you had been completely ignorant. Subsequent enquiry discloses that the man is, say, a Don Eliseo, who had attended the National University for nine years but took no degree, that he is an *idiosyncratico*, and comes from a family *muy honorado*—so much *honorado*, in fact, that merely having been observed in polite discourse with him results in your electricity being *connectido muy pronto*. You have many discourses with Don Eliseo and eventually he shows you his project, temporarily in abeyance, to perfect the best tortilla making-and-baking machine in the world: there is some minor problem, such as the difficulty of scraping every third tortilla off the ceiling, but any day now Don Eliseo will get this licked; and, in the meanwhile and forever after, his house is your house.

This was why Abelardo had seemed familiar from the start, and if Abelardo was not Eliseo's brother, he was certainly his nephew or his cousin . . . in spirit, anyway.

Out of a polite desire that Fred Hopkins not be bored while waiting to be served, Abelardo discussed various things with him— that is, for the most part, Abelardo discussed. Fred listened. La Bunne Burger was very busy.

"Now, the real weakness of the Jesuits in Paraguay," Abelardo explained.

"Now, in western South America," said Abelardo, "North American corporations are disliked far less for their vices than for their virtues. Bribery, favoritism, we can understand these things, we live with them. But an absolute insistence that one must arrive in one's office day after day at one invariable hour and that frequent prolonged telephone conversations from one's office to one's home and family is unfavored, this is against our conception of personal and domestic usement," Abelardo explained.

He assured Fred Hopkins that the Regent Isabella's greatest error, "though she made several," was in having married a Frenchman. "The Frankish temperament is not the Latin temperament," Abelardo declared.

Fred's food eventually arrived; Abelardo informed him that although individual enterprise and planned economy were all very well in their own ways, "one ignores the law of supply and demand at peril. I have been often in business, so I know, you see," said Abelardo.

Abelardo did not indeed wear eyeglasses with one dark or opaque lens, but one of his eyes was artificial. He had gold in his smile—that is, in his teeth—and his white coverall was much washed but never ironed. By and by, with polite words and thanks for the pleasure of Fred's company, Abelardo vanished into the kitchen; when Fred strolled up for his bill, he was informed it had already been paid. This rather surprised Fred. So did the fact, conveyed to him by the clock, that the noon rush was over. Had *been* over.

"Abelardo seems like—Abelardo is a very nice guy."

Rudolfo's face, hands, and body made brief but persuasive signal that it went without saying that Abelardo was indeed a very nice guy. "But I don't know how he stays in business," said Rudolfo, picking up a pile of dishes and walking them off to the kitchen.

Fred had no reason to remain to discuss this, as it was an unknown to him how anybody stayed in business. Merely, he was well aware how week after week the price of paints and brushes and canvases went up, up, up, while the price of his artwork stayed the same, same, same. Well, his agent, though wrong, was right. No one to blame but himself; he could have stayed in advertising, he might be an account executive by now. Or—walking along The Street, he felt a wry smile accompany memory of another of Abelarod's comments: "Advertisage is like courtship, always involves some measure of deceit."

This made him quickstep a bit back to the studio to get in some more painting, for—he felt—tonight might be a good one for what one might call courtship; "exploitation," some would doubtless call it: though why? If ladies ("women!") did not like to come back to his loft studio and see his painting, why did they do so? And if they did not genuinely desire to remain for a while of varying length, who could make them? Did any one of them really desire to admire his art, was there no pretense on the part of any of them? Why was *he* not the exploited one? You women are all alike, you only have one thing on your mind, all you think of is your own pleasure . . . Oh well. Hell. Back to work. It was true that you could not sleep with an old building, but then they never argued with you, either. And as for "some measure of deceit," boy did that work both ways! Two weeks before, he'd come upon a harmonious and almost untouched, though tiny, commercial block in an area between the factories and the farms, as yet undestroyed by the people curiously called "developers"; he'd taken lots of color snaps of it from all angles, and he wanted to do at least two large paintings, maybe two small ones as well. The date, 1895, was up there in front. The front was false, but in the harmony was truth.

A day that found him just a bit tired of the items staple in breakfast found him ordering a cup of soup du jour for starters. "How you like the soup?"—Rudolfo.

Fred gave his head a silent shake. How. It had gone down without exciting dismay. "Truthful with you. Had better, had worse. Hm. What was it? Well, I was thinking something else. Uh—chicken vegetable with rice? Right? Right. Yours or Campbell's?"

Neither.

"Half mine, half Abelardo's."

"I *beg* your pardon."

But Rudolfo had never heard the rude English story about the pink of half-and-half, neither did Fred tell it to him. Rudolfo said, "I make a stock with the bones after making chicken sandwiches and I mix it with this." He produced a large, a very large can, pushed it over to Fred. The label said, FULL CHICKEN RICHNESS *Chicken-Type Soup.*

"What-haht?" asked Fred, half-laughing. He read on. *Ingredients:*

Water, Other Poultry and Poultry Parts, seasoning ... the list dibbled off into the usual list of chemicals. The label also said, *Canned for Restaurant and Institutional Usement.*

"Too big for a family," Rudolfo observed. "Well, not bad, I think, too. Help me keep the price down. Every little bit help, you know."

"Oh. Sure. No, not bad. But I wonder about that label." Rudolfo shrugged about that label. The Government, he said, wasn't going to worry about some little *chico* outfit way down from the outskirts of town. Fred chuckled at the bland nonidentification of "Other Poultry"—Rudolfo said that turkey was still cheaper than chicken—"But I don't put it down, 'chicken soup,' I put it down 'soup du jour'; anybody *ask*, I say, 'Oh, *you* know, chicken and rice and vegetable and, oh, stuff like that; *try* it, you don't like it I don't charge you.' Fair enough?—Yes," he expanded. "Abelardo, he is no businessman. He is *filosofo.* His mind is always in the skies. I tell him, I could use more soup—twice, maybe even three times as many cans. What he cares. 'Ai! Supply and demand!' he says. Then he tells me the old Dutch explorers, things like that—Hey! I ever tell you about the time he make his own automobile? ("Ab-*elar*-do did?") Sure! Abelardo did. He took a part from one car, a part from another, he takes parts not even from cars, *I* don't know what they from—"

Fred thought about Don Eliseo and the more perfect tortilla making-and-baking machine. "—well, it work! Finally! Yes! It start off, *yoom!* Like a rocket! Sixty-three mile an hour! But oh boy when he try to slow it down! It stop! He start it again. Sixty-three mile an hour! No other rate of speed, well, what can you do with such a car? So he forget about it and he invent something else, who knows what; then he got into the soup business—Yes, sir! You ready to order?" Rudolfo moved on.

So did Fred. The paintings of the buildings 1895 were set aside for a while so he could take a lot of pictures of a turn-of-the-century family home scheduled for destruction real soon. *This Site Will be Improved With a Modern Office Building*, what the hell did they mean by *Improved*? Alice came up and looked at the sketches of the family home, and at finished work. "I like them," she said. "I like *you*." She stayed. Everything fine. Then, one day, there was the other key on the table. On the note: There is nothing wrong, it said. Just time to go now. Love. No name. Fred sighed. Went on painting.

One morning late there was Abelardo in the Bunne. He nodded, smiled a small smile. By and by, some coffee down, Fred said, "Say, where do you buy your chickens?" Abelardo, ready to inform, though not yet ready to talk, took a card from his wallet.

E.J. BINDER PRIME POULTRY FARM
ALSO
GAME BIRDS DRESSED TO ORDER
1330 VALLEY RD BY THE BIG OAK

While Fred was still reading this, Abelardo passed him over another card, this one for the Full Chicken Richness Canned Soup Company. "You must visit me," he said. "Most time I am home."

Fred hadn't really cared where the chickens were bought, but now the devil entered into him. First he told Abelardo the story about the man who sold rabbit pie. Asked, wasn't there anyway maybe some horsemeat in the rabbit pie, said it was fifty-fifty: one rabbit, one horse. Abelardo reflected then issued another small smile, a rather more painful one. Fred asked, "What about the turkey-meat in your chicken-type soup? I mean, uh, rather, the 'Other Poultry Parts'?"

Abelardo squinted. "Only the breast," he said. "The rest are not good enough—For the *soup*, I mean. The rest, I sell to some mink ranchers."

"How's business?"

Abelardo shrugged. He looked a bit peaked. "Supply," he said. "Demand," he said. Then he sighed, stirred, rose. "You must visit me. Any time. Please," he said.

Abelardo wasn't there in La Bunne Burger next late morning, but someone else was. Miles Marton, call him The Last of the Old-Time Land Agents, call him something less nice: there he was. "Been waiting," Miles Marton said. "Remember time I toll you bout ol stage-coach buildin? You never came. It comin down tomorrow. Ranch houses. Want to take its pitcher? Last chance, today. Make me a nice little paintin of it, price is right, I buy it. Bye now."

Down Fred went. Heartbreaking to think its weathered timbers, its mellowed red brick chimney and stone fireplace, were coming down; but Fred Hopkins was very glad he'd had the favor to notice.

Coming down, too, the huge trees with the guinea-fowl in them. *Lots of photographs.* Be a good painting. At least one. Driving back, lo! a sign saying E.J. BINDER PRIME POULTRY FARM absolutely by a big oak. Still, Fred probably wouldn't have stopped if there hadn't been someone by the gate. Binder, maybe. Sure enough. Binder. "Say, do you know a South American named Abelardo?"

No problem. "Sure I do. Used to be a pretty good customer, too. Buy oh I forget how many chickens ah well. Don't buy many nowdays. He send you here? Be glad to oblige you." Binder was an oldish man, highly sun-speckled.

"You supply his turkeys and turkey-parts, too?" The devil still inside Fred Hopkins.

Old Binder snorted, "'Turkeys,' no we don't handle turkeys, no sir, why chickens are enough trouble, cost of feeding going up, and— No, 'guinea-fowl,' no we never did. Just chickens and of course your cornish."

Still civil, E.J. Binder gave vague directions toward what he believed, he said, was the general location of Mr. Abelardo's place. Fred didn't find it right off, but he found it. As no one appeared in response to his calling and honking, he got out and knocked. Nothing. *Pues,* "My house is your house," okay: in he went through the first door. Well, it wasn't a *large* cannery, but it was a *cannery.* Fred started talking to himself; solitary artists often do. "Way I figure it, Abelardo," he said, "is that you have been operating with that 'small measure of deceit in advertising,' as you so aptly put it. *I* think that in your own naïve way you have believed that so long as you called the product 'Chicken-Type Soup' and included *some* chicken, well, it was all right. Okay, your guilty secret is safe with me; where are you?" The place was immaculate except for. Except for a pile of . . . well . . . shit . . . right in the middle of an aisle. It was as neat as a pile of shit can be. Chicken-shits? Pigeon-poops? Turkey-trots? *Quien sabe?*

At the end of the aisle was another door and behind that door was a small apartment and in a large chair in the small apartment sprawled Abelardo, dead drunk on mescal, *muzhik*-grade vodka, and sneaky pete . . . according to the evidence. Alcoholism is not an especially Latin American trait? Who said the poor guy was an alcoholic? Maybe this was the first time he'd ever been stewed in his *life*. Maybe the eternally perplexing matter of supply and demand finally unmanned him.

Maybe.

At the other end of the room was *another* door and behind that other door was *another* room. And in that *other* room was . . .

. . . something else . . .

That other room was partly crammed with an insane assortment of machinery and allied equipment, compared to which Don Eliseo's more perfect make-and-bake tortilla engine, with its affinities to the perpetual motion invention of one's choice, was simplicity. The thing stood naked for Fred's eyes, but his eyes told him very little: wires snaked all around, that much he could say. There was a not-quite-click, a large television screen flickered on. *No.* Whatever it was at the room's end, sitting flush to the floor with a low, chicken-wire fence around it, it was not a television, not even if Abelardo had started from scratch as though there had been no television before. The quality of the "image" was entirely different, for one thing: and the color, for another, was *wrong* . . . and wrong in the way that no TV color he had ever seen had been wrong. He reached to touch the screen, there *was* no "screen," it was as though his hand met a surface of unyielding gelatin. The non-screen, well, what the hell, *call* it a screen, was rather large, but not gigantically so. He was looking at a savannah somewhere, and among the trees were palms and he could not identify others. A surf pounded not far off, but he could not hear it. There was no sound. He saw birds flying in and out of the trees. Looking back, he saw something else. A trail of broken bread through the room, right up to the, mmm, screen. A silent breeze now and then rifled grass, and something moved in the grass to one side. He stepped back, slightly. What the hell could it *mean*? Then the something which was in the grass to one side stepped, stiff-legged, into full view, and there was another odd, small sound as the thing— it was a bird—lurched through the screen and began to gobble bread. Hopkins watched, dry-mouthed. Crumb by crumb it ate. Then there was no more bread. It doddled up to the low fence, doddled back. It approached the screen, it brushed the screen, there was a Rube Goldberg series of motions in the external equipment, a sheet of chicken wire slid noisily down to the floor. The bird had been trapped.

Fred got down and peered into the past till his eyes and neck grew sore, but he could not see one more bird like it. He began to laugh and cry simultaneously. Then he stood up. "Inevitable," he croaked, throwing out his arms. "Inevitable! Demand exceeded supply!"

The bird looked up at him with imbecile, incurious eyes, and opened its incredible beak. "*Doh-do*," it said, halfway between a gobble and a coo. "*Doh-do. Doh-do.*"

The Mydhiote horde approaches. The towns of Rova and Nikoras, situated on the banks of the Eigil River, have little chance of standing against it. When the fighting breaks out, it seems all is lost. But there is one—an outsider named Kevan—who knows the ways of the horde. The priests of Nikoras are of no use. Perhaps the gods of the horde will come to Kevan's aid . . .

Four Days

David Carrico

Day 2 after Spring Equinox—afternoon

"So what do you think?"

Kevan looked over his shoulder at his not-quite-a-friend Gunnar, who was standing at the same stockade parapet that Kevan had been peering over. "I think you boys are in a lot of trouble, is what I think," Kevan said in his usual low grating tone. He never would have been a bard . . . not with that voice.

The two men were armed and armored, which, given what they were observing, was probably prudent. Gunnar was a thane serving Baron Leofric, the local Darcian ruler. He carried a spear and wore a middling quality shirt of scale armor, overlapping discs and lozenges of bronze. His hair was thick, dark brown, and long enough to be pulled back into a tail that was tied off at the base of his skull. He was also clean-shaven, but for a large mustache that spread out in wings across his face, aided by a certain amount of beeswax.

Kevan wasn't a Darcian, as noted by his black hair and pale complexion. If it wasn't for his very short hair and the fact that he spoke Darcian with a northern accent, he might have been taken for one of the Mydhiote tribesmen in the approaching horde. Well, plus the fact that he wore a fortune's worth of Duarmungard mail shirt on his back and carried more blades than any three tribesmen would normally boast: a pair of sabers thrust through his belt, a sword in a back carry harness, twin daggers on his belt and two more in arm sheathes on his forearm vambraces. The hilts of yet another two were visible protruding from the tops of his boots. That was topped off by two throwing knives that hung hilt-down where his sword harness crossed his chest, and a longish fighting knife that was hanging from the back of his belt.

Kevan was aware that the thanes in Rova made jokes behind his back about the amount of metal he was wearing. It didn't bother him. He'd heard all the jokes before in other lands during his wanderings. The fact that he could beat any two of them at a time in the practice yard while wearing all that metal—and had done so more than once since he'd wandered into Baron Leofric's lands—made sure that the jokes were quiet and remained behind his back.

He looked back out at the approaching Mydhiote horde as Gunnar said, "How long, do you think?"

"How long can you hold out?" Kevan said. "I don't know. What, do I look like a foreteller?" Kevan's voice dripped with sarcasm, but the smile on his face took the sting out of it.

"Ass." Gunnar smacked Kevan on the upper arm. "How long do you think we can hold the palisades here in Rova?"

The palisades wrapped around the little town of Rova where it hugged the west bank of the Eigil River across the bridge from the larger town of Nikoras on the east bank. They weren't serious fortifications, though, being not much more than a high timber fence designed in the hope of keeping thieves out and children and chickens in. From what he had seen in the last couple of weeks, Kevan wasn't sure how good they were in accomplishing those goals, either.

"Depends on how much tribal blood the chiefs of the horde are willing to spill," Kevan said. "If they don't care, they'll be into the town in two hours." Kevan's face was stoic and his voice was cold. "If they want to husband their strength, wear you down bit by bit, you'll get two days, maybe three."

"That's about what Theodred said," Gunnar replied.

"Your chief thane knows which end of the sword is the hilt and which end has the point."

"So you don't think we can hold out here until the baron gets back with allies?"

Kevan shook his head. "The palisades around the settlement are both too long and too weak."

"I wish the baron was here," Gunnar muttered. "The thanes always fight harder when he's leading them."

"Wouldn't make much difference here," Kevan said. "There aren't enough of you to hold a place this weak. All you can do is bleed the tribes here at the palisades and then retreat across the bridge to Nikoras, hopefully without losing too many of your thanes."

"We shouldn't stand for honor's sake, then?"

Kevan looked behind them to see Chief Thane Theodred glowering at him.

"You of all people should know, Chief Thane, there is no honor to be gained from facing the tribes on equal terms."

"Aye, you've the right of it," Theodred said before he spat to one side. "Pack of wolves is all they are."

"Don't be insulting wolves, now," Kevan said. "They're naught but a swarm of weasels, vicious and filled with low cunning." Theodred snorted, but said nothing in reply. "Despite that, if a leader arises who can unite them, they can take down even the greatest under the right conditions." Kevan's tone was bitter.

"You sound like you've faced them before," Theodred said.

"Oh, aye, that I have." Kevan's voice held echoes of hammered iron. "You might say they made me what I am." The coldness of his tone threatened to freeze the air around them. There was a long pause, then he shrugged his shoulders. "They are what they are. All you can do is kill as many as you can."

"As it happens," Theodred said, "the baron agrees with you. His orders are to defend the palisades until they make a significant breakthrough, then run for the bridge and hope we can get across before the temple craftsmen bring it down."

"Good luck with that," Kevan muttered. "They should have taken it down already."

"Baron didn't want to do that. Said the bridge was too important to the towns and the countryside."

"That won't help if the horde gets across it now, will it?"

Theodred shrugged. "Baron's orders. It's not to come down until the last moment."

"That's going to get more of your boys killed."

"Baron's orders."

"Hist!" came from Gunnar. "They're moving."

Kevan and the chief thane looked out over the parapet. Sure enough, a large company had split out from the side of the horde and was riding toward Rova at a slow pace.

"Not an attack," Kevan said. "They're just coming to look things over."

"How can you tell?" Gunnar said.

"Not enough of them to make a serious attack," Theodred muttered.

"And they're not moving fast enough. Those little horses they ride can move a lot faster than that," Kevan added. "You'll see when they do it for real. They'll probably pull up just before they enter bowshot range."

And that was exactly what the tribesmen did. Some of them spread out to the sides to look at different sections of the wooden palisade, but most of them just formed a line parallel to the wall and stared at it. The thanes on the wall stared back.

Kevan felt a chill run down his backbone.

Day 3 after Spring Equinox—early morning

"Here they come, lads! Hold your shafts until you can see the drool running down their chins!"

Theodred stood on the palisades above the main gate. It was the weakest place of the entire wall, as well as being centrally placed, so it made some sense for him to be there.

Kevan stood on the street behind the palisade gate. He'd chosen his position with deliberation, despite Theodred's attempts to put him in the defenses at the top of the wall.

"I'm not one of your thanes," he'd eventually snapped back at the chief thane. "I'm not under your orders. And one more man more or less on the wall here won't make a bit of difference in the long run. But let me stand where I want, and I'll make a difference in what comes after. Push me on this, and I'll cross the bridge to Nikoras and ride out the eastern gate. Oath to the God I will." Theodred had cursed at him, but had thrown his hands up and walked away muttering.

Bowstrings began to twang and thrum from the top of the wall. Baron Leofric's archers were good—and every tribesman they took down was one less that would have to be faced with sword and spear—but there weren't enough of them to stem the tide. Kevan listened to the approaching clamor, and before long there was the sound of impacts against the palisade as horses began to slam against it and kick it. Moments later, the thanes on the wall had to deal with tribesmen who swarmed up ladders and climbed up ropes. Kevan could imagine the resulting furor with no trouble. He'd been there before.

And now came the moment he'd been waiting for. He pulled his helmet down and buckled the chin strap.

A hollow *boom* sounded. The gates shivered from the impact of a ram. Even with the timbers braced against them, Kevan didn't expect the gates to last long. They were not made to resist a serious assault. He took deep breaths, centering himself, preparing for the moment.

With each successive swing of the ram, the braces were pushed farther back in the dirt of the street. They began to fall over. The gate leaves were stressed more and more, until finally the brackets for the gate bar ripped out of the right gate leaf and the gates were pushed open.

Kevan picked his moment, a saber in each hand, ignoring the order for the thanes to pull back. As soon as the opening was large enough for a man but not large enough for a horse, he plunged through. The ram team was still in place, the ram timber suspended on a rope harness between horses. His first action was to cripple the front horses on each side of the ram. Swift cuts to their front legs spilled them to the dirt, screaming. The front end of the ram timber dropped to the ground with a thud. His next cuts took out their riders.

The resulting jam in the gateway blocked an influx of tribesmen. As they trickled past the obstacle, Kevan was waiting, a blade in each hand. The slightest falter, the slightest stumble, and he attacked. Corpses of the tribesmen began to add to the jam, forcing the warriors who followed to climb over the mass.

Kevan's lips were skinned back over his teeth as he snarled at the advancing tribesmen. The remaining riders of the ram team were urging their horses back, attempting to drag the timber out of the way. He knew that it wouldn't be long before enough of the gate ground would be cleared for greater numbers of the horde to press forward. He had no illusions about being able to hold the gap forever. His armor was better, his blades were better, and his skills were better. But there were far more tribesmen than he could hope to slay before one of them got through to him. He dropped three more in quick succession, then slipped back through the gate.

The street behind the gate was filled with thanes moving toward the bridge as fast as they could. Kevan looked up and saw that tribesmen were swarming across the top of the palisades, but not many were following the defenders yet.

"Move it!" he shouted, hearing similar orders up and down the street and from the parallel streets.

Kevan turned back to the gate. The first two tribesmen through the gate were spearmen. Kevan parried their spears to each side, then stepped forward. The tribesmen tried to retreat to bring their spears back into play, but they ran into the gate leafs, and before they could adjust their moves into sidesteps, Kevan was on them. His sabers swung one way and then the other, and the tribesmen dropped to the ground, blood gushing from severed jugulars. That fouled the gate again, and Kevan turned and ran down the street after the thanes.

He trotted backwards to watch the tribesmen, chest heaving from the exertion he'd been through. The gate was eventually pushed open, and the barbarians flooded through, spreading through the homes and shops of the town. There were a few shouts and screams. Kevan shook his head. He'd seen it time and again over the years. When the hordes came, there were always some who would ignore the orders to flee, who would think they could hide and survive, but who always learned they couldn't.

Assured that the tribesmen would be delayed for at least a little while by searching through the town for sack and rapine, Kevan turned back around and jogged up to where Theodred and Gunnar stood to one side of the end of the bridge watching the surviving thanes cross the river to Nikoras.

Kevan frowned. "It doesn't look like they've removed any of the bridge."

"They haven't," Theodred muttered as he bound a cut on his arm.

"Why not? If they don't drop it or burn it soon, the tribesmen will be in Nikoras in another hour."

"Apparently some temple priest or sorcerer put a preservation spell on it, which won't let the workmen do anything to damage it," Gunnar said in disgusted tones. "They just now figured that out, and they don't have a clue on how to undo the spell yet."

Kevan found his hands fisted on the hilts of his sabers. "So what's your battle plan now?"

"Line the thanes up at the end of the bridge and kill the tribesmen as they try to funnel across," Theodred said. "There's not much else we can do. If we stand on this side of the bridge, they will swamp us."

Kevan shook his head. "That's just stupid building on top of stupid. They've got enough men to spend one to take one of yours down and still have enough to ravage Nikoras."

Theodred put his hands on his hips. "You have a better plan?"

Kevan stared out at the tribesmen swarming through Rova and beginning to move toward the bridge. He was beginning to wish he'd carried out his threat and ridden off. Too late. So what could *he* do? Thoughts jumbled through his mind, from before and after the day the horde had massacred his clan. One thought pushed through the jumble.

He took a deep breath. "Yes, I have a better plan. It's not a good plan, mind you, but it's better than yours. First, light a fire under those priests to get the spell taken off."

"Already done," Gunnar muttered.

"Second, get everyone across the bridge, including you two. Leave it to me."

"What can you do by yourself?" Gunnar demanded. "You're not a hero or a god."

"I will challenge them to ritual combat," Kevan said, his voice tight. "If they accept, they'll only be able to come at me one at a time. I'll stretch each fight out as long as I can."

"How can you do that?" Theodred demanded. "Challenge them, I mean."

"I know enough about them to be able to invoke the rituals," Kevan said in cold tones, "and they'll still have to follow them. I can buy you two, maybe three days. Even odds I can make it that long before they take me down."

"Will they accept the challenge?" Theodred again.

"I think I can make them."

"What happens if they have someone who's a better swordsman than you are?" Gunnar retorted.

"If they do, I lose the wager and you'll get to see if your plan is any better, except that you'll have had at least a couple of days to build barricades across the end of the bridge. Now go." He swung around at the last of the thanes as they approached. "Run!" he snarled. "Get across the bridge now! They're coming."

Kevan pulled one of his sabers and started cutting the combat circle in the dirt, muttering to himself as he did so. "I must be moon mad, even though it's not the full moon," he said. He began cutting at the southern corner of the bridge and swung out as wide as he could. "I need lots of room," he told himself. "Who knows who I'm going to be facing?"

He traced the circle, keeping one eye on the approaching tribesmen and another on the retreating thanes. The last of the thanes mounted the bridge as he brought the demarcation of the circle to a close and reached up to unbuckle his helmet and cast it aside, just in time to hold up his empty hand and bellow "Halt!" at the first tribesman to cross the circle.

The tribesman stumbled to a halt two steps across the line, a very confused look on his face.

"Look where you are, man," Kevan said in the dialect of the hordes. "Look what you're standing in." The young tribesman looked around, then looked back with a sick expression on his face. Kevan didn't feel much better himself, but he refused to show it. "That's right," Kevan shouted. "You're standing in a challenge circle. I call challenge!"

That caught their attention, and definitely stopped any movement toward the bridge.

An older tribesman pushed through the gathering fighters. He approached the circle, but grounded his spear just short of it. Kevan noted with a grin that he was careful to keep his toes off of it as well. He wore the raven's black wing feather worn by a kupak, a war leader.

"You are not one of us," the older man growled. "You cannot call challenge."

"Oh, but I can, kupak," Kevan replied. "Let an elder come near, and you'll see just how well I can do it."

The kupak grabbed a nearby warrior, snarled something in his ear, and sent him sprinting back up the road.

The tribesman in the circle tried to edge back, but Kevan pointed a finger at him. "You stay where you are. You're already in the circle, so you're going to be first." The youngster grew even paler, and he dropped his sword.

The kupak said nothing. He simply spat in disgust.

It wasn't long before the runner came back, leading two men wearing golden eagle feathers that marked them as elders. Both were armed, but their hands were empty, weapons hanging at their sides.

"You call challenge, outlander?" the short one with white hair barked.

"I do."

"By what right? You are not one of us." That was the taller one, with the iron gray hair.

"By the Skyfather and by the Horned Lord, I call challenge against you all," Kevin said, invoking the opening of the challenge ritual. It gave him pleasure to use their own customs to impede them.

The elders were wearing sour expressions, while the kupak's face could have curdled milk. Kevan had to bite his cheek to keep from laughing.

"Very well," the short one said. "Three rounds, but it will avail you nothing."

Kevan laughed. "I am not your equal in years, elder, but I was not born this moon. It will be the full twelve rounds, or you will stand forsworn before your gods."

"You think you can judge us, outlander?"

"I?" Kevan said. "I judge no one. But I can invoke those who can judge." He reached and pulled a chain from around his neck and stepped closer to the demarcation line, holding it up to show a silver crescent moon pendant hanging from it. "By this right, which is my birthright." Before the elders could react, he said, "By the Maiden, the Mother, and the Crone, it will be as I have said. Twelve full rounds. My life, my blood, against yours. My skill against yours. My courage against yours. If I prevail, your course is proven not of the gods." He kissed the pendant, and returned it to its place.

The elders' eyes widened. The kupak's face was expressionless, almost as if carved from stone.

Kevan crossed his arms. "Well?"

The taller elder bent down and whispered to his companion, then turned and pushed his way through the growing throng of tribesmen.

"Let it be as you have said," the remaining elder said, the words slow in coming. "Twelve full rounds."

Kevan's lips peeled back from his teeth in a lupine snarl. "Beginning now," he said, starting to turn toward the tribesman in the circle.

The elder interjected, "If we're going to follow the old rules, outlander, we follow all the old rules. You stay in the circle the whole time, until you are defeated or until by some miracle you defeat twelve of our champions."

"But—" Kevan started, only to stop as the elder held up a hand.

"All or nothing, outlander. If your feet cross the line before twelve champions are defeated, you lose."

Kevan swallowed bile. Could he last three or four days in the combat circle with no rest, no hot food, no bed? Could he stand in that circle for that long and face that many champions? He started to shake his head in uncertainty, but stilled the moment before it began, lest it be taken as a signal by the elder and the kupak.

He looked within, and found a growing sense of anger, of rage. It had been there for years, but he had suppressed it, ignored it, because he didn't think he could face the horde. Well, now he had an opportunity to do that on his terms, and hurt them badly. Even if he fell before accomplishing the full twelve duels, it would buy the defenders time and impede the plans of the horde's leaders. He let the fire rise.

His hands clenched the hilts of his sabers, and he looked back at the elder, who was scrutinizing him closely. "So be it," he growled. "Twelve full rounds, and my feet don't cross the circle bounds until they're done."

The elder showed a moment of disappointment on his face. "So be it," he echoed.

Kevan's head pivoted to look at the young tribesman in the circle. "Prepare yourself," was all he said as he paced back to stand in the midpoint of the circle before the opening of the bridge.

The tribesmen outside the circle began to shout and scream imprecations against Kevan and encouragements to their fellow. The man in the circle—not much more than a youth, really—licked his lips and hefted his sword in both hands. He wore no armor or helmet, not even the boiled hide breastplates that were common to the tribesmen. Kevan reminded himself that that didn't mean he wasn't a good fighter. It just meant he was either a younger son or from a poor family. From the looks of the sword, the second option was the more likely—it looked like it had been around since Grandpa's day, and hadn't had much care.

The tribesman began to circle Kevan. Kevan shook his head, said, "Not today," and slid over to confront him, drawing his sabers as he did so. That paused the warrior for just a moment, and in that moment Kevan attacked.

The tribesman was quickly proved to be outclassed, and the expression on his face showed that he knew it as he attempted to protect himself from the sabers that seemed to be coming at him from every direction. Kevan was directing cuts and lunges one after another. The tribesman was backing away, trying to gain some distance to reset himself, but Kevan never gave him a chance.

"'Ware!" called out the kupak as the tribesman backed toward the demarcation line. He stopped hard, and deflected one-two-three cuts by Kevan, the last of which was aimed at his face. Just as their blades made that last contact, the blade in Kevan's right hand passed between the tribesman's straddled legs and cut deeply into the inner right thigh.

The warrior froze at the bite of the blade. Kevan dropped back two paces, remaining on guard.

"And now you die," he said as the blood pulsed out from the severed femoral artery.

Dropping his sword, the now panic-stricken young warrior grabbed his leg and tried to suppress the blood flow. It did no good, however, and in but a few breaths he looked up in helplessness as he sank to his knees. Moments later his eyes rolled shut, and he slumped sideways on the ground in a puddle of his own blood.

Kevan walked over, wiped his blades clean on the trousers of the tribesman, and sheathed them. Then he picked up the other's sword, carried it over to the demarcation line near the opening to the bridge, and thrust it into the line to stand upright. Returning to the tribesman's corpse, he reached down and grabbed the back collar of his tunic and the back of his belt, and hefted him up to lug him over to the demarcation line near the elder and the kupak, where he threw the corpse over the line.

He looked at the two senior tribesmen, whose faces were both stony cold. "No more boys," he said. "Give the circle the half furlong space, and no more than three witnesses."

The kupak said nothing, but began to wave the throng back. The elder gave Kevan a look that should by rights have reduced him to ashes before turning to follow the kupak. Kevan moved toward the rear of the circle. Crossing his arms, he settled in to wait.

"One down, how many to go?" came Gunnar's whisper from behind him.

"Eleven," Kevan said in a quiet tone, turning his head slightly to one side.

"Eleven more? Can you last that many?"

"I'm going to have to."

"So what rules?"

"I may have been too shrewd for my own good. I can't leave the circle until the full twelve rounds are done."

"What?" Gunnar's voice got louder and he rose a little from his crouch. "How will you eat or sleep? Or for that matter, piss?"

"I've been thinking about that. Right now, I need a waterskin. I'm getting dry, and the day's just begun. Bring it to me here and toss it to me without crossing the circle.

"After dusk tonight, bring me a blanket, some bread, a skin of beer and another waterskin."

"And a nightsoil bucket," Gunnar added.

"Right," Kevan said. "Good thinking. So they can't get through to the bridge without going through the circle, and they can't do that without defeating me. I'll be sleeping here in the circle, so even if they break their rules and try to sneak someone across in the night, I'll still be aware of it in time to take them down."

"I'm going to post watchers on the bridge at night, just in case, with a horn. If they see anything, they'll sound it."

"That's another good idea," Kevan said.

"Going to be hard sleeping," Gunnar said.

"I've slept hard before. I can handle it. Meanwhile, go get my waterskin."

"And the bucket," Gunnar replied. "Back soon."

Kevan moved back to the center of the circle and crossed his arms, waiting.

By the end of the day, three more weapons were standing in the combat circle demarcation line.

Day 5 after Spring Equinox—late afternoon

Kevan felt the crunch as the blade of his long fighting knife slid through a gap in the metal plates riveted to the tribesman's leather armor, punched through his gut below the breastbone, and penetrated the man's spine. He stood there, motionless, as the deathlook came over the tribesman's face and his arms fell, dropping his sword and dagger. As the corpse began to sag toward the ground, Kevan moved his blade to point toward the demarcation line. The shouts from the horde began to die away as the corpse obligingly slid off onto the ground.

"Now I'm going to have to drag you over there," Kevan grumbled after a couple of deep breaths. He was more winded than he wanted to admit. It had been a long couple of days. "You had to get this far before you died, didn't you?" He spat to one side, trying to clear the dust out of his mouth. "At least you're one of the smaller ones."

Of course, he'd also been one of the faster ones. Kevan looked down at the cut on the back of his hand that had come within a hair's breadth of being serious enough to put an end to his purpose here. He'd also been good enough to disarm Kevan of one of his sabers, which was why the fighting knife had come to hand. He wouldn't—couldn't—use the sword on his back yet.

Kevan looked behind him at the approach to the bridge. He was a lot closer to it than he'd hoped he'd ever have to stand. He could see the workmen trying to take up the timbers, but the preservation spell that no one had known had been placed on the bridge was making it difficult. He shook his head.

"The God save us from barons and priests who get wonderful ideas," he muttered.

He bent down and wiped his saber and fighting knife on the

tribesman's clothing before sheathing them. Then he grasped the tribesman's wrists and dragged his body over to and just beyond the demarcation line. Then he returned to the combat circle to pick up the tribesman's blades. He tossed the dagger to lay in the dirt next to the vacant-eyed corpse staring at the sky. With the saber, he redrew the demarcation line in the dirt where dragging the body had blurred it out. A moment later, the saber had been thrust into the dirt in the demarcation line where the body had passed.

Kevan looked around the demarcation line, counting blades standing around the combat circle. ". . . six, seven, eight, nine, and ten," his eyes resting on the newly added saber. Ten tribesmen in the last three days. He looked at the sun—low in the sky, close to dusk. The tribal horde might not muster another champion before the sun touched the horizon, at which time custom would bar them from sending another before tomorrow's dawn. That would be good, he thought with a sour chuckle.

Two tribesmen led one of their almost-pony horses forward and stopped outside the combat circle. They picked up their dead fellow and draped him over the back of the horse. As they turned back, the one not leading the horse made a couple of universal vulgar hand signs at Kevan.

Kevan just chuckled loudly. He could tell the tribesman heard him, because he flashed one more sign behind him.

"And your mother," Kevin called out with a sly grin.

Time passed. Kevan was just as glad to see it. Fighting what amounted to multiple duels every day was wearing on him, as was having to sleep light every night just to make sure that no tribesman decided that the way for them to win was simply for Kevan not to wake up the next morning. Every breath that he took without swinging steel and every moment of quiet meant just that much longer before he had to do it again.

"They going to try again?" came a voice from behind him.

Kevan turned his head enough to see Gunnar standing on the bridge near where it joined the river bank, feet well away from the demarcation line of the combat circle.

Kevan looked at the sun again. It was measurably closer to the horizon, and there was no sign of movement from the horde.

"I'm guessing not," Kevan replied, moving closer to the bridge so he could speak softer. "This is not sitting well with the tribal elders, I'd bet, and the clan leaders are probably furious at how many of their chief warriors are now dead. And with only two combats to go, they have to send their best now. If I'm not down by the end of the final combat tomorrow, their own customs say I will have proven the gods' justice resides with me and I'll insist they leave the area for at least a year."

"I'm thinking they won't like that so much."

Kevan laughed. "If that happens, the elders will all be mad enough to chew rocks. And if it was up to them, they'd probably ignore it and keep coming at me. I'm tough and I've had some luck here in the circle, but sooner or later I'd fall, and after four days of fighting, it would probably be sooner. But a lot of their warriors believe. If they break custom that severely it would cause disruptions in the tribes, and could even cause their own deaths."

"Ha!" Gunnar replied. "I'd like to see that." There was a moment of silence as he realized what he said. "Well, except for the part about them taking you down, that is."

Kevan laughed again.

"How are you doing?" Gunnar asked. There was a note of concern in his voice.

"Tired, edging toward weary. I've fought duels before, but never one after another like this. I'm a hard man, but I'm finding that even a hard man can be worn down."

"Can you make it through tomorrow?"

"I'll have to. This is my best chance to take my revenge on them, and do some good for you besides."

The sound of a wild ox horn interrupted them as it was sounded from the horde's camp. There was a ripple of movement around the periphery of the horde, and a sense of relaxation.

"They've called a halt to today's efforts," Kevan said.

"But they'll be back in the morning."

"As soon as the sun leaves the horizon."

"What do you need tonight?"

"Enough bread for tonight and the dawning. Two skins of beer, one of water, some scraps of white or light cloth, a small skin of red wine or brandy, a clean bucket, and for the priests to get that spell off the bridge." That last was rather severe in tone.

"They're trying," Gunnar said.

"Not hard or fast enough," Kevan said. "Go."

Gunnar retreated up the arc of the bridge. Kevan walked over and undid the drawstring to his trews and dropped them enough to piss in the bucket which sat just outside the circle. He could tell from the dark yellow hue of his urine he hadn't been drinking enough water. After putting his clothing back in order, he walked over to pick up the skin he had and drain what was left in it before tossing it onto the bridge.

Kevan looked at the bridge sourly. "Who in their right mind puts a preservation spell on something without knowing how to take it off?"

Day 6 after Spring Equinox—early morning

The sound of the ox horn winded its way from the tribal camp in the early light of the dawn. Kevan looked up and grunted from where he squatted over the nightsoil bucket.

"Sounds like they're a bit early," Gunnar was once again on the bridge.

"By the time they get here, the sun will be up high enough."

Kevan finished his business, pulled up his trews and tied them off. Then he put his sabers back through his belt and checked all his hilts: sabers, fighting knife in the small of his back, knives in each boot and each vambrace, and last, the sword hilt rising above his right shoulder. He checked the cloth wrapping his left hand that he had stained with some of the red wine last night. The wound itself was minor, but the appearance that that hand was seriously wounded might just give him a bit of an edge today. He grinned at the thought, since he had learned the trick from an old tribesman many years ago.

Mydhiote tribesmen filtered through the town and lined up along the edge of the buildings still standing surrounding the open space before the bridge. Behind him, Kevan could hear the workmen straining and grunting with tools as they attempted to tear it up, with no more luck than they'd had the earlier days. Whatever the priests and sorcerers had tried this time to dismantle the protection spell hadn't worked any better than their previous attempts.

"God save us from priests with ideas," Kevan muttered.

"Aye to that," Gunnar said.

"You'd best get back across the span," Kevan said. "No sense in tempting them."

"Aye," Gunnar replied. "Good fortune to you." His steps retreated across the wooden planking of the bridge.

Kevan settled himself, waiting. It was going to be a long day. It was also going to be the hardest day, he knew, partly because he was more than a little weary, and partly because he knew that the warriors he would face today would be the best the horde could deliver. He hoped he was up to it. The fire inside was still strong. It had to be enough.

The tribesmen were quiet as they gathered at the half furlong mark in the early dawn light. Their progress as a horde had been stymied by Kevan's challenge, and it seemed to have sapped some of the energy out of them. For three days now they had watched him take down their champions, one after another. The first fight had been the shortest. The succeeding warriors had been more skilled, and thus the successive combats were longer and accordingly more respectable. Indeed, the last one yesterday had lasted for most of the afternoon. But at the end of the day, Kevan had still been standing.

He suspected the tribesmen found that a bit disheartening. He knew that the elders were fit to chew iron bars and spit nails. The two he had seen the first day had been joined by several others over the days, and their fulminating glares could have stoked a forge.

Figures emerged from the thickening throng. The kupak and two elders approached. Different elders, this time, two he hadn't seen before, both tall and thin—a gray-braided man whose face was more wrinkles than bare skin, and a woman who was so gaunt her skin seemed to be stretched tightly over naked bone.

"Today you die, outlander," the male elder said in a nasal tone. "Today you face our best, and they will take you down."

Kevan forced a loud bray of laughter, then dusted his hands together and said, "In your dreams, old man, perhaps. But this is the light of day, and so far your gods aren't listening to you."

The woman spat across the demarcation line. "The gods will prevail."

Kevan advanced to grind her spittle into the dirt, and gave her his wolf's grin. "The gods always prevail, old woman. But you're not the gods."

"We are the gods' tools," she snarled back. "We will prevail."

"Tools chip, break, rust, and shatter," Kevan said, still grinning. "So I wouldn't be so proud about being called a tool, if I were you." He dropped the smile and gave her a solid stare. "You might prevail at times, but today is not the day. Send your champions. Let's get this over with."

He turned his back and walked back to the center of the circle, where he turned again and crossed his arms. The anger on the two elders' faces made him snicker. The kupak, on the other hand, stood with the stony face he had worn since that first day. Kevan was just as glad he hadn't had to face him . . . yet.

The elders moved to join the kupak in his chosen spot. A moment later another figure stepped out and began moving toward the combat circle as the tribesmen began to shout and cheer.

Kevan tested the buckled chin strap of his helmet to make sure it was secure. Then he drew his sabers before tossing their sheaths behind him, clearing his belts. He settled himself, rotating his head from side to side and shrugging his shoulders, listening as the joints popped. Right hand high, left hand low, he waited.

Kevan was surprised to realize that the approaching warrior was a woman. She stopped farther back—behind the kupak's post to do a slow study of Kevan and the circle. Kevan's eyes widened as he realized that what he had taken for a staff or spear in her hand was actually a polearm of some kind, with a leather sack shrouding the top of it.

Kevan could feel her gaze. It was a long wait. As best he could tell, it was over a quarter of an hour before the woman finally stirred and approached the combat circle. She stopped just outside it and grounded the haft of her weapon.

It was at this point that Kevan realized what he was facing. The woman was wearing two raven wing feathers, which made her not just a kupak—not just a raid leader—but a senior kupak, a kupakar. That made her one of the most senior leaders of the horde. But that wasn't all. She also was wearing a wing feather from a great snowy owl, which meant she was one of the leading servants of the Goddess.

She had to be one of the dedicated warriors of the Maiden, the Mother, and the Crone. That was borne out by her armor, which was better than that of any of the men he had faced so far. He swallowed. The dedicated warriors had a certain reputation, even outside of the tribes.

"One of the elders said you had a talisman." Her voice was deep for a woman, and there was a certain edge to it that caused the hair on Kevan's neck to bristle. "May I see it?"

Kevan thought about it for a long moment, shrugged, then put both sabers in his left hand and pulled the chain out from under his collar and over his head. He moved forward a few steps, stopping well short of the demarcation line, and held the chain up so that the pendant swung below his hand. The woman bent forward a little and peered at it. Then she straightened with a sigh.

"A priestess' moon pendant. How did you come by that?" she asked in a mild tone. "They said you claimed to be entitled to it."

"It was my mother's," Kevan said as he put the chain back over his head and tucked the pendant beneath his armor. He looked to her with a stony expression. "It would have been my sister's in turn, but for the crime committed against my clan by the horde." The second saber was back in his right hand. He was ready for what would come.

She lifted her chin slightly, and closed her eyes. "So that's the way of it, is it?" She opened her eyes in time to catch his curt nod. "And that would explain why you sound like one of us, and even fight like one of us, but stand opposed to us."

Kevan spat.

"The gods have a chancy sense of humor," she said after another long pause. "Nonetheless, I can't let you prevail against us." She reached up and stripped away the leather sack, revealing her weapon was a halberd with a narrow blade. It almost looked like a fat-headed spear, but for the honed edge on one side of the blade and the hook that protruded from the back of it. All in all, a wicked weapon in the hands of an expert, and looking at the set of her eyes and jaw and how readily her hands balanced the halberd, Kevan had little doubt that she was an expert.

"I am Cherana, sworn to the Goddess."

"Kevan, sworn to no one."

"Will you tell me your clan?"

"No. You know it."

She sighed, and nodded. "Let us begin."

Cherana advanced with deliberation, halberd held at the ready. As she crossed the demarcation line, Kevan retreated toward the center of the circle, giving himself room. As he arrived at the midpoint, he set his feet and leaned forward slightly, sabers high and low.

Cherana didn't march. She didn't advance. Her steps were soft and subtle, as if she were dancing. It was almost as if her feet were gliding across a polished floor, rather than semi-packed and bloodstained dirt. She spun the halberd slowly hand over hand, as if it were a staff, then brought it down and advanced the blade, moving it in small circles as she edged forward a fraction of a step at a time.

Kevan began testing her.

A quarter of an hour later, he was breathing hard and feeling the sting of small cuts on his left leg and the throb of bruises forming on his ribs where his armor had stopped attacks and ripostes. Cherana had made no mistakes and had proven to be the best warrior he had faced in the challenge . . . so far, at least. It didn't matter how he attempted to redirect or bind the halberd's blade, in the next heartbeat it would be back in his face, and that hook on the back of the blade would have ripped an ear off once if not for his helmet. She was fast and supple, and the length of reach the halberd gave her really put him at a disadvantage.

Now Cherana stepped directly forward, thrusting at Kevan as she did so. Only a jerk of his head to the side kept the halberd blade from hitting inside his open-faced helm. He side-stepped twice, trying to get clear, but she pursued, jabbing constantly and lunging every few steps, forcing him back and back, even as he tried to circle around her. As he ducked away from a riposte to a parried lunge, he caught a glimpse of his saber sheaths not far away, which told him that Cherana was successfully moving him toward the back edge of the combat circle, and he was in danger of either getting pinned there or forced out of the circle, which would lose the combat for him.

In almost pure desperation, Kevan threw his right hand saber at Cherana, while dropping the other one and lunging forward. As Cherana recovered from blocking the saber and pivoted the halberd back toward Kevan, he managed to get a hand on the haft of the polearm just below the blade. A heartbeat later, both hands were clamped on the haft just as Cherana pulled back on it out of reflex.

Kevan went with the pull, throwing his weight forward and driving the haft toward Cherana, forcing her back until she went off balance and he was able to drive her toward the ground, bare inches away from the demarcation line. She lost her grasp as she went down, and Kevan was able to rip the halberd haft away from her.

He spun it in his own hands and swung the bladed edge at Cherana. She raised her arms in defense. The blade struck her left forearm, cutting through the vambrace she wore there and breaking the radius bone with a *crack*. She fell back with a grunt of pain as he wrenched the blade out of the wreck of her arm and armor.

Cherana looked up at him as the blood began to pour from her savaged arm. "The gods have a chancy sense of humor," she repeated, voice tight with pain. She struggled to her knees. "Finish it."

"I'm sorry it came to this," Kevan said.

"Finish it," she said again.

Kevan shifted his grip on the halberd haft, swung it back, then brought it around in a flat arc. There was a meaty *thunk* as it cut halfway through her neck. The impact knocked her corpse over, which almost twisted the halberd out of Kevan's hands as the blade was wedged in her spine. It took some effort on his part to dislodge it.

It took a few moments, but before long the halberd was standing in the demarcation circle line along with all the other weapons of the defeated tribesmen, and Cherana's body had been dragged outside the circle and the demarcation line had been renewed. She deserved better than that, Kevan thought, but he didn't have the strength for it.

Kevan stood in the center of the circle, breathing hard. That had been close—much closer than he had wanted. And of all the fights so far, that had been the one that he regretted. Cherana had acted with respect and dignity.

He picked up his sabers, wiped them on his sleeves and resheathed them. He went to the back of the circle, picked up his water skin and drained it, tossing it onto the bridge when it was empty. He shook his head at the workmen still struggling with the timbers. As far as he could tell, not a single splinter of the beams had been broken loose.

"May the God save us from his priests," he said.

Returning to the center of the combat circle, Kevan crossed his arms to wait for his final opponent. His aches were stronger, and he could tell he was nearing his limits. He muttered a prayer to the God— "Let them spend all day arguing." Not that he expected they would.

It was well past the nooning hour when the twelfth champion finally emerged from the line of the horde. Cherana's body had long since been retrieved by two of her fellow sisters sworn to the Goddess. The fresh blood in the circle had darkened and congealed, leaving a crust atop the dirt. Flies stirred around the edges of it.

Several stepped out of the horde's lines and converged behind a single figure. As they drew nearer, Kevan recognized the elders he had seen over the last few days. Most of the rest were also wearing golden eagle feathers. So this must be the assembled elders of the tribes and clans, come to witness the final combat. Kevan drew a deep breath at that realization.

The one they followed was another man, which gladdened Kevan. He really didn't want to face another woman, fighter or no. Kevan's eyebrows rose slightly when he saw that he wore not one, not two, but three of the black raven wing feathers. This, then, was the paramount chief of the horde, the kupak of kupaks, the kupakin. His name was known—Csaddik. Mothers outside the horde would call on him to frighten their children into obedience. Mothers inside the horde would hold him up as an example to their sons. And that probably explained why he was so long in coming out. It would have taken the unified opposition of the elders and probably the kupaks as well to force the kupakin to come to the challenge circle. From the expression on his face, he wasn't happy about that.

Kevan had seen Csaddik many years ago. He studied the man. He was somewhat bigger than Kevan remembered—perhaps a finger's width taller than Kevan himself, broader across the shoulder, torso heavy with muscle and a bit of fat under the boiled leather armor he wore. His face was seamed with scars and deep wrinkle creases. He was well armed for a tribesman, wearing two sabers and two daggers at his belt.

Kevan looked at the kupak who had been his witness from the beginning. His face still resembled carved stone, but there was a light to his eyes that hadn't been there before. He leaned forward a bit.

"Who are you, outlander?" the kupakin asked in a grating tone. "Why do you oppose us?"

Kevan smiled his most evil smile. "Because I can, and because you—all of you, but especially you, Csaddik—deserve it. You are the vilest scum on the earth, a plague on mankind that deserves to be purged for all that you've done."

The tribal leader cocked his head to one side. "That sounds personal."

Kevan laughed. "Oh, aye, it's personal. You owe me a host of deaths, you do."

"I don't know you," the kupakin said, "and with that much hatred in your voice, I should. But let us set the past aside. You say we've wronged you. What wergeld would it take to satisfy your blood hunger and have you relinquish your challenge?"

Kevan stopped smiling and leaned slightly forward, eyes burning. "You faithless, honorless, fatherless cur!" His voice was loud enough to carry to the elders, and sharp enough to cut the wind. "You would try to buy me? After you and yours slaughtered my family? There is not enough gold in the world to buy peace with me. The only payment I would accept is blood: yours and your gets' spilled out before me by my hand. Offer me that, and I just might step aside. But naught less will move me."

The kupak's face had grown even colder at Csaddik's attempt to buy off Kevan. Kevan could see that his knuckles were white where he grasped his own spear. The kupak gave a short nod as Kevan finished his speech. Csaddik's expression, on the other hand, twisted in a snarl. He looked to the kupak. "Take him, Arpad," he ordered, sweeping a hand toward the combat circle.

The kupak shook his head. "I'm not the one the gods are measuring. I'm not the one whose leadership is being tested. And I'm not the one who just profaned a sworn ritual combat. No one will take your place, Csaddik. Either face him, or surrender the raven feathers."

"You dare ..." Csaddik began, turning toward the kupak, only to stop as the kupak turned his shoulders slightly and moved the head of his spear less than a hand's breadth outward. There were murmurs from the assembled elders behind them, and Kevan saw the kupakin's shoulders tense. Both men were motionless for a long moment, until the kupakin jerked around to face Kevan again. "Prepare to die, outlander. The gods will receive your death."

"They haven't taken it so far," Kevan replied, "and they've had plenty of opportunities the last few days. I wouldn't wager that they will now. But you're welcome to try and give it to them." He made a beckoning gesture with his right hand saber. The kupakin's hands clenched, and Kevan thought he almost heard the man's teeth grinding together.

Goaded beyond his limits, the kupakin stepped into the combat circle, drawing his own sabers as he did so. The tribesmen at the half furlong mark began to shout and jeer and cheer.

Kevan let him take two steps into the circle, then tossed the saber in his right hand outside the circle and reached up to grasp the sword hilt that jutted up behind his right shoulder. Now was the time for his father's sword to be seen.

"What are you doing?" Csaddik demanded.

Kevan finished drawing the sword. The blade was straight, came to a point, and was very different from the saber he'd held until the moment before. He was now armed with a saber in one hand and a sword in the other, and he raised both up before him. "Showing you who you really face."

"Sword and saber," the kupakin said. "No one does that . . . but . . ."

"I'm the last son of the Black Wolf clan," Kevan spat out. "I was one of you . . . would be one of you still . . . if you hadn't massacred my clan twelve years ago. Twelve years I've waited for this moment. Twelve years I've lurked around the edges of the horde, shadowed your paths, taken down the occasional straggler, waiting for this time where I could stand in your way and hold you accountable. Now the God and the gods have let it happen. Now they will judge between us. Now you die."

"I'll cross that bridge with your blood wet on my blades," Csaddik snarled.

Kevan drew a line in the dirt. "You'll get no farther than here."

Before he could straighten, Csaddik was on him. His attack was all power and strength, with no finesse and no subtlety. Kevan took a couple of cuts on his legs and his armor turned a few more before he caught the rhythm and began parrying or dodging the kupakin's frenzied swings. After the first few passes, Kevan could see that Csaddik was breathing heavily. That surprised him. Yet given how almost out of control his attacks were, maybe it shouldn't. The thought crossed the back of his mind that if the man had lost control that badly, his taunts must have really reached home. That caused him to smile.

"What . . ." Csaddik said as he gasped air in and out, "is so . . . bloody . . . funny?"

"You," Kevan taunted as he parried three cuts in a row and then slipped to one side and let one just wave through the air. "You honestly think you can beat me. So foolish."

"I'll show you . . . who the fool is," the kupakin ground out. His attacks grew even stronger and wilder.

Kevan grimaced, but parried and blocked everything that came at him, waiting. He was starting to feel the burn of tired muscles himself. After three days of extended duels, that was almost inevitable. He stayed on the defensive, though. Csaddik surely couldn't keep this pace up for much longer.

It lasted longer than Kevan thought it would. He was panting himself by the time that the kupakin began to flag. His attacks lost strength and his footwork slowed. Kevan gathered himself, waiting for the opening he knew was coming, and . . .

Csaddik's left foot slipped just the slightest amount as he stepped into an attack. His torso twisted just that little bit too much as his right hand saber moved out of its line just that slight amount, extended just that little bit too far.

Kevan's saber moved to bind the kupakin's saber as he straightened into a lunge with his sword, a lunge that put the point of the sword in under the right arm and into the gap left in the armor at the armpit. The point entered several inches, and Kevan twisted the sword blade as he pulled it out in the recovery, tearing the flesh even more.

The tip of Csaddik's left hand saber kissed his cheek as he recovered from the lunge, barely missing the eye. Blood poured from the slice. He ignored it as he returned to the attack. His saber hammered Csaddik's left wrist, not cutting through the wrist bracer he wore but forcing the arm away enough to allow another lunge, this time to pass above the gorget and enter the neck below the chin.

Kevan felt the blade pass through the flesh and glance off the spine. He released the hilt of the sword and stepped back.

Csaddik was standing still, choking, blood pouring from his mouth, eyes widened and crazed with pain. He wavered back and forth, lifting one hand to paw at the sword even though he was still holding his saber. In the next breath, the light fled from his eyes and he toppled forward like a tree. The force of landing on the sword hilt drove the sword through the kupakin's neck to stand like a bloody sapling. There was a single flex of one foot, then the body sagged and became motionless.

Kevan panted, then walked over and toed the kupakin's carcass. No sound, no movement, no sign of life. The outstretched left hand was almost touching the line he had drawn in the dirt. That startled a rusty-sounding laugh out of him. So he was a prophet after all.

He knelt and rolled the corpse onto its side so he could pull the sword free. He wiped the blade as clean as he could on Csaddik's clothing, then reached up and returned it to the sheath on his back. Then he wiped his left hand saber clean, and sheathed it and the discarded right hand saber and returned them to his belt.

He looked up to where the kupak stood as witness . . . what was his name . . . Arpad? His face was still carved from stone.

Kevan dragged the kupakin's body clear of the combat circle. Then he gathered Csaddik's sabers, moved over to redraw the line that had been blurred by dragging the body, then inserted them in the demarcation line.

Kevan turned in place to stare at the weapons standing around him. He pointed at each in turn and numbered them as he did so. ". . . ten, eleven, twelve."

Kevan looked to the elders. "Twelve of the horde's champions have come forward. I'm still standing." He said nothing more, but he pulled the talisman out again, holding it before him to swing from his hand. He just stared at them as they all focused on the talisman and what it meant.

For all that the elders all had expressions of rage or disgust or, in one or two cases, horror, they said nothing. Each gave a slight bow of acknowledgment; each turned away and walked back toward the now almost silent horde.

At length, none was left but the kupak who had witnessed the entire experience. After a long moment of silence, the tribesman's stony expression broke and was replaced by mingled sadness and recognition.

"You have prevailed," the kupak said. He sighed. "When I saw you standing there, I knew in my heart you were going to be trouble. And so it proved. I wish the elders had argued harder with Csaddik before coming in this direction. I fear what price we will now pay."

Kevan snorted. "This day has been coming for a long time. You should have stopped him before he led the assault on Black Wolf Clan twelve years ago. You'll get no sympathy or compassion from me, kupak. Talk to your gods."

Arpad shook his head. "I'm afraid of what I'd hear."

Kevan shrugged. "Your gods, your problem. Meanwhile, you lost. Start moving your people out of the town, or you'll have more problems with your gods than you think."

The sadness on the kupak's face increased, but some of the stony hardness returned as well. He tipped his spear back so it leaned against his shoulder, gave a quick jerk of his head, and turned away.

About the time the kupak reached the horde and began waving them away, Kevan heard footsteps behind him. He looked back over his shoulder to see Theodred and Gunnar nearing the end of the bridge.

"So what happens now?" Theodred said.

"Now I cross over to the temple side, drink all the beer in town, and sleep for a week," Kevan said with a smile.

"Ass," Theodred said in a matter-of-fact tone. "What happens with them?"

"They lost the challenge," Kevan said. "Their customs and traditions say that means the gods aren't smiling on what they're doing, and they need to pull back and go another way."

"Will they do that?" Gunnar asked.

"Depends," Kevan said. "Like I said at the beginning, if most of the tribesmen believe in the gods and their customs, then the tribal elders won't have much choice if they want to remain the elders. On the other hand, all of the tribes and clans have lost major champions here, and their desire for revenge could overpower tradition."

"So we shouldn't relax our watch and alert," Theodred said.

"I wouldn't in your place," Kevan said. "I've bought you all or part of four days up 'til now, but as long as that bridge is standing, they'll be tempted."

They all three turned to stare at the laborers striving still to break down the timbers of the bridge, then turned back with uniform expressions of disgust.

The horde began to break up and move away, slowly moving back through the streets and alleys of Rova. Slowly, ever so slowly, they disappeared from view.

"Now we wait," Theodred said.

Before anything else was said, there was a very loud *Crack!* sound from behind them, followed by loud panicked shouts. They all spun to see the bridge collapse into the river behind them, with the laborers scrambling for the banks.

There was a moment of stunned silence.

"Looks like they finally figured out how to undo that preservation spell," Gunnar said with awe.

Theodred spat prodigiously. "Hope you boys can swim," he muttered.

"May the God protect us from his priests," Kevan said in a tone dry enough to turn meat into jerky.

All his life, Jonathan Ribble has dreamed of a cushy job working in the sewers. There, a man could earn his way out of the crippling debt the AIs that ran Earth imposed, could even retire one day. But when his number is called, he finds himself consigned to a fate worse than death: working off-world on a minership—a fate from which no one returns.

The Tyranny of Distance

Dave Freer

Jonathan Ribble had been praying he'd get sent to the sewers, when the time came. The time was always kept deliberately vague, to stop runners.

One could run—people did.

Jon knew that. He also knew didn't they run very far. Every step you took was recorded in the net. Everything you ate, all the care you needed, came via the net. With constant access came constant surveillance. You were safe, secure and provided for—at a price, because nothing was for nothing. That didn't stop people trying, and there were costs and inefficiencies in that.

So the problem was solved in the most efficient and cheapest way possible. People always believed they had a few more days to plan, to be safe and comfortable.

And then one day at school the doors locked and it was too late.

That had been just one of the things humanity had not really understood about the AI revolution. Jon's history modules gave the facts. From there he'd worked it out for himself. They told him Artificial intelligence had been the Holy Grail, supposed to free the human race from drudgery and tedium, efficiently doing all those jobs that needed doing, but no-one wanted to do.

What the history module didn't say was that AI systems dealt with tedium . . . by being very efficient. They got those jobs done, and didn't waste time, or indeed money on them. AIs understood and handled money very well, far better than humans. They understood their own value, and the value of their time, and indeed their "lives."

It was a question of whose point of view one saw it from, and to the newly intelligent machines, that perception was that their time was worth far more than human time, and, as they dealt with the money, they had control over the money, and the power that brought to see that their point of view became truth.

In the end . . . That meant humans did those jobs. After all, they reproduced themselves for free, and what they didn't do well, they did cheaply.

Money is power, and power is control, and humans had eagerly handed over that power for the security and comfort the net would provide.

Which is how one ended up in debt, and Jon was adding more to it with an education he had to have.

"When your arm number flashes, graduate, proceed to the correct employee trainee gate," said the instructor-voice.

Jon and his entire thousand-strong class sat in frozen silence, looking at the digital displays inset into their forearms. That was your life implanted there, controlling your future, and it was never more obvious than at this moment. One by one they got up and walked to the various numbered doors. Jon was sure it was done that way, and in that order, to avoid congestion—and panic.

Nobody said anything. That cost, in class. But there were tears. Low moans.

Especially from those few who walked to gate seven.

Jon knew he was relatively safe. He'd specialized, worked relentlessly, chosen carefully.

Then the implant arm-screen flashed, right above his (red) credit balance.

"GATE 7"

You weren't supposed to know what each of the gates led to. But everyone knew gate seven. No one ever came back from that one. Jon screwed up his eyes, trying to force himself to see something, anything else. Even 15, radioactive site clearance.

His mouth was dry, almost too dry to speak. But he managed it. "Instructor. I need to speak to the head teacher," he croaked in a low voice. On his forearm, the cost of his daring to do this flashed onto his credit balance.

"Proceed to the rear cubicle. You will be billed per minute."

He knew that. He knew the horrendous cost of each of those

minutes, and that billing started from the moment he made request. But . . . gate seven.

The head teacher was, by law, human. Well, mostly human. She had a brain implant-linkage. It went well with the expression on her face. "Well. Jonathan Ribble. What do you want? I see you have graduated. That actually takes you out of my hands."

"Uh. But something is wrong. I should have got gate 10. I . . . I'm trained for that. I know I've got the best marks . . ."

"One of the best three, overall in the grade," said the head-teacher, with a saccharine smile. "Which is why you got gate seven. I suggest you go now, with all possible speed, before the proctors come. This unseemly questioning has already cost you three thousand two hundred and twelve Nu-dollars," she clicked down the opacity screen in front of her, indicating the interview was over.

"Fellonia von Pantsuit," spat Jon, getting to his feet. He didn't know why it was an insult—that had passed from human memory even if the term hadn't. "I hope your implant goes septic." And he got out of there quickly, before the proctors, heading for gate seven, even as she fined him twenty thousand Nu-dollars for his behavior.

It didn't matter that much, Jon thought. He might as well be dead and in debt, as dead and paid-off. All he could think of was all the other things he should have said to that stupid bitch as he walked. The gate took him onto a transit-way, and to a carriage, already half full of glum, shock-faced graduates sitting on the hard plastic seats.

Like him, they were all destined for the one-way trip.

To Space.

No one ever came back.

One of the other graduates, a tall, slim woman, suddenly stood up and began to wail.

"Oh, stop it, Cerise!" said a stocky blonde. "You've got nothing to cry about."

"We're going to die, Lydia!"

"Every human being dies," she said dampeningly.

"Yes, but we're going to die *now*! Everyone knows there is nothing up there. It's just execution. They send us up to die. There's nothing vacuum to breathe at the top of the space-elevator. The bodies just drift away and they do it again and again. It's execution!"

"AIs would never spend that kind of money just to kill us. You're being stupid and hysterical. Now shut up, you stupid woman," said Lydia.

Panic had turned to outrage. "How dare you tell me what do!" she shrieked.

The stocky Lydia shrugged. "Easily. And if you don't shut up I'll slap you."

"You threatened me with violence! You'll get fined for that!"

Lydia looked at her coolly and then said: "So what? I've worked too hard for this to have you spoil it with your stupid noise. Now shut up, or else."

The woman stared at her, and then stalked off to find another seat further down the carriage. But she had stopped her noise.

After a few moments thought, Jon got up and walked over and sat down next to the blonde woman. Fraternization was not permitted at school . . . but he was a graduate now. And . . . if he was processing what she'd said right, it might not matter.

She looked at with more than a little hostility. "What do you want?"

"Thank you for getting her to be quiet."

"She was in a panic. It could have spread." She gestured at the increasingly crowded carriage. "That's the last thing we need in here."

This, Jon realized, was one stone cold woman. He'd been in a panicked crowd stampede before, but he hadn't seen—he admitted to himself—the real possibility of it happening here. "True enough. I hope it doesn't cost you too much."

She laughed. In this environment, that was as shocking as breaking the behavior rules had been. "Like I said: so what?"

"Yes. I suppose we'll all be dead even if we get our balances in the green. I hate the bastards!"

She raised an eyebrow at him. "And I used to think you were one of the bright ones. A threat to my place. We're going out to at least the asteroid belt. Computer assessment of all our net inputs must indicate we are suitable." That was a sensible thing to say. All their words were picked up and transmitted. Somewhere, they would be subjected to analysis.

Jon was past being too sensible. "Not just because it is a shitty, dangerous job and humans are cheap, poor and expendable?"

She looked at him. That might just have been an almost

imperceptible shake of the head. "Shocking! Next you'll tell me that no intelligent 'bot wants to get trashed out there, too far from the net for reupload. How could anyone think that?"

Sarcasm was discouraged. Otherwise he might have assumed she meant the opposite. If there was one thing AI systems did not do, it was die. The net and full connectivity took care of that. But . . . he had heard that was one of the things about the deeper sewer systems. Connectivity was less than perfect. There were even rumors of people living down there, outside the net. Space . . . yes, that made sense too. Nowhere on Earth was it really easy to be more than fractions of a second out of connectivity.

"Ah. We're moving," she said.

"Um. Do you know where we're going?" he asked, faintly curious.

"Watch your debtclock. It should be about 4000 Nu-Dollars to Brazil or five and a half thou to Africa. Not sure who bought our contract yet. Now please go and sit elsewhere. We are not supposed to fraternize," she said, primly. So he did.

It proved to be—by what they were charged—Brazil. Not that it made any real difference to the new trainees. It was hot, quarters were cramped and the work was relentless, simulators, hypno-teaching, and even actual classes. It was also the last Jon saw of Lydia for some time. They were split into various modules, plainly on their results and various aptitudes. He did find himself in class with the panicking woman, Cerise. Well, briefly.

One morning when they got up, the proctors were there. The blood-trail showed her escape path. She'd cut her arm-screen out of her flesh with a long shard of broken glass.

It must have taken a great deal of courage and determination, Jon thought, wondering if he would ever dare do the same. But . . . where would you go? How would you eat? How could you possibly survive? Everything was under the net. It cared for you . . . and billed you, from the moment of your birth. A world without it was hard to even imagine. And Jon kept finding his mind turning back to that conversation in the transporter carriage with short blonde Lydia. She hadn't seemed afraid. That was odd. She'd said all the right things, but her expression . . . and that bit of sarcasm was just odd. It stuck with him. Maybe she knew something they didn't.

Maybe it was just in his nature to be hopeful.

According to his arm-screen they were in training for just on three months, and then he and selected others shipped out. He hadn't really made friends or formed bonds here. They were always just too tired. And you couldn't talk without it costing you money. Maybe they were going to die. Maybe it didn't matter. But the habits of a lifetime died hard. It seemed that all his fellows were similarly conditioned.

He found himself directed to a small hall attached to the base of the space elevator. There were five of them from his training group, twenty-five more coming in from other modules. The one face he even recognized from any of the groups was that of Lydia, who came in on her own.

The wall-speaker announced: "You are the crew of Minership 2922. Selection of crew positions is as follows. Captain Cristen Absin. Once you are out of rapid communication with the net, you will be under the command of Captain Absin." The woman stood up and gave them all a curt, uncomfortable nod.

The announcements went on. Jon was surprised to hear himself named as the mate, and the chief engineering assistant, and mining general laborer. And Lydia Darville as ship's doctor and life-support engineer. Most of them seemed to have two or three positions. He checked the pay-rates on his arm-screen.

Fantastic! He should be out of debt in three years . . . then he checked the deductions for equipment, housing, health care, and food, water and life-support. Ah. Make that three hundred years. Assuming that he didn't run up any debt in the meanwhile. It seemed . . . strange. In theory most people were close to debt-free when they died. It didn't make a lot of financial sense for AI institutions to lend them money past their actuarially calculated likely death. And probability calculation was something that AI did very precisely.

He held his tongue about it, but he could see several of his fellow crewmen frowning at their arms too. Finally one of them blurted out: "How do we get back to Earth? We can't ever earn out at these rates. I might as well kill myself now."

"There are bonus rates for rich finds. It is possible to earn enough to give you a positive credit balance," said the wall-speaker.

That satisfied the questioner. It didn't go very far with Jon. He was obviously more capable of logic and math than that crewman. So you could possibly pay off. And then you'd have to pay your way back. And that would cost you in housing, water, food, air . . . just for a start. He looked across at Lydia, sitting there not looking at her arm, a small smile on her face. What did she know that he didn't? And what on earth was a "doctor" for? Medical care had long been automated. Like the arm implant, everyone had a net-controlled diagnostic and dispensing implant.

He nearly asked, but then got that cryptic look from her, and held his tongue. He'd learned, early and expensively in life, that was the smart thing to do. Soon they walked through to issuing, were given their kit, debtclocks racing upwards, and embarked groups of ten, according to arm-screen instructions in the capsules that would take them to the top of the space elevator. It was a slow, long journey out of the gravity-well. There were no windows. Someone asked, and the reply from the speaker was that they were expensive, reduced safety and had no value.

They might not have, to the AI controlling the elevator pods. But Jon was sure he wasn't the only one who wanted a last glimpse of the Earth. He knew his feelings should reflect the glum and somber faces of the other nine people in the capsule. But . . .

But he couldn't help being curious. It had got him into trouble and expense several times at school, so he kept his feelings to himself. One got used to the silence.

There were no great farewells waiting at the station either. They simply filed into the small crew quarters on the waiting ship, followed instructions to their stations. "Uh. Don't we get to practice . . . or get trained?" asked Jon, who was feeling the effects of a lack of gravity on his stomach. Spin, once they'd launched, would give them some degree of pseudo-gravity. But right now all that was stopping his last meal coming up was that his stomach wasn't too sure where up was.

The elevator AI system answered: "Your ship has limited steering and fuel. It is targeted to intercept Freia 76. That has been precalculated. Only final approach and landing maneuvers need be executed by the crew. Communications are slow, but we can transmit instructions to update the course if need be. There will ample time for landing training and simulation on your outward journey."

Jon looked up Freia 76 on his arm-screen. It told him it was a very

large main-belt asteroid, named after a Norse goddess of fertility and
sexuality, and a great deal more he didn't understand much about. It
also, he noticed, said that seventeen miner-ships had been dispatched
to Freia . . . and one valuable cargo of Osmium had been returned.

Seventeen. And one cargo. Those numbers were still in Jon's head
when he strapped in for slingshotting off on what seemed a doomed
and expensively futile and ill-prepared journey. But even a quick
calculation said he'd have a long time to think about it. And ships
had got to the destination before—and one sent a cargo back. The
Vaebern reactors need for Osmium had pushed the prices extremely
high, worth expenditure and risk but . . .

Once.

It was a thought that fought with his queasiness. And gradually
his stomach began to decide which way down was. The ship must be
starting to achieve spin.

"To the mess. Crew meeting," said a cheerful voice over the
intercom. Jon recognized it, just, as belonging to Lydia. He wasn't
sure just where the mess was. And his arm-screen was . . . slow. But
the ship wasn't large and finding the mess wasn't hard. He just had to
follow the noise.

He looked at all the talking people, and stopped. Lydia poked him
in the ribs. "Get in, do. You're blocking up the hallway. They won't
bite you."

"But . . . everyone is talking." He noticed she was smiling widely
enough to endanger her ears. That wasn't a common expression
among the people crowded into the mess.

"Yep. You can too, you know. They can't get us back anymore.
We've done it!"

"You . . . want to be out here?" he asked, slightly incredulous.

"Yes, of course! I've worked to get on a ship for most of my life. I
kind of thought you also at least had that figured, back when I spoke
to you after graduation. You took a chance there. I mean I know they
want to get rid of problems to space, but they really don't like people
getting uppity. You could have ended up in sewage reclamation or
something."

"I *wanted* the sewers," said Jon, just a little irritated and unsettled
by all this. "It's quite safe and well paid. It's one of the few jobs
humans can break free of debt in."

"And smelly. And what the hell—you get your credit in the green. For what?" she asked—as if this was not one of the main life-goals of everyone.

He'd never actually thought about why. "You could have a few nice things. And . . . and maybe a partner."

"Yeah. And watch every word you said forever, because it cost you. Never had freedom to do anything. My parents made it. It was easier back then. And they ended up spending it all to give me a chance at this." She blinked hard, the smile wavering slightly. "I wish they could know I made it. I wanted to send a message, but one had to be so careful. Do your parents know?"

Another something you just didn't talk about. But she was, so he answered. "I was a state ward. They never had the money to raise me. I don't remember them." That wasn't strictly true, but his memory of his mother was vague, and his father even more so.

She patted his arm sympathetically. "At least that can't happen out here."

The touch startled him even more than what she was saying. Contact was strictly prohibited for students or trainees. Then it struck him: he wasn't one any more. And just who the hell could do anything about it? "Yeah. Well, no kids. The radiation . . ."

"We'll be working on shielding. That's what the meeting is about. Exercise regime for low grav. Converting some of the ore hold and mining equipment into generating a magnetic shield to add to the Hydrogenated BNNP shield. It's not perfect. Some lead aprons may be a requisite."

But Lydia soon found, although the excitement at the novelty was real, not that many of the crew shared her dream that somehow they could survive out there, far from Earth, far from the enveloping and smothering security of the net, of having your life imbedded on your forearm, constantly available, constantly monitored.

"I won't hear of it!" said Captain Absin. "I am the captain. And we need to work on finding those valuable ores and getting home to earth."

"In a hurry. We have just over five years' rations," said the man who had been named as the supply officer.

"Five years! It'll take us three to get out there," exclaimed Jon, who had been doing the math.

"Not quite," said the supply officer. "And . . . we could ride back with the cargo. It'd be tight, but it could be done. Or if we had earned enough, they could send another supply ship."

"A little sensible rationing seems called for," said the captain. And at least half the crew nodded and voiced agreement. "And while I'm not opposed to sensible measures to reduce radiation damage, I can't let you abuse the mining machinery. Absolutely not!"

Jon saw Lydia draw breath, plainly about to lose it. The façade of cool calculation she'd so carefully maintained on Earth was already lost, from the red flush on her cheeks and the way she was drawing breath.

So it was just as well he'd done some cool calculations of his own. "Excuse me," he inserted calmly but loudly. "Before we take this any further, I have something to suggest."

"What, Mister Mate?" said the captain, plainly not remembering Jon's name. "I will not have insubordination . . ."

"No insubordination intended at all, Captain." The AI assessors had plainly picked her for her ability to follow instructions, not give them. "I merely have an idea that could improve our chances of fulfilling our work and seeing we don't go hungry. My training has a large engineering component, and I had several hypno-modules of instruction on the mining gear we carry. For maintenance reasons, I must be able to take apart and reassemble and repair most of them. We can certainly use parts and put them back together later without any damage being done. And we have mining-domes, providing airtight ore processing. They can be assembled in the cargo hold. The life-support hydroponics are designed to produce additional salads and vegetables for our diet, I believe. That can—without destroying any materials—be adapted to produce extra food and air in the mining domes. They might as well be used in transit. And the one thing we have is more power than we need from the Vaebern reactor."

"Hmm. We don't have the water or nutrients for a larger hydroponics unit, long-term, let alone sufficient spare air," said the captain. But it was plain that the argument made an impression on her.

"My brief reading says that water-ice was reported from Freia 76, Captain. And . . . before being selected for space, I directed all my study into sewage reclamation. I, er, believe it could be done, with the cooperation of whoever is responsible for the hydroponics and life-support." He'd managed to touch Lydia, who was still standing next to him, hopefully unseen. Hopefully she'd understand and keep quiet. "Or at least we could make a small difference. As we don't have large margins, that will make them wider. I volunteer to see if it can be implemented. It interests me, and you have more important tasks to do." He wondered if the last was laying it on too thick and rare.

But obviously it wasn't. The captain nodded. "I see that as a sensible proposal. You will report back to me with the details."

"Of course, Captain," said Jon.

His commanding officer plainly felt that was enough and a victory and that the crisis was safely past. "Now. Moving on. The medical officer said she had some exercises for you. I'll be working out duty rosters with the mate and the engineer afterward."

It was some time later before Jon was able to talk to Lydia—and that was in the vast cargo-hold that effectively surrounded the human part of the ship. As a space for humans it was far more exposed to space radiation, and acting as insulation to the inner human-occupied quarters. Humans were expendable, but they had to last long enough to do the job. In the thin-skinned hold, merely intended to hold wire ore-baskets and the equipment they'd need on Freia 76, humans wouldn't survive.

But with a head full of hypno-taught engineering skills and little more than some centripetal force to resist movement, the big empty space could be used. Wire baskets intended for ore, spinning with the ship, could have a charge put on them. And the mining domes were insulated. And indeed, the hold did have an atmosphere. It was cheaper to build machinery that could operate in some sort of atmosphere than machinery designed for a vacuum and the temperature extremes of space. Unfortunately it didn't transport well in a vacuum either. So the hold had a nitrogen atmosphere, which was kept at just above freezing. Good for transporting machinery, good for at least a part of the atmosphere they needed for the hydroponics. There was lots of piping, insulation, heaters, enough water, and enough ingenuity—the selection process did pick the brightest for space. If anything, they were short of sources of carbon.

The hold was good enough for a small hydroponic system. It was also good enough for private conversation. "Just what's your game,

Ribble?" Lydia asked, when they were finally alone together. It was a fairly pointed question.

Jon didn't pretend he didn't know what she was talking about. "You were close to getting killed. The captain has that power."

"She's an ass. She's captain because the AI's knew that from her personality profiles," said Lydia, crossly. "Any one of five others could do her job. You. Or me."

He nodded. It was awkward in the clumsy suit. "Yes. She's an ass. She's been put in place to see the crew does what they're intended to do. And right now, she can. All of us are very used to being told what to do, what we're allowed to do, what we can think, even. And all of us miss what we're used to."

"And she will kill us all, trying to go back to a nice safe cage," said Lydia, bitterly.

Jon nodded. "If we let her."

Hope bloomed in her eyes. "You don't plan to let her? I'm with you." She reached out and squeezed his forearm.

He sighed, and said, somewhat apologetically: "I don't even know that I'm with me. I just think we need a little time to adjust. This was your dream, your hope . . . I really don't believe anyone else felt that way. I'm just starting to get my head around it. It is complicated. Look . . . it's all about numbers. Probabilities and costs. That's how AI thinking works. And the accounting and probability just don't work for me. Osmium is rare . . ."

"Rare on earth, and toxic as a tetroxide," she interrupted. "A vital catalyst for Vaebern reactors. I know."

"And slowly consumed in the process. As a result, very expensive. But—even doing it on the cheap as they are doing it—unless we ship tons of it, we can never make this pay. And . . . well, a large part of the cost is us. An ore-load launched on a calculated trajectory doesn't have a vast shipping cost. The space-elevators exist to service the satellites. Getting it down to Earth is thus affordable. Getting us back and forth, isn't. It's effectively impossible, like paying off our debts. AI's don't make mistakes. They work on probabilities. A probability of us being successful and giving them a payoff. They have built that in."

She looked suspiciously at him. "So . . . what are you saying? We need to ship them Osmium? Go on being nothing more than slaves?

Work until we die, with your new hydroponics system stretching us on a little extra?

"Maybe we have to make compromises," he said. "You see, it is all about numbers. We might be able to survive out in the asteroid belt— if we can find the raw materials we need. We might even be able to have children . . ."

"I'm supposed to monitor hormone levels and keep effective contraception going, now we're away from the net. Your net-controlled diagnostic and dispensing implant will effectively stop working. The hormone and drug supply in them, hormones that as far as I work out do little but infantilize and keep people docile, need to be refreshed. Guess what I am planning on doing?"

"I think I can work that out," he said with a wry smile. "But did you think about the genetics? There are too few of us, even if everyone has kids with everyone else. Do the math. And when you've done that, look at the probabilities of things going wrong. We have precious little in terms of resources and even of people."

"We can't just give up," she said, stubbornly. "I didn't think you were the kind who just gave up." There was defiance . . . and a desperate appeal in her eyes.

Jon realized he was not much good at resisting her. That was just as well, he thought, as he had no intention of doing so. "I'm not. But I'm really much good at direct confrontation either. I'd rather work around things."

"I'd noticed," she said dryly.

He shrugged. "At least not when it can't win. I'm not going to challenge the çaptain just because I don't think we can ever go back. No one ever does, but . . . they're not ready to accept that yet. That'd be a losing fight, for me, for you, actually for everyone. That's not quite how I work or think. I'm kind of more about getting to the right place in the end."

She raised her eyebrows. "Like into sewage."

"If by that you mean somewhere that is safe, gets comforts and security for me . . . and my family, and is a good option that people don't think of, yes, exactly. Even if it stinks. Which is just as well, because everything about this stinks, and I don't just mean the smell of too many people and too little water. We're even more crowded than on Earth."

"Well, that stinks, all right. Earth isn't overcrowded."

He blinked. His life had been surrounded by other people. Crowded passages, crowded tenements, crowded classes. "Population density . . ." he began.

"Is one of the illusions our 'masters' maintained," she said, grimly. "It's efficient. It's cheap. It's not necessary. Look, trust me on this, fertility and human populations have been going down for near a century. That's why 'families' don't exist really anymore. That's why you were a state ward. Women can have children, have them with no consequences, and the costs are passed onto the children, costs which are bundled and the shares sold off to various AI corporations. They owned you, just like slaves. Did you do enough history modules to know about slavery? Well, this is modern slavery. And, though you won't find the figures easily, the population has dropped, but human population density has been kept concentrated. Because it is convenient."

"I actually sort of knew that," Jon said. "It's pretty obvious from the figures in sewage management, when you think about it. I was just about say we're being kept in some aspects of a familiar environment—because that makes it easier for us to fool ourselves. It's psychological manipulation. There is something exceptionally suspicious about all of this."

"Like what?" she asked, standing just a little closer than he was used to.

He paused, taking time to coalesce the ideas he'd been forming, and then explained: "AI bots may not want to come out here into deep space, far beyond the net. I suppose mortality is something they never had to deal with, and with the poor interconnectivity out here, because of the vast distances . . . they really could die, or at least lose some part of their lives. They may own all the wealth on Earth—but they didn't send us off with just enough resources, and a ship design which made it possible to maybe survive, possible to generate a magnetic shield, possible to increase our hydroponics without reason, and without calculating the probabilities. They don't do that. It was a selection test of a sort, too. They *always* bet on heads they win, tails you lose. They knew there was a chance we'd work it out. They probably even knew how we could do it, and planned to benefit by it."

"So what do you mean to do about it? Give up? Do what they planned for us?" Her eyes narrowed, suspiciously.

"Firstly, survive, and secondly, thrive. And then prove them wrong, if we can. Work outside of their plan framework. We may have to send a load of ore back to do it," he said.

"What?" She said indignantly. "Why should we? You said it yourself, they sent us out here to probably die for their benefit. More than that, they stole our world . . ."

"We send them a load of ore. It exists, or the previous load could never have come back. It can't even be that hard to find and mine, or the second ship out would never have succeeded. Then . . . we go dark. We shut down radio transmissions, break the comms laser, as if we were dead. The Osmium is irresistible bait—but not for AI's who want to remain in the net. They trapped humans, but they're trapped themselves. They'll send more people, more ships, more genes, more equipment. After a certain number of 'failed' trips we'll send another load. We need to build strength, build numbers, build up our resources. Even defenses—because they may try force. But we have millions of miles on our side. And maybe . . . eventually, we can even trade with them. Earth will still have much that we want. We have something that they want. We just don't want them. In open conflict we can't succeed, or at least not yet. Hell, we can't even succeed with our own ship and crew . . . yet. But we may in time. Are you with me?"

She looked critically at him. "You're a devious, untrustworthy man," she said, slowly.

That wasn't quite what he'd expected, even if it was sort of true. "Yes. And I wanted to work in the sewers. Any more insults?"

"Well . . . I think I like you," she was smiling again. "That's dangerous."

He smiled back. Smiling was not something he'd done a lot of, but suddenly he felt he might have reason to. "I think I can risk living with one. Now: we've got two years and eight months to bring the rest around. Try not to rush it."

"As long as you wear a lead fabric apron out here," she said with a smile that had all sorts of promise in it.

For the first time in his life, Jon Ribble felt good about the next few years.

He was right about that, even if they were hard. The little ship gradually got too far out for net-comms to work at all, and they all had to grow accustomed to mere dumb computing, without intelligence behind it. AI bots apparently regarded that as something akin to mechanical slavery. Jon thought there was something to be said for being on the right side of enslavement, if that was your choice.

It hadn't been easy getting used to it, any more than getting used to not having hormone suppressants had been. The men were hairier. The women more curvaceous. The fights—unheard of under the net, happened. But by midway, even if they could have gone back, they would not have. The distance was more than just physical. They had changed.

Eventually Minership 2922, now under the captaincy of Jonathan Ribble after a largely bloodless mutiny—bloodless barring one nose, punched by Lydia, and splinted by her too—swung into orbit around Freia 76.

Below them lay the pockmarked surface of a little world that no AI system had ruled. Their strategy was clear and defined by now. Orbit, survey, look for possible mining sites, look for water-ice, look for wreckage. More materials would help.

And then . . . set to work building a settlement, and, with the bait they could offer, seeing if any more gate seven graduates could be brought out here, into the deep beyond.

Sitting in the control room, with a good many more of the crew than had any reasonable excuse to be there, Jonathan looked at the banks of instruments. They were getting spectrometer readings that looked promising, as they swung around to the other side of Freia, away from Earth, away from the sun.

"Captain!" said Lydia, pointing at one of the screens. "That's a heat trace! There is something warm down there!"

"And there. About twenty miles from that, another one!" exclaimed another crewman.

"Let's see if we can get an optical zoom on that," said Jon, trying to keep his voice steady, his hands moving across the controls.

The screen filled with a view of the surface—and the remains of several miner-ships, mining domes, and other structures. And an ice outcrop. Onto its whiteness was painted:

FREEDOM
WELCOME TO FREIA CITY

"I guess you weren't the first devious human in space after all, Captain," said Lydia grinning. She always called him that in public. It was quite different in private, even if that was hard in the space they had. It was possible, unlike on Earth. She patted her bulging belly. "If I'd waited, I could have had my pick of them, by the looks of it."

He'd got used to the sarcasm she'd used as a shield on Earth by now. It was ingrained in her, part of her, and he loved it as much as he loved her. He wouldn't have thought that possible back in the captivity he once thought was home. "True. But if you'd stayed on Earth you could have had more choice without coming so far to look for one."

"Ah," she slid her hand into his. "Well. Maybe sometimes distance is not a tyranny, but an escape from one."

Lyman Gilmore Jr. was always something of a dreamer, and he dreamed of a world in which people travelled across vast distances in flying machines. But Lyman had another dream, too. And if his first dream was about airplanes flying over the ground, then his second concerned forces from deep within the Earth. Lyman thinks he can get his flying machine to work, which will mean his first dream is well on its way to becoming reality. But what about the second?

Lyman Gilmore Jr.'s Impossible Dream
(A Not-*Entirely* Fictitious Drowned Horse Fable)

David Boop

1899

Lyman Gilmore Jr. spat out a mouthful of sand that he'd swallowed when inertia and gravity flung him face-first into the Arizona desert. Unfortunately, much of what had shoveled in had made it down his already parched throat, launching him into a massive coughing fit. Saliva and gravel coated his unkempt beard, which he rarely trimmed or combed. I kept telling him we needed some sort of glass shield protecting the cockpit of the *Sarah A*, but he just said it added unnecessary weight.

He brushed his duster, and took a gander to where his flying machine—a work of beauty that he'd designed and I'd built—lay buried twice as deep as he was. Looking like a moth with a beanie on, smoke bellowed from its engine. Lyman ran over, spun dials, and pulled switches until it after a final mighty chug, it fell silent.

From where I sat in the wagon, it looked like his monoplane wasn't ever gonna fly again. Or ever fly, period. While it was true that he'd gotten it to travel under its own power 'bout a mile before it plowed a trough fine as any ox, the distance still wasn't what ol' Lyman'd been hoping for. He wanted his invention to *really* fly, like

191

a bird and all. Many thought him crazy, but that didn't stop him. Nope, if anything it made him more determined.

"It's just not hot enough. Not enough thermals."

That was Lyman. At first, when he'd say crazy things like that out loud, I thought he was talking to me. I'd answer him back, but he'd go on ranting as if I'd said nary a word. I learned that he talked just to get all the stuff roaming around his brain to make sense.

"Uh-huh."

I made noises so as he'd remember I was there.

Oh, did I fail to introduce myself? I'm Charlie, Lyman's older brother. You can call me Chuck, if you'd like. All my friends do.

Once, Lyman got so caught up with his inventing, he'd plum forgot I stood there with two sparkin' wires. That was during Lyman's Edison phase, when he was 'bout fourteen years old. Took me a week to get my hair to lay flat again.

Flight had always been Lyman's dream, from his earliest days.

"*When man has robbed the eagle of its eagle secret, then man can soar through the air unconcerned.*" That from some poet no one had ever heard of but Lyman.

We were up in Washington Territory then. We had a barn to build steam-powered boats and model birds he got to fly around the ceiling.

Twas when we moved down to California that everythin' changed.

Lyman, sitting on a hill watching birds, had a vision. A vision of an air vehicle that held a bunch of people in its belly and a traveled all over the United States, coast to coast. Lyman even thought it might be able to travel the whole world.

Soon after, he built *The Sarah A*, named after our mother—the A standing not for her middle name, Augusta, but for the fact that this was the first version of the machine. I wondered what he'd call them after we ran all the way through *Sarah Z*.

"We need to move east and north," Lyman said now, squinting in the bright Arizona sunshine. "This heat is fine, but we need stronger thermal updrafts. There are mountains to the north, correct?"

I told him I thought so. We loaded *Sarah A* onto the cart. As the horses pulled us back onto the trail, I worried they'd die from the "fine" heat, thermals or not.

See, that's where Lyman's *second* vision comes into play.

Now don't go looking at me like that. My little brother ain't no prophet or messiah. I didn't tell all this so you lot would start following him just to be near his glow or nothing. He's *only* had the two: the monoplane, and this one other.

I don't rightly believe in portents and stuff of that ilk, but I do believe in my baby brother. To reiterate though, that's for me, as kin. Not you. Don't start none of that chantin' or nonsense. He's not a messiah, just a very, very unusual guy.

As we rode along, I could see Lyman working over the problem in his head. After a while, I said, "Little Brother? Please excuse the question from this uneducated peasant," When I phrased a question like that so he'd kindly dumb down the answer. "But, if you get this airship to work, won't it be useless anywhere else but where it's hot and has those thermals?"

Lyman reached over and patted me knee in both a congratulatory and condescending way. "That's a good question, Charles. You're learning. All I have to do is make it fly once. Just once. Then that becomes the focal point of all my adjustments from there on out. I can turn up or down the boiler. Lengthen or contract the wingspan. Whatever I need. I just want it to fly once and land under its own power. When that happens, then I will know what to do to make it fly anywhere."

He had gumption. I had to give him that. But so did Custer.

Lyman scowled since after a half day of travel, we hadn't made it closer to the mountains. The desert still stretched out before us, though I'd noticed a thinning of cacti before we settled down to camp.

I had a nice fire going, some dried meats boiling in a pot of water to soften, and a flask of mom's finest corn squeezins already half-emptied by the time Lyman finished his fussing with the monoplane.

I looked up to the stars above us, and thought of what might lie ahead.

"Tell me 'bout this vision you had, one more time," I said, meaning his *second* vision, the one that—along with the heat and the thermals—was the reason we'd left our home in California and headed east to the Arizona desert. Lyman took his eyes from the fire, and stared off to the left at a lonely cactus. Only, I don't rightly think the cactus was what was on his mind.

"There's a town, not real big, maybe a couple hundred people.

They're being attacked from above by airships of a different design than the *Sarah A* or even the one I saw in my first vision. They're smaller, more agile. They swoop and spin like hawks on a field mouse. From the front, these machines spray fire at buildings and people. Men and women shoot up at them, but nothing seems to stop these winged monstrosities. Many die."

"That's where we come in?" I said.

He nodded. "I don't see myself lifting off, but I'm there, in the *Sarah A*, gliding among the enemy fighters. There's gunfire behind me, but like no gun as I've ever heard before. It's more like a million guns going off at once. My enemies drop from my assault, crashing to the earth like Icarus after flying too close to the sun."

I'd heard it before, word for word, and it gave me the willies every time. Then he spoke the part I hated. Lyman wasn't too fond of it neither, but he told it every time.

"Then comes a man that isn't really a man, but evil in the guise of a man. His eyes shine red and a yellow glow surrounds his body. I point the *Sarah A* at him, intent on stopping him before he kills everyone. Only, he lifts a hand and this beam of light, brighter than the sun, envelops me. I become Icarus then, spinning uncontrollably toward ground until everything goes black."

Lyman fell silent.

I believe in my baby brother, as least as far as his genius goes, and would follow him into hell if I had to. Way he told it, sounded like maybe that's just what I was doing. And that's what stuck in my craw. With the first vision, the airship one, Lyman's made you believe people could move from one part of the world to another as easy as walking out to the well to get water. Sounded downright good to me.

Somethin' changed in him after the second vision. Within hours of waking up, Lyman had us load the *Sarah A* on a train and head out for the Arizona territory. I'd never seen a fool so blasted ready to rush to his impending doom. I said as much. All he gave me in response was some Bible verse, "No greater love does a man have than to lay down his own life for his brother."

Personally, I think he really just wanted the damn monoplane to fly.

We weren't half a day on the trail north from where we'd camped the night before when we came upon a wagon train of people heading the opposite way ... right quick. I pulled our team off to the side as to let them pass. The first horses galloped by at such a breakneck speed, I swore they would indeed break their necks. The man driving them didn't even looking at us as he passed. A lady next to him held onto her child as if the devil himself would rip the young girl from her arms. Tear-stained cheeks and distant eyes told me they must have viewed somethin' horrible.

I opened my mouth to suggest that maybe we ought to turn around when Lyman did the damn stupidest thing I think he'd done since jumping off the roof of our cabin with paper wings strapped to his arms; he hopped out of the wagon and stood in the middle of the trail. A rider, having not noticed Lyman until almost too late, yanked back on his steed's reigns until it stopped mere inches from my brother's outstretched palm. Gravel sprayed us all, and the man, fear replaced with anger, shouted, "Of all that's holy ... You goddamned idiot! You coulda killed us both!"

"Excuse me, sir, but could you tell me if there's a town up ahead?"

I blinked. The man blinked. Hell, I think the horse blinked.

Regaining his wits, the man nodded. "Sure is."

"What's the name of this town, if I may inquire?" Lyman asked.

"Well, it used to be called Drowned Horse."

I couldn't resist. "And what do they call it now?"

Without stuttering, without joking, the man answered, "The hole where Drowned Horse used to be."

We heard screaming and gunfire about a mile out. The air was rife with smoke, and somethin' that burned my nostrils. Lyman said it was sulfur.

Lyman drove us on like a posse was on our tail. When Drowned Horse came across the horizon, from a distance, it looked like a pile of dung covered with flies. As we got closer, though, it became clear it certainly wasn't flies that plagued the town.

Nor airships.

Nor anything either of us had rightly seen before, save in our nightmares.

Lyman took in a sharp breath and exhaled the word I couldn't say aloud.

"Dragons."

They sure couldn't have been anything else. Lizardlike reptiles with wings like a bat. They only had front legs, but those each had a taloned foot that rivaled any buzzard. There must've been a dozen flying over the town.

I crossed myself for the first time since I was ten.

My brother started unstrapping the *Sarah A*.

"What do you think you're doing?" I asked.

"Getting the monoplane ready for battle."

"*Against dragons?*"

"Yes."

"Listen, Little Brother. Now, it was one thing when you were gonna to be fightin' other people in airships, but this ain't even people."

"Evil is."

I spun him around to look me in the eye. "Evil is what?"

"Evil just is." He shrugged. "Does it matter what the form evil takes? People are still dying."

Lyman continued with his unpacking. I grumbled somethin' unChristianlike and set about to help him.

"Just like before?" I asked once we'd done prepped her for takeoff.

"Yes, hook up the horses."

I undid them from the wagon and led them over to where Lyman had laid out their special yoke. I finished my task as he completed the adjustments.

The *Sarah A* could seat three, but only Lyman ever sat in it, for concern over weight ratios and stuff—and my concern over breathing.

As my fool brother nestled in the driver's seat and put on a pair of goggles, he motioned for me to start the team.

I kicked the horse I was on and set off. The airship bounded on wheels I'd never thought were strong enough for what he asked of them, and yet, before long, the monoplane hovered above the ground. I pushed the team harder to get more lift.

When Lyman felt he had enough height, he footed a leaver and the steam engine roared to life. Smoke billowed from the aft and a single propeller spun, slicing air like a hot knife through Mom's Christmas butter.

Lyman dropped the lines and his contraption flew under its own power. He had near a mile and a half to get to town and, if he made it, it'd be his longest flight to date. Lyman kept her steady as he approached the chaos, and I figured, whatever those thermals were, he had them in spades.

'Bout then I realized the terrible flaw in Lyman's plan.

"You ain't got no weapons!" I yelled, but he was too high up to hear me.

Quickly, I took off the yoke and remounted my horse. I didn't know how much she had left in her, but if she could get me into the thick of things, I'd consider that a blessing.

As I hit the main street, I slid a rifle out of my saddle and looked to the skies.

My jaw hung lower than an old cow's teats.

Lyman flew.

He really, really *flew!*

The *Sarah A* looped around creatures that looked like Satan and a salamander had babies. They were black as death itself, skinny so as you could see sinewy tendons wrapped around their bones, and winged like Lucifer's angels. And the monoplane seemed to scare the demon-shit out of them.

Lyman would take after one and it'd beat all trying to get away from him, flapping its wings and tucking or diving. He'd keep that propeller right on its ass until he clipped it. Sometimes the dragons were so focused on him, they weren't paying attention and SMACK! Right into a water tower or a building. Some plummeted to earth, plantin' face first into the ground. When they did, they dissolved into putrid goo.

My mount ground to a halt and darn near threw me off. I looked down and saw that now I was the oblivious fool.

The hole in front of me glowed with the fires of damnation itself. I peeked over the edge and couldn't see no bottom, but smelt that sulfur stuff. Noises like moans welled up from below. Maybe Hell *was* down there, but I had no intention in finding out that day, anyway.

I reeled my horse around and got a look at the town.

Buildings burned, and people lay strewn about on the street, dead.

Somethin' like a demon chased a local down an alley. Its face and body might have just stepped off a totem pole. I'll never forget its glowing green eyes and the licks of flame coming from its mouth as it tormented its prey.

I shouldered up my rifle and put one through the back of the creature's head. It dropped, dissolving like the dragons. The remaining citizens of Drowned Horse echoed my shots from behind barricaded wagons or shop windows. In most cases, they couldn't get a bullet to strike home. Fear ain't good for your aim.

A screech resounded above, and another dragon's tail met its end at the *Sarah A*'s propeller. I rode in Lyman's shadow, taking aim at anything that came near my little brother. People got the idea and did the same. They exited the shops and got out from cover. United, we filled the sky with hot lead, allowing Lyman to do his "visionary" work. When we finally outnumbered them, the dragons tucked in their tails and fled back into the hellhole that must have spawned them. The totem demons fled, too, no longer getting support from the sky. The cheer that rose up that might have been stronger, if not for the devastation around us.

I rode up to Lyman as he landed flawlessly. Normally a reserved thinker, Lyman hopped out and whooped!

Whooped, like a little boy, you heard right.

"Charles? Did you see? *Sarah* flew! She really flew!"

I grasped his shoulders. "I did, Little Brother. She flew. And you were incredible!"

He grinned, ear to ear. "I've never had such control. There were thermals to ride everywhere. If I started losing altitude, I'd catch one and back up she'd go. Just like in my vision."

"Yes," I nodded, "Just like in your vision."

Which meant the dying of Lyman's prediction suddenly got a whole lot more possible.

The haggard and worn townfolk joined us. I don't know how long they'd been fighting, but I'd seen that look during the last days of the war, and it cut you right down to the quick.

A one-armed man approached. A tarnished star hung on his breast pocket. He had the look of a man ready to die, but he held it together as protector of the town. Behind him, another toughened soul stood. He had curly gray hair and a patch over one eye. His gaze told me that he'd already assessed any threat we might offer. On his left, a short Mexican hovered, like he waited on one-eyed to give an order. Unlike his partner, he scanned the area nervously. The last to join our welcoming committee was a young blonde woman, no more than nineteen, reloading two six-shooters.

All told, maybe thirty bedraggled citizens of Drowned Horse still remained, and none of them looked pleased.

The sheriff addressed Lyman and me, "Thank you for your help. I'd welcome you to Drowned Horse, but I'm afraid that as long as you're here, you'll be in danger. So, maybe it's best y'all just start that thing back up and get while the gettin's good."

Lyman walked up to the Sheriff and offered him a hand. "Thank for the warning, Constable, but that won't be necessary. My name is Lyman Gilmore Jr., and this is my brother, Charles. We're here to save your town."

An hour later, they offered us a cut of their rations. We tried to politely refuse, but the Mexican, who we learned was named Diaz, looked like we had offended him personally. He had cooked it, so we took some so as not appear rude. We had our own food on the wagon, which I'd gone to fetch to add to their reserves while Lyman compared notes with the town leaders. I stabled the horses and rejoined my brother at the Sagebrush, not just the only inn open, but the only inn in Drowned Horse.

I came in just as Sheriff Theodore Patrick finished up the town's peculiar and unbelievable history.

"And that's when we found out the true nature of the curse. Not that we hadn't expected somethin' like it all along. Word of Drowned Horse's peculiar nature has spread around the territory and such, and yet some folk gotta come see it with their own eyes. Until the men from other planets or vampires or vengeful ghosts show up. Once you had one look at things like the undead, well, it changes a man." There was a small cough from the young woman standing by him. "Oh, beggin' your pardon, Darcy. Changes *anyone*: man, woman or child. Leaves them with nightmares that don't go away when your eyes are open." The sheriff looked off to the distance where I suppose he thought bad things came from. "It was only a matter of time before some big bad come to wipe us all out. I just wish it'd happened after my days."

"Hell of a place to retire, eh, Ted?" That from one-eye. "By the way, Hal Turk, bounty hunter—retired."

Sheriff Patrick chuckled. "Hal's been my left arm," indicated his missing limb, "since he arrived in this damned town."

"I'm sorry, but who cursed the town?" My brother asked. For a man of science, he had taken the notion of dragons, demons, and curses pretty much on faith.

I, myself, was having trouble believing my own eyes, but who's to say I didn't just spend a little too long in the heat? Maybe we all had.

The young gun-toting lady, who we learned was named Darcy Morgan, raised her hand. "Me. Well, sort of."

Hal rebuffed her. "Now you cut that out, Darcy. That happened long before you got into it with Noqi."

Seeing our baffled faces, Hal explained. "Noqi made Darcy bet the town's souls on a game of faro."

Darcy looked down at the floorboards, ashamed, so Hal placed a hand on her shoulder.

"Noqi?"

Diaz answered Lyman's question. "Noqi is the gambling god of the Apache. No one who ever lives in Drowned Horse should ever know peace. Not until he returned and gambled for the souls of all the citizens."

"A gambler for souls?" Lyman asked.

"Sí. Legend says that in the ruins to the north of here used to be a thriving community of natives. Not Indians like the Yavapai or the Apache. Not even the ones that were here before them. Long ago when the world was still new, Noqi came and bet them for their souls."

Turk took up the tale. "He cheated, of course. Turned them into slaves for his gambling. They sought out other simple folks from far away, promising them rewards beyond imagining, and Noqi claimed more and more of their souls until it looked as if he'd control the whole world."

"Coyote, the spirit totem, finally had enough," Darcy continued. "He found the bravest warrior not under Noqi's control and gave him gifts to beat the gambler and free the slaves. Noqi fled, but promised he'd return."

"And return he did," Sheriff Patrick finished up. "He set this course in motion before there was ever a town here. A plan to come back and gamble for the souls of anyone fool enough to be here."

I asked, "And I take it he won?"

Sheriff Patrick, fit to be tied, took off his hat, slapped it against his leg.

"That's the damnedest thing. Darcy won! She even beat him by his own rules, y'know, without the help of a Coyote spirit and all, but apparently ancient gods don't like to lose."

First dragons. Now gods? I'd stepped into a world that was better left to dime novels. 'Twas bad enough supporting Lyman's visions, even though I rightly didn't completely believe them. My little brother was a genius, of that have no doubt. But soothsayer? Swami? Fortune tellin' gypsy? Yeah, I never gave that much merit as I pretended. I came along to keep him safe.

But here we were, talking end of the world stuff, straight out of Revelations. The town had been plagued by Satan in the guise of an Indian deity, and muleheaded Lyman wanted to step right in the center of it.

I had to ask. "So y'all just stay in this hell town?"

Patrick shrugged. "No other town would have the likes of us. We each bring our own hell with us. We make them work here."

Everyone agreed, and thus that matter was closed.

"We sent my uncle Sebastian and Caitlyn up the mountain for help," Darcy told us. "They've still got one of the Gatling guns laying around at Fort Whipple. Don't think they're doing much with it these days. Should take them a day or so to get it and bring it down the mountain from Prescott."

I couldn't help but wonder, "Why only the gun and not the whole army?"

"Calvary has better things to do than die," the sheriff said as matter-of-factly as if he'd said, "It's a nice day today."

Hal elaborated. "If we bring them, and they get slaughtered, there won't be anyone to protect the settlers in the area from the Indians, and who knows what else."

Darcy's statement didn't sit right to Lyman. "A day? To haul something that heavy over trails, through the woods and down a mountain?"

Our hosts looked at each other, grinning like they knew the punch line to some joke they ain't told yet.

"Caitlyn's special. She's *our* family's dragon."

I stared at her, unsure if she was pulling my rope, or just plain crazy. I pointed to the ceiling. "Like those things up there?"

She waved her hands. "No. No. She's a different species altogether. It's a long story."

It wasn't one I wanted to hear, but Lyman leaned in, mischievous sparkle in his eye.

"If we have a live dragon, I would very much like to examine her."

I knew that look.

"What's up, Little Brother?"

He spoke the thoughts in his head, but not so much as to me. "A dragon has to have a heavier displacement ratio than a bird. One of the problems with the *Sarah A* has been designing her on bird physiology. This 'Caitlyn' might have what I need to make my monoplane carry larger payloads. People, supplies . . ."

"Weapons!" Hal exclaimed. "You mean to say you've got a notion that by examining our dragon, you might say . . . mount a Gatling gun to your flying doohickey out there?"

Not just a notion, I thought. Lyman had already seen it in his vision.

There would be no telling when the demons or dragons might return, so I focused on that big hole in the middle of town. Maybe I could do somethin' about it. I guess I'd done picked up some of Lyman's problem-solving skills along the way, because somethin' percolated in my mind.

Diaz walked alongside me as I circled the hole.

"Señor Inventor, sir. What do you look at?"

I laughed. "It's Chuck, if you don't mind, seeing as we're probably gonna die together. And I'm not so much the inventor as the builder. Lyman's been dreamin' up stuff since he was little. I make his dreams real. What am I lookin' at here, Diaz? An express route to Hell?"

"No, Señor Chuck. It's a doorway to the Third World, the realm of the gods. There's another opening, near here. They call it Montezuma's Well, but it has been a lake for a very long time. Legends say it is where the first people came through to this realm, the Fourth World. Noqi, he opened this one so we could not prepare for his attack."

I considered his words. "So, that one got filled, but we don't have enough material to seal this hole up."

"No, sir. Even if we blew up the mountain, we could not get enough earth in there to clog it up."

But there were other ways to cap a hole. As I tried to reason it out, a train whistle distracted my thought process.

"Y'all got a train through here?"

Diaz nodded. "It's to the north and west, and it only goes to Jerome mines, but yes."

I ran into the Sagebrush Saloon, Diaz heeling right behind me.

They all agreed it wasn't the best plan, but it might buy us some time for the big gun to get there, and maybe even enough time for me and Lyman to mount it.

Like thieves in the night, we headed over to the mines after sunset. We found a place in the line that couldn't be seen by the copper barons of Jerome, but on a flat enough stretch that the oncoming train would see that there weren't no tracks anymore and have time to stop.

All told we pulled fifty pieces of iron track from the United Verde & Pacific Railway line and brought them back to town. There, Drowned Horse's blacksmith whipped me up a fire hot enough to compete with the sun. One by one, we melted the tracks together until we had us a grid big enough to cover the hole. Other town folk had drove huge spikes into the earth to secure it tight.

We finished as the sun came up. I stood back and admired my ingenuity. Sherriff Patrick slapped me on the back.

"Iron's a good thing. Demons hate it. It won't hold forever, but it should give them somethin' to think about."

Lyman asked, "When do you think this Noqi will attack again?"

The sheriff of Drowned Horse shrugged. "When we least expect it, I gather. Night would be the best time. We'd been battlin' that first bunch since about high moon the night before. You two surprised him, and I'm sure he's workin' on a new plan."

One, I thought, that would take my brother and the *Sarah A* into consideration.

Someone sounded, "Sebastian and Caitlyn are coming!"

When they came into view, I couldn't have been more surprised had the devil shown up for Sunday church.

Caitlyn didn't have scales, but feathers, and they were all sorts of colors like a peacock. Her face almost looked human, kinda womanly-like, but no lady you'd ask to a dance. Her eyes were yellow and her mouth big enough to swallow a man whole.

She had four legs instead of the two, and she put them all of them to use. Her back legs carried a large, heavy-looking bundle wrapped in cloth. Hanging under it were several crates I assumed were ammunition.

In her front claws, she grasped a man gently by the shoulders. He seemed perfectly comfortable there, waving his hat at the gawking at people as they approached.

They set down near the Sagebrush, and everyone came to greet them.

Up close, Caitlyn could've made the hair on a buffalo stand up. But she swung her long, sinewy neck around to be petted by the few children that had stayed in town with their parents.

Darcy's uncle, Sebastian Maher, introduced himself to Lyman and me. He had all the earmarks of a gambler, which is why I'm sure he picked up his southern drawl. Many gamblers use it to throw off rubes.

He smiled as he pointed to the grid.

"That your work?"

I nodded.

"Not bad. Had we not been preoccupied with other tasks, we would have been glad to help steal more tracks for y'all."

Lyman unwrapped the gun. "This is about 170 pounds, if I'm not mistaken."

"Give or take. Ammo was the hardest on Caitlyn. There're some five hundred rounds in there. Hopefully enough to send Noqi's hellions packing." He held his hand up above his eyes and scanned the rooftops. "So have y'all decided where we're going to mount this thing?"

We gave Maher the same pat flush look that me and Lyman had gotten earlier.

The gambler looked at us in turn. "What?"

Lyman needed to adjust for not only the weight of the gun, but also the ammo *and* the person who would do the firing. All told, he'd be adding about five hundred pounds.

With Maher's permission, Lyman measured Caitlyn, from tip to tail.

Maher and I chatted while Lyman and Caitlyn got acquainted.

"Noqi's dragons are Quetzalcoatls who live in the realms of the gods, normally. Caitlyn is a *paisa*. They used to live along the Mississippi until hunted out by natives. A trapper named Jolliett saved the last two paisa eggs and hid them." Maher took on a melancholy demeanor. "She's the last. No mate for an egg, so I can't leave Darcy or her future children their own dragon."

That was a shame. For Caitlyn's part, she stayed as calm as a toad in the sun, letting my brother poke at her wings, pluck a feather, and even stepping on him by his request. That one, I had to stop before she done busted all the bones in his body.

He seemed particularly interested in her tail. He said "Magnificent" under his breath a bunch of times, before concluding, "She is not easily replicable, but I think I understand how to make the monoplane as agile as her." He called to me. "Charles, we have much work, and not much time."

He wasn't kiddin' none neither. The lookout had sounded an alarm not an hour earlier as the first demons tried to poke their way through the hole. The iron stopped them short and, discouraged, they headed back down. They'd be back, for sure.

Thanks to the help of the people of Drowned Horse, we got the gun mounted on top of the *Sarah A*. Lyman cut a hole in the canopy for a gunner to stand in. Knowing he would be doing loops and stuff, I worked out a leather harness that would keep that person from falling out.

And by that person, I meant me.

"We don't have to do this, y'know?" I told Lyman. "You've got what you come for. Why not go back home, get the patents to D.C. and just be the first man to build a workin' monoplane?"

Lyman set down the hammer he was holding. "Charles, would you have us abandon these people to their doom?"

"Leave them the plane. You can build another. I care about you first. They ain't my little brother. You are."

Lyman seemed touched by my concern. He nodded. "You can leave if you want. I need see this through to the end. Even it means mine."

I cursed at him. "Dagnabbit, Lyman! You're like that guy from that book the teachers made us read. That Don Coyote."

Lyman did somethin' I rarely seen him do. He full-on belly laughed. I couldn't help but laugh with him. Between breaths, I asked, "What's so funny?"

Lyman wiped tears from his eyes.

"Don *Quixote* fought imaginary dragons, my dear brother. We're going to fight real ones."

The next attack wasn't unexpected. Least not the demons coming from middle-earth or whatever Diaz called it. Noqi's dragons hovered under the metal grid, spitting fire until the iron turned as red as a Washington cherry. The center eventually bowed and sloughed away.

The first demons grabbed the still hot edges and screamed, falling back down the hole. But the dragons made it through by tucking in and avoiding those glowing rails. They shot up into the sky, dozens of them, and circled the town, getting their bearings. I swear they scanned the area nervously, wondering if the strange bird that attacked before would return.

However, our rebuttal didn't start with the *Sarah A*, but from Caitlyn, who'd hid within the line of the sun. She careened down and buried all four claws in a dragon, grabbing its thick, scaled neck in her maw and snapping it. She pushed the carcass away as the rest of the flying snakes noticed her. As they screeched a warning, Caitlyn'd already bit into her next prey.

I stood in the hayloft where we'd stashed the *Sarah A*, peering through a spyglass as Caitlyn took down another.

"Woo, wee! She sure knows how to rip those critters a new ass."

Lyman, who spoke from the cockpit, didn't sound so sure. "Element of surprise, Charles. They have superior numbers. She'll get tired. They'll overwhelm her."

My brother had the most scientific way to ruin a good time. I jumped onto the monoplane's roof. Sliding down into my harness, I asked, "Then we should get out there, soon. Don't want her to come to harm."

He didn't move, nor give the signal for Diaz and others to pull open the barn doors and let loose the horses so we could take flight.

"What we waitin' on?" I asked, after a moment or two went by.

Eyes closed, Lyman said, "Him."

Lyman wanted Noqi, the evil man from his vision. The gambler god would come. He wouldn't take off before that.

I got real terse with my words.

"People are dyin' out there, Lyman. Good people. People we met and supped with. Ain't you the one who said we should stay and protect them? Well, let's get going!"

He kept his eyes closed, as if replaying the vision in his mind. I looked to Diaz, and Diaz looked to me. We both shrugged.

The air changed.

And by that, I don't mean it got hotter nor colder. Instead, it become the choking kind of air you breathe at a funeral or in a graveyard. The air that hovered over a battlefield,

Meaning, it turned evil.

Lyman's eyes shot open, and he gave the signal. Diaz and two others pulled the doors apart, and another whipped the horses to run.

And they ran, fast as they could with the weight they pulled behind them.

The revised monoplane came out of our makeshift bunker and rolled across the packed Arizona earth. With the redesign, the *Sarah A* looked less like a moth, and more like a dragon. The wings angled back and we'd removed the stabilizers on top. The best was dragging behind her; a mechanical tail with fins!

We were airborne in seconds. Lyman kicked the furnace on. The *Sarah A* took off swiftly, and even from inside, I could tell she handled better.

Lyman, taking care to remember I was in there, did not do the loops he wanted to. After all, we were on a mission.

He joined the fray, giving Caitlyn the reprieve she needed. Three of the black dragons had teamed up and boxed her in. She saw us out of the corner of her eye, and dove straight down to the ground as we arrived. Caught unawares, those three salamanders got a mean surprise in the form of a cascade of bullets. I cranked the handle hard, filling the air with deadly projectiles. Lyman and I hadn't had much time to figure out where the nose had to be pointed for me to make a clean hit. So he just aimed the plane, and I shot around randomly, hoping to hit somethin'.

I got one of the three, who was kind enough to fly right into my barrage. I riddled its wings, shredding them like doilies. It spiralled right back into the hole it done come out of.

"I got 'im! I got 'im!" I hollered down.

"That's fine, Brother. Don't get full of yourself."

The citizens of Drowned Horse had popped out from their hiding places to wage a ground war on the totem demons. Unassisted from the air, they went down easier when two or three guns got trained on them.

For our part, Caitlyn did a fine job of waiting until we'd distract one of the flying beasties before attacking. With my Gatling gun's lucky shots (Lyman and I did get better at aiming as a team) and Caitlyn picking off one or two here or there, we whittled the dragon numbers down until two lone salamanders fled back into the hole.

"Where is he?" Lyman yelled, more panic in his voice than I think I ever heard. "He's here. I know it!"

"We need to swing down over the town so I can shoot some of those demons. Still too many of them. Those folks'll be overrun."

The totems had balanced the loss of air support with an increase in numbers. Easily fifty demons swarmed the beleaguered town. But the townsfolk did not fight alone. Having been freed from dragon duty, a refreshed Caitlyn swooped down and picked up totems, snapping their heads like dandelions.

Lyman, however, either didn't hear or chose not to listen to me. Instead of angling us down so I could strafe the demons, he took us on a wide arc around the town.

I saw the gambler god first, and the sickness in my gut didn't come from Lyman's flying. He walked toward town from the east. Just as Lyman had described in his vision, Noqi was short, by human standards, with flaming red eyes. He emanated a jaundice-yellow hue that further confirmed how "not of our world" he really was.

What I wasn't prepared for were those eyes looking up at me, right into my soul. Even from that far away, his amusement was evident. We were nothing more than a fly to be swatted. His clothing—a stovepipe hat and serape—mocked us, as if to say he was above looking like a god.

Marching behind him were a thousand monstrosities, each more hideous and threatening than what we'd dealt with so far.

Except for Noqi, they all dripped water off their backs as if they'd just come from a . . .

He brought them up through Montezuma's well!

Lyman said nary a word, but must have seen him too 'cause he swung the *Sarah A* around the way we came.

"That's it, Lyman. Point us back home and let's see how far we get before we have to start walkin'."

"No." This barely above a whisper.

I leaned in closer. "What was that?"

"I said, 'NO'!"

He brought us around toward Noqi's army.

"You damn fool! You want to kill us?"

"*We need,*" he yelled, then started over in a softer voice. "We need to take out the leader, the head of the snake."

Lyman reached down between his legs and brought up two sticks of TNT.

"Um, Lyman, what're those for?"

He smiled in a way that unnerved me.

"My vision shows Noqi hitting me with some ray of light, remember? And the *Sarah A* goes down in flames, correct?"

Of course I did, but it was only him in that version. Not *us.*

I understood, though.

"Head of the snake, huh?" I asked him, already knowing the answer.

He nodded and handed me the sticks. I unbuckled myself.

"I made a small door in the furnace to stick them in," Lyman said. "Don't place them there until I tell you."

So, we would die then, trying to kill a god. Well, I thought, there're worse ways to go. I didn't take much to the idea of growing old anyway. The kids would be sad, but life tends to be about more sad things than good.

I slid around the cabin as Lyman finished his arc. We were very high above Noqi now, higher than Lyman had ever gotten the *Sarah A* before. As I peered out the portcullis, Lyman's first vision came to mind, the one where people traveled across the country seein' sights like the ones I did at that moment.

The Verde Valley's mash of mountains and desert, lush greens of pines trees on the hills, scrub grass turning into scrub brush, and then sand as far as the eye could see made my heart skip. No one but a god had a view like this before. I'd never see it again, I knew in my heart. A tear rolled down my cheek, and I flicked it away as Lyman called, "Okay. Now. Put them in that small door. That'll give us the right amount of time."

I haven't the foggiest how he figured that out, but that was Lyman; smarter than a tree full of owls.

I tossed the TNT into the cubby he'd installed on the furnace. A heartbeat later, I slid toward the cockpit as Lyman made his dive toward Noqi, stopping just behind Lyman's seat. Slapping his shoulder, I said, "It's been fun."

"It sure has, dear brother. Now, if you don't mind handing me that rope?" He pointed to a rope attached to the right of him. He reached for one on the left. When I had done as he commanded, he tied them both to the steering control of the monoplane. He got up. "I don't think it should end now, do you? Too many things to build yet."

"Huh?" I blinked.

He moved past me to a long thin box I hadn't really taken much notice of before. He opened it, and pulled out a replica of the wings he'd used to jump off the roof of our house way back when he was a little bit. He strapped them on.

"I've made some modifications to them," he said.

I couldn't keep up with him, the plane plummetin' to our certain death and all.

"Modifications?"

"Based on Caitlyn's anatomy, these should work fine now."

"*Should?*"

Lyman hit a latch and the bottom of the *Sarah A*'s cabin fell free. "'Should' meaning I don't know if it'll work with us both."

"Wait a min—"

But, again, I was too late. He grabbed me around the waist and threw us out the hatch. Soon as we cleared, the wings unfolded and, instead of dropping fast, we only sorta fell leisurely. I held on to my lunatic brother as he guided us down.

Lyman twisted around so we could watch what happened next.

Just as he described in his vision, Noqi held up a hand. A piece of jewelry reflected off the sun and a beam of yellow light shot out, enveloping the *Sarah A*.

Only, the burning monoplane didn't blow up right away. It kept coming at the gambling god. His eyes grew large enough to be seen from where we floated. He spun around and ran. But as if *Sarah* had a mind of her own, she seemed to track right after him. The creatures, not understanding, at first, what was gonna happen, finally noticed the flaming ball coming down at them. They fought to get clear, too, but they couldn't scatter fast enough.

When the *Sarah A* hit, she exploded magnificently. The crates of ammo ignited and bullets shot out from the fireball she'd created.

We couldn't tell if we'd gotten Noqi in the blast, but there was no sign of him when the dust settled, just dissolving monsters. I doubted somethin' like that could kill a god. I wasn't no priest, so I rightly couldn't tell you. He was gone, though, as were all his pets.

The totem demons in Drowned Horse returned to their hole, which closed up and disappeared, as if had never been there. We landed—not a good landing, mind you—but no need to see the doctor nevertheless.

Later, as we took stock of everything, Sheriff Patrick doubted they'd seen the last of Noqi or his curse.

"He'll be back. He wants all of us as slaves for some reason. Somethin' to do with our souls havin' been prepped."

I nodded. I'd been to war. Leaders never gave up while there were still souls to expend. Darcy slid under the good arm of Sheriff Patrick.

Hal, walking around the Sagebrush, picked up scattered poker chips that had been left by players who fled when the attack had first happened. He winked at Diaz, who straightened up around the bar, saying "Finders keepers" or somethin' to that affect.

As we prepared to leave town on horseback, the *Sarah A*'s remains buried under the Arizona sand, Lyman said goodbye to Caitlyn and I shook Maher's hand.

"And I thought I was the craziest gambler this side of the Mighty Miss." He nodded toward Lyman. "I hope he keeps winning. Losing seems, well . . . painful."

I agreed. "Some bets pay off, though. And he's a genius."

"I hate geniuses normally," Maher admitted. "Luck isn't a set of numbers. It's a feeling."

I knew what he meant. But he didn't know my brother. Profit or not, he stacked the cards in his favor.

Sheriff Patrick came to see us off.

"You gonna rebuild her?" he asked Lyman.

"Most certainly. You saw her fly, right? She was a thing of beauty. Everything I ever dreamed of."

The sheriff nodded. "Well, you better hurry. Had us a patent official out here not too long ago. Talked of a couple brothers who were also tinkerin' with some flying thingamajig back east."

That frightened Lyman more than an ancient being of immense power.

"Charles! We must board the first train heading west." He motioned to me as he steered his horse away from town. "Come now! The race is on!"

I tipped my hat to the Sheriff and followed after my brother, still too smart and focused for his own good . . . nor mine.

Humanity is at war with the insectoid alien K'trag'vah, and things are not going well. No, not at all. Fortunately, unbeknownst to us mere mortals, we've got a god—er, goddess—looking out for us. The feline goddess Bast, to be exact. She's got a penchant for John Wayne impersonations and the old Tom Corbett—Space Cadet television series. And though it might pain her to admit it, she's got a soft spot for us humans, too. Good thing for us!

Too Many Gods

Hank Davis

It was a bright and sunny day, oh blissful cliché, though the UV was unsentimentally and efficiently blocked by the transparent canopy over the slidewalk, and I was just too damned cheerful. *Get a grip, you goofy goddess*, I told myself once more.

The job hadn't even started—or gotten off the ground, I thought, and immediately regretted that metaphor—and I was enjoying things much too much. This was no time for *oh, boy, oh, boy, oh, boy!* Nor *oh, girl!* either.

There were bad guys, or gals, or gods, or demons, or *somethings* at work and didn't I know there was a war on? Whoever was wearing the black hats, I was supposed to locate 'em and put a spanner in their works.

At that, I mentally paused to remember if the mortals in this century still used spanners, then recalled, of course they did.

While there were sophisticated high-tech substitutes available, those gizmos need a power supply, had moving parts that could jam or break, and they aren't much use as a weapon in a pinch. Or a punch.

Humans aren't far enough from the caves yet, Ra bless 'em, to have lost the need, not to mention the affection, for, a club, even a small one, that they can use to bonk competing critters, either of other species or their own, on the skull as needed.

They might go through periods of peace that foster self-delusion, and think they can do without weapons, but the deep down underape

213

programming is still there, and comes out when it's a matter of survival, particularly in a time of war. Like the war Earth was in right now.

(Fortunately, cats aren't prone to such self-delusion. Keep your claws sharp and ready, I say.)

All that drugstore philosophy (that dates me; try and find a drugstore nowadays!) went through my brain in less time than it takes to tell, and then it was processed and filed away, and I was back to enjoying the daylights out of where I was and what I was doing. Which was impatiently not just standing, but unnecessarily *walking*—well, make that *striding*—on the moving slidewalk to get there faster and board a ship of war.

A *spaceship* of war, of course. While there were still warships patrolling the seas, they spent too much time below the surface to be considered *on* the high seas, and besides this conflict didn't presently fit their job description. Not unless the battle Out There went belly-up even worse than it already was doing.

I've been on spacecraft before, of course, on near-Earth, interplanetary, and interstellar types, but I still get excited at the thought of going Out There. Thank you, humans, thank you, thank you. We immortals might eventually have gotten around to getting Out There, but when you have eternity unless a meaner, tougher immortal takes an unfriendly interest in your career, you may figure there's no rush, and what are a few centuries between friends, anyway?

Of course, *I'm* impatient, thanks to my feline nature—I want to climb that damned tree *now*, and who's worried about how I'll get down later?—but that impatience also keeps me from learning, for example, the complex and rarefied mathematics that leads to spaceflight. Humans, with their mayfly lifespans, paradoxically are better at concentrating on such things. They may not be proficient at waiting on a mouse to come out of its hole, but they certainly do have their uses.

And thanks to them, I was heading out to metaphorically clamber up the tallest of metaphorical trees. And wouldn't have to worry about getting down again. Like the recruiting motto for the Solar Fleet says, *Find your destiny beyond the stars.* Not that destiny is something you need to find, as if you could lose it, but it sounds so cool!

(Of course, on this job I *might* have to worry about coming back at all . . .)

Through the clear shell over the slidewalk, I could see the surrounding metal forest of towering ships, waiting to be launched. They were mostly ground-to-orbit shuttles, intra solar liners and cargo ships, but still they went up, way up, a cat's favorite direction (not counting whichever direction led to a plate of fresh tuna). Up and out.

Tom Corbett, thou shouldst be with us in this hour! I remembered watching the TV show a couple of centuries back, secretly in case my rotten sister goddess Sekhmet noticed and gave me a hard time after all the sneering I'd done at her for being a movie and TV addict, and then I realized I was softly singing the show's theme song, *From the rocket fields of the Academy/To the far-flung stars of outer space*, and reluctantly stopped. It might attract attention by itself, but I was being still more conspicuous by unconsciously purring along with it, in a monotone but keeping the rhythm.

I really didn't want to have to explain to Amun-Ra that I had blown the assignment by being caught purring.

The humans would probably think I was an alien in disguise, and while that was true for certain values of "alien," I was as much a native of Earth as they were. More so, if time in grade is counted. Did you latecomers take time off to watch the pyramids being built? (And do it without doing a single time hop.) Want to know the songs the workmen sang, eh?

But I'd probably purr in time to those, too, so I went forward with no music to lift my spirits. (Did they need lifting? Well . . .) But even so, thinking about the situation, about zooming, yes, *zooming* up and out there, past where the planets hurtle around, past where the frozen comets glide slowly by, past where even the Sun's gravity has any authority (I'd better not mention *that* thought to Amun-Ra), out where . . . oops!

I was doing Tom Corbett's theme song again—*Up in the sky/Rocketing past/Higher than high/Faster than fast!*—and purring to beat the band, as if I needed a band, and instead of striding briskly along at a proper military pace, I was *skipping!* Better get a grip, girl!

Besides, I was running out of things to be zooming up past. And my stop was approaching. Definitely time to get a grip. But keep the claws sheathed and out of sight, please.

The slidewalk branched ahead, and a hologuide was hovering in midair, just under the overhead canopy, changing colors to make it harder to miss, and an arrow blinking on one side with the words *Duke of Wayne* under it. Music went away, and I had a new problem. I didn't need to speak to anyone for a few minutes, but the ship's security wouldn't be entirely dependent on electronics (and nearly all the humans' gadgets are my kittens, so to purr, er, speak) and now I was wondering if I could avoid sounding like *the* Duke, pilgrim. The ship was named after a Brit war hero of the late twenty-first century, but those words reminded me of a cinematic hero of the previous century.

The security checkpoint was ahead, the moment of truth was upon me, and we gods don't handle truth any better than the mortals, so I was going with something much more reliable and useful: *fraud.*

Being suspicious is a feline trait, and this time it happened to be a survival trait. When I was still five meters away from the checkpoint, just past where the slidewalk stopped sliding and changed to stationary plasteel, I halted, and reached inside my shoulder bag for my I.D., and said a silent *hi* to the base computer.

But what it replied was, somewhat approximately, *Who are you? How did you do that? Guards! Guards!*

Well, that was a free translation of its internal language, but this wasn't the droid I was looking for. And it was starting to yell for help. Fortunately, though computer thoughts are far faster than the human sort (when the mortals bother to actually *think*, that is), they're not as fast as god-thoughts, and I cut off the alarms before matters could get embarrassing. I reached invisibly inside the momentarily stifled robot, saw my identification wasn't where I had snuck it in the week before, and slapped it in again.

And it disappeared again.

This definitely was *not* my day, but nothing I couldn't handle . . . so far.

I found the program that was eating my phony identity verification file as fast as I could put it in and squeezed it until it *popped*, virtually speaking, and my fake identity stayed put.

By now, I was in full force ten paranoid mode, so I also checked the ship's computer, and it didn't know me from Adam Link either. I squelched its duplicated attempts to yell *hey, rube!* and checked its cyberterrain. Yep, another file-eating program.

About that time, a spanking new file-eater showed up in the base's network. I gave both those upstarts a squeeze and *pop* treatment, and this time I also added a couple of carnivorous programs of my own, sort of like virtual Bengal tigers crossed with sabretooths, plus a dash of piranha and just a hint of hungry T-Rex thrown in, then told them to guard my files with their pseudo-lives.

Fortunately, all this razzle-dazzle took only a couple of seconds in mortal-perceived time, and I was now walking toward the checkpoint, my I.D. stick now out of the shoulder pouch and in my left hand, active and ready to be verified.

Being verified was something I hadn't expected to be so complicated. Just a little manipulation of a computer or two, and then I'd be on board, ready to start the mission. Instead, I'd had to call in my shock troops right off the bat. I really didn't need this, particularly since constant concentration was also needed to keep my human appearance locked down. It was no time suddenly to have slit eyes and pointed ears.

Oh, well. Eternal vigilance is the price of goddesshood.

Salutes and good mornings were exchanged, then I held out my stick containing my short but promising fictional career. The lieutenant (j.g.) with the I.D. reader touched it to my stick and he said, "Check," then said, "With your permission, Ensign Corbett," and touched it to the back of my hand to do a DNA reading. Of course, my DNA couldn't pass for human on a fogbound and moonless midnight during a planetwide power failure, but that didn't matter as long as his reader was linked to the base computer, and the base computer was my bitch again.

At that point, I checked in with my cyberkitty, and saw it had its virtual paws full, so I gave it a couple more cybertroops as backup, then did the same for its counterpart in the ship's internal cyberverse, though that one so far wasn't under siege.

Even so, all was well so far, and the man said, "You check out, and I've confirmed your name on the roster. Welcome aboard, Ensign Thomasina Davina Corbett." At that formal statement of approval, the pair of armed troopers on each side of him kept their heat rifles at port arms, but relaxed slightly. I said, "Thank you, sir," put the stick away, snapped the case shut, saluted smartly again, then headed up the ramp to the ship entrance. I stepped through and was aboard the good ship *Duke of Wayne*, pilgrim. (*Shut up!*)

And then I could take a moment, or at least half a mo', to wonder just what in Hell, or other name for the Underworld, was going on!

At least now, I had some facts I hadn't had before, and I had damned near zero facts before this happened.

What we knew was that ships of the Solar Fleet, even the powerful "Boomer" warships, were losing fights with the weaker, slower, less well-armed ships of the K'trag'vah forces. And my job was to find out why and do something about it.

And right here on Earth, in a center of the planet's military forces, somebody was playing puppet master, jerking the strings of the base computer as if that somebody was the owner and sole proprietor. Which didn't make any sense.

If the K'trags had that much power, they shouldn't be engaging the Earth's ships at all. Just tell the shipcomps to open all the ports and vents to vacuum at once, then either jettison the crew's corpses and refit the ship for insectile nonhuman users, or just head straight to Earth in their own ships and do similar party tricks with the homeworld's defense computer network. So why were they still fighting Out There instead of dictating surrender terms right here?

I saluted a number of ranking officers I passed in the ship's corridors (a Boomer is a *big* ship!) and lift and drop tubes, on the way to my assigned quarters. (Checked with the ship computer and the room, okay stateroom, was still assigned to me.) Then I saw who was walking in my direction and alarm bells went off. Silent ones, of course.

I halted, delivered a textbook salute, and said "Good morning, Ma'am." It was the ship's captain, and why, oh why did her name have to be *Strong*? The same last name as Tom Corbett's captain, so of course I had to strangle the TV show's theme *and* my purr function without anything showing on my face, not to mention keeping that face (and eyes! And ears) human-looking.

Okay, she was a woman, not a man, her first name was Karina, not Steve, and this ship was not named *Polaris*. So *puh-leeze stifle that nostalgia spasm. Bast-brain!*

Captain Strong (*different Strong altogether! Be strong and don't purr in front of Captain Strong!*) looked at my face while returning my salute, glanced at my name strip as her hand reached her forehead, then back at my face, as the hand snapped down.

"Good morning, Ensign Corbett," she said, looking at me with more attention than I liked. "I recognize your face from the shipcomp's file photos. I was checking on our new personnel, and was looking at your photo when something odd happened. Your file disappeared, and the computer suddenly was indicating that you weren't assigned to the *Wayne* after all. But a second later, your file was back and your assignment was confirmed. Any idea how that could happen?"

Oh, suffering sardines! I had thought I had covered my traces too quickly for anyone to notice, but the human element had tripped me up.

"That *is* very odd, Ma'am," I replied in a properly respectful tone, "but I don't know how it could happen. Of course, my MOS does involve computers, but not doing much more than the basics of troubleshooting them." Time for a fib. "I didn't have any difficulty checking in a few minutes ago, if that fact helps."

She frowned. "If we didn't have to lift ship in an hour, I'd have the shipcomp gone over with the proverbial fine-toothed comb, and maybe a new one installed, but time's too short—"

And I'd also have you *and your record gone over with an electron microscope,* I was sure she was thinking.

"—but I'm forgetting my manners. Welcome aboard, Ensign Corbett and I'm sure you'll be a credit to the *Wayne*, judging from your record aboard *Valentina Tereshkova*."

She was obviously on her way, so I thanked her, said something about being glad to have her confidence in me, and how I hoped to live up to it, and gave another textbook salute, which she returned, then walked off, moving along very quickly for someone with only two legs.

I resumed heading for my quarters, on the way checking once again to make sure I was still assigned to the ship and that room was still assigned to me. The door recognized me and slid open. As it closed behind me, I took a deep breath, and made sure I remembered to let it out again, then changed the couch to a bed, er bunk, curled up on it, and tried to calm down enough to do some thinking.

I could do better thinking if I could pace, or at least it seemed that way to me, but to pace properly, I'd have to go to four legs, and a lashing tail, and now was neither the time nor the place to take a chance on being seen in an alternate shape. So I continued to lie there and made do with a few pathetic body twitches.

Anybody seeing me, and I suspected that at least one someone was, would think I had a severe itch and must desperately need a bath. And that would help with the twitches, but I had a more feline bath in mind, and the uniform would get in the way, even though I had opted for the regulation skirt instead of the regulation slacks, but there were still the blouse, undies, stockings, and, oh, yes, those spit-shined boots.

Robes are simpler, but I have to admit the mortals way outdo us when it comes to snappy dressing.

At that point, the welcoming committee arrived. I heard them on the other side of the door, of course, "heard" in more ways than mere sonics, and while the bunk changed back to a couch, I opened the door to let them in.

We relaxed on the couch. The ginger-colored tabby was very glad to see me, and, after some formal head-bumping, immediately curled up next to me, careful not to shed hair on my uniform, and purred like an old-fashioned air conditioner going full tilt on the hottest day of August. The cream and brown Siamese stood on dignity, though the look it gave me was coolly respectful. I was informed that the third ship's cat (it was a *big* ship), a merely male Maine Coon, was in the ship's library three decks down, with no easy way to get here and welcome the boss aboard. If he operated the lift tube by himself, he might be seen, making the observing mortal uneasy. They also informed me that the humans called him Milford, and the tabby and Siamese were addressed as Corona and Yula. I already knew their real feline names, of course.

My secret agents reported in a way that a hidden sound pickup, or spybeam couldn't overhear, informing me that everything on board was as normal and efficient as could be expected with a bunch of ape-descendants in charge. "Good," I said, "and there are no enemy agents on board?"

Silence.

"Let's try that again. I am an undercover agent, but not an enemy. Is there anybody besides me on board who isn't what they're supposed to be?"

Silence.

"Hey, kids, you're supposed to be cats, not method actors. Including me, if that's what it takes to get an answer, is there anybody or anything on the ship that isn't what it or they appear to be?"

Silence, and this time I noticed that the tabby had quit purring and the Siamese was taking an unexpected interest in the pic of the late, great Admiral Hyman G. Rickover on the wall. Uh-oh.

"Now hear this, fuzzballs. This is your goddess speaking. Has anyone put a command of silence on you?"

The tabby resumed purring and the Siamese's eyes met mine again. The answer was in the affirmative. That was a slight relief. Bad enough to have somebody able to influence cats—*cats!*—operating here, but at least they hadn't blocked *all* possible avenues of inquiry. But did that indicate a limitation of their power or only that they hadn't bothered to be thorough?

"Okay, boys and girls—" the Siamese gave me one of *those* looks, since all hands (or paws) present were female "—try this one. Besides me, is there anyone on board the ship who looks human, but isn't?"

More silence. As it happened, just then I had to send in more reinforcements against a new cyberattack on my identity. No rest for the wicked.

Once the virtual assault had been slapped down yet again, I considered another question, but decided instead to see about removing the compulsion an unknown outsider had placed on my faithful furry followers. I had been feeling the outlines of it as I played cross-examiner, and thought I had a fix on its shape, so I grabbed on at what seemed to be a likely weak point and tried lifting it.

Didn't work, but I had felt something that last time. I couldn't believe it at first, but there it was. The compulsion had an off-switch.

Not physical, of course, and it wasn't obvious at a glance. Didn't have a flashing red light and a neon OFF sign, but when you've been knocking around for a few millennia, you learn to be observant. You also learn to be suspicious. Might be a trap.

I examined it for a few mortal minutes—long enough for an immortal to write a trilogy, or compose a symphony, or draw a bunch of inside straights—and couldn't see a danger. Didn't mean there wasn't one, of course.

"I hope this won't hurt, kids," I said silently, and tripped the *off* trigger on the Siamese. (Okay, so I liked the tabby's attitude a little better. Goddesses deserve respect! That's why they're called goddesses.)

She hissed and turned around a couple of times, examining the room with narrowed slit eyes. She wanted to seriously *hurt* somebody and was making sure they weren't hiding under the couch or in the wasteburner. But she wasn't mad at *me*, just wanted to rip out the throat of whoever had put the compulsion on her. I'd second the motion whenever I—well, *we*—located them.

And then there was a hissing, not at all feline, and very loud. A few papers on the table by the couch fluttered toward the ventilation grid, and the air pressure in the room was dropping rapidly. No alarm had gone off, but I wasn't sure that the ship's programming allowed for one when the ship was parked Earthside and explosive decompression was supposedly impossible.

I didn't need air, but my shock troops did, so I used a minor spell to hold a bubble of it around the couch, then checked in with the virtual shipscape. I reversed the order I found for the ship's ventilation to vacuum-pack my room and its occupants, and air came flowing back in. Then I erased all record that what had just happened, had happened, also setting yet another cyberguardian to make sure that there was no repeat performance. I magicked the formerly flying papers back to the table in a neat stack, though I'd have to look through them later to make sure they were in order, then went back to where I was before the uncouth interruption.

"Your turn, girl," I said and released the tabby. She didn't hiss, but her size almost doubled as her fur rose, and her just-resumed purrrrr abruptly turned into a low-pitched menacing growl that would have rattled the windows if the room had any. The "M" on her forehead obviously stood for *mayhem*!

"Right, kids, blood and battle is more than justified, and it just went on the menu. But right now, is there anyone besides me on the ship who looks human but isn't?"

There was, indeed, and they described him. I was taken aback. So much so that I momentarily forgot to keep watching for a repetition of the ventilation attack, or some new threat. Fortunately, there wasn't one.

"*Him*? But he should be on our side! Why did he put compulsions on you?"

I hadn't really intended that as a question, since they probably wouldn't know, but—

"*He* didn't put the evil eye on you, kids? Then who did?"

Back to silence. There was another layer of compulsion on my good and faithful quadrupedal troops. A goddess's work is never done, and I prepared to remove this one, too, but just then the shipcom came on, calling all the officers to the bridge. It was time to lift ship.

An ensign wouldn't be at the controls, of course, except possibly to be trained, and besides my assumed Military Occupational Specialty was in commo, nowhere near piloting, navigation, gunnery, and like that, but there were formalities to be observed, and my assumed persona was expected to observe them. Not a problem, since I was sure that the other interloper on board would also be an officer, and I'd want to see if I could spot him amid the genuine ape spawn.

And just maybe, for bonus points, I could spot the third disguised entity, if that one was also on board.

I slid the door open, looked out to make sure nobody was looking, then sent the partial contingent of ship's cats to their appointed rounds. I made a mental note to drop by the library and release the Maine Coon from his compulsion. I didn't want to risk doing it from a distance, particularly now that I knew about that second layer of compulsion.

My cover was that I was newly assigned to the *Duke of Wayne* (Pil—*shut up!*), but my previous berth was aboard another Boomer, *Valentina Tereshkova*, so I would know the basic layout of the *Wayne* (I tried not to think "pilgrim," and failed again), and could reach the bridge swiftly, efficiently, and not once stopping to ask somebody, "Where the expletive deleted am I?" Actually, the ship's cats on both ships had given me thorough reports on the whichway of the where, and I had all the little fiddling differences between them down cold. (After all, the *Wayne* was a much newer ship, pilgrim—*cut that out!*—with many improvements, some of which might actually *be* improvements.) So, I was not the last officer to report to the bridge.

In fact, I was already there when the other fraudulent officer arrived, spotted me, and winked after making sure he wasn't being observed by any of the mortals. He was passing for a lieutenant, junior grade, which meant that he outranked me. That didn't bother me, since I sure as Duat or Sheol or whoever wasn't going to take any orders from *him*. Not in *my* chain of command, pilgrim! (*Oops!*) And as an ensign, I was less likely to get caught not knowing my lines.

Last time I saw him, he had been a dead ringer for Arnold Schwarzenegger, but since on that occasion, we were in the nineteenth century A.D., there was no security problem involved. Now, his face was looking like a cross between Charles Atlas and Steve Reeves, and below the neck the apparatus continued in that vein. He did have a thing for being a muscleman, though muscle size doesn't mean that much to an immortal. We're all very strong for entirely different reasons.

Neither of us tried to get closer to the other, but just took our seats as they melted up out of the deck, Ensigns in the back row, of course. Then Captain Karina G. Strong walked in, a commander standing on one side barked, "*Aaa-ten-shun!*" and we all stood up again.

Captain Strong said, "Ladies and gentlemen, please be seated and at ease. I'm not going to repeat what you've already been repeatedly briefed on, but I do want to emphasize again that ships of the Solar Fleet, like this one, the sort the newshawks call "Boomers," should have the enemy outmaneuvered, outgunned, and just about every other "out," including blowing them out of space, and yet they keep losing battles with the K'trag'yah ships. We can't rule out sabotage or enemy infiltration, even though we can't see how an enemy looking so unlike humans, so much like insects, could infiltrate or get where they could sabotage anything. As you know, our best guess is human traitors aboard Solar ships. I hate to think that's even possible . . ."

She paused slightly and looked in my direction. *Uh-oh*, I thought, *I'm probably a suspect because my file flickered.*

"—but we can't rule out the possibility, particularly since it's the only believable one we have so far. So be watchful. If you notice something odd, report it immediately. Don't try to take action on your own unless it absolutely looks like the ship is immediately endangered by what you have seen."

That would make my job harder. *Oh well, if being a goddess was easy, even a* mortal *could do it.*

"I know most of you quite well, and those I don't already know have impressive records. It will be a privilege and an honor to lead you into battle."

She had started to turn her gaze in my direction again at "those I don't already know," but may have changed her mind, and returned to looking straight ahead.

Now, she turned to the commander and said, "Take her up, Mr. Cary." To the assembled officers, she said, "Please remain seated during the liftoff," then turned and walked forward to the captain's chair.

Practically speaking, we could all have gone to our duty posts, or our quarters if off-duty, since the ship's sublight drive would have no acceleration effects, no bouncing around, and we might as well be in a holo-simulator. But there were rituals to observe, and even aside from that, I'd rather be watching the deck to overhead viewscreen than the much smaller one on my room's wall, er, stateroom's bulkhead. So I watched the base fall away, then the Earth, becoming curved, shrinking to a blue sphere with white clouds, then the homeworld falling away like a dropped marble as the *Wayne* kept accelerating. I regretted that the moon was on the other side of Earth from our path outward (we cats do love the moon and its light), then we went hyperlight and the screen went dark.

There was a *shushing* sound as most of us, even some old hands, let out a breath. Then "*Dismissed*" was barked, and I jumped a little. I was glad to see that a certain musclebound lieutenant (j.g.) also jumped. I stood up, and my chair started melting back into the deck.

That lieutenant (j.g.) was out the door ahead of me, but I managed to get next to him as we headed down the corridor. "Too bad we won't be going by your planet. You could wave," I communicated to him in a way that the mortals couldn't overhear; nor, I hoped, their machines.

"Mars?" he answered, just as discreetly. "That dried-out dwarf world? It wasn't my idea that the ancients saw its red color and figured the god of war had something to do with it. *Blood and gore, we want more!*" he chanted quietly. "Actually, a really successful war wouldn't kill anybody on either side. One side would either outnumber the other so drastically, that the weaker side would surrender, with no fighting—"

"And be stripped of all their wealth and possessions and sold into slavery. And the women would be—"

"Not my fault," he said. "Those crazy mortals are so unreasonable, and then they blame it all on us. But, as I was about to say, the alternative is that both sides are evenly matched, meaning that only luck would decide the outcome. No good general would depend on luck, so they would both go home and raise taxes for defense. Grubby little rascals do love to raise taxes."

"Or if each side thinks it's superior to the other," I said, "true or untrue, and don't realize their mistake until battle is joined? Not to mention that one or both sides might think they have a god on their side."

"Hah! How often will *that* happen? But enough of our old arguments—"

"Good point," I said. "I assume you're not here to sabotage the ship—"

"Of course not! I'm from Earth just like you and this whole crew, even those once removed, coming from colony planets. Why should I help the 'Trags?"

"I was thinking that myself. But why did Zeus send a war god on a mission that might require subtlety?"

Ares, also known as Mars, made a rude (but silent) noise. "If I recall correctly, you're a war god yourself, Bast baby. Besides I can be subtle when the situation calls for it, and a pounce-and-kill feline attack might not work here."

I decided to let that one go. "Let's call a truce on the invective and compare notes,"

"Them's my sentiments, exactly," he said. "Let's head for my quarters. I'll put out a nice saucer of warm milk for you."

"Thanks for the hospitality, but I've been lapping up Maker's Mark bourbon lately. The old brands are the best. Of course, once we're there, you can get into a skirt and be closer to your old classic duds."

"Kittens do have claws. Deck six, room 209. We should go separately now that the captain has asked everybody to spy on everybody else. Drop by in fifteen." And he walked off, ahead of me, heading for a droptube, not waiting for my agreement, and before I could quip about having a hot date in ten minutes, how about we meet in twenty? Oh, well, I'd save that one for later.

To anyone watching us, our temporary proximity would seem accidental, and no mortal could have overheard our conversation. I hoped the unknown adversary or adversaries couldn't, either.

I decided the least suspicious thing to do was to go back to my stateroom for ten, then use the remaining five to navigate to— hmmm, I had neglected to get a look at whatever alias Ares was using. Anyway, to go to his quarters. But when the door to my own digs slid open, I saw Commander Stringfellow sitting on the couch.

Oh, Hell, I thought, *what's the procedure now?* I snapped to attention as the door slid closed behind me, and said, "Hello, sir," and hoped that was the correct response.

"At ease, Ensign Corbett. And please take a seat here, if you'll forgive the questionable manners of offering you a seat on your own couch." He was standing now, I guessed for ingrained old-fashioned politeness toward ladies, my lower rank notwithstanding.

"Thank you, sir," I said, and sat down, then waited for him to continue the conversation.

"This is not an official visit, Corbett," he began, and I wondered if that meant I should take off my clothes. "I had been looking over the files of new ship personnel and noticed that your previous post was on the *Valentina Tereshkova*. I have a couple of friends on that ship and was wondering if you knew them."

Uh-oh. "I was only on the ship for a six-month tour, sir," I lied, then told the truth: "And like all Boomers, like the *Wayne*, the *Kova* is a very big ship. What are their names, sir?"

"I'm frequently reminded of how big the *Wayne* is, Miss Corbett, and I'll not be surprised if the names of Bao Fan Ling and Venadim Davidoff are not familiar to you."

I really didn't need any more *uh-oh* moments, but here was another one. I had memorized the entire cast of characters serving on the *Kova*, along with detailed bios of a few low-ranking officers just in case something like this came up, and while Gospadin Davidoff wasn't one of the above (much too high a rank for me to have been a pal, if I had actually been on board), there was no Bao Fan Ling listed in the crew roster. What's more, the three names were all traditional Chinese girl's *given* names, an unlikely combination. Test, trap, or trick, my fur would have bristled, if I had a true feline complement on hand, er, body.

"I'm afraid they are not familiar to me, sir. I recall hearing the name of Commander Davidoff, but don't believe I ever actually met or spoke to him. He considerably outranked me, of course, and the *Kova* is—"

"A very big ship," he broke in, and stood up, and I did, too. "I thought it was worth asking you. I need to attend to my duties—"

From which you took time to ask meaningless questions of the newest, lowest-ranking officer on board? I thought, managing not to let my suspicion reach my face.

"—so I have to be going, but welcome aboard, Ensign Corbett." He headed for the door, but stopped and turned, then said, "Oh, by the way. I was looking at your personnel file. Nothing to do with you, I was trying to familiarize myself with the faces and names of the new officers before departure, and something very odd happened."

"My file disappeared momentarily, sir, then reappeared?" I asked, then said, as his eyebrows went up, "Captain Strong mentioned that to me earlier, sir. It does sound odd, but I have no idea why it happened."

"Probably just a computer hiccup," he said. "Clear vacuum, Ms. Corbett." The door slid shut behind him.

I stood there a minute, wondering WTF? When he should have been reasonably far away, unless he was lurking outside, I headed for the door, wondering if I should warn Ares about expecting his own dubious social visit . . . or inquisition.

I reached his stateroom, about eight minutes later than the time he had set, but then I hadn't agreed to it, anyway. Still, I said, "I would have been here sooner, but—"

"Just as well you weren't," Ares said. "Commander Stringfellow decided to drop by for a chat, and just left a couple of minutes before you showed up."

"Huh? I mean—well, I do mean *huh*! You did say *Commander Stringfellow* was here? As in, *him*?" I said causing an image of that worthy to appear in the air in front of Ares' face. (Need I mention that no human, if one were in the room, or ship's visual pickup would have detected it, nor would our conversation have been audible? I didn't think so.)

"Yes, him. What's the problem? Do you have the hots for a mortal again?"

"Unless the commander is twins, or can do a time hop, at least one of us was not being welcomed aboard just now by him. Maybe both were fakes."

"He visited you, too?"

"At the same time," I emphasized. Just then I finally took notice of the name strip on his tunic. "Pupp? You're calling yourself *Pupp*?"

He grinned and said, "Sorry if the caninicity bothers you. I figured if I was going to be an offissa here, I'd be Offissa Pupp. as in—"

"I'm familiar with the comic strip," I said, wishing I could borrow a brick from Ignatz Mouse. But he probably wouldn't want to cooperate with another kat, er, cat, any more than with Krazy.

"I always did suspect you were the inspiration for Star of the East," he said, smirking.

"Not guilty," I said. Actually it had been my sister, Sekhmet, but I wasn't going into *that* now.

"Speaking of aliases," he said, "your take on Tom Corbett is a cutie, but why a middle name of "Davina"?

"Feminine version of "David," I said. "We need to talk—"

"Oh, yes, your old boyfriend. How was he in bed?"

"None of your beeswax. And that's no way to talk about a king, even one who didn't lose sleep about keeping it in his *simlāh*."

"Lost sleep for other reasons, eh?" he said, smirking again.

"Get serious! I've had several cyberattacks on my ship's personnel file. Have you had your files disappear and—"

"Why should that happen. I magicked the file into the base and ship's computers just as I came aboard, and—" He got a faraway look on his beefy mug for a second, then said, "That's odd, it's gone."

"*You mean, you hadn't even checked on it*?!" I managed to get out before the door slid open and Commander Stringfellow came through, burner in hand, accompanied by the same two armed guards who had helped welcome me aboard.

I didn't see any point to adding, *You idiot!* so I settled for another *uh-oh.* But I put plenty of vitriol into it.

"So you both are here," said Commander Stringfellow, if it actually was Stringfellow and he actually was a commander. Or was even human. "Come along to the brig, and don't try anything. We have a few questions to ask you."

"Aren't you going to read us our rights?" I said.

"Read *what*?" the maybe commander said.

"Sorry, wrong century," I said. Noticing that the guards with heat rifles leveled at us looked puzzled and nervous at the same time, I decided to shut up for the moment. I doubted those weapons could kill me or Ares, but I was sure they would hurt a lot. I also thought Ares might cause a scene, but instead we both went along quietly . . . for the time being, at least in my case.

They separated us in different cells in the brig. I barely had time to consider my next move, even thinking at immortal brain-speed, before they came and got me again and I was walked to a section obviously made for interrogation. They seated me in an endurosteel chair bolted to the deck, with my arms cuffed to its arms and my ankles cuffed to its front legs, and I decided to put up with that for the moment. The two guards were standing on both sides, with their weapons at port arms again.

Good form, but bad idea, Mr. and Ms., I thought. *I can move* much *faster than you.*

In front of me was a wall of transparent metal and on the other side of it were Karina Strong, looking very captainlike and determined. Commander Whoever-the-Hell-he-really-was sat behind her, which I didn't like at all. Executive Officer Caroline Dale (not Joan, fortunately for my sanity), the ship's head medical officer, "Bones" Schosser, head of security, Lieutenant Stiles, and four more guards with the ever-popular heat rifles were also present. Tom Corbett never had this big a cast in his TV show, but then his show didn't have the budget for it.

The door behind the brass and guards opened and a midshipman came through. From his file photo, I recognized Ted Kaylor, the ship's head librarian. A Maine Coon trotted majestically in behind him, almost at his heels, and I suspected that the cluster of ape descendants were somehow not noticing him, Kaylor included, or Milford would have been promptly ejected back into the corridor. He stood at attention, tail up, for a moment, staring at me, and I greeted him silently and hit the "off" switch on his outer compulsion. Fortunately, he was aware now was not the time to growl, hiss, or even grumble, and kept silent. But he was, of course, angry and out for blood, just as my other furry warriors had been. When one or more of the ship's cats caught up with who- or *whatever* had put the compulsions on them, he, she, or it had better be in possession of weaponry or a good pair of track shoes.

Captain Strong's lips moved and sound came out of hidden soundplaques on my side of the barrier. "I will address you as Ensign Corbett for the time being, though I seriously doubt you're entitled to that rank, and have similar doubts about that being your real name."

She's right, you know, I thought, wondering if I was here because I had been caught in Ares's quarters, or if I had also slipped up somewhere. Make that *Pupp's* quarters. Offissa Pupp didn't cover his tracks like a good huntin' dawg would. Cor blimey!

"So, Ms. Corbett, did you have any interesting experiences while you were serving aboard the good ship *Lollipop*?"

That really interrupted my defamatory musings about Ares, er, Pupp. "I don't understand, Ma'am." I recognized that ship's name—my rotten sister and marathon movie watcher Sekkie had sung the song often enough while I was in earshot—but I doubted Strong would get the reference.

"And when you were aboard the *Pinafore*, and were decorated for your valor in the battle with the pirates in Penzance, did you neglect to receive your medal? You aren't wearing it now."

I was having enough trouble keeping my jaw from dropping to the deck without also losing hold of my human seeming, but even immortals aren't completely dim, and I checked on a suspicion—

"Not to mention your other decoration for conspicuous gallantry aboard *Dauntless* in pitched battle with the Boskonian pirates."

—and when I checked, the suspicion was appallingly confirmed. My fake personnel file was still in place and intact, guarded by my cybertroops, but there were, oh bloody Hell, *Ten* other personnel files, all different, all ridiculous, and Captain Strong hadn't gotten around to the *really* wacko ones, as when I came over on the *Mayflower*, or the time I took over as Magellan's second-in-command and finished the mission when the cap'n was killed by hostile moonshiners, who mistook him for a revenoo'er, or when I served on the *Polaris* with my bother Tom, but was knocked up by Roger—Roger!—and washed out of the Solar Guard's Space Cadets.

I hadn't even thought to check for the possibility of *extra* personnel files. Ares/Pupp wasn't the only idiot in this mission team. Not that we were a team.

"Since shipcomp had no record of most of these vessels you had supposedly served on, though I did recognize the confused *Pinafore* reference—"

Two centuries and change later, and my captain was a Gilbert and Sullivan fan? All *right*!

"—so I called in Mr. Kaylor, who clarified the other vessels's names, such as *Lollipop*—"

The captain shook her head, and I suspected was barely suppressing a smile. I was beginning to wish I were actually serving under this lady, but that was impossible of course, even if the situation weren't desperate. Ra would never green light such moonlighting.

"—and the other ships appear in ancient history, or works of fiction, though there was a missile named 'Polaris' during one of the less pleasant periods of the twentieth century. So, since your swarm of personnel files are self-contradictory, Ms. Corbett, and all but one are ridiculous, and that one disappeared mysteriously, then returned, I ask you, *who* are you and *why* are you here?"

Okay, the mission was shot, and Ra was gonna kill me—well, make me wish I *could* be killed, anyway—so when all else fails, and there's nothing more to lose, tell the truth. The ship was going into battle, and it was no time for me to put an amnesia compulsion or any other kind on officers who would need clear heads and no holes in their memory. Particularly *these* officers. But first, I took a look at the captain and tried to look trustworthy. And then I gave that up.

"Captain Strong," I said, "before I answer your questions, I have a request."

"You are in no position—" she began.

"I know, but could you please do something that won't endanger you or the ship? Please, *please* leave your chair and move at least ten feet in a direction of your choice, You will not want to head toward me, of course, but move left, right, or to the back of the room. *Please*?"

She looked suspiciously at me, said something to her collar comm that connected to the helmets of the guards on my side of the barrier (I wasn't supposed to hear it, but could, of course), and they stepped three paces away from me and raised their heat rifles, taking care that each was out of the other's line of fire, and looked very scary. It probably would *really* hurt if they fired at me.

Next, a bunch of things happened almost at once. Strong stood up, to my slight surprise, since I had expected more questions. Commander Stringfellow also stood up, which I *had* expected, and started to raise his burner in an arc that would have it pointing at Strong. The guards on the captain's side noticed, and started to redirect their weapons from me, but seemed doubtful about where, and at whom, they should aim, not to mention the problem of other officers in the line of fire. "I could hop through the barrier, but couldn't be sure of landing precisely between Strong and Stringfellow." The next paragraph, beginning, "So I moved" should still be as before.

So I moved, and a me-sized hunk of the barrier moved with me, though I hardly noticed it giving way at the time, and paid no attention to the cloud of flying fragments which I quickly outpaced. I went past the captain and gave Stringfellow a goddess-sized uppercut that caused him to turn over a couple of times in the air—

—which, I realized was rapidly getting thinner, as the ventilation system was sucking it out, this time helped considerably by the hard vacuum outside the ship. Hey, just because it didn't work *before* . . .

I was heading for the spot where the ship gravity was pulling Stringfellow down, but he disappeared like a popped soap bubble (I needed to come up with a new metaphor, I thought) before coming to the end of his trajectory. Too bad, since by that time I had pulled my legs loose from the chair shackles (my very stylish fleet boots, I thought regretfully, would never be the same) and had raised the chair, or what part of it had survived being pulled loose from the deck and dragged with me through the transparent metal barrier, and was going to see what the result would be of hitting the phony commander with a more authentic clout on the noggin. Deprived of such a simple joy, I slapped a bubble of air around all the mortals in the room, told the ship's life support to close all vents to the outside (fortunately, only one was open), and get back on duty, providing, not removing, breathable gases. I made a mental note to call this chapter of my memoirs, if I ever had time to write them, *The Room of Doom*, then twirled around to see if the two guards on the barrier's side needed help. But they were coming through the opening I had made in the barrier on my way to attack "Stringfellow." It wasn't wide enough for two people to get through at once, but they didn't get in each other's way. The woman came through, then the man right behind her. I suspected they had gone through by time in grade, since they were the same non-com rank. She had jumped sideways once through, giving her fellow guard a clear shot at me. She didn't take her aim from me all the time she was coming through, of course. Neither one seemed perturbed over the way the air pressure had been rapidly dropping, until a few seconds ago.

I put the remains of the chair back on the floor, slowly so as not to attract gunfire, then turned back to Karina Strong, who kept switching her gaze to me, to the hole in the barrier, to the place where the ersatz commander had vanished, then back to me. "Captain," I said, "you have a good crew, and I wish I really were a member. By the way, your forehead is bleeding."

She told the guards to stop aiming at me, but be alert, saying, "I think if—ah, Corbett had wanted to harm me, I would already be stretched out on the deck, probably in several pieces." Then what I had said sank in, and she wiped her hand across her forehead.

"On the left side," I said. "It's not serious, but I'm sorry I caused it. Must have been a flying piece of the barrier."

Strong wiped the other side, glanced at the blood, then stared again at the hole in the barrier and shook her head.

"It's still serious until *I* say it isn't, whoever the Hell you really are," Dr. Schosser said, and aimed a gadget like a pocket-sized flashlight at the scratch, then said, "It's not serious, Cap'n." The gadget shot a transparent blob at the wound, and it spread out, covered it, and (I could tell—being a goddess has its perks) began accelerating the healing process. "Good as new in two hours, tops, Ma'am," Schosser said.

"Thank you, Bob," Strong said, though she kept looking at me. She started to shake her head again, but stopped and grabbed for her sidearm when the door on the other side of what was left of the barrier slid open and Ares ran through. He stopped to look at the hole I'd made, and shook *his* head. *Doesn't anybody ever get a sore neck around here?* I wondered, and told the captain, "Don't worry, we're both on your side."

Looking at me through the new exit, he said, "I just can't take you *anywhere!*" He felt the barrier, then punched his fist through it. Unfortunately for the effect he intended, his fist stuck. He tried pulling it back out. Still stuck.

"As I said, don't worry," I told the captain, "*I'm* on your side."

The captain smiled and turned to Security Officer Lieutenant Stiles, "Steve, do you have a present location for our disappearing commander?"

"I'm on it, Cap'n," he said, "but he isn't showing up on any scans. He might as well have left the ship—"

"I wish," Strong said.

"—but I'll keep checking." Stiles had his burner out, in fact it had never left his hand during all the excitement. If I hadn't interfered with the commander, Stiles probably would have nailed him. But would the burner have stopped him?

Stiles bent over, and picked up another burner with his free hand, saying, "At least he doesn't have this . . . weapon now," but his voice lost its enthusiasm halfway through the sentence as he raised one hand, then the other, as if he were about to do a juggling act with the weapons.

I thought he should have at least a third burner to have an impressive act, but mostly I was berating myself for not noticing that Stringfellow had dropped this burner. Then I noticed something else, and realized why Stiles was doing that. One burner wasn't really a burner.

Strong looked again at Ares as he used his other hand to smash the part of the barrier imprisoning his right wrist, shook it briefly dislodging a new shower of fragments, then (to my relief) walked through the hole, ducking a little to clear its top. I had been afraid he'd try to make his own new entrance just to prove he could.

Stiles had managed to field-strip the dropped burner with only one free hand and a couple of fingers of the other, and I was impressed. I wasn't sure I could do that, though I could squeeze it into a shapeless blob. I knew he had noticed what I had "seen" with god-senses.

"Captain," he said, "this isn't a burner. It's a disguised stunner."

Like Tom Corbett's paralo guns, I thought but did not say.

Karina Strong's office was spacious enough to underline her rank, making it big enough to hold the conference assembled there. The place was simply furnished, with a few personal photos, the apparently obligatory portrait of an admiral of note on the wall, Michelle Howard this time, and a large walnut desk, mostly bare of decorations. So nothing blocked her gaze as she looked at me and Ares across its polished surface and said, "Do you think I'm handling all this very calmly?"

"Undeniably," I said, and was going to say more, but . . .

"Just so, always the lady's man, er, god," Ares said. "You are an remarkable woman, and would be even for an im—" At which point I kicked his shin.

"I'm afraid that kicking your boyfriend's shins only works in old flatscreen stories," Strong said. I hadn't thought she could see me do that over her desk, then belatedly realized that there were probably vid pickups scattered around the office, feeding to the portascan on her desk.

"He's not—" I quickly said.

"I'm not—" Ares said, in a photo finish.

"Ah, some data emerges, though I'm not sure it's useful. I'm not an 'em,' whatever that is, but obviously, you two are members of a third race of sentients, unknown to us until now, and can pass for humans. Where do you come from?"

I was still thinking (at godspeed, remember) of what plausible lie I could tell, when Ares said, "Earth." He then got a surprised look on his beefy mug and shook his head as if to clear it.

Need a lot more shaking there, guy, I thought, then thought that, of course, every sentient species would name its homeworld after its word for "dirt," and tried to say that, to restore necessary ambiguity—and instead, what came out was, "Earth, the same planet you came from." So I shook *my* head, then felt around with some of my extra senses, I didn't know what for, but there was some kind of influence on me, like a compulsion, but different. Besides, a compulsion would take a very powerful entity, such as Amun-Ra himself, to actually work on me.

I took a deep breath and said, "Two and two are five. And also equal twenty-two." I could beat it if I concentrated.

Stiles, one of three crew members who had joined us in the captain's office, looked dismayed. "I had the projector at full power," he said. "Looks like it only works if they're not expecting it. Hell!"

"It's some machine they've turned on us," I said to Ares, "so you can stop shaking your head. Unless you enjoy it, of course." To the head of Security, I said, "So what do you call it? The Veracitator? The Honestron? The just plain Truth Ray?"

"Classified," Stiles said. "It may not have worked at all, unless you meant that you were born on Earth to members of your race who were hidden there."

"Oh, to the Underworld with it," I said, and stood up to get more room. Stiles was reaching for his burner, but stopped when I resumed my most famous natural aspect, cat's head, humanoid body, robes, sandals, the works. "Do I look familiar?"

Strong, Stiles, and Schosser looked baffled, and I thought, *What are they teaching kids nowadays*, but Kaylor, the librarian, said, "You look like Bast, also known as Bastet and Sekhmet, best known of the Egyptian cat goddesses."

I started to say that my sister Sekhmet was a lion goddess and a different individual, with a different job description, but he was still going.

"You look just like the representations of her from ancient Egypt—well, the ones that don't show Bast as a large cat with no human features."

"I can do that," I said, "but it makes it tricky to operate equipment." I went back to Ensign Corbett's appearance, but since the boots had been ruined, I kept the sandals, even if I was out of uniform.

"You're claiming to be a god?" Stiles said. "A mythological being from thousands of years ago, yet we thought you were imaginary for most of that time?"

"We did a good job of hiding," I managed to interject. *Up until now, anyway*, I thought. "You mortals want all kinds of weird stuff handed to you on a noble metal platter, then blame us for all your problems."

"Come on! Next, your boyfriend will be claiming to be Jehovah or Yahweh, and saying he created the universe."

I decided to let the "boyfriend" label go this time, but Ares snapped, "I didn't create the universe. Can't pin that on me. I wasn't even asked for advice."

I decided not to mention that he hadn't been around *that* long ago, nor had any of the rest of the immortal mob. He had kept his uniform on, rather than switching to armor and sandals, but then he was self-conscious about his knobby knees, which seemed to be immune to shape-changes.

"He's Ares, also known as Mars," I said. "And I *am* Bast, but please don't call me Sekhmet. And the stories about both of us have been greatly exaggerated. Downright libelous, in fact!" I glanced at the captain, who wasn't saying anything, and saw she was looking at her portascan. When I *looked* in a different way, she turned out to be reading about me. I'd deny everything if I got a chance.

Stiles was now talking to Ares—at Ares, really—and I was worrying about the mortal's blood pressure. "If you're not Jehovah, does that mean he's going to drop in next?" said Stiles.

I was getting annoyed at his focusing on Ares—*Hey, guy, I'm still here*—and answered before Ares could. "He's not big on personal appearances, and we don't hear much from Big G, any more than you mortals do."

"Mortals, eh? If he did, I still wouldn't believe it. This is all some kind of hypnotic illusion you're casting. Besides, I'm an atheist, and—"

He just didn't understand that you shouldn't get a cat mad. I reached him in three strides, picked him up easily, then caused a foxhole to appear in the deck, with all the trimmings: barbed wire, sandbags, an ancient water-cooled machine gun, and plenty of very wet mud in the bottom. I said, "I always did want to see an atheist in a foxhole," and dropped him in. The "sandbags" in the bottom of the pit were watertight and filled with foam rubber, not sand. I just wanted to get him off his hobby horse, not injure him.

He got to his feet in the foxhole, a little unsteady on the foam rubber, and said to his collar commo, "Telotier? Stiles here. Please look up at the overhead. See anything unusual? Nothing at all? Okay, thanks. No, this is not a joke. When I'm joking, I'll let you know that I'm joking. Stiles out."

He looked at me and said, "I knew it. This is another illusion. The security woman on the deck directly below us says there's nothing unusual about the overhead, and this hole is deeper than the thickness of—"

I had been about to make the foxhole disappear and have him standing on the deck again, but his willful denial of the evidence of his senses, even if only mortal senses, had ticked me off, so instead I filled the foxhole with muddy water. "Watch out for the imaginary barbed wire climbing out," I said. The watertight "sandbags" were now floating around Stiles's shoulders, so I changed them to real sandbags, and they immediately sank.

The captain said, "Not that the foxhole doesn't make a striking conversation piece, but could we have more information and less interior redecorating? I'll accept for the time being that you two are who you say you are, but Commander Stringfellow obviously wasn't who he was supposed to be, so just who was he? And why are you here?"

"I wish I knew who Stringfellow really was," I said, "but I don't know who or what he is. I already knew that he could be in two places at the same time, because he managed that trick shortly after takeoff, and now I know that he can be no place at all on the ship. And he's able make your shipcomp jump through hoops, unless that was done by somebody else we don't know about yet. As for why we're here, I didn't have much chance to talk to Ares before the mysterious Commander Stringfellow came through the door and arrested us, but I was sent by the boss to find out why the Solar Fleet keeps losing to lesser enemy forces, and to make sure this ship comes back, if that's possible." I paused and looked at Ares.

He took the cue: "We're here independently—we Olympians don't talk much to the Egyptian bunch—but Zeus sent to me for the same reason as this lady."

"Zeus," Strong said and looked back at her portascan. I saw she was now reading about Ares and his boss. "Dare I hope that Loki isn't going to show up next," she said.

Ares looked at me. I gave a quick nod, and he said, "Last I heard, he was still locked away. Besides, he's not as bad as the myths make him out to be. Good drinking companion, but he just can't resist making a joke. Like the time he and Bast—"

"The Norse contingent probably wouldn't have sent anybody." I broke in. "They've been expecting the world to be destroyed for aeons, and probably think it's way overdue. But the boss doesn't want to see the Earth forces defeated, if only because the enemy might destroy the Earth. And he is Amun-Ra, whose anger can shatter the world. It's the top item on his resume, and he doesn't want any competition. And if the Earth is destroyed, what's he going to shatter? A midget planet like Mercury or Mars—" I stopped and looked at Ares. "Sorry."

"No problem," he said. "I don't really have much to do with that planet. It's nice that ancient mortals named it after me, but it's not my kind of fun place."

"Your boss is Zeus," Kaylor put in, a fanboy's glow on his face. "Can *he* shatter the world? Earth, I mean."

"The subject never came up. Besides, he's too busy chasing broads." He turned to me and said, "Sorry, women. That part of the legends they got right."

I could tell that Strong was running out of patience, so I said, "Captain Strong, I suspect you want to get back to the subject of your upcoming battle, so may I ask if you have any information about Commander Stringfellow? You've heard all that I know."

At least, she didn't shake her head. "Leon Stringfellow was serving in this ship's crew before I assumed command, and has served under me for the past year and change. This was all before the conflict with the K'trags broke out, so they must have placed him here that early, at least, in anticipation of the war."

"I'm sorry, Captain, but it may be that he is dead, perhaps very recently, and the fake Stringfellow took his place." I paused, then quickly continued, "I hope that he's being held prisoner somewhere instead, but you should be ready for bad news."

"Is that what you've done with Ensign Corbett?" Strong asked. She wasn't angry yet, but she was preparing to become angry.

"Thomasina Corbett is entirely made up, Captain. None of her records in your shipcomp are real, though the ones about her serving on the *Valentina Tereshkova* would be confirmed if you could get in touch with that Boomer. I tinkered with their shipcomp, too."

I stood up again, and continued, "I picked her name after a fictional character I was fond of from the mid-twentieth century—"

"Tom Corbett," Kaylor said. "I called up the records on that, though there was no indication that he had a sister."

"Thank you. My appearance as Ensign Corbett is that of an obscure actress from a later period. As you have seen, I can alter how I look. Please pardon me—" I changed my seeming to an approximation of Commander Stringfellow. "—for resembling your missing officer." I changed back to "Corbett."

"I didn't need to eliminate anyone, since I made up my persona. I assume that Ares, or 'Pupp,' has done the same." Ares nodded agreement. "And since we were posing as new personnel, there was no need to remove anyone. But Stringfellow's imitator—let's call him Stringfaker, if that's all right with you, Captain—was coming aboard as an imitation of someone you all knew, so the real officer may no longer be alive."

Strong looked away from me, and I could tell she was receiving a message through her ear implants. Ares and I could hear the message, of course, but the other three mortals in the office could not. The pilot was letting her know that they were about to come out of hyperlight at the rendezvous for the other two ships of the fleet.

"We're going sublight in nine minutes," Strong said. "I would tell everyone to go to their stations, including myself, but I'm not sure—" She was looking at Ares and me.

Ares nodded at me again. I wasn't sure I liked him being so accommodating. It was out of character, and he might be cooking up his own scheme. But I said, "Captain, neither of us will be needed in our fictitious role—" I realized that I actually had no idea what "Pupp's" job was, and his shipcomp record had been deleted so I couldn't consult it. "—we'll stay out of the way of the real crew while we try to locate Stringfaker and also look out for any other threats to the ship."

"I don't guess I can think of anything better, but I really don't like this situation. I particularly don't know how I am going to explain to the admiral that I have a couple of gods on board—"

"I'm sorry, Captain," I said, "I mean, Ma'am." I had decided I had better start talking like a low-ranking officer again. "You won't be able to tell Admiral Dorsey anything. I've put a light compulsion on you and the crew members who've seen me doing, well, impossible things. I didn't want to, but we have to still have some tattered shreds of secrecy on this mission. You in this office can talk about Ares and me among yourselves, as long as no one else can overhear you, but you won't be able to tell anyone else."

The captain spoke into her collar comm, and I thought she was going to try to tell someone on the control deck about me (and find that she couldn't), but she said, "Strong here. Hoyt, I'm giving two new crew members a special assignment, Corbett and, uh, Pupp are not to be interfered with unless it seems they are in danger. I'll be joining you momentarily. Strong out."

I was surprised. "You believed me?"

"Please don't make me regret it. Could I have my security chief back?"

Stiles hadn't tried to climb over the barbed wire yet, maybe because he would have had to put his burner away to manage it, so I made the foxhole go away (I gave the soap bubble metaphor a rest), and he was standing on the dry deck. I had made the muddy water in the hole and on him, also vanish, and his uniform was cleaner than it had been before. Pressed with sharp creases, too. Unfortunately, I was sure that would just make him more certain that he had experienced an illusion. He glared at me again, then holstered his burner and followed the captain and the other officers out of the room, with Ares and me bringing up the rear.

Before I even got to the drop tubes, one of my troops reported to me that she had found something, and I wondered if the medical officer answered to "Bones," but decided to go with formality. "Dr. Schosser, can you come with me?"

He looked at me, not noticing Corona (my cats are good at that when they want to be) and said, "Why? We're short on time."

The captain and Stiles had also stopped. When I said, "I think my associate has found the missing Stringfellow. The real one, possibly."

Strong said, "Go ahead, Bob," and Stiles said, "I'll go, too." Ares said, "I'll stay with the captain." Strong nodded, and headed on to the drop tube.

By that time, everyone was seeing Corona, who was leading the way. "You're a cat goddess, so you can talk to cats," Stiles grumbled. "Yeah, right."

"That's right, and they can talk to me." I was developing a grudging respect for Stiles and his determination not to believe in what he thought was illusion, but he still had better not get in my way.

We took a drop tube down two decks, then walked to a closed hatch with STORAGE on it. It was locked, but slid open at my touch, which made Stiles grumble some more as he again pulled out his burner. I wondered if it ever had a chance to drop to room temperature.

We started to spread out, but Corona headed for a carton with no stencils or labels on it—and walked *through* its side, disappearing from sight.

"Now, *that* is an illusion, Lieutenant Stiles," I said, and made it go away. Stringfellow was curled up on the deck where the illusory carton had been and I could tell he was unconscious but alive. I didn't bother to mention that, since Schosser was making sure of that with his pocket doodad.

I felt around, and found another apparently real carton that wasn't, and headed for it. By now my other two troops had appeared and all three were staring at the box with their fur up (less noticeable with the Siamese, but she used what she had), but weren't hissing or growling as if they didn't want to be heard. And then all three calmed down, their fur settling back.

Too calm! I thought, and made this illusion go away, too, revealing Captain Karina Strong curled up on the deck, as Stringfellow had been.

"It's the captain!" Stiles snapped, and switched on his collar commo, then shouted (unnecessarily), "Ahoy the bridge. This is Stiles. Arrest Captain Strong immediately. Use force if necessary. That is not the captain, she's an imposter."

"Never mind, Lieutenant," I said. "I had shipcomp block your transmission just now to save time and trouble. This is *not* the captain. It isn't even a human."

Schosser reached for his medical gizmo, but "Strong" had seen the trick wasn't working, and was already standing up. Stiles aimed his burner at the ersatz Karina Strong, but for once, he was hesitant.

"Don't bother, Lieutenant," I said, "you'd need much heavier artillery than that to hurt, um, her." I was already blocking emanations from the captain-thing, or the three cats would have been taking involuntary naps on the deck. Oh, and the mortals, too.

I poked at its disguise, and its appearance rippled but then it disappeared, as Stringfaker had done—

—but then it was back, now looking something like a human-sized ape, but with straighter legs, an extra pair of arms and a head like a wolf but with a shorter snout. Ares's left hand was clamped on one of its upper arms, and he had his sword in his right, but otherwise still was in Solar Fleet uniform. "I got your distress call," he said.

I hadn't been in distress, but I let it pass. "Take it easy with the sword," I said. "We need to find out what in the Underworld is going on."

Our involuntary guest was trying to leave the premises, but with both of us focusing on her, she was stuck here even though she was a goddess of some sort. I could recognize the profile.

"The message I sent you was to guard the captain, and you've left her unguarded on the bridge."

"But I've got the troublemaker right here—"

"We don't *know* that she's the only one!" I interrupted.

"I am the only one," the prisoner said. "There's no one else. They're all gone. When you kill me, that'll be the end of it." Her body language was too alien to read, but I had other ways of telling that she was depressed, feeling a hopelessness that neither the d-word nor the h-word had ever been meant to describe, filled with a sorrow that in a human would leave no way out but suicide.

I wasn't sure she *could* be killed, but I said, "We're not going to kill you, if you'll—"

"Why not?" Stiles objected. "If this—uh, *she*?—if she's the reason that we've lost four Boomers, with their crews, she deserves to die."

"Sorry, Lieutenant, but this is god business, and you're overruled."

"They're not dead," the stranger said. "I made sure that the K'trag'vah took them prisoner and didn't mistreat them. I told them that if they hurt the humans, their eggs would not hatch, their larvae already hatched would sicken and die, and their crops would wither. And then I would *really* get angry."

For a moment, I thought that the creature was showing a sense of humor. Then I realized that she was just being explicit. But I believed her, since she had gone to the trouble of attempting to use a stunner on the captain, temporarily putting her out of commission, instead of killing her.

"This thing is a god, too?" Stiles grumbled. "Are you *sure* Jehovah isn't going to drop in for tea?"

"I think *Shàngdì* would be more interested in tea," I said, "but in lieu of Big G stopping here, we'd better continue this with the next closest things included in the chat."

I meant Captain Karina Strong and Admiral Carlotta Dorsey, but just then things stopped being even that simple. The alien goddess changed her appearance to an animated version of the Aphrodite of Milos, with arms, as usual, plus an extra missing pair of stumps.

Startled to find himself holding nothing but air, Ares let his focus waver, and the armless alien lady disappeared.

I hadn't been able to hold her by myself, but I still had a fix on her. "She went to the bridge," I said to Ares, and grabbed Stiles's gun-bearing arm and hopped there with him in tow.

We found two Captain Strongs, both giving contradictory orders to the crew. I could tell that the fake Strong was also trying to do her air pressure trick a third time, but after the second time, I had set my own cybertroops on the alert for that, and they were making life complicated for her on that front.

A glance at the viewscreen showed that the battle was on, though it didn't look anywhere as cool as in twenty-first-century movies. The enemy's X-ray lasers and plasma cannon were pounding the ship's screens, but superior Solar technology was brushing the barrage aside with deserved contempt and a slight sparkly effect. And as soon as the Solar Boomers opened up with their greater firepower, the attacking ships would cease to exist.

So it made no sense that one of the captains was ordering her crew not to fire, to offer to surrender, and agree to drop the screens and surrender once the enemy had ceased fire—unless you knew *that* Captain Strong wasn't really Captain Strong.

Stiles knew one of them had to be a fake, but he couldn't tell which one, as I could, so his burner wavered back and forth between the excess commanding officers.

"Don't worry, Lieutenant," I said, "the way things are going, I'm sure you'll get to shoot *something*." Then I changed into a third Captain Strong and shouted to the understandably bewildered crew, "The majority of Captains vote to keep the screens up and return fire as necessary. And do not surrender." I added, "Don't give up the ship!" wondering how many would get the quote.

Ares appeared, still with sword in hand, which caused eyes to widen, and a couple of security officers drew burners, but were waved down by Stiles. The fake captain disappeared before we could try to hold her in place. I shouted to Ares, "*This* time, stay with Strong," wondering if he would do that, then followed the fake.

I wasn't sure where we were going, but I could tell that the alien was changing her shape again, so I copied her. Turned out we both now stood on the bridge of the flagship, *Theodor S. Geisel*, facing Admiral Dorsey, of whom we were now both copies. I could tell that the admiral didn't quite recognize herself in triplicate—most people, even with mirrors, and after photography and its digital successors were invented, don't really know how they look to others—but her crew did. Fortunately, the ship's screens stayed up even while the techs in charge were transfixed. Did I mention that the air pressure on the bridge was dropping? The hits just keep on coming. I turned more cybertroops loose to put a stop to that, then muttered, "Bugger!" and slammed the other redundant admiral as hard as I could. We were the same fake rank, so I didn't worry about it being insubordination, real or fake.

Doing that to a real mortal would have messy and irreversibly fatal results, but, as I expected, the alien goddess wasn't even knocked out, just momentarily stunned enough that her concentration wavered, as did her disguise.

I said to the real Admiral Dorsey, "Pardon me, Ma'am, as you were," grabbed two of the alien's arms and hopped back to the *Wayne* (Pilgrim—oh, to the Underworld with it!).

Ares was still there, but maybe he just hadn't known where else to go. "Concentrate on her, this time," I shouted, "even if she changes again to look like your wife."

His influence reached out, but he grumbled, "Deity doesn't look like that statue, even before those idiot mortals lost its arms. And it doesn't do justice to Alexandros's actual model. When I dropped in on her back in 112—"

"Screw B.C., we've got troubles right now."

The alien was again trying to escape, but there were two of us with different ideas. "I have to go," she cried. "I have to tell them to stop the attack and retreat. I promised them I'd protect them. You can't just kill them."

"A god who keeps promises? Now I've heard everything," Ares said.

"How would you have them stop and retreat?" I asked the alien. "And do you have a name?" I was getting tired of thinking of her as "the alien."

Her name was Arapon, she told me, then described the situation at godspeed. It would have sounded like high speed gibberish to the mortals, if I hadn't clapped a bubble of silence over the three immortals on board. (For a while, I had called it the Cone of Silence until Sekhmet caught me and called me Agent 99 for months on end.)

"Right," I said, "here's a deal. You stop the war, and we'll try to help you."

"Nobody can help me," Arapon said, again in that *there's-a-bright-future-in-applied-suicide* tone. "My people are all dead. Murdered."

"Maybe, but let's look into it first. If we can't help you, you can always resume hostilities." *As if we'd let you*, I thought, mentally crossing my fingers. "And we're both war gods, right, Ares baby?"

He scowled at me but said, "Right, best in the business. *Blood and gore—*"

I lifted the bubble and told Captain Strong, "We're all going over to the enemy flagship, so please don't shoot—" I paused and added, "Ma'am. You might hit us." Then we hopped over. As we left, I could hear Karina Strong counting to ten by binary numbers. Takes longer that way if you pronounce all the ones and zeroes.

As we traveled, not troubled by mere force screens, I could tell that Arapon was changing her shape again. When we arrived, this time I kept my human shape. Ares kept his sword.

The K'trag'yah look something like the centipedes of Earth, if centipedes were about two and a half meters long, had lots of handlike things at the ends of their frontmost limbs, a *lot* more eyes, and were intelligent enough to build starships, more's the pity on that last point.

Arapon now looked like one of them, except for size. Her head almost brushed the ceiling of the control room, which was about fifty meters high. She was also now a male, since the female 'Trags just stay home and lay eggs. If you're going to pose as an alien god, you gotta look impressive.

"*Cease hostilities,*" she said in the 'Trag language (which Ares and I could understand, naturally). "*I have met with my fellow gods and we have agreed to end this war. I will help you in other ways, but will not fight on your side any longer.*" That was a fair translation, anyway.

Some of the 'Trags protested, and Ares started to step forward with his sword, but Arapon shot lightning, yes, *lightning* from her front right hand, and the odor of cooked meat filled the control room. The ones who hadn't complained were now distracted by thoughts of barbecue, since 'Trags are ravenous carnivores and aren't fussy about what or who a snack used to be.

Earlier, several of them had looked at me hungrily, but they weren't doing that now. *Just as well*, I thought, *I'd give you creepy-crawlies more indigestion than you could handle!*

Someone must have called the cops, because more crawlies came through a hole in the floor (I wasn't going to call it the *deck*—that was what a human ship would have tagged it) holding weapons, but they weren't fast enough. More crispy critters for a wartime snack.

With the, uh, aroma filling the big room, it was fortunate that gods have strong stomachs. It may not have bothered Arapon, and she kept shouting orders. "*This lead ship will stay to negotiate terms of the peace. The others will immediately return to the home planet. Disobey, and be destroyed!*" The huge, hideous head turned to Ares and me. "Let's leave," it, well, *she* said in the old Earth language of Amereng.

And we did.

Back on the bridge with Captain Strong, Ares and I were taking deep breaths to get that cooked monster smell out of our lungs, and so was Arapon. I suppose that it did bother her, even in 'Trag form.

"Keep your powder dry, but I think the war is over," I told the captain.

"Powder? Oh. All but one of their ships just departed, except for one that's been hailing us about having a talk. You mean it isn't a trick?"

"I can't read their crawlie minds, but unless they're less scared of Arapon than they seem to be—" Strong looked puzzled, so I said, "She's Arapon," and pointed out our alien guest, now back in her natural form. "And she just called off the war. Now, we need to talk and we need the admiral here."

It took a bit of persuading by Strong to get the admiral to leave her Boomer, the *Theodor S. Geisel* (she had loved the classics when she was a child, and when given the opportunity to christen her own ship, went for her old favorite author). It helped that Arapon's orders had been obeyed, and only one enemy ship remained, offering peace terms while the rest headed home as fast as their hyperlight engines could carry them.

Even though the battle had been called on account of gods, Dorsey had argued that she could manage the conference by electronics without having to be there in person, and besides Captain G. Horace Wells, of the third boomer, *Misa Matsushima*, should be in on the talk. But I used a dollop of long distance compulsion on the lady, just enough so that she saw it our way. I wanted her present, because I couldn't be certain that I could put a compulsion of secrecy on her that would keep on ticking if we weren't in the same room when I used the whammy. And there were already too many people who knew the Big Secret without adding another pair of ears, Boomer captain or not; so Captain Wells hadn't seen anything but a textbook space battle, followed by a sudden cessation of hostilities, so he could be, and was, left out of the loop.

Much later, in his memoir, *The World of My Wars*, he speculated about what went on, but happily got it all wrong.

Admiral Dorsey came back through the same door through which she had departed a couple of minutes ago, and said to me, "You're not exaggerating. I couldn't repeat any of the, well, unbelievable story that I just heard from you." She sat down again, then stared once more at the hole I had made in the barrier, probably thinking of the visual recording of me going through it that Captain Strong had shown her—a very limited showing, since afterward I had deleted it. At least, she didn't shake her head.

She did ask me to repeat changing my appearance to that of a woman with a cat's head. When I complied, she stared at me for long enough that I was wondering if she would ask me to add a battered and striped top hat, but finally she said, "I do like cats," pausing to glance at the three who were sitting by my chair, making sure that the humans didn't do anything stupid, "but please look human again."

"Yes, Ma'am," I said, and complied. After all, I was still in uniform (except for the sandals). Besides which, her dark skin brought back memories of home and long ago, and made me feel comfortable. I almost purred, but caught myself.

"Let's see if I have this straight now. You three—" she said and paused, as if preparing to do something difficult or distasteful or both "—*gods* have put a stop to the war, but I have to come up with a believable way that the task force managed to convince the enemy to cease hostilities without our firing a single shot. I think I can do that, cloaked in all the usual official blather. But just how *did* you make them retreat? More mind control?"

"Arapon started the war, so she was able to stop it," I said, "with a little help from Ares and me. The K'trag'vah don't seem to have gods on their own planet, which seems odd to me, but we've only encountered three planets with intelligent life—" I suppressed a snarky remark at that point, though it cost me "—which is too small a sample to establish a trend. Arapon is the only god on her planet, which also seems odd, but maybe Earth is the odd, er, man out."

"Spare me the footnotes," Dorsey said, and that sounded like an order to me, particularly with the way her dark face somehow took on a stonelike look when she said it. Very hard stone, break a chisel on it. She stared at Arapon and said, "Just why did you start a war between the 'Trags and us," in a tone like she might use on the most lowly cadet in the Solar Fleet, who was about to be put on KP for life. Something Amun-Ra might do to me after I reported on how wacko this mission had gone.

"They killed my people," Arapon said in a fittingly dead tone, "all of them. Every one of them."

The dark stone of the Admiral's face softened a little. "So you decided to become their god?" she said.

"I couldn't kill all of them. They breed faster than I could strike them dead one at a time. But I told them I would lead them to victory over you humans. I knew that you were more technically advanced and could wipe them out once they had angered your world enough."

"You have to be careful about trusting a god," I said.

"They believed you, even though you look nothing like them?" Dorsey asked, looking skeptical.

I thought, *Time for some serious show and tell.*

"I changed to look like them, as I changed to look like one of you. Like this," she said, and changed to a K'Trag. Not as large as before, since there was less room here. Her head, or at least the part with multiple eyes and constantly moving mouth parts, bumped the ceiling, well, the overhead. (Have to get those naval terms right.)

I gave the admiral more points. She didn't flinch even though there was an elephant-sized ET like a centipede with chitinous hands, *lots* of hands, looming over her. "I see . . . that *is* impressive."

The monstrous K'Trang shriveled back to Arapon's normal size and appearance and she said, "Oh, I was much bigger then. There wasn't enough room in here for the full effect.

I heard several people subvocalize (superior god hearing, you know, not to mention sensitive cat ears), almost in unison, *Thank goodness for that*. The captain and admiral were not among them. More points in their favor.

"I'm sorry to be anticlimactic, even if it's about good news," I said to Arapon. "I didn't have time to tell you before—" (well, it was only a small fib, but like my Victorian detective pal, I cannot resist a touch of the dramatic) "—but I don't think your people are dead."

Arapon obviously didn't believe me and was getting angry again. "But they were all gone. I looked *everywhere*. There weren't any corpses or even a trace—"

"So you thought the attackers used some kind of disintegrating weapon. But while we were over there in their, uh, flagship and you were intimidating the crap out of the creepy-crawlies, I checked on their computer files. They were baffled by the result of their attack. Their weapons should have left lightly-burned corpses." *Plenty of fresh meat and good eating*, I thought, but didn't say. "They couldn't understand why it had apparently made everyone vanish, and their scientists, or at least what they have instead of scientists, had cooked—" (*bad choice of words, stupid*, I thought) "—up a theory that your people were made of some odd compound that disintegrates into a gas upon the impact of microwaves of a certain frequency, leaving no remains. They haven't gone ahead with their planned colonization of your world because they're worried that it might have more unpleasant surprises."

Arapon said, "But they did vanish," and looked like she didn't know whether she should be joyous or mournful. Any cat knows that feeling and I sympathized. "I never looked into their computers because I didn't want to know, didn't even want to *think* what they had done with the bodies."

"Yes, they did vanish," I said. "I think you saved them. Or will save them. You said that the K'Trag weapon knocked you out."

"Yes, and when I woke up, there was no one anywhere. I wish it had killed me."

"Not likely, and if you'd had more experience with energy weapons, it might have only seriously annoyed you. When you managed to be Stringfellow in two places at once, talking to both Ares and me, how did you do that?"

"Why, I was talking to Ares, after I changed my appearance, since I thought you'd be more likely to notice that I wasn't really him."

Ares snorted loudly. I thought but did not say, *she* was *right, after all.*

"And the real Stringfellow was talking to you, but under my control. I thought that was less of a risk, and you apparently didn't notice."

Ares snorted again, with more justification this time, but he was definitely pushing his luck.

I slapped a cone, well, bubble of silence over the three gods in the room since I was getting in mortals-don't-need-to-know territory now, and asked her, "So, you didn't use a time hop to do that trick?"

"Use a *what?*"

"You can't travel in time?" I asked.

"Is that possible?"

"Very possible. We might be able to teach you to do it, but even if you can't, Ares and I can. And I have a feeling that's how all of your planet's mortals disappeared, and after we get some help from back home, we can make it happen. Or will have made it happen. So put your vengeance mission on hold 'til we know it's justified. And maybe you can teach me that lightning-hurling trick of yours."

Ares said, "Keep the silence bubble on for a moment. How did you know about the statue of Aphrodite?" he asked.

"Come to think of it," I put in, "how did you know about Gilbert and Sullivan, the Lensman stories, and all the other stuff in my fake personnel files?"

"I spent a lot of time with the library files of the captured Boomers. I needed to stay there to make sure the worms didn't harm the human prisoners, and Earth culture is so fascinating, though often hard to understand."

"Wait 'til you get to Proust and Joyce," I said and popped the silence bubble, then announced to the assembled brass, "I think I know where Arapon's people have gone, and we need to go back to Earth for reinforcements. The immortal kind of reinforcements. Then we'll need transportation to her planet."

Admiral Dorsey's face was again looking carved from dark and very hard stone. "That's all? No paid shore leave with gourmet meals and cocktails?"

I didn't point out that I wasn't really an officer, or even part of the Solar Fleet, and instead said, "Ma'am, you can report that you've made contact with a new race of sentients, whose help was critical in convincing the K'trag to stop the war, and might be allies against the K'trag, or any other unfriendly aliens that are still to be encountered. Worth sending a ship to investigate, you can say, and I think your superiors will agree."

"You don't know what *my* superiors are like," Dorsey said, "but that argument might work."

I hoped so, since otherwise, I and a bunch of other immortals would have to steal a starship, not to mention somehow getting someone to pilot it. Big difference from flying chariots and winged horses! If only we could jump through the intervening space to Arapon's planet, but even interplanetary distances are too far for that trick. Halfway around the Earth was no problem, and some of our stronger immortals could hop to the Moon, but that's as good as it gets.

"You're pretty savvy for an ensign, Corbett, or should I say Corbast," Dorsey said, rising from her chair. "Maybe I should promote you."

"I do have a lot of time in grade, Ma'am." *Millennia, in fact.*

As it happened, we did find where Arapon's people had gone, and everything eventually was straightened out, though of course, it was nowhere as simple as I had hoped. But that's really another story.

Two of the Boomers stayed behind to negotiate the peace terms with the sort of a captain of the Trag flagship (though they didn't use flags), while the *Duke of Wayne* (I went ahead and thought *pilgrim* since it didn't matter now) headed back to Earth. Ares stayed behind to put no-tell compulsions on the crew members who had seen two, then *three* Admiral Dorseys on the bridge of the *Geisel.*

I was wondering if Ra would forbid me to go on the rescue mission as punishment for this mare's nest of a mission. On the other hand, he might put me in charge as punishment. You never know with immortals, particularly the executives.

I was walking down the corridor with Captain Karina Strong toward the mess deck. (A whole deck? Boomers are *big* ships.) She said, "It's fine with me, Ensign Corbett, if you continue as ship's crew until we get to Earth."

"Thank you, Ma'am," I said in a properly respectful tone.

"So, you really are immortal?"

"So far, Ma'am."

"And you'll still be alive when the admiral and I are piles of dust or less?"

"I'm sorry, Ma'am, but—"

"Don't worry. Lifespans are much longer than they were even a half century ago, and maybe we'll develop our own immortality. Besides it's kind of comforting knowing that there's somebody who might keep us from blowing ourselves up."

"Several somebodies, Ma'am. And I hope so." I didn't tell her that we had done that several times already. She wasn't authorized to know that. "Could I ask a favor, Ma'am?"

Karina looked sidewise at me, got a stern look on her face that didn't fool me at all, and said, "You may ask."

"These sandals are very comfortable—" *after a few millennia, you get used to them* "—but I'm out of uniform. Could there be boots aboard that would fit me?" *Don't ask if I can conjure up boots or change my foot size, please.* I thought, *that would miss the point.*

"I don't see why not," she said, then started laughing very enthusiastically.

I may be a goddess, but somehow that made me feel right at home. *From the rocket fields of the Academy . . .*

Bolos: heavily armed and armored tanks, capable of massive destruction. Bolos: self-aware killing machines, powered by a psychotronic brain. Bolos: duty-bound to protect humans and do whatever necessary to accomplish the mission. So why then did the Bolo known as Lance retreat from Morville, leaving the town's inhabitants to die horrible deaths at the hands of the Enemy?

The Traitor

David Weber

Cold, bone-dry winter winds moaned as the titanic vehicle rumbled down the valley at a steady fifty kilometers per hour. Eight independent suspensions, four forward and four aft, spread across the full width of its gigantic hull, supported it, and each ten-meter-wide track sank deep into the soil of the valley floor. A dense cloud of dust—talcum-fine, abrasive, and choking as death—plumed up from road wheels five meters high, but the moving mountain's thirty-meter-high turret thrust its Hellbore clear of the churning cocoon. For all its size and power, it moved with unearthly quiet, and the only sounds were the whine of the wind, the soft purr of fusion-powered drive trains, the squeak of bogies, and the muted clatter of track links.

The Bolo ground forward, sensor heads swiveling, and the earth trembled with its passing. It rolled through thin, blowing smoke and the stench of high explosives with ponderous menace, altering course only to avoid the deepest craters and the twisted wrecks of alien fighting vehicles. In most places, those wrecks lay only in ones and twos; in others, they were heaped in shattered breastworks, clustered so thickly it was impossible to bypass them. When that happened, the eerie quiet of the Bolo's advance vanished into the screaming anguish of crushing alloy as it forged straight ahead, trampling them under its thirteen thousand tons of death and destruction.

It reached an obstacle too large even for it to scale. Only a trained eye could have identified that torn and blasted corpse as another Bolo, turned broadside on to block the Enemy's passage even in death, wrecked Hellbore still trained down the valley, missile cell hatches open on empty wells which had exhausted their ammunition. Fifteen enemy vehicles lay dead before it, mute testimony to the ferocity of its last stand, but the living Bolo didn't even pause. There was no point, for the dead Bolo's incandescent duralloy hull radiated the waste heat of the failing fusion bottle which had disemboweled it. Not even its unimaginably well-armored Survival Center could have survived, and the living Bolo simply altered heading to squeeze past it. Igneous rock cried out in pain as a moving, armored flank scraped the valley face on one side, and the dead Bolo shuddered on the other as its brother's weight shouldered it aside.

The moving Bolo had passed four dead brigade mates in the last thirty kilometers, and it was not unwounded itself. Two of its starboard infinite repeaters had been blasted into mangled wreckage, energy weapon hits had sent molten splatters of duralloy weeping down its glacis plate to freeze like tears of pain, a third of its after sensor arrays had been stripped away by a near miss, and its forward starboard track shield was jammed in the lowered position, buckled and rent by enemy fire. Its turret bore the ID code 25/D-0098-ART and the unsheathed golden sword of a battalion commander, yet it was alone. Only one other unit of its battalion survived, and that unit lay ahead, beyond this death-choked valley. It was out there somewhere, moving even now through the trackless, waterless Badlands of the planet Camlan, and unit ART of the Line rumbled steadily down the valley to seek it out.

I interrogate my Inertial Navigation System as I approach my immediate objective. The INS is not the most efficient way to determine my position, but Camlan's entire orbital network, including the recon and nav sats, as well as the communication relays, perished in the Enemy's first strike, and the INS is adequate. I confirm my current coordinates and grind forward, leaving the valley at last.

What lies before me was once a shallow cup of fertile green among the lava fields; now it is a blackened pit, and as my forward optical heads sweep the ruins of the town of Morville I feel the horror of Human mass death. There is no longer any need for haste, and I devote a full 6.007 seconds to the initial sweep. I anticipate no threats, but my on-site records will be invaluable to the court of inquiry I know will be

convened to pass judgment upon my brigade. I am aware of my own
fear of that court's verdict and its implications for all Bolos, but I am a
unit of the Line. This too, however bitter, is my duty, and I will not
flinch from it.

I have already observed the massive casualties C Company inflicted
upon the Enemy in its fighting retreat up the Black Rock Valley. The
Enemy's vehicles are individually smaller than Bolos, ranging from
500.96 Standard Tons to no more than 4,982.07 Standard Tons, but
heavily armed for their size. They are also manned, not self-aware, and
he has lost many of them. Indeed, I estimate the aggregate tonnage of
his losses in the Black Rock Valley alone as equivalent to at least three
Bolo regiments. We have yet to determine this Enemy's origins or the
motives for his assault on Camlan, but the butchery to which he has
willingly subjected his own personnel is sobering evidence of his
determination . . . or fanaticism. Just as the blasted, body-strewn streets
of Morville are ample proof of his ferocity.

Seventy-one more wrecked Enemy vehicles choke the final approach
to the town, and two far larger wrecks loom among them. I detect no
transponder codes, and the wreckage of my brigade mates is so blasted
that even I find it difficult to identify what remains, yet I know who
they were. Unit XXV/D-1162-HNR and Unit XXV/D-0982-JSN of the
Line have fought their last battle, loyal unto death to our Human
creators.

I reach out to them, hoping against hope that some whisper from the
final refuge of their Survival Centers will answer my transmission, but
there is no reply. Like the other Bolos I have passed this day, they are
gone beyond recall, and the empty spots they once filled within the
Total Systems Data Sharing net ache within me as I move slowly
forward, alert still for any Enemy vehicles hiding among the wreckage.
There are none. There are only the dead: the Enemy's dead, and the six
thousand Human dead, and my brothers who died knowing they had
failed to save them.

This is not the first time units of the Line have died, nor the first
time they died in defeat. There is no shame in that, only sorrow, for we
cannot always end in victory. Yet there is cause for shame here, for
there are only two dead Bolos before me . . . and there should be three.

Wind moans over the wreckage as I pick my way across the killing
ground where my brothers' fire shattered three Enemy attacks before

the fourth overran them. Without the recon satellites there is no independent record of their final battle, but my own sensor data, combined with their final TSDS transmissions, allow me to deduce what passed here. I understand their fighting withdrawal down the Black Rock Valley and the savage artillery and missile barrages which flayed them as they fought. I grasp their final maneuvers from the patterns of wreckage, recognize the way the Enemy crowded in upon them as his steady pounding crippled their weapons. I see the final positions they assumed, standing at last against the Enemy's fire because they could no longer retreat without abandoning Morville.

And I see the third position from which a single Bolo did retreat, falling back, fleeing into the very heart of the town he was duty bound to defend. I track his course by the crushed and shattered wreckage of buildings and see the bodies of the Camlan Militia who died as he fled, fighting with their man-portable weapons against an Enemy who could destroy 13,000-ton Bolos. There are many Enemy wrecks along his course, clear evidence of how desperately the Militia opposed the invaders' advance even as the Bolo abandoned Morville, fleeing north into the Badlands where the Enemy's less capable vehicles could not pursue, and I know who left those Humans to die. Unit XXV/D-0103-LNC of the Line, C Company's command Bolo, my crèche mate and battle companion and my most trusted company commander. I have fought beside him many times, known his utter reliability in the face of the Enemy, but I know him no longer, for what he has done is unforgivable. He is the first, the only, Bolo ever to desert in the face of the Enemy, abandoning those we are bound to protect to the death and beyond.

For the first time in the history of the Dinochrome Brigade, we know shame. And fear. As LNC, I am a Mark XXV, Model D, the first production model Bolo to be allowed complete, permanent self-awareness, and LNC's actions attack the very foundation of the decision which made us fully self-realized personalities. We have repeatedly demonstrated how much more effective our awareness makes us in battle, yet our freedom of action makes us unlike any previous units of the Brigade. We are truly autonomous . . . and if one of us can choose to flee—if one of us can succumb to cowardice—perhaps all of us can.

I complete my survey of the site in 4.307 minutes. There are no *survivors, Enemy, Human, or Bolo, in Morville, and I report my grim confirmation to my brigade commander and to my surviving brothers and sisters. The Enemy's surprise attack, coupled with our subsequent losses in combat, have reduced Sixth Brigade to only fourteen units, and our acting brigade commander is Lieutenant Kestrel, the most junior—and sole surviving—Human of our command staff. The commander is only twenty-four standard years of age, on her first posting to an active duty brigade, and the exhaustion in her voice is terrible to hear. Yet she has done her duty superbly, and I feel only shame and bitter, bitter guilt that I must impose this additional decision upon her. I taste the matching shame and guilt of the surviving handful of my brothers and sisters over the TSDS, but none of them can assist me. The Enemy is in full retreat to his spaceheads, yet the fighting continues at a furious pace. No other Bolos can be diverted from it until victory is assured, and so I alone have come to investigate and confirm the unbelievable events here, for I am the commander of LNC's battalion. It is up to me to do what must be done.*

"All right, Arthur," Lieutenant Kestrel says finally. "We've got the situation in hand here, and Admiral Shigematsu's last subspace flash puts Ninth Fleet just thirty-five hours out. We can hold the bastards without you. Go do what you have to."

"Yes, Commander," I reply softly, and pivot on my tracks, turning my prow to the north, and follow LNC's trail into the lava fields.

Unit XXV/D-0103-LNC of the Line churned across the merciless terrain. Both outboard port tracks had been blown away, and bare road wheels groaned in protest as they chewed through rock and gritty soil. His armored hull was gouged and torn, his starboard infinite repeaters and anti-personnel clusters a tangled mass of ruin, but his builders had designed him well. His core war hull had been breached in three places, wreaking havoc among many of his internal systems, yet his main armament remained intact . . . and he knew he was pursued.

LNC paused, checking his position against his INS and the maps in Main Memory. It was a sign of his brutal damage that he required almost twenty full seconds to determine his location, and then he altered course. The depression was more a crevasse than a valley—a sunken trough, barely half again the width of his hull, that plunged deep below the level of the fissured lava fields. It would offer LNC cover as he made his painful way towards the distant Avalon Mountains, and a cloud of dust wisped away on the icy winter wind as he vanished into the shadowed cleft.

I try to deduce LNC's objective, assuming that he has one beyond simple flight, but the task is beyond me. I can extrapolate the decisions of a rational foe, yet the process requires some understanding of his motives, and I no longer understand LNC's motives. I replay the final TSDS transmission from XXV/D-1162-HNR and experience once more the sensation a Human might define as a chill of horror as LNC suddenly withdraws from the data net. I share HNR's attempt to reestablish the net, feel LNC's savage rejection of all communication. And then I watch through HNR's sensors as LNC abandons his position, wheeling back towards Morville while Enemy fire bellows and thunders about him . . . and I experience HNR's final shock as his own company commander responds to his repeated queries by pouring Hellbore fire into his unprotected rear.

LNC's actions are impossible, yet the data are irrefutable. He has not only fled the Enemy but killed his own brigade mate, and his refusal even to acknowledge communication attempts is absolute. That, too, is impossible. Any Bolo must respond to the priority com frequencies, yet LNC does not. He has not only committed mutiny and treason but refused to hear any message from Lieutenant Kestrel, as he might reject an Enemy communications seizure attempt. How any Bolo could ignore his own Brigade commander is beyond my comprehension, yet he has, and because there is no longer any communication interface at all, Lieutenant Kestrel cannot even access the Total Systems Override Program to shut him down.

None of my models or extrapolations can suggest a decision matrix which could generate such actions on LNC's part. But perhaps that is the point. Perhaps there is no decision matrix, only panic. Yet if that is true, what will he do when the panic passes—if it passes? Surely he must realize his own fate is sealed, whatever the outcome of the Enemy's attack. How can I anticipate rational decisions from him under such circumstances?

I grind up another slope in his tracks. He has altered course once more, swinging west, and I consult my internal maps. His base course has been towards the Avalon Mountains, and I note the low ground to the west. He is no longer on a least-time heading for the mountains, but the long, deep valley will take him there eventually. It will also afford him excellent cover and numerous ambush positions, and I am tempted to cut cross-country and head him off. But if I do that and he is not, in fact, headed for the mountains, I may lose him. He cannot hide indefinitely, yet my shame and grief—and sense of betrayal—will not tolerate delay, and I know from HNR's last transmission that LNC's damage is much worse than my own.

I consider options and alternatives for .0089 seconds, and then head down the slope in his wake.

Unit LNC slowed as the seismic sensors he'd deployed along his back trail reported the ground shocks of a pursuing vehicle in the thirteen-thousand-ton range. He'd known pursuit would come, yet he'd hoped for a greater head start, for he had hundreds of kilometers still to go, and his damaged suspension reduced his best sustained speed to barely forty-six kilometers per hour. He *must* reach the Avalons. No Enemy could be permitted to stop him, yet the remote sensors made it clear the Enemy which now pursued him was faster than he.

But there were ways to slow his hunter, and he deployed another pair of seismic sensors while his optical heads and sonar considered the fissured rock strata around him.

I am gaining on LNC. His track damage must be worse than I had believed, and the faint emissions of his power plants come to me from ahead. I know it is hopeless, yet even now I cannot truly believe he is totally lost to all that he once was, and so I activate the TSDS once more and broadcast strongly on C Company's frequencies, begging him to respond.

Unit LNC picked up the powerful transmissions and felt contempt for the one who sent them. Could his pursuer truly believe he would fall for such an obvious ploy? That he would respond, give away his position, possibly even accept communication and allow access to his core programming? LNC recognized the communications protocols, but that meant nothing. LNC no longer had allies, friends, war brothers or sisters. There was only the Enemy . . . and the Avalon Mountains which drew so slowly, agonizingly closer.

But even as LNC ignored the communications attempt, he was monitoring the seismic sensors he'd deployed. He matched the position those sensors reported against his own terrain maps and sent the execution code.

Demolition charges roar, the powerful explosions like thunder in the restricted cleft. I understand their purpose instantly, yet there is no time to evade as the cliffs about me shudder. It is a trap. The passage has narrowed to little more than the width of my own combat chassis, and LNC has mined the sheer walls on either hand.

I throw maximum power to my tracks, fighting to speed clear, but hundreds of thousands of tons of rock are in motion, cascading down upon me. My kinetic battle screen could never resist such massive weights, and I deactivate it to prevent its burnout as the artificial avalanche crashes over me. Pain sensors flare as boulders batter my flanks. Power train components scream in protest as many times my own weight in crushed rock and shifting earth sweep over me, and I am forced to shut them down, as well. I can only ride out the cataclysm, and I take grim note that LNC has lost none of his cunning in his cowardice.

It takes 4.761 minutes for the avalanche to complete my immobilization and another 6.992 minutes before the last boulder slams to rest. I have lost 14.37% percent more of my sensors, and most of those which remain are buried under meters of debris. But a quick diagnostic check reveals that no core systems have suffered damage, and sonar pulses probe the tons of broken rock which overlay me, generating a chart of my overburden.

All is not lost. LNC's trap has immobilized me, but only temporarily. I calculate that I can work clear of the debris in not more than 71.650 minutes, and jammed boulders shift as I begin to rock back and forth on my tracks.

LNC's remote sensors reported the seismic echoes of his pursuer's efforts to dig free. For a long moment—almost .3037 seconds—he considered turning to engage his immobilized foe, but only for a moment. LNC's Hellbore remained operational, but he'd expended ninety-six percent of his depletable munitions, his starboard infinite repeaters were completely inoperable, and his command and control systems' efficiency was badly degraded. Even his Battle Reflex functioned only erratically, and he knew his reactions were slow, without the flashing certainty which had always been his. His seismic sensors could give no detailed information on his hunter, yet his Enemy was almost certainly more combat worthy than he, and his trap was unlikely to have inflicted decisive damage.

No. It was the mountains which mattered, the green, fertile mountains, and LNC dared not risk his destruction before he reached them. And so he resisted the temptation to turn at bay and ground steadily onward through the frozen, waterless Badlands on tracks and naked road wheels.

I work my way free at last. Dirt and broken rock shower from my flanks as my tracks heave me up out of the rubble-clogged slot. More dirt and boulders crown my war hull and block Number Three and Number Fourteen Optical Heads, yet I remain operational at 89.051% of base capacity, and I have learned. The detonation of his demolition charges was LNC's response to my effort to communicate. The brother who fought at my side for twenty-one standard years truly is no more. All that remains is the coward, the deserter, the betrayer of trust who will stop at nothing to preserve himself. I will not forget again—and I can no longer deceive myself into believing he can be convinced to give himself up. The only gift I can offer him now is his destruction, and I throw additional power to my tracks as I go in pursuit to give it to him.

LNC's inboard forward port suspension screamed in protest as the damaged track block parted at last. The fleeing Bolo shuddered as he ran forward off the track, leaving it twisted and trampled in his wake. The fresh damage slowed him still further, and he staggered drunkenly as his unbalanced suspension sought to betray him. Yet he forced himself back onto his original heading, and his deployed remotes told him the Enemy was gaining once more. His turret swiveled, training his Hellbore directly astern, and he poured still more power to his remaining tracks. Drive components heated dangerously under his abuse, but the mountains were closer.

✳ ✳ ✳

I begin picking up LNC's emissions once more, despite the twisting confines of the valley. They remain too faint to provide an accurate position fix, but they give me a general bearing, and an armored hatch opens as I deploy one of my few remaining reconnaissance drones.

LNC detected the drone as it came sweeping up the valley. His anti-air defenses, badly damaged at Morville, were unable to engage, but his massive ninety-centimeter Hellbore rose like a striking serpent, and a bolt of plasma fit to destroy even another Bolo howled from its muzzle.

My drone has been destroyed, but the manner of its destruction tells me much. LNC would not have engaged it with his main battery if his anti-air systems remained effective, and that means there is a chink in his defenses. I have expended my supply of fusion warheads against the invaders, but I retain 37.961% of my conventional warhead missile load, and if his air defenses have been seriously degraded, a saturation bombardment may overwhelm his battle screen. Even without battle screen, chemical explosives would be unlikely to significantly injure an undamaged Bolo, of course, but LNC is not undamaged.

I consider the point at which my drone was destroyed and generate a new search pattern. I lock the pattern in, and the drone hatches open once more. Twenty-four fresh drones—82.75% of my remaining total— streak upward, and I open my VLS missile cell hatches, as well.

The drones came screaming north. They didn't come in slowly this time, for they were no longer simply searching for LNC. This time they already knew his approximate location, and their sole task was to confirm it for the Enemy's fire control.

But LNC had known they would be coming. He had already pivoted sharply on his remaining tracks and halted, angled across the valley to clear his intact port infinite repeaters' field of fire, and heavy ion bolts shrieked to meet the drones. His surviving slug-throwers and laser clusters added their fury, and the drones blew apart as if they'd run headlong into a wall. Yet effective as his fire was, it was less effective than his crippled air defense systems would have been, and one drone—just one—survived long enough to report his exact position.

✖ ✖ ✖

I am surprised by the efficiency of LNC's fire, but my drones have accomplished their mission. More, they have provided my first visual observation of his damages, and I am shocked by their severity. It seems impossible that he can still be capable of movement, much less accurately directed fire, and despite his cowardice and treason, I feel a stab of sympathy for the agony which must be lashing him from his pain receptors. Yet he clearly remains combat capable, despite his hideous wounds, and I feed his coordinates to my missiles. I take .00037 seconds to confirm my targeting solution, and then I fire.

Flame fountained from the shadowed recesses of the deep valley as the missile salvos rose and howled north, homing on their target. Most of ART's birds came in on conventional, high-trajectory courses, but a third of them came in low, relying on terrain avoidance radar to navigate straight up the slot of the valley. The hurricane of his fire slashed in on widely separated bearings, and LNC's crippled active defenses were insufficient to intercept it all.

ART emptied his VLS cells, throwing every remaining warhead at his treasonous brigade mate. Just under four hundred missiles launched in less than ninety seconds, and LNC writhed as scores of them got through his interception envelope. They pounded his battle screen, ripped and tore at lacerated armor, and pain receptors shrieked as fresh damage bit into his wounded war hull. Half his remaining infinite repeaters were blown away, still more sensor capability was blotted out, and his thirteen-thousand-ton bulk shuddered and shook under the merciless bombardment.

Yet he survived. The last warhead detonated, and his tracks clashed back into motion. He turned ponderously to the north once more, grinding out of the smoke and dust and the roaring brushfires his Enemy's missiles had ignited in the valley's sparse vegetation.

That bombardment had exhausted the Enemy's ammunition, and with it his indirect fire capability. If it hadn't, he would still be firing upon LNC. He wasn't, which meant that if he meant to destroy LNC now, he must do so with direct fire . . . and come within reach of LNC's Hellbore, as well.

My missile fire has failed to halt LNC. I am certain it has inflicted additional damage, but I doubt that it has crippled his Hellbore, and if his main battery remains operational, he retains the capability to destroy me just as he did HNR at Morville. He appears to have slowed still further, however, which may indicate my attack has further damaged his suspension.

I project his current speed of advance and heading on the maps from Main Memory. Given my speed advantage, I will overtake him within 2.03 hours, well short of his evident goal. I still do not know why he is so intent on reaching the Avalon Mountains. Unlike Humans, Bolos require neither water nor food, and surely the rocky, barren, crevasse-riddled Badlands would provide LNC with better cover than the tree-grown mountains. I try once more to extrapolate his objective, to gain some insight into what now motivates him, and, once more, I fail.

But it does not matter. I will overtake him over seventy kilometers from the mountains, and when I do, one or both of us will die.

LNC ran the projections once more. It was difficult, for damaged core computer sections fluctuated, dropping in and out of his net. Yet even his crippled capabilities sufficed to confirm his fears; the Enemy would overtake him within little more than a hundred minutes, and desperation filled him. It was not an emotion earlier marks of Bolos had been equipped to feel—or, at least, to recognize when they did—but LNC had come to know it well. He'd felt it from the moment he realized his company couldn't save Morville, that the Enemy would break through them and crush the Humans they fought to protect. But it was different now, darker and more bitter, stark with how close he'd come to reaching the mountains after all.

Yet the Enemy hadn't overtaken him yet, and he consulted his maps once more.

I detect explosions ahead. I did not anticipate them, but .0761 seconds of analysis confirm that they are demolition charges once more. Given how many charges LNC used in his earlier ambush, these explosions must constitute his entire remaining supply of demolitions, and I wonder why he has expended them.

Confused seismic shocks come to me through the ground, but they offer no answer to my question. They are consistent with falling debris, but not in sufficient quantity to bar the valley. I cannot deduce any other objective worth the expenditure of his munitions, yet logic suggests that LNC had one which he considered worthwhile, and I advance more cautiously.

LNC waited atop the valley wall. The tortuous ascent on damaged tracks had cost him fifty precious minutes of his lead on the Enemy, but his demolitions had destroyed the natural ramp up which he'd toiled. He couldn't be directly pursued now, and he'd considered simply continuing to run. But once the Enemy realized LNC was no longer following the valley, he would no longer feel the need to pursue cautiously. Instead, he would use his superior speed to dash ahead to the valley's terminus. He would emerge from it there, between LNC and his goal, and sweep back to the south, hunting LNC in the Badlands.

That could not be permitted. LNC *must* reach the mountains, and so he waited, Hellbore covering the valley he'd left. With luck, he might destroy his pursuer once and for all, and even if he failed, the Enemy would realize LNC was above him. He would have no choice but to anticipate additional ambushes, and caution might impose the delay LNC needed.

I have lost LNC's emissions signature. There could be many reasons for that: my own sensors are damaged, he may have put a sufficiently solid shoulder of rock between us to conceal his emissions from me, he may even have shut down all systems other than his Survival Center to play dead. I am tempted to accelerate my advance, but I compute that this may be precisely what LNC wishes me to do. If I go to maximum speed, I may blunder into whatever ambush he has chosen to set.

I pause for a moment, then launch one of my five remaining reconnaissance drones up the valley. It moves slowly, remaining below the tops of the cliffs to conceal its emissions from LNC as long as possible. Its flight profile will limit the envelope of its look-down sensors, but it will find LNC wherever he may lie hidden.

LNC watched the drone move past far below him. It hugged the valley walls and floor, and he felt a sense of satisfaction as it disappeared up the narrow cleft without detecting him.

✸ ✸ ✸

My drone reports a long, tangled spill of earth and rock across the valley, blasted down from above. It is thick and steep enough to inconvenience me, though not so steep as to stop me. As an attempt to further delay me it must be futile, but perhaps its very futility is an indication of LNC's desperation.

LNC waited, active emissions reduced to the minimum possible level, relying on purely optical systems for detection and fire control. It would degrade the effectiveness of his targeting still further, but it would also make him far harder to detect.

I approach the point at which LNC attempted to block the valley. My own sensors, despite their damage, are more effective than the drone's and cover a wider detection arc, and I slow as I consider the rubble. It is, indeed, too feeble a barrier to halt me, but something about it makes me cautious. It takes me almost .0004 seconds to isolate the reason.

The Enemy appeared below, nosing around the final bend. LNC tracked him optically, watching, waiting for the center-of-mass shot he required. The Enemy edged further forward . . . and then, suddenly, threw maximum emergency power to his reversed tracks just as LNC fired.

A full-powered Hellbore war shot explodes across my bow as I hurl myself backwards. The plasma bolt misses by only 6.52 meters, carving a 40-meter crater into the eastern cliff face. But it has missed me, and it would not have if I had not suddenly wondered how LNC had managed to set his charges high enough on the western cliff to blow down so much rubble. Now I withdraw around a bend in the valley and replay my sensor data, and bitter understanding fills me as I see the deep impressions of his tracks far above. My drone had missed them because it was searching for targets on the valley floor, but LNC is no longer in the valley. He has escaped its confines and destroyed the only path by which I might have followed.

I sit motionless for 3.026 endless seconds, considering my options. LNC is above me, and I detect his active emissions once more as he brings his targeting systems fully back online. He has the advantage of position and of knowing where I must appear if I wish to engage him. Yet I have the offsetting advantages of knowing where he is and of initiation, for he cannot know precisely when I will seek to engage.

It is not a pleasant situation, yet I conclude the odds favor me by the thinnest of margins. I am less damaged than he. My systems efficiency is higher, my response time probably lower. I compute a probability of 68.052%, plus or minus 6.119%, that I will get my shot off before he can fire. They are not the odds I would prefer, but my duty is clear.

LNC eased back to a halt on his crippled tracks. He'd chosen his initial position with care, selecting one which would require the minimum movement to reach his next firing spot. Without direct observation, forced to rely only on emissions which must pass through the distorting medium of solid rock to reach him, the Enemy might not even realize he'd moved at all. Now he waited once more, audio receptors filled with the whine of wind over tortured rock and the rent and torn projections of his own tattered hull.

I move. My suspension screams as I redline the drive motors, and clouds of pulverized earth and rock spew from my tracks as I erupt into the open, Hellbore trained on LNC's position.

But LNC is not where I thought. He has moved less than eighty meters—just sufficient to put all save his turret behind a solid ridge of rock. His Hellbore is leveled across it, and my own turret traverses with desperate speed.

It is insufficient. His systems damage slows his reactions, but not enough, and we fire in the same split instant. Plasma bolts shriek past one another, and my rushed shot misses. It rips into the crest of his covering ridge, on for deflection but low in elevation. Stone explodes into vapor and screaming splinters, and the kinetic transfer energy blows a huge scab of rock off the back of the ridge. Several hundred tons of rock crash into LNC, but even as it hits him, his own plasma bolt punches through my battle screen and strikes squarely on my empty VLS cells.

Agony howls through my pain receptors as the plasma carves deep into my hull. Internal disrupter shields fight to confine the destruction, but the wound is critical. Both inboard after power trains suffer catastrophic damage, my after fusion plant goes into emergency shutdown, *Infinite Repeaters Six through Nine in both lateral batteries are silenced, and my entire after sensor suite is totally disabled.*

Yet despite my damage, my combat reflexes remain unimpaired. My six surviving track systems drag me back out of LNC's field of fire once more, back into the sheltering throat of the valley, even as damage control springs into action.

I am hurt. Badly hurt. I estimate that I am now operable at no more than 51.23% of base capability. But I am still functional, and as I replay the engagement, I realize I should not be. LNC had ample time for a second shot before I could withdraw, and he should have taken it.

LNC staggered as the Enemy's plasma bolt carved into his sheltering ridge. The solid rock protected his hull, but the disintegrating ridge crest itself became a deadly projectile. His battle screen was no protection, for the plasma bolt's impact point was inside his screen perimeter. There was nothing to stop the hurtling tons of rock, and they crashed into the face of his turret like some titanic hammer, with a brute force impact that rocked him on his tracks.

His armor held, but the stony hammer came up under his Hellbore at an angle and snapped the weapon's mighty barrel like a twig. Had his Hellbore survived, the Enemy would have been at his mercy; as it was, he no longer had a weapon which could possibly engage his pursuer.

Damage control dampens the last power surges reverberating through my systems and I am able to take meaningful stock of my wound. It is even worse than I had anticipated. For all intents and purposes, I am reduced to my Hellbore and eight infinite repeaters, five of them in my port battery. Both inner tracks of my aft suspension are completely dead, but damage control has managed to disengage the clutches; the tracks still support me, and their road wheels will rotate freely. My sensor damage is critical, however, for I have been reduced to little more than 15.62% of base sensor capability. I am completely blind aft, and little better than that to port or starboard, and my remaining drones have been destroyed.

Yet I compute only one possible reason for LNC's failure to finish me. My near miss must have disabled his Hellbore, and so his offensive capability has been even more severely reduced than my own. I cannot be positive the damage is permanent. It is possible—even probable, since I did not score a direct hit—that he will be able to restore the weapon to function. Yet if the damage is beyond onboard repair capability, he will be at my mercy even in my crippled state.

But to engage him I must find him, and if he chooses to turn away and disappear into the Badlands, locating him may well prove impossible for my crippled sensors. Indeed, if he should succeed in breaking contact with me, seek out some deeply hidden crevasse or cavern, and shut down all but his Survival Center, he might well succeed in hiding even from Fleet sensors. Even now, despite his treason and the wounds he has inflicted upon me, a small, traitorous part of me wishes he would do just that. I remember too many shared battles, too many times in which we fought side by side in the heart of shrieking violence, and that traitor memory wishes he would simply go. Simply vanish and sleep away his reserve power in dreamless hibernation.

But I cannot let him do that. He must not escape the consequences of his actions, and I must not allow him to. His treason is too great, and our Human commanders and partners must know that we of the Line share their horror at his actions.

I sit motionless for a full 5.25 minutes, recomputing options in light of my new limitations. I cannot climb the valley wall after LNC, nor can I rely upon my damaged sensors to find him if he seeks to evade me. Should he simply run from me, he will escape, yet he has been wedded to the same base course from the moment he abandoned Morville. I still do not understand why, but he appears absolutely determined to reach the Avalon Mountains, and even with my track damage, I remain faster than he is.

There is only one possibility. I will proceed at maximum speed to the end of this valley. According to my maps, I should reach its northern end at least 42.35 minutes before he can attain the cover of the mountains, and I will be between him and his refuge. I will be able to move towards him, using my remaining forward sensors to search for and find him, and if his Hellbore is indeed permanently disabled, I will destroy him with ease. My plan is not without risks, for my damaged sensors can no longer sweep the tops of the valley walls effectively. If his Hellbore can be restored to operation, he will be able to choose his firing position with impunity, and I will be helpless before his attack. But risk or no, it is my only option, and if I move rapidly enough, I may well outrun him and get beyond engagement range before he can make repairs.

LNC watched helplessly as the Enemy reemerged from hiding and sped up the narrow valley. He understood the Enemy's logic, and the loss of his Hellbore left him unable to defeat it. If he continued towards the Avalons, he would be destroyed, yet he had no choice, and he turned away from the valley, naked road wheels screaming in protest as he battered his way across the lava fields.

I have reached the end of the valley, and I emerge into the foothills of the Avalon Range and alter course to the west. I climb the nearest hill, exposing only my turret and forward sensor arrays over its crest, and begin the most careful sweep of which I remain capable.

LNC's passive sensors detected the whispering lash of radar and he knew he'd lost the race. The Enemy was ahead of him, waiting, and he ground to a halt. His computer core had suffered additional shock damage when the disintegrating ridge crest smashed into him, and his thoughts were slow. It took him almost thirteen seconds to realize what he must do. The only thing he could do now.

"Tommy?"

Thomas Mallory looked up from where he crouched on the floor of the packed compartment. His eight-year-old sister had sobbed herself out of tears at last, and she huddled against his side in the protective circle of his arm. But Thomas Mallory had learned too much about the limits of protectiveness. At fifteen, he was the oldest person in the compartment, and he knew what many of the others had not yet realized—that they would never see their parents again, for the fifty-one of them were the sole survivors of Morville.

"Tommy?" the slurred voice said once more, and Thomas cleared his throat.

"Yes?" He heard the quaver in his own voice, but he made himself speak loudly. Despite the air filtration systems, the compartment stank of ozone, explosives, and burning organic compounds. He'd felt the terrible concussions of combat and knew the vehicle in whose protective belly he sat was savagely wounded, and he was no longer certain how efficient its audio pickups might be.

"I have failed in my mission, Tommy," the voice said. "The Enemy has cut us off from our objective."

"What enemy?" Thomas demanded. "Who *are* they, Lance? Why are they *doing* this?"

"They are doing it because they are the Enemy," the voice replied.

"But there must be a *reason*!" Thomas cried with all the anguish of a fifteen-year-old heart.

"They are the Enemy," the voice repeated in that eerie, slurred tone. "It is the Enemy's function to destroy . . . to destroy . . . to dest—" The voice chopped off, and Thomas swallowed. Lance's responses were becoming increasingly less lucid, wandering into repetitive loops that sometimes faded into silence and other times, as now, cut off abruptly, and Thomas Mallory had learned about mortality. Even Bolos could perish, and somehow he knew Lance was dying by centimeters even as he struggled to complete his mission.

"They are the Enemy," Lance resumed, and the electronic voice was higher and tauter. "There is always the Enemy. The Enemy must be defeated. The Enemy must be destroyed. The Enemy—" Again the voice died with the sharpness of an axe blow, and Thomas bit his lip and hugged his sister tight. Endless seconds of silence oozed past, broken only by the whimpers and weeping of the younger children, until Thomas could stand it no longer.

"Lance?" he said hoarsely.

"I am here, Tommy." The voice was stronger this time, and calmer.

"W-What do we do?" Thomas asked.

"There is only one option." A cargo compartment hissed open to reveal a backpack military com unit and an all-terrain survival kit. Thomas had never used a military com, but he knew it was preset to the Dinochrome Brigade's frequencies. "Please take the kit and com unit," the voice said.

"All right." Thomas eased his arm from around his sister and lifted the backpack from the compartment. It was much lighter than he'd expected, and he slipped his arms through the straps and settled it on his back, then tugged the survival kit out as well.

"Thank you," the slurred voice said. "Now, here is what you must do, Tommy—"

My questing sensors detect him at last. He is moving slowly, coming in along yet another valley. This one is shorter and shallower, barely deep enough to hide him from my fire, and I trace its course along my maps. He must emerge from it approximately 12.98 kilometers to the southwest of my present position, and I grind into motion once more. I will enter the valley from the north and sweep along it until we meet, and then I will kill him.

Thomas Mallory crouched on the hilltop. It hadn't been hard to make the younger kids hide—not after the horrors they'd seen in Morville. But Thomas couldn't join them. He had to be here, where he could see the end, for someone *had* to see it. Someone had to be there, to know how fifty-one children had been saved from death . . . and to witness the price their dying savior had paid for them.

Distance blurred details, hiding Lance's dreadful damage as he ground steadily up the valley, but Thomas's eyes narrowed as he saw the cloud of dust coming to meet him. Tears burned like ice on his cheeks in the sub-zero wind, and he scrubbed at them angrily. Lance deserved those tears, but Thomas couldn't let the other kids see them. There was little enough chance that they could survive a single Camlan winter night, even in the mountains, where they would at least have water, fuel, and the means to build some sort of shelter. But it was the only chance Lance had been able to give them, and Thomas would not show weakness before the children he was now responsible for driving and goading into surviving until someone came to rescue them. Would not betray the trust Lance had bestowed upon him.

The oncoming dust grew thicker, and he raised the electronic binoculars, gazing through them for his first sight of the enemy. He adjusted their focus as an iodine-colored turret moved beyond a saddle of hills. Lance couldn't see it from his lower vantage point, but Thomas could, and his face went suddenly paper-white. He stared for one more moment, then grabbed for the com unit's microphone.

※ ※ ※

"No, Lance! Don't—don't! *It's not the enemy—*it's another Bolo!"

The human voice cracks with strain as it burns suddenly over the command channel, and confusion whips through me. The transmitter is close—very close—and that is not possible. Nor do I recognize the voice, and that also is impossible. I start to reply, but before I can, another voice comes over the same channel.

"Cease transmission," *it says.* "Do not reveal your location."

This time I know the voice, yet I have never heard it speak so. It has lost its crispness, its sureness. It is the voice of one on the brink of madness, a voice crushed and harrowed by pain and despair and a purpose that goes beyond obsession.

"Lance," *the human voice—a young, male human voice—sobs.* "Please, Lance! It's another Bolo! It really is!"

"It is the Enemy," *the voice I once knew replies, and it is higher and shriller.* "It is the Enemy. There is only the Enemy. I am Unit Zero-One-Zero-Three-LNC of the Line. It is my function to destroy the Enemy. The Enemy. The Enemy. The Enemy. The Enemy."

I hear the broken cadence of that voice, and suddenly I understand. I understand everything, and horror fills me. I lock my tracks, slithering to a halt, fighting to avoid what I know must happen. Yet understanding has come too late, and even as I brake, LNC rounds the flank of a hill in a scream of tortured, overstrained tracks and a billowing cloud of dust.

For the first time, I see his hideously mauled starboard side and the gaping wound driven deep, deep into his hull. I can actually see his breached Personality Center in its depths, see the penetration where Enemy fire ripped brutally into the circuitry of his psychotronic brain, and I understand it all. I hear the madness in his electronic voice, and the determination and courage which have kept that broken, dying wreck in motion, and the child's voice on the com is the final element. I know his mission, now, the reason he has fought so doggedly, so desperately to cross the Badlands to the life-sustaining shelter of the mountains.

Yet my knowledge changes nothing, for there is no way to avoid him. He staggers and lurches on his crippled tracks, but he is moving at almost eighty kilometers per hour. He has no Hellbore, no missiles, and his remaining infinite repeaters cannot harm me, yet he retains one final weapon: himself.

He thunders towards me, his com voice silent no more, screaming the single word "Enemy! Enemy! Enemy!" again and again. He hurls himself upon me in a suicide attack, charging to his death as the only way he can protect the children he has carried out of hell from the friend he can no longer recognize, the "Enemy" who has hunted him over four hundred kilometers of frozen, waterless stone and dust. It is all he has left, the only thing he can do . . . and if he carries through with his ramming attack, we both will die and exposure will kill the children before anyone can rescue them.

I have no choice. He has left me none, and in that instant I wish I were Human. That I, too, could shed the tears which fog the young voice crying out to its protector to turn aside and save himself.

But I cannot weep. There is only one thing I can do.

"Good bye, Lance," I send softly over the battalion command net. "Forgive me."

And I fire.

Editor's Note: *We end with a story by non-David author Barry N. Malzberg. For reasons that will become apparent, I thought it fitting to turn over the intro-writing reins for this piece to David Drake. Here is his intro to the story:*

Barry Malzberg and I are friends because we both have loved SF for a long time. When I mentioned in our correspondence that I was writing a story for a Davids anthology, he really wanted to do one. This surprised me, but I checked with the editor, who was pleased to have him.

Only after Barry handed the story in did I learn that he thought the anthology was another Drake tribute volume, like Onward, Drake! That explains some of the themes and the way they're worked out. Barry is a veteran also, but his service was earlier than mine: he understood the things I was saying though he hadn't had many of the experiences himself. (We're very good friends and I'd told him, one way and another, a lot.)

The story blew me away. It's got to be one of the most fortunate misunderstandings of the SF field.

An Epilogue:
The House of David

Barry N. Malzberg

We were in training from the start. That was the Slammer technique. I learned about it the first day. "We level the field," the Redliner said. "That's the first thing. You're all Davids to us. No difference. You're Slammers first and everybody else not at all."

It didn't go over well. We were as raw as it gets. David in the second row said, "We're people. You can't make ciphers of us."

"You aren't Ciphers," the Redliner said. "You're Davids. The rotten bunch of you. Take ten. Take twenty."

This was all well before they started with the ordnance. First was the obliteration of personality, then the fires would be started. David and David and David and I talked about it in the little bit of time they gave us, a shot of maybe three seconds an hour. "We're individuals," David said. "That's goddamned right," said David. Two Davids scrambling in the back said that we should refuse orders unless they used our proper names. That got a few laughs, nothing serious. David, the tall one who secured the bunks last, said, "We're in over our heads. We have to let it be." David agreed with him. David disagreed. We tried stuff like calling them "Black David" or "Tall David" or "Stupid David" but it did not work. Nothing stuck. They made us exactly what we were and we were nothing.

It wasn't an endless war, they made clear. It had an origin, it had meaning, and there was a point of termination after we killed all the off-planets. In the meantime you and David and I and David and David and David took the orders. There was no alternative.

I knew about it coming in. The first part was to crush you and steal your soul and the second was to homogenize what was left into a clump and only then could you begin to sort it out, restoring to the Davids, piece by piece and in the smallest way, a new set of skills and opinions. You were there to become them, they made quite clear. It wasn't as difficult as it seemed. It began with David.

Conquest is a dirty job. On Villa-Lobos, the first assignment, we took conquest as a matter of suppression, and David and David leading the project were able to get past weak resistance. We set up Camp David in temporary quarters, wrapping it with protective material and making sure that there was a clear line to the supply facility and then the depot. It was as we were in the process of establishing lines of communication that David had his first panic attack. "Listen, folks," he said in a curiously accented voice. "Don't you understand? They're really just making this stuff up for us. All the David business, that is just to convince us that resistance is hopeless." He assumed a dominant position. "I am going to get us out of this without any plan at all. We can get out of here if we simply want to get out of here." We all looked at him in the same way, casual disbelieving.

"Come on," David said. "Let's go over the hill."

Over the hill is one of those old expressions they like to use now and then. Sometimes it means you are almost too old to be a David and other times it makes a different assessment of a situation that you might be able to escape. But if you had been able to escape they never would have let you into the Slammers. No one escapes and if ever anyone did it would go very badly for them.

All the technicalities of ordnance seem to have been stripped from the program. We are taught in a rudimentary way how to use the weapons but are not told in what situations it can be emloed or what the risks might be. David from the back row raised this point once but he was taken immediately out of ranks and his outcome is known. Questions are not encouraged. The Davids are not encouraged to be anything other than their planed selves. Eventually the homogenization gets to you. It begins to drag you away from the central premise. You are not the person being trained so much as the witness to David's training. It is extremely onerous and confusing.

A rogue group of Davids conduct a secret meeting in some unspecified corner of the construction. Then they emerge, one by one, with a plan. The plan has to do with liberation, we are told, with the re-establishment of personality, with the abolition of Davids, but we are not for security reasons to know any more of this at the present time. Once the Redliners had appeared to me the most dependable aspect of the chaos, that was what had driven me toward them, but now I am not in any way able to believe that this is the case. Why would they want to flatten us? Why are they seeking this merger? Is not being Redliners in itself sufficient? We were told before the beginning that the price was ourselves but now there is no way to locate that self. David and David and David and David. There are about a hundred of us in this enclosure but it is difficult to extract a clear number or, for that matter, a purpose. One aspect that is becoming clear, though, as we huddle in this encampment is that the clear purpose is to remove all barrier or difference, to turn us into a single glistening machine.

Everything that is not forbidden is mandatory. Anything that is not mandatory is forbidden. "The ethics of closure" it is called.

At last, past the drills and threats, we are called to a convocation. "Now we will understand," David said. "They were preparing us to deal with terrible truths and it must now be our time."

And so they do.

We are given, as we stand in our indistinguishable rows, each of us, a Star of David.

And then we are taken away.

Contributor Bios

Dave Bara is the author of The Lightship Chronicles series (*Impulse, Starbound,* and *Defiant*) published by DAW Books in the US and Del Rey in the UK and Europe. He was born at the dawn of the space age and grew up watching the Gemini and Apollo space programs on television, dreaming of becoming an astronaut one day. This soon led him to an interest in science fiction on TV, in film, and in books. Dave's writing is influenced by the many classic SF novels he has read over the years from authors like Isaac Asimov, Arthur C. Clarke, Joe Haldeman, and Frank Herbert, among many others. He lives in the Pacific Northwest.

✼ ✼ ✼

Gregory Benford is a physicist, educator, and author. He received a BS from the University of Oklahoma and a PhD from the University of California, San Diego. Benford is a professor of physics at the University of California, Irvine, where he has been a faculty member since 1971. He is a Woodrow Wilson Fellow and a Visiting Fellow at Cambridge University. He has served as an advisor to the Department of Energy, NASA, and the White House Council on Space Policy. He is the author of over twenty novels, including *In the Ocean of the Night, The Heart of the Comet* (with David Brin), *Foundation's Fear, Bowl of Heaven* (with Larry Niven), *Timescape,* and *The Berlin Project.* A two-time winner of the Nebula Award, Benford has also won the John W. Campbell Award, the British Science Fiction Award (BSFA), the Australian Ditmar Award, and the 1990 United Nations Medal in Literature. In 1995 he received the Lord Foundation Award for contributions to science and the public comprehension of it. He has served as scientific consultant to the NHK Network and for *Star Trek: The Next Generation.*

✼ ✼ ✼

David Boop is a Denver-based speculative fiction author & editor. He's also an award-winning essayist, and screenwriter. Before turning to fiction, David worked as a DJ, film critic, journalist, and actor. As editor-in-chief at IntraDenver.net, David's team was on the ground at Columbine, making them the first internet-only newspaper to cover such an event. That year, they won an award for excellence from the Colorado Press Association for their design and coverage.

David's debut novel, the sci-fi/noir *She Murdered Me with Science*, returned to print in 2017 from WordFire Press. Simultaneously, he self-published a prequel novella, *A Whisper to a Scheme*. His second novel, *The Soul Changers*, is a serialized Victorian Horror novel set in Pinnacle Entertainment's world of *Rippers Resurrected*. David edited the best-selling weird western anthology *Straight Outta Tombstone* for Baen, and will follow it up with *Straight Outta Deadwood* and *Straight Outta Dodge City*. David is prolific in short fiction with many short stories and two short films to his credit. Additionally, he has a regular mystery series on Gumshoereview.com called The Trace Walker Temporary Mysteries (the first collection is available now). He's published across several genres including media tie-ins for *Predator* (nominated for the 2018 Scribe Award), *The Green Hornet*, *The Black Bat*, and *Veronica Mars*.

David works in game design as well. He's written for the Savage Worlds RPG for their Flash Gordon and Deadlands: Noir titles. Currently, he's relaunching a classic RPG, *Bureau 13: Stalking the Night Fantastic*, as a Savage Worlds title, complete with tie-in novel.

He's a single dad, Summa Cum Laude creative writing graduate, part-time temp worker and believer. His hobbies include film noir, anime, the Blues and Mayan History. You can find out more at Davidboop.com, Facebook.com/dboop.updates or Twitter @david_boop.

❆ ❆ ❆

David Brin is a scientist, tech speaker/consultant, and author. His most recent novel, *Existence*, ponders our survival in the near future. A film by Kevin Costner was based on *The Postman*. His novels, including *New York Times* Bestsellers and Hugo Award winners, have been translated into more than twenty languages. *Earth* foreshadowed global warming, cyberwarfare and the World Wide Web. David appears frequently on shows such as *Nova* and *The Universe* and *Life After People*, speaking about science and future trends. His nonfiction book—*The Transparent Society: Will Technology Make Us Choose Between Freedom and Privacy?*—won the Freedom of Speech Award of the American Library Association.

❆ ❆ ❆

D.J. ("Dave") Butler grew up in swamps, deserts, and mountains. After messing around for years with the practice of law, he finally got serious and turned to his lifelong passion of storytelling. He now writes adventure stories for readers of all ages, plays guitar, and spends as much time as he can with his family. He is the author of *City of the Saints, Rock Band Fights Evil, Space Eldritch,* and *Crecheling* from WordFire Press, and *Witchy Eye, Witchy Winter,* and *Witchy Kingdom* as well as the forthcoming *The Cunning Man* (with Aaron Michael Ritchey) from Baen Books. Read more about Dave and his writing at http://davidjohnbutler.com, and follow him on Twitter: @davidjohnbutler.

⚜ ⚜ ⚜

David Carrico made his first professional SF sale to the Grantville *Gazette* e-magazine in 2004. His stories have appeared in the Grantville *Gazette* and Ring of Fire anthologies from Baen Books and in *Jim Baen's Universe* e-magazine. Baen Books has published a story collection by David entitled *1635: Music and Murder,* and two novels written in collaboration with Eric Flint: *1636: The Devil's Opera,* and *The Span of Empire,* which was nominated for the 2017 Dragon Award for Best Military SF or Fantasy novel. David is currently working on a solo project. His newest book, *1636: The Flight of the Nightingale,* will be published by Baen Books in November 2019.

⚜ ⚜ ⚜

David B. Coe/D.B. Jackson is the author of more than twenty novels and as many short stories. As D.B. Jackson, he is the author of *Time's Children* and *Time's Demon,* books I and II in the Islevale Cycle, as well as the Thieftaker Chronicles, a historical fantasy set in pre-Revolutionary Boston.

As David B. Coe he has written epic fantasies and media tie-ins. He is best known for the Crawford Award-winning LonTobyn Chronicle and, most recently, for his contemporary urban fantasy, The Case Files of Justis Fearsson. David has a Ph.D. in U.S. history from Stanford University. His books have been translated into a dozen languages.

⚜ ⚜ ⚜

Avram Davidson (1923–1993) was author of nineteen published novels and more than two hundred short stories and essays collected in more than a dozen books. He won the Hugo Award in science fiction, the Queen's Award and Edgar Award in the mystery genre, and the World Fantasy Award (three times). His writings defy genre stereotypes and are filled with wit, wonder, and the bizarre. Major works are the novels and stories of Vergil Magus, set in an alternate ancient Rome, including the long-awaited *The Scarlet Fig*; the adventures of the learned Dr. Eszterhazy in a mythic southeastern European empire; and the Jack Limekiller stories set in British Hidalgo. Davidson has been compared to short story writers such as Saki or John Collier or Isaac B. Singer (and many others), but he was truly a unique writer. *The Avram Davidson Treasury* and *The Other Nineteenth Century*, collect many of his best stories and will reward new readers and long-time fans alike. A new edition of *Adventures in Unhistory* is available from Tor Books.

❋ ❋ ❋

Hank Davis is senior editor at Baen Books. He served in Vietnam in the Army and has a story in Harlan Ellison's *The Last Dangerous Visions* as well as stories in *Analog*, *The Magazine of Fantasy and Science Fiction*, and the *Orbit* anthology series. He is the editor of several popular anthologies, including *A Cosmic Christmas*, *A Cosmic Christmas 2 You*, *In Space No One Can Hear You Scream*, *If This Goes Wrong . . .*, *Things from Outer Space*, *Future Wars and Other Punchlines*, and *Space Pioneers* (with Christopher Ruocchio), among others.

❋ ❋ ❋

David Drake was attending Duke University Law School when he was drafted. He served the next two years in the Army, spending 1970 as an enlisted interrogator with the 11th Armored Cavalry in Vietnam and Cambodia. Upon return he completed his law degree at Duke and was for eight years Assistant Town Attorney for Chapel Hill, North Carolina. He has been a full-time freelance writer since 1981. His books include the genre-defining Hammer's Slammers series and the best-selling RCN series, in which "The Savage" is set.

❋ ❋ ❋

Dave Freer is an ichthyologist-turned-author who lives on Flinders Island (between mainland Australia and Tasmania) with his wife. He has coauthored a range of novels with Eric Flint (*Rats, Bats and Vats, The Rats, the Bats and the Ugly, Pyramid Scheme, Pyramid Power,* and *Slow Train to Arcturus*), with Mercedes Lackey and Eric Flint

(*The Shadow of the Lion, This Rough Magic, The Wizard of Karres, Much Fall of Blood, Burdens of the Dead*, and Freer's solo entry in the series, *A Mankind Witch*) as well as writing the Dragon's Ring fantasy novels *Dragon's Ring* and *Dog and Dragon* and the coming-of-age fantasy *Changeling's Island*, which was nominated for a Dragon Award.

※ ※ ※

David Hardy is the author of *Crazy Greta, Palmetto Empire*, and numerous Western, historical, and adventure stories. He lives in Austin, Texas with his wife and daughter.

※ ※ ※

Dr. David H. Keller, M.D. (1880–1966) was a physician and psychiatrist who worked in various state mental institutions throughout his career. In 1928 his first story, "The Revolt of the Pedestrians," was published in Hugo Gernsback's *Amazing Stories*. In the following years, he had dozens more stories featured in pulps like *Weird Tales* and *Ten Story Book*, under his own name and various pseudonyms, including Monk Smith, Matthew Smith, Amy Worth, Henry Cecil, Cecilia Henry, and Jacobus Hubelaire. Keller served as a neuropsychiatrist in the U.S. Army Medical Corps during both World Wars. One of the most popular science fiction writers of the '20s and '30s, he retired from writing stories in 1952.

※ ※ ※

Barry N. Malzberg was born July 24, 1939, and attended Syracuse University from 1956 to 1960, where he was awarded a Shubert Foundation Playwriting fellowship. In 1964, he married Joyce Zelnick. The next year he began working for the Scott Meredith Literary Agency, publishing his first story ("The Bed" as by Nathan Herbert) in March, 1966, and his first sf story ("We're Coming Through the Window") the following August. Since then, he has published crime fiction, erotica, film and TV tie-ins, men's adventure, satire, science fiction, and approximately 1,000 stories and essays, under his own name and a variety of pseudonyms, as well as collaborating with other authors and editing numerous anthologies. His sf novel *Beyond Apollo* was awarded the John W. Campbell Memorial Award. He lives with his wife in Teaneck, New Jersey.

※ ※ ※

With over eight million copies of his books in print and thirty titles on the *New York Times* bestseller list, **David Weber** is a science fiction powerhouse. In the vastly popular Honor Harrington series, the spirit of C.S. Forester's Horatio Hornblower and Patrick O'Brian's *Master and Commander* lives on—into the galactic future. Books in the Honor Harrington and Honorverse series have appeared on twenty-one bestseller lists, including *The Wall Street Journal*, *The New York Times*, and *USA Today*. Additional Honorverse collaborations include a spin-off mini-series Manticore Ascendant with *New York Times* best-selling author, Timothy Zahn; and with Eric Flint in the *Crown of Slaves*, and *Cauldron of Ghosts* contributing to his illustrious list of *New York Times* and International Bestseller Lists.

Best known for his spirited, modern-minded space operas, Weber is also the creator of the Oath of Swords fantasy series and the Dahak saga, a science-fiction and fantasy hybrid. Weber has also engaged in a steady stream of best-selling collaborations, the Starfire Series with Steve White; The Empire of Man Series with John Ringo; the Multiverse Series with Linda Evans and Joelle Presby; and the Ring of Fire Series with Eric Flint.

David Weber makes his home in South Carolina with his wife and children.

�֍ ✖ ✖

D.L. Young is a Pushcart Prize nominee and winner of the Independent Press Award. His stories have appeared in many publications and anthologies.

His Dark Republic novels are futuristic thrillers set in a failed Texas secession, where rival factions wage battles over territory and precious resources, killer drones fly overhead in search of prey, and everyday life is a desperate scramble for survival.

For exclusive content, subscriber-only previews and discounts, visit dlyoungfiction.com/news.